the
states

the
states

norah
woodsey

Published and Manufactured in the United States in 2024.

Excerpt of the poem *Geimhriú* by Ailbhe Ní Ghearbhuigh, originally published in The Coast Road (2016), used with permission from Gallery Press. For more information, please visit http://www.gallerypress.com/

Edited by Kara Aisenbrey
Cover art and design by Anna Morrison
Irish translations by Andrea Brown
Author portrait by Lauren Naylor
Interior design by Zoe Norvell

ISBN 979-8-9884457-0-8

norahwoodsey.com

Ná labhair focal,
ná féach im threo,
tá duifean ar mo chroí
nach n-ardófar.

Géillim don ngeimhriú.

Ní aithneofar mé
go péacadh na mbachlóg.

Table of Contents

chapter
one

The patriarch of the Sullivan family sat in his home office at an impressive mahogany desk, an heirloom passed down from his father's father. Across the antique plush carpet, also from his father's father, his eldest daughter lounged in silk pajamas on a European sofa, flanked by matching elegant armchairs, and played on her phone. Beside him hovered his lawyer, a man more firefighter than legal scholar, who stood and stared at an awaiting financial portfolio in anticipation. The rest of the modern room was sparsely furnished. The glamour of the floor-to-ceiling windows, which revealed the New York City skyline from fifty-five stories up, perfectly complemented the mixture of antique and modern furnishings. When Patrick Sullivan did speak from this desk, the vibrations of his voice bounced off the glass windows, returning to him the sounds he liked best in the world. His only remarks were no longer on the topic of the family meeting, but instead praise for his accomplishments in the past, parties of the past, celebrities and models of the past. The scars on the desk that bore witness to his father's work, or his father's father's construction of the cosmetics empire of which he was king, were ignored. That was not a past that interested him.

At the nearest window, to the left of the elegant seating area and antique desk and lawyer and portfolio, his middle daughter, Tildy, stared down at the people on the sidewalk below. Her shoes rested in the permanent depressions her father's feet had made in the carpet. He'd stand at this window often, looking at this view. From here, her father would say the people below moved like insects. He would see their smallness without acknowledging that he, too, was small when looked on from high above.

And Tildy knew that when he was down there, face-to-face with others, he would hate the people more, for their ugliness or poverty or whatever evidence of humanity he saw on their faces. The untidiness of life offended him. Everything he saw and touched must be immaculate, or it was a personal offense. Tildy knew this better than most. She was called from herself by her father's voice.

"Gisele, come see," he called to his eldest daughter. On his desk were various items, including a tablet, mainly used for photos and screenshots of news clippings, alongside the updated financial portfolio for Aibell Cosmetics. With a single manicured index finger, Patrick Sullivan swiped through the photo album on his tablet in perfect contentment. His daughter rose and joined the men at the desk. "Lee, you too. Something you said made me think of this photo. I love this photo of my wife. Do you see? The way she knew just the right angles for the light to catch her face. She was always 'on' when we did events. Kids these days do not understand how to be 'on,' to always think of your angles."

"Oh my god, is that Kate Moss behind Mom?" Gisele leaned in to examine the photo from her father's shoulder.

"Yes. This was the Met Gala, after we launched the Vitality line. We flew in all the best for our after-party. I heard Madonna wanted to attend, but no. She was a smoker in those days." Her father said the word as if it were a dead rat in a crosswalk.

Tildy, satisfied with being ignored, turned back to the view. Block after block of grey and glass spears stood like fortifications between her and the rivers and bay and ocean. The old photos he cherished were not the mother she knew. Her mother apologized to paperbacks as she dogeared them, played Tetris on an old Game Boy to calm herself before big events, and would always take a deep breath when they exited Shannon airport and say, "Do you feel it, Tildy?" And Tildy would nod because whatever "it" was, she felt it, too. No, those airbrushed photos held nothing for her.

Peter Lee cleared his throat. "Mr. Sullivan, we should really return to the issue of… The, well, how we should proceed. Mr. Sullivan."

"Lee, just sell off some shares and be done with it. I don't know why you are bothering me with this nonsense. Your job is to handle the money. So handle it! Sell some shares! Not too many. Don't risk my control of the company."

Mr. Lee, a lawyer of some competence and more patience, looked to Tildy for support. She chose not to see this. Her gaze was focused beyond the people and the buildings and the boroughs, to the horizon, east of here.

"Mr. Sullivan, we can't handle this the usual way. Your debt is considerable. Selling that number of shares will not cover it all. Perhaps we need to explore ways to reduce monthly expenses. The slip fees and maintenance for the Coronet, and of course the loan and insurance payments, are…"

Gisele folded her arms. "You want Daddy to sell the yacht? Lee, he couldn't sell the Coronet."

Tildy imagined helping Lee. She'd say, "If we don't make the minimum payment, you stand to lose everything." She imagined his indignation and her sister's disgust, currently directed at Lee, turned to her instead, only sharpened by her father's disappointment in her. The flow of anger outward preventing the inward flow of information. Tildy was independent of her father, but his family pride and the shares she'd inherited from her mother meant that she was, more often than she liked, called into the day-to-day operations of his life and the business, the two of which were hopelessly intertwined. No, she would remain silent. He would never listen to her.

She checked her watch.

Her father cleared his throat. "Well, then. We should… Gisele, what can we do?"

With a dramatic sigh, as if an entire day of work was just asked of her, Gisele flopped sideways into a designer armchair. "How should I know! You have to work, and I'm doing the branding for the new line."

Tildy knew that Gisele had very little involvement in branding, beyond approving one of three options, but she said nothing.

Gisele threw her arm over her eyes. "We can uninvite Alexandra and her family from our trip to St. Barths."

"Good thinking, Gisele dear. That's for the best anyway. Alexandra is always at the beach in the Hamptons. She gets too much sun. Skipping this year will be good for her."

Lee removed his glasses and pinched the bridge of his nose. "Mr. Sullivan, that won't be enough."

Her father raised his voice. "And what exactly is enough, Lee? I can't maintain the relationships I need to maintain for this business to operate unless I keep up a certain lifestyle. Do you expect me to spend my whole life slaving away, with everyone knowing that I've sold homes and my yacht and canceled vacations?"

Tildy checked her watch again, willing it to move faster. She knew what flaws she harbored that kept her here, but she often wondered why Lee didn't escape. Was the pull of her father's image so strong, that even this was worth tolerating?

"We start small, Mr. Sullivan. What about that farm in Ireland? The real estate market there is very different than here. There was a telecom company that wanted it. Or was it green energy? And we had another offer to rent. A local. A chef or something, wanted to grow local produce. Let me pull up that email."

Tildy's watch on her wrist and the view outside were forgotten. Her family resentment, the financial portfolio — all of it, forgotten. She listened, flushed, as Lee continued.

"Some young guy, I looked him up. One of these modern restaurants with a moral theme. Oh, I can't find it now. I can find it later. Either case, we can sell the land to someone for good money. No one would know, and I would be discreet."

Her father was leaning forward, interested in this idea. Or, rather, his understanding of the idea.

"Now, if the land has value, Lee, perhaps this is a possible revenue stream. We can exploit it. I'm Irish, as you know. My mother's people come from Cork, and my father, he was mostly Irish. His family were some of the Irish slaves that the English brought over."

"Not slaves, Dad. Jesus," Tildy muttered, unheard.

Her father nodded. "We could pitch it as a way to

come home, return and help the locals. Bring sophistica-tion and industry to a, uh, job creation project. It would be simple to get the necessary approvals and things. I know many politicians there, the former president was a good friend. I went to his daughter's wedding. I know Bono, you know. Everyone knows everyone. It's so much smaller there. They'll love what I'd bring, because I'm one of them."

"Well…" Lee began.

"Sorry, Daddy. That land is in Nana's name, and Matilda has power of attorney. She won't let you do a thing with that land, just like all the shares she refused to give you," Gisele said, deploying Tildy's full name as if it were a dagger. It didn't hurt to be addressed formally by someone who she didn't respect or love.

Lee joined Tildy at the window.

"No."

Before the lawyer could try to convince her, she presented the word as a complete fact. Not as an argu-ment—more like a locked door without a key. There would be no negotiation, no discussion on this topic.

"We're up against it here, Tildy. You know that."

"We always are. And it wouldn't be enough," she whispered.

The tension in the room had been noticed by a device on her father's desk, ever present and always listening. The faint white light at the base turned blue.

"May I offer my assistance?" a woman's voice inquired. It wasn't a real human voice, but it was familiar to the family as though it were real.

Lee looked to his boss and Gisele, saw their interest in what the artificial assistant had to say, and jumped on the offer. "What should we do, Russell?"

"Have you asked Tildy?"

Gisele and her father rolled their eyes as Tildy returned her gaze back to the city view.

"She doesn't want her grandmother to sell the land," Lee said.

"The land wouldn't be enough, as I'm sure Tildy has pointed out."

Gisele yawned. "We have to solve this problem with as little inconvenience as possible, Russell. Mommy designed you to make our lives easier. And Matilda doesn't understand how to be comfortable. She's too busy working and having a career in data mining."

"Data science," Tildy corrected.

"Whatever."

The sensor light indicated the device was processing the information. A dark blue line chasing a faint blue line, hounding it as they went round and round together. Tildy remembered how it looked, once. She remembered asking it her own impossible question, on a day that seemed like a lifetime ago. And what following that advice had cost her.

Russell spoke. "What about a relocation to Palm Beach? A discreet sale of New York City assets will look more like preparation for retirement than symptoms of financial trouble."

Gisele clapped and bounced in her seat. "Oh, I love Palm Beach!"

Mr. Sullivan frowned. "Retirement? I'm far too young for that. No one would believe it. No, I'm not sure. All of my business is here."

"Present it as a way to spend time with your children, then. If Gisele and Tildy relocate with you, and you make space for Alexandra and her children, no one will think of it as a retirement. It is common knowledge your daughters will inherit the business."

Tildy's stomach clenched. There were many places she did not want to live, and Palm Beach topped the list. Nothing about the climate, the politics, or the memories of the place appealed to her.

"Palm Beach," her father said reflectively. "I do find it so peaceful, you know. We could buy a second jet for the commute, I suppose."

Lee grimaced. "I'm afraid you couldn't afford a, uh, *second* jet."

Russell's light turned dark blue again. "You could comfortably afford your existing jet by renting it out for private use by others when it is not of use to you."

"Like a *taxi*?" Mr. Sullivan spat. "You want my Gulfstream to be used in the *gig* economy?"

"I can provide you with names of thirty-seven people on Financial Analysis's list of the top fifty wealthiest Americans who rent out their jets when not in use, including Percy Weathers."

"Oh. Percy does it? That's interesting. Percy rents out his jet. I didn't know that. That is interesting. Palm Beach."

Tildy's hand was cramping. Looking down, she realized her fist was clenched and forced herself to relax each finger, then stretch them all out and return her hand to a languid position. She checked her watch.

"Leaving so soon?" Lee asked desperately.

"I have a meeting." Tildy crossed her father's office and collected her coat and purse from the armchair in the far corner.

"Oh yes, Matilda has a *job*." Gisele laughed.

"I do, yes. And you have a branding meeting downstairs in ten minutes. Remember?"

"Oh! Why didn't you tell me! You could've told me! Just standing there, like a stupid sad mannequin! Now I have to rush to get dressed."

Her sister ran from the room, snapping her fingers as she yelled, "Constance! Constance, get here now! Did you steam the silk jumpsuit?"

Her father ignored his eldest's outburst and his middle child's departure. "Lee, if we did this Palm Beach idea, would we still need to sell the Coronet?"

Tildy passed through the office and let the enormous wooden door swish shut behind her. In the dimly lit corridor, with the soft sconce lighting at each side, Tildy relished the quiet. She needed this moment to be alone, before the rush of the sidewalk and subway. As she often did here, in private, she touched the wallpaper with her fingertips.

Her mother had picked this pattern: an ocean in the midst of storm, etched on a dark matte blue, the lines accented with silver foil. As a girl, Tildy would trace her fingers over the shiny metal details as she and her mother left the residential wing and walked to the elevator, her touch part of the waves as they crashed into rocky shoals. When she was older, the water's high crests reminded her of the sea on a day long ago, a day when she broke two hearts with one terrible choice. And now, he might be back in her life, her grandmother's land bringing them together once more.

No, she told herself as her hand fell to her side. Not together. He needed something from Nana. He wanted nothing from her. She had been weak and foolish. When he had offered her love and acceptance, she had chosen to listen to her father, to Gisele, to Russell, and abandon him. Now? Now she was simply a part of his past.

Tildy continued down the hallway and hit the elevator button. As she waited, she shook her head and laughed.

"I know Bono."

chapter
two

Tildy slipped into the stream of pedestrians on the busy sidewalk. A delivery truck had double-parked, blocking cyclists from use of the bike lane. Two rideshare drivers honked at one another as they jockeyed for position to get onto Fifth Avenue. Workers hustled to get lunch, either for themselves or their bosses. Heavy booms of distant construction, nearer traffic, loud conversations, and far-off arguments made focus difficult.

Her phone buzzed with an incoming call. Tildy grimaced. This call should have been expected, and yet for old, familiar software, Russell was always able to surprise her.

"Hey."

"Tildy, darling. You seem stressed."

"What makes you say that? Are you tracking my heartrate?"

Russell's laugh was kind and warm and almost real. "Oh, that would be rude."

Tildy noted the omission but said nothing. It helped to have the AI know everything about her and her family. It saved Tildy the time from having to explain it all. Russell continued. "You seemed distressed in your meeting with your father and Lee today."

"I'm fine."

"Tildy, what did they say that upset you? Was it Palm Beach?"

Tildy passed by a hot dog vendor, and a group of tourists stopped in the middle of the sidewalk to take a photo of a building. They could find thousands of photos of it online, of course, but she just stepped around them.

"I do hate Palm Beach."

"There's something else." Russell said it with conviction.

Why bother denying it? "He wants to buy Nana's land."

"He who?"

Tildy grimaced. "Never mind."

A short pause ensued. It would take a moment, but Russell would know. Gisele and her father might have forgotten, but not Russell. "Oh. The young man."

"Aidan. Yes."

"Tildy, darling. That was years ago."

"It was." Eight years ago, she added silently.

"He must be married by now," Russell continued.

"He's not."

Russell went silent. Tildy could almost see her light, dark blue chasing the light blue, as the virtual assistant processed the information.

"And he hasn't reached out to you. Not on social media, not by text."

Tildy's cheeks burned with petulant anger. She hung up and shoved the phone into her jacket pocket. It was so stupid, to talk about her problems to her mother's college project. But who else did she have? No one who cared.

She walked to the 42nd street station and descended the concrete stairs. A gust of grimy, hot wind blew her hair back as a train, likely one she wanted, departed the station. She tapped and passed the gates, then checked the countdown clock for her train. As she waited, she took out her phone again and checked social media. Animal photos, news stories, people who were internet famous joking with other internet famous people. It was a temporary yet welcome respite from her current concerns. A post from Evelyn Tournay caught her eye.

Looking for participants for a therapy study for the sleep cognition lab. $20 gift card per night of completed sessions! New York City only. Please repost!

There was a link, which Tildy clicked right away. Evelyn had been a classmate from high school. Evelyn, her then-boyfriend Benito and their friends were clever, kind people who hadn't fit in. Tildy hadn't fit in either, so they stuck together. Tildy had spent each school year waiting for her turn to go to Ireland, to see her Nana, and by senior year she had neglected her friendships. All she had wanted was to see Aidan again.

Tildy skimmed the material. Lucid dreaming on demand. The possibilities presented themselves in a flash. She cast a furtive glance around the platform, in case her excitement was noticeable. Everyone else was absorbed by their phones. She returned to the documents and scrolled through. A mesh cap of electrodes and a little transmitter was all it took, and she could sleep in her own bed. It could be like time travel, only better—there were no consequences, no social cost. What if her days of failure with her family, the monotony at work, and the regret in her peaceful moments were only half her life? What if, at night, she could go to Ireland and do all that she wished, without having to face who she had been, or who she had become?

The train pulled up to the platform. Tildy tapped out a direct message as she boarded, then stared at her words. She wasn't brave enough to shape her conscious life the way she wanted, but she would do this. She would do this for herself.

She reached work in time to get a coffee from the micro café underneath the office. Tildy sighed as she faced the three flights of carpeted, narrow stairs. She began her ascent and thought, as she often thought, of the people who had once called this building home. Dozens of people crowded into tight, dark spaces, with only curtains to separate them. Now, all the walls had been torn down, and the splintering wood floor, bearing scars from toys played with by children long dead, gave the space "industrial character." Tildy set down her jacket and purse and took her coffee into the glass conference room.

This meeting had representatives from all product teams in attendance. Tildy greeted the others, sat in her usual chair, and sipped her coffee. Meetings were fine, if you were used to looking pleasantly blank while keeping your thoughts to yourself. Tildy was an expert at that.

A coworker she knew only superficially greeted her as he sat down and took out his laptop. Everyone here only knew her superficially. When people asked about her background, they either let themselves be deflected by her questions about them or were surprised by her curt replies. It wasn't that she kept her family a secret, exactly. She simply chose to make it not worth discussing.

And it really wasn't worth discussing.

She was the unwanted middle daughter in a family known for it's cosmetics empire. It had been a global force. In every trip to every country, there were billboards with airbrushed faces and Aibell branding. But the years had gone by, and new companies had taken more and more of the market share. Her dad hadn't toned down his spending. If anything, it accelerated after the death of her mother.

Instead of lurking in his shadow, Tildy had earned a degree that might help, if she was asked. As she waited, she built a career apart from them. If the family ship went under, she wasn't going to be pulled down with them. Besides, it was a good job and she enjoyed the work. She used concrete math to explain how decisions were made. The people behind the decisions were abstract, described as users and visitors and clients. They weren't neglectful parents or vain siblings.

The meeting began, and a problem was presented to the group: did their website need a feed or a timeline? It wasn't just a question of how to best present information for consumption. This website, like every website, needed interaction. It needed to elicit a response from the user. Would providing a feed increase user engagement? Would it increase user retention, minutes on page, click-throughs, and social media shares? How could they best guarantee that users became loyal, forgiving when issues arose, and eager for new content?

Tildy jotted down some notes about possible experiments they could run, wondering at how the decisions made in a room like this might influence the choices of thousands of strangers. They needed to consider questions such as whether they wanted to show this only to logged-in users. Logged-in users differed in behavior from logged-out users, even those who reliably visited. Additionally, she needed to consider the duration of the experiment. Was this a one-month, three-month, or six-month timeline? Who would set the goals?

While those around her continued to speak, she thought of her older sister's remark. "Matilda has a *job*." She didn't feel the need to tell Gisele the hard truth: if she fell outside her father's orbit, or more likely, if their father sunk the business, the trust fund their mother and Lee had established wouldn't cover the bills. And if things continued as they were going, even Gisele would need a job.

The UX designer asked a question, calling Tildy from herself. If she was going to work, she needed to be present. Her family took up enough of her life as it was. No reason to give them everything.

It was nearly 8 p.m. when her keys hit the bottom of the ceramic bowl by her front door. The orchid beside the bowl was drooping. The crush of the subway, the hurried foot traffic on the sidewalk, and now this. She felt irritation blossom in her chest, wild and unwelcome. She needed to stop buying plants. Just another living thing she was letting down.

She slipped out of her shoes, set them carefully to the side, and stepped into her slippers before she entered her living room. The familiar rush of love brushed away thoughts of her dying orchid. She loved her home. The large living space, with floor-to-ceiling windows, opened before her. It was very much like her father's penthouse, only smaller and with more character. The view on a rainy day was perfect. Grey and harsh, air conditioners and tarred roofs and fire escapes crawling the sides of brick and stone buildings. Today a bright sunset struck across the sky, in gashes of orange and pink, but the buildings surrounding her blocked most of the view. It was a relief to be ensconced in grey. The color palette didn't suit her mood.

Like her place in New York City society, she had inherited the apartment, too. This was her mother's apartment, kept for when her parents fought. It was ridiculously extravagant to have a whole apartment for fighting in a city with a housing crisis, but it wasn't unheard of in her family's circles. In the early days, she and her younger sister, Alexandra, would join their mother here. Gisele always stayed with their dad, and before long Alexandra did too. She had fond memories of this place, but not because of her mother. When they were here her mother was consumed by despair, by what and in what amounts, she never fully articulated. She rarely noticed her daughter in that state, but Tildy appreciated the quiet, then and now.

As Tildy stood at the kitchen sink, cleaning her hands and cell phone, she imagined giving up this apartment to move to Palm Beach. Giving up her job. No more art gallery openings, private tours of museums, or meetings for her mother's charity. All the advantages she gained from her family that held meaning to her would disappear. She would never. And yet, she knew something about herself that she kept in the darkness. If her family demanded it, she would go. Her strength to resist them ended at the land and stocks, and even that was simply family loyalty turned elsewhere. How she spent her time was within their power. And what was life, if not allocating the precious resource of time?

She went to the bathroom and started filling her tub. It was a very small bathtub. Sometimes, when her father insisted that all the children join him for overseas conferences or meetings or weddings, she would check the website for their accommodations and ensure that there was a good-sized bathtub. Then she would agree to go, as she would anyway, and she would quietly remain in the background of their splendor, waiting for her time to take a bath.

She threw in salts and watched the water reach as high as it would go. She turned on music on her phone, threw her clothes into the hamper, and sank into the hot water. No matter what bathtubs her family had there, she told herself not to join them in Palm Beach. She wished she would listen.

One short breath, and Tildy dropped her head below the surface, reveling in the hollow sound of her own body suspended in a warm embrace. The ever-present ache in her shoulders softened, but did not ease. It would take more than warm water to make that tension disappear.

After her bath and a dinner of pasta, her phone buzzed. A text from Gisele.

    ◯ Going to Palm Beach in the AM.

Tildy rolled her eyes and her finger hovered over the keyboard, typing the first letters of many different phantom replies. To her relief, her phone showed Gisele was typing again.

○ We're flying with Stu and his parents, no room for you. :(

Tildy thumbs-up'd the message and lowered the phone in relief. But then she felt a vibration.

○ When you visit Alexandra on Sat, bring her babka from that place near you.

Tildy walked into her bedroom with resignation. She shut her eyes and slumped onto the bed, the perfect boredom of her weekend destroyed before it had begun. The babka sold out before 9 a.m. The train to the Hamptons took two hours. She pulled up the message to reply.

Thumbs-up.

chapter
three

The rideshare met her right as she disembarked the train at the quaint Southampton station. The air was fresh and crisp in a way that is impossible in the city. The car drove south, toward the water, as houses became more spaced apart. They all looked a bit the same. Green bushes offered privacy, bars fencing in cobblestone driveways, bookended by two columns of brick, faux gas lanterns on top.

For generations, Tildy's brother-in-law's family had lived here. Their primary estate, sprawling and decadent, was a few miles north. They kept an apartment in

Manhattan for when the children were little and needed a good private education, but the summers had been spent here. Tildy had only seen their estate twice, once for a graduation party and another time for her sister's wedding. That family liked to complain about the expense of the upkeep, of the difficulty in finding good help, and all the other sorts of irritations that made up the lives of people who had always been wealthy.

She relished her last moments of solitude. Over two and a half hours on the train had given her the chance to read, to rest, and to not be home. If she felt sorry for herself, she only had to think of Palm Beach and be relieved they hadn't tried to force her to go, because she would have gone. Her will was not that strong. Not anymore.

No one greeted her when she exited the car. Her knock was answered by the tired household manager, who offered a smile in advance sympathy. Tildy handed over the babka and allowed herself to be led to the guest suite upstairs, where she washed her hands and changed her clothes. She splashed water on her face, toweled it off, then gripped the counter and stared at her reflection. She examined her smooth black hair, fair eyes, and pale skin. Her features were all appropriately sized and in the correct places, but somehow mismatched. There was a hardness to her that neither Gisele nor Alexandra shared. It certainly hadn't come from their mother. She found no comfort looking at her reflection, so she left it behind and went downstairs.

The first day of visiting her sister was always the hardest.

Tildy found Alexandra lying on a couch in the library. Today, for fun, she tried a new approach: bubbly.

"Hey! I just got in!"

"Tildy. Ugh. You just missed the kids. I had the nanny take them to the shoreline. I can't deal with all the noise and complaints today. I was up all night and I'm exhausted."

"What happened?"

"I was researching. I read a thing online that cuticle loss is associated with this horrible autoimmune disease that I'm pretty sure I have. Doesn't Dad have cuticle loss?"

"I think that's because he gets manicures too often."

"No, that's not it. Whatever it is, he doesn't have it as bad as I do. That would explain why I can't seem to shake this baby weight."

If anything, Tildy thought her sister looked too thin. She kept that to herself. "How are the kids? Is George liking his new school?"

"Sure. Of course they want mothers to do all kinds of work. Volunteer in classrooms and bake sales and help with fundraiser galas. I tried to explain to them that I'm not available for manual labor, that my in-laws will send them a check. They don't care. It's *expected*. Even asking me is so insensitive."

Tildy sat and looked around. "Where's Charlie?"

"He was in his office shed. Probably just playing video games. These work from home days are just an excuse. He could be sitting with me, making sure I feel better, but he'd rather fight goblins or orcs or whatever it is he does all day."

"He has a job, honey. Why don't you get a personal assistant?"

This was the wrong reply. Alexandra took the throw on the couch and pulled it over her head. From beneath the folds of fabric, she moaned, "You don't understand. No one understands."

Tildy rose and read book titles on spines, a slight pain in her heart at all they revealed about the owner of them. Biographies of artists and translations of Greek classics and a full collection of the Hardy Boys mysteries. Her brother-in-law loved to read. It was the thing that could've drawn her to him. They'd grown up in the same circles, joined the same clubs, avoided the same activities. He had even liked her once. There had been some polo tournament his family was forcing him to attend, and he had asked her to join him. They could've pursued something, if she had forgotten to look forward to her summers elsewhere. But she felt no regret for herself. She only wished her sister deserved him.

"Charlie loves to just lock himself in here. He's started bringing George in here too. They play games or they read. Like I'm some sort of monster they need to get away from."

"They want to give you some peace and quiet."

Her sister only grunted in reply. Tildy walked back to Alexandra and put the back of her hand to an abandoned cup of tea. The porcelain was cool.

"Do you want to eat lunch here or downstairs? I brought babka."

Alexandra lifted slightly. "Babka? From the little place?"

"Just for you."

"Oh, good. Right next door, you're so lucky."

Tildy carried the teacup for her sister as they made their way to the breakfast room, where they usually had lunch.

And the visit went on much like this. One argument threaded to another, her sister's demands for sympathy bringing up as much sympathy as such demands often do. The pair of children arrived and added to the presentation. They were evenly divided in personality; one was quiet and reserved like their father, the other impulsive and selfish like their mother. Tildy loved them, though she often checked her watch to gauge when bedtime would relieve her of their attention.

After dinner, when Alexandra was busy doing her skin-care routine, Charlie and Tildy sat in separate corners of the living room. He was reading a book about the history of Japanese role-playing video games, she a new paperback she had purchased before boarding the train. They had failed to turn on enough lamps to light the space this late into the night. Blue moonlight shone in, the cool tone fighting the golden glow of a desk lamp opposite the large windows. If she stood up and looked out, she would see hints of the moon's glow dancing on shards of water. It reminded her of the nighttime view from her Nana's land, a place she loved that lay so far from here. She hoped the dream experiment would match the beauty and quiet of that place, even if the man she wished to be with was out of reach.

"Thanks for coming out to visit us, Tildy. Alexandra has been… you know," Charlie said with a smile. Tildy didn't meet his eyes, but she nodded. They stayed quiet, enjoying that quiet, while nothing moved around them and they remained stationary, a part of their surroundings in blissful inertness.

"Charlie? Charlie!" Alexandra called. "It's time for bed."

Charlie set down his book with a sigh and left his chair. Tildy rose as well. He shut off his lamp, she shut off hers, and she closed the curtains to block out the moonlight. She stayed behind a moment while Charlie ascended the stairs to where his wife waited. He didn't look downcast or sad. He had made his choice and wasn't miserable, not really.

It was good that Tildy had let him go. No matter how hard he had tried, he couldn't have satisfied her. He would never have understood her. There was only one person who could, and he was lost to her now.

The next week, when schedules permitted, Evelyn greeted Tildy in the lobby of the university's human studies building, then guided her through a large, heavy door to a stairwell, ascended one flight, and exited into a carpeted hallway. The blue floor, the soft grey walls, and the tastefully vague artwork gave the place a sterile serenity.

"It was so great to hear from you! How many years has it been?"

Tildy adjusted her purse strap as they walked. "I think

it was Madison's farewell party."

"That's right! That was, what, junior year of college? And you've been in this city this whole time?"

"Yeah, I'm pretty bad at keeping in touch."

"Oh I hear you, school, family, drama. It's hard. Ok, this is our office. After you," Evelyn held the door open to a surprisingly small space. "We'll need to go over the experiment, and if it all sounds good to you, I'll ask some preliminary questions, and then we'll fit the cap and map the electrodes. The mapping can be tedious sometimes."

Tildy sat in the chair as instructed and gripped her hands in her lap. A stone white mannequin head on the desk, covered by a netting of electrodes and wires, faced her. She tried to mirror its inertness, hiding the tangled web of feelings she held inside.

Evelyn turned her monitor towards Tildy, and clicked through a slide show. Zylegxer, a drug used to treat nightmares, had been found to cause deep and sustained sleep. This was not unexpected. However, patients had reported facts and events in their dreams that were believable, accurate depictions of what they knew from their day-to-day life. This is unusual. In a typical dream experiment, dreamers may forget prompts or missions, and details from the past few days may not reliably appear in a dream state, while inaccuracies occur at random to derail the dreamer's sense of reality.

Importantly, the drug also increased the frequency of lucid dreams. Patients reliably remembered their intended goal within a dream, could communicate through eye movement back to researchers, and navigated near-real worlds to achieve the goal while they slept.

After the medication slides were finished, a card titled simply DREAM MACHINE remained in place. Tildy leaned forward, the plain bold text calling to her.

Evelyn clicked on and showed a young woman wearing the cap currently on the mannequin. It was a device filled with low-frequency signal emitters, sensors, vibration devices, held together with gold and grey coated wiring, with a chin strap like a bicycle helmet. Earlier iterations of lucid dreaming devices used focused ultrasound to stimulate the prefrontal cortex, but the results were unreliable. Ultrasounds do not pass through the hard bone of an adult skull very easily and prefrontal cortex activation is likely only an artifact of our measuring systems, not because it is generating dreams.

In this study, the radio emitters and vibration devices could pass through the bone of the skull. They were programmed to activate at set intervals, stimulating neurotransmitters and biomechanical feedback that replicated the action of Zylegxer. Evelyn explained something about suppressing delta activation to trigger cortical stimulation, but Tildy didn't pay much attention. Only one message, playing through her head on repeat, came through – these tools guaranteed her hours of lucid dreaming, which she could use to build her own world, one that forgave and accepted her.

The next slide covered applications. Unsurprisingly, recreation and creative endeavors were listed.

"We all know tech bros are going to want to use this to replace their psychotropic drugs, but my primary interests are folks who need therapy for trauma. A lot of the despair people feel, either in domestic violence situations, abusive work environments, things like that, is an inability to imagine a better life for themselves—a way to get out of the situation that is killing them. The strain of surviving, of getting through the day-to-day, is all too much. They don't have time to think about the future. Imagination takes time and space, and both are a luxury. Talk therapy has its own problems. People in lower economic classes are more likely to report that they don't trust therapists, they don't want to share their secrets, they don't want to invite investigations into their private lives.

"What this therapy can give clients a few hours of space to freely imagine their future. They can make decisions, see how it will play out to the best of their abilities, without interference or supervision. We plan to submit for FDA approval in the fall. As we said, Zylegxer has already been cleared for use by the FDA for certain applications, nightmares and other disordered sleep conditions. There are no safety concerns there, though we do tell participants they need a safe place to sleep for a full eight hours before taking the drug or using the cap."

"Wouldn't it be difficult to convince people to take medication that isn't necessary?" Tildy asked. "Especially people in domestic abuse situations?"

Evelyn nodded. "That was a concern we had as well. The cap can work alone through physiological feedback, without the medication, but it needs fine-tuning. We're still in development on that front. For now, we need both the medication and the cap to achieve the desired results consistently. We're confident we can complete the device without relying on the medication."

Tildy knew she should be thinking about this technology as Evelyn intended, as a tool to help people without the privileges of free time and private mental healthcare. But she couldn't. She stared at the final slide, her own thoughts selfishly consumed with possibility.

Evelyn gathered the papers Tildy needed to review and tapped them into a neat pile. She smiled and shook her head. "I knew your sister was, you know, a SULLIVAN. But I didn't realize you were related to her. All those years in school, I never put two and two together."

Tildy shifted in her seat. "She and I didn't spend much time together when we were kids."

Evelyn seemed to sense the unease and steered the conversation elsewhere. "You hung out with Lin Okamoto? How's she doing?"

"She and Chloe got together after high school. They moved up to Syracuse, I think."

Evelyn gasped. "Chloe! Wow, that takes me back. She was with Daphne forever. Whatever happened to her?"

"She married a senator."

"Oh shit, is she that Daphne?"

"Yeah."

"Damn. All these people moving away," Evelyn said. "Girl, why are you still here in the city? You were going to move too, weren't you? To live with your grandma?"

Tildy looked down at the mottled industrial carpet. "I thought I would. I didn't, in the end."

Evelyn shook her head and her tone dropped. "Growing up that fast isn't fair."

"No." Tildy forced a smile. "But you're doing great! I love this project."

"Thanks. So glad we don't have to work out of the lab for this—the device is take-home, so no long lab nights for me, and no trying to convince people to let me spy on them. People don't like being watched when they sleep, even if we don't really know what they are dreaming."

Evelyn looked down at her desk and smiled. "You know, one of the reasons I joined Dr. Cutting's lab was your mom's charity. They helped my aunt and little cousins through some shit, with free therapy and home visits and what not. Your mama was a good woman. Ah, and she was beautiful, too. I remember seeing her on a billboard for something. A charity or an awareness campaign, I can't remember, in Times Square. Times Square! And I thought, 'Hey, that's Gisele's mom! She's alright!' It makes more sense that she was your mama. She was so good."

Tildy put on the stony, kind face she always used when something attacked this wound in her heart. "Thanks."

"Okay, anyway! I better stop talking and get back on task here. Let me just give you a rundown of the experiment—I know you know already, but I need to follow the outline here. This is a study in the Cutting Lab for Psychology. The purpose of the study is to learn whether an external device can consistently activate lucid dreaming with factual details, from both distant and recent memories. Participation in this experiment is entirely voluntary. You may withdraw your consent at any time. Data will be stored here at the lab, and you have the option to opt into sharing with researchers within the university, outside of it, and/or with media and the general public. Those consents are found here, on this page."

Tildy reviewed the page, checked boxes, and signed.

"Okay, first question. Your name is Tildy Sullivan, single, born in NYC, same year as me, right?"

"Right."

"Dating in this city is like trying to find an organ donor, I'm telling you. Okay, question one. Would you say you are good sleeper?"

"Yes."

"Any difficulty falling asleep?"

"No."

Evelyn frowned, reoriented her cursor, clicked, and nodded. "Sorry about that. Do you feel refreshed after sleeping?"

"Yes."

"Do you often wish you could sleep more when you wake?"

Tildy paused, various replies coming to her, before she said, "Yes."

"Do you replay events in your dreams?"

A momentary flash of memory interrupted her, not of him, but of a simple event. How often had she dreamt of learning to ride the Coyne's pony, Gandalf? Her mother had watched from a picnic blanket beneath a tree, along with Mrs. Coyne and her toddler Niall, while Mr. Coyne led Tildy round and round on their daughter Fionnuala's steady, if a bit small, Connemara pony. Tildy had dreamt this many times, with little variation, as if her brain was giving the memory a quick polish at night.

"Yes, I do."

"Can you lucid dream?"

"Sometimes. Rarely."

"Okay, great. How many hours a night do you sleep?"

"Seven to nine. Depends. Nine on the weekends."

"Can you maintain a quiet, safe space to sleep for at least three nights?"

"Yes."

"Great. Participants are asked to think of a realistic scenario to explore while they are dreaming. This can be, like, going back to school for a different degree, moving upstate, taking a promotion, these sorts of things."

"Got it."

"It works by extending and modifying the dreaming stages of sleep. You will dream for more than three hours each session, beginning immediately after you fall asleep.

And you will have perfect recall of your dream."

"Each time?"

"Hopefully, or else we screwed up. Here's some paper-work going over what we discussed. Standard experiment disclosures and an information release. There's also another page here where you affirm you will not use the cap more than fifteen times in a one-month period."

Tildy's pen hovered over the line. "What happens if you do?"

"The cap activates memory and rational thought, and overuse may have an effect on your recall abilities during the day. We've only seen that in animal studies, though. The cap gives you trippy dreams way before it starts affecting your memory."

Tildy had done some superficial research the night before. Patent applications, journal articles, newspaper interviews. But she still didn't understand how this tech-nology worked. She listened to Evelyn read the very long list of possible serious side effects and struggled to take it seriously. She signed.

"Alright, what scenario are you going to be exploring?"

"Moving to Ireland."

Evelyn looked up and gave her a sad smile. Then she nodded and typed. "What are the obstacles and challenges you expect to encounter in the dream?"

Tildy shifted in her seat. "My father's whole… deal, adjusting to the different style of living over there, uh, learning how to drive on the wrong side of the road. Stuff like that."

"And stick shifts, too? No thank you. I've been in New York City my whole life. I don't even drive. I'd take the bus."

"I hear you. My nana's village doesn't have much public transportation, though."

Evelyn left her seat, lifted the cap from the mannequin's head, and grabbed a set of pliers. "Good point. That country is so tiny. We flew over it when we went to London for a psychology conference last year. Took no time at all."

Tildy only smiled and waited. Evelyn set the cap on Tildy's head and adjusted the size with the pliers. Once it fit snugly, she sat back at her computer and pressed some keys. In the reflection of a metal desk lamp, Tildy could see a green light turn on.

"When you use this for the sessions, that light will be on for the first minute, then it shuts off. It'll stay on for now because we're just getting things calibrated. You might feel some slight vibration through the cap, but it shouldn't be uncomfortable."

The little devices in the cap began to buzz. Through her hair, Tildy found it only faintly perceptible. Unsure what to do with herself, she shut her eyes. She thought of a trip to Galway with her mother, long ago. They had gone shopping for a birthday, or was it a baby shower? They stopped over in Cupán Tae before heading back to Nana's. Tildy still remembered the delight of the tea service; delicate little sandwiches on fine china, porcelain cups with dainty handles waiting patiently to be filled with tea, cream, and sugar. It must have been winter. She remembered the smell of the seasonal blend, gingerbread and dark berries. And she remembered her mother smiling at her fondly, just the two of them, a little reprieve from the stresses that would one day pull them apart.

Tildy sighed. Her composure was almost complete. She was going to do this. She just had to hold on a little longer.

"Alright, I'm going to ask you to visualize some things. Can you think of your granny's house?"

The little fence and beyond it the half-and-half door, whitewashed walls on either side, the window frames painted, one layer over another, the first laid down by her great-great-grandfather as a young boy. The original glass panes like a gentle sea, light glittering off the wobbly surface. Flowers in the flower box, and inside, her nana's shadow as she crossed the floor she had walked across since she was a child, in a room that had sheltered her family for generations.

"Wow, that came through nice and clear. Okay, now think of a rock falling to the ground."

A rock thrown off the Wolfe Tone bridge, the Corrib dark, strong and threatening. The rock causing a splash, and the childish squeals of laughter that followed. The frightening sense of doom, of *what if next is not a rock but me, what if I climb up and I totter and I fall, down, down, down into the rushing black-blue water beneath us.*

"Little noisy. Let's try what happens at the beginning of the day. In the sky."

The sun rises across the hills, where I want to be.

"Great. Wow, we may not even need Zylegxer. Excellent. Now say your name?"

"Tildy Halleran Sullivan."

"All done, nice and easy. You can take the cap off now. Here's a little bag for it, and inside is a secondary cap to wear over the net, so it doesn't snag on your pillows or anything. You may want to tie your hair back in a low pony, just to keep it out of the way."

"Okay."

Tildy shivered a little as she put the device in the bag. What had happened inside her brain? What if something had been knocked loose?

"Here's the device that the recordings will be transmitted to, sending them back to us. Just keep this by your bed, and it'll do all the work for you. The box will have little lights telling you if it is transmitting or in standby mode. But that's not important—you don't need to worry about that. I know I keep repeating myself, just want to make sure everything is clear so far."

"It is."

"Okay, and here's the Zylegxer. It's just five days' worth. I think you may be able to get by without it, but I'd use it for the first couple of sessions. Give you something to compare it to, when you go without."

Tildy took the small bottle and stuffed it into the bag with the net. Evelyn smiled and leaned back against her desk. "Well, lady! I think that's all!"

"Any advice for getting these dreams to be as accurate as possible? Like, research and stuff? You said that memory will be more activated with this device."

"It will, yeah. I wouldn't go too deep. Look up the weather, maybe, and some spots you'd think you'd like to go to but haven't been to recently."

Tildy rose, looked into the bag, and paused. She made herself ask a practical question, one she would ask if she was being a professional or even rational. "You said more sessions will help the study?"

Evelyn snorted. "Girl, we need all the help we can get. We put so much work into this kit, and no one wants to use it."

She looked down at the bag in her hand. "That's a shame."

"It is! If you can give me five sessions in the next two weeks, I'm telling you, I'll be so grateful to you, you don't even know!"

"I'll do it. And you'll want notes about what I see and stuff?"

"Yeah, as detailed as you can," Evelyn said, then added with more meaning, "and if you find any peace, you know, from thinking through this, let me know. That's what this is all about."

With her eyes lowered, Tildy nodded, holding the bag with a firm grip. They said their goodbyes, and she left—back to work, back to her commute, back through her routine until she was home again and in bed and ready, holding the dream machine, eager to see if it could make her whole again.

Tildy looked up the weather forecast and a hotel with availability in Galway, Ireland. Lots of availability and a disappointing forecast. She took extra care getting ready for bed, shut off the lights, turned up her noise machine, and sat in the dark.

She held the cap in her hand and looked down at it. The electrodes caught the streak of light coming in from her hallway. This was going to run currents through her brain. It was an untested medical device. With her family history, it might not be safe. What was she thinking?

No, she knew what she was thinking. She sipped some water, put on the cap, and lay down on her pillow.

The green light on the transmitter turned on, stayed on, and then shut off.

chapter
four

The heat of the sun was an unwelcome, flat pressure against Tildy's face. Her skin tingled. There was more. She closed her eyes and tugged at an invisible string, unravelling the knot. A soft breeze moved in from the sea and lifted strands of hair from her face. A fragrance of fuchsia, warmed, mixed and coiled about her in perfect proportion to the salt mist. It didn't smell like New York.

The loving laughter of friendships, in accents both surprising and familiar. From somewhere nearby, she could smell smoke escaping a flung cigarette. The rough bench under her hands had only hints of paint remaining. Gulls cried in the distance. The luggage against her legs was heavy and pressed against her sweaty skin. A couple on vacation bickered in Italian nearby.

Tildy opened her eyes and looked around. What she saw matched what she smelled and heard—unpleasant details, but they added to the realism. She immediately accepted this world, sighing a sigh of near-contentment, a calm with conditions. She would invest herself in this dream; she would treat it as real, and see where it led.

Tildy's mind filled in the gaps of the dream. She had changed into a soft, expensive sweater before leaving Shannon airport. Yes, of course. It had been an eager preparation for the sweater weather of Galway – a steady mist and chilly gusts that she remembered from childhood. Yet it was warm here; locals strolled in shorts and tank tops. A last heatwave before the end of summer. She peeled off the cashmere and stuffed it into her carry-on bag. It would get used tomorrow, if the forecast was to be trusted. If not tomorrow, later in the week, or some day in the future. This was home now.

Home. She listened to the camaraderie around her, the way locals seemed to know everyone, their confident familiarity with their surroundings. Maybe it would become home. Growing up, Tildy had been moved from one part of New York City to the next, with quick jaunts in Santa Fe and Florida, but always back to the city. She'd had no other permanence than the city and, in the end, a vague American accent. What had allowed her to passively participate in any conversation across the Atlantic now bloomed black whenever she used her voice. As she had during childhood visits, Tildy was determined to be silent, unless speaking could not be reasonably avoided.

If she didn't speak, she blended in quite well. Drunk men on a stag party, evidently from Liverpool, based on their soccer jerseys, had leered at her as she walked to the airport bus stop, shout-singing "Galway Girl" in her wake. The attention unrequited, she accepted the practical information within it; she looked like an object for tourists. Like she belonged.

Now alone on a bench, she should be overlooking the water. Instead, she averted her gaze from the backsides of the strangers who wandered about her in clusters, soaking in the warm sun. To her left, Spanish Arch, next to the museum and a restaurant, beyond a row of houses snuggled tightly along a dead-end road to the water's edge.

Tildy paused. Was it Spanish Arch? Spanish Arches? There were two arches in the structure. Was it only the raucous downtown area known as Spanish Arch, or was it the section of wall, with the actual, physical arch, known as Spanish Arch? Now that she looked at it, she recalled an old photo from her grandmother's house, or a museum, or the internet. It showed the original Claddagh village, women in worn grey-brown dresses and great patterned shawls huddled in groups as fishmongers set up their stalls. At that time, there was only one arch. Tildy could feel her grip on the dream slipping. Her insecurity made the realism waver.

She puffed out a breath. She didn't know, and that was normal. She filed the question away. Nana might tell her, if she didn't belittle her too much for asking.

She was here, and it was summer again. Disjointed childhood snapshots formed her memories of this place. Playing fetch with a dog named Countess, learning rude phrases in Irish from her cousins, her first game of volleyball, oddly enough. She remembered hearing of the swans in the water—the souls of lost fishermen—and to never interfere with them or else she'd be cursed. The swans had scared her, so avoiding them was no problem. Her trips to Ireland had given her endless material for cocktail conversations at her father's parties and company galas. She told stories of sheep blocking her great-uncle's car for two hours, locals who refused to speak to her family in English, and the beauty of the ocean as seen from the Wild Atlantic Way.

She had secrets, too. Unlike those early memories, which lived in her as moments without time, the later events were clear, fixed in place.

The weather was too hot. Exasperated, Tildy yanked the handle of her rolling suitcase into the extended position and hoisted her purse onto her shoulder. She'd just go to the hotel and insist on an early check-in. Judging by the time on her watch, it would be a very early check-in. The jostling of her unruly suitcase on the narrow, busy sidewalks begged her to step into the street, where she would meet certain death. The people behind the wheel of many compact cars were friendly, as most Irish were, yet their assertive driving was worthy of Manhattan streets.

By the time she reached the hotel, her shirt and slacks were secured into uncomfortable places by a layer of sweat. She was grateful to have removed the sweater when she had. Why had the dream included all this? Was it *really* necessary?

The lobby, clean but dated, smelled faintly of hospital soap left inside a cedar chest. Dark red carpet, dark wooden paneling, and antique blown-glass lights gave the space a warm, timeless air. She steered her suitcase to the desk and waited. The bored receptionist, a young man with red hair, fair skin, and no hope of growing facial hair, continued his work for a moment. He wore a smart vest and a tie, colors matched to the décor of the hotel, over a crisp white button up shirt. He flashed a sincere smile when he noticed her.

"How may I help you, miss."

"I've arrived early, reservation under Matilda Halleran."

He looked over his screen. "May I see your passport and method of payment for incidentals, please."

Tildy handed him her Irish passport and credit card. He looked from her to the passport, with her parents' surnames hyphenated, permanently bound together, and back to her face. Then he processed her payment and returned the items.

"Your room will be on the second floor, left from the elevator, room 28. We have you down for ten nights. The elevator is just beyond the restaurant. I'll help you with your things."

"That's okay."

He pointedly looked to the empty lobby, the vacant doorway, then back to her.

"What else have I to do?"

The walk gave her the opportunity to look over the dining area, populated by grey heads and deployed news-papers. The clerk seemed to sense her thoughts.

"We're quite popular with the pensioner set."

They reached the highly polished brass elevator, and he pressed the button. What followed was a sound like a mining cart rubbing against a chain-link fence. The illumi-nated number changed from 3 to 2. After an uncomfortable pause, it changed to 1. They waited. The young man sighed. They waited longer. One of the double doors slid open slowly, as if it were pantomiming fatigue. Then the second door jerked to life, sliding open as well. Tildy looked at the clerk.

"Ready to live dangerously, then?" he asked with a grin as they squeezed into the incredibly tiny, incredibly reflec-tive space. The doors closed as noncommittally as they had opened.

He cleared his throat. "Lost your accent, I see. California?"

Tildy frowned. She didn't want to waste her time dreaming about small talk with a stranger. "New York City."

"New York. My mum has a cousin in, ah, Newark, was it?"

"Oh?"

"Sure. Married a local, stayed. Broke her brother's heart. I'm moving to Florida myself. Haven't any brother's hearts to break. Only my sister, and she emigrated to Belgium."

Tildy looked him full in the face, taking in his pale skin and overt friendliness. "Florida?"

"You don't recommend it?"

"It's hot. And…" The elevator had released them into the hallway, and she turned left and scanned for her room number. She wanted to end this conversation and close the door. She did not want to discuss Florida. She was here so she wouldn't have to think about Florida. She finished weakly, "So many tourists."

"Nothing I can't handle, I think. Get a lot of sunburns there, I take it?"

"It is the tropics," she answered quietly as they approached door 28. He led her into her cozy home for the next ten days; the decor included wine-colored carpet, tiny buds blooming on floral wallpaper, and a vintage television.

She handed him a €1 coin. He accepted it with warmth. "We'll speak on Florida more, maybe, eh? Good afternoon, then, Miss Halleran."

He shut the door behind him. When his retreating footsteps grew faint, Tildy locked the door and set the security latch. She turned and faced the hotel room. She could just settle down. She was safe here. But her brain felt this was real. The carpet beneath her shoes, the smell of the wood polish, the gentle sway of the curtains in the air conditioner breeze all matched her expectations, so the impulse to do what she always did when she traveled swept over her. Maybe it was the dream telling her to put in the work. That, if she treated the dream as real, it would be more real for her.

Inside the bathroom, she slid open the frosted glass door. A standard-size tub and matching blush tile greeted her. She checked the closet—nothing there but spare blankets and a pillow. Almost lying down, she paused. She dropped to her hands and knees and checked under the bed. A solid platform. The room was definitely empty. Satisfied, she rose, shut the curtains, peeled off her sweaty clothes, and then collapsed back onto the pillows with the remote control.

The station was set to local news, the volume muted, subtitles displayed. Tildy half-heartedly attempted to turn on the volume. The remote was old and confusing, and the TV remained silent. She gave up, snuggling in and letting herself doze as she watched the screen. The headlines covered a hurling tournament, Brexit fallout, and a plowing championship. Tildy listened, and didn't listen, and felt the air conditioning on her skin. Darkness wrapped itself around her, obscuring the world she had carefully constructed.

Time had passed in New York.

Tildy woke to her faint grey wall and modern

floor-to-ceiling curtains. She lay still, processing what she was seeing, disoriented by the contrast. When she felt ready, she sat up. Early spring. Sunrise blooming through buildings, rising far beyond her street, beyond Long Island. It was only one or two in the morning in Ireland right now, not late afternoon. It wasn't real.

She put her face in her hands and rubbed, trying to increase her circulation. They smelled of her hand soap. Because she was in New York, in her apartment.

She grabbed her journal and noted details of the dream, including the elevator. Why was the elevator broken? And the valet moving to Florida? Was that just to ground the dream with feelings she had now? She wasn't sure. There had been a sense of her own power there, in the dream, but incomplete power. The dream was a train. She could choose a destination, ride it or not, but how she got there was beyond her control. It was exactly what she had hoped for.

Tildy went through the motions of her day. She dressed, commuted to work, completed her tasks, attended to all the details, ran the experiments the executives wanted her to run, but she felt her attention pulled in too many directions. Lee had texted her, asking her to join another family meeting. Alexandra had left a voicemail, asking for childcare. There was nothing to say to any of them. All Tildy wanted to do was go home and sleep.

At lunchtime, just as she entered her favorite Japanese curry shop for lunch, a text buzzed her phone. It was from Russell.

○ How are you, Tildy?

She set the phone back in her purse. She asked herself the question. *How am I?*

The text had no special significance. It was likely the product of some subroutine, a programmatic way to maintain her emotional connection. Now, though, the question seemed impossible to answer. How could she answer? She didn't know herself.

Lunch, then emails, then a meeting, then checking early results on the test feed. Her calculations for interactions were off. If she couldn't measure this correctly, the entire experiment was pointless. She spent a few hours diagnosing the issue as the day grew darker. In the end, it was a careless oversight. One she hadn't made in years. She tidied it up and read through the product spec once more, feeling as though she owed the company this extra bit of attention.

At six, coworkers asked if she wanted to join them for drinks. Tildy declined and said she would another time. She had plans tonight. They left all together in one direction, she alone in the other.

She went home, showered, took the medication, set the cap on her head, and stared at the green light until it shut off.

Tildy entered the dream at night, hot and dry. The overambitious hotel air conditioner had switched to heating mode at some point. The television was still on. The room looked exactly the same as her last dream. She was still hastily undressed, her teeth felt slimy, and her hair was frizzy. Had a version of her slept here? Had any time passed? Or had the dream paused? She checked the clock. It was 9 p.m., and her jet lag felt so real. She wondered if it was it possible to dream here.

Outside were the sounds of a city come to life. Tildy shut off the television and stretched. She was here, so she'd go out. It was dark, but she couldn't get hurt here. Could she get hurt here? She passed her tongue over her unbrushed teeth and hesitated. Just how realistic could this become?

The dream soothed her. She knew it had a plan for her, that it needed her to go outside, that it would keep her safe. Perhaps this would be the only time in her life that she could walk somewhere at night without any fear.

She washed her face and combed her hair, then changed into fresh clothes: a pair of jeans that fit perfectly, high-top sneakers that were really too cool for her, and a loose white T-shirt. She put on what her mind told her was her favorite jacket, a worn leather in warm brown. She didn't own this jacket in real life. Where she had pulled these clothes from, she didn't know, but she didn't dwell on it. Her black hair was half up, allowing the waves to curl slightly against her shoulders. She applied basic makeup, going back over her work with extra mascara. After her makeup was applied, her hand hovered over the small fabric bag containing her mother's ring, then retreated.

The young woman in the mirror was the best version

of herself. Even still, despite the whimsy of the dream, she looked like an attractive woman's friend, a handsome man's cousin, the disappointing child of a beautiful couple. Not a heartbreaker who had fallen to age, a stunning creature brought low by sorrow. The woman Tildy saw in the mirror was a plain, unoffensive person, with none of the charms of youth to lean on. A background character to someone else's story.

On her way through the lobby, she paused. She didn't know where she was going. If the Spanish Arch area was busy in the daytime, evening would be a disaster. Tildy felt her enthusiasm fading; she didn't know anyone here, and she didn't have anyone who could help her if she needed it. The dream began to feel too large, with hidden corners and long shadows all around her. She hadn't thought this through.

"What's the craic?" the clerk asked. He was still wearing his vest, but his tie was missing, and his top button undone. As if he had gone on break and hadn't quite put himself back together. As if he was real.

"Erm," Tildy said softly, her voice squeaking slightly from disuse. "I was hoping to get a pint and some food, nothing fancy. Really hoping for a quiet place? I don't want any trouble."

He nodded. "You'll want to stay clear of Eyre Square and Spanish Arch. Lots of drunk fellas up to no good. I've a place in mind." And he took out a well-used notepad, nearly three-quarters full. He flipped to the next blank sheet, scribbled the pub's name, a map, and added a name at the bottom. "Ask for Eli. He's working tonight, he'll keep the boys off you. You shouldn't have trouble, though."

"No…"

He blushed. "Oh, no. No! I only meant it's quiet that part of town. I, er, here now. Here's the front desk number, ring me if you need anything. I'm here until midnight, then Misha takes over until 6 a.m."

She thanked him, took the slip of paper, and left. In real life, would this be a text message? Or were notes on paper still common in Ireland? Tildy shook her head. *Accept this,* she told herself. *Accept that this is how it should be. This is your dream.*

The enormous seagulls from the daytime were gone. Their groups had been replaced by teenagers in black clothing, each holding bottles in paper bags. She saw women lined up outside of a bar, barking laughs as they tottered in high heels on cobblestone streets. Tildy stopped her cruel thoughts and chastised herself. Those were the kinds of things her father would say, and he was not here. She didn't need to bring his negative in. She continued on her walk, letting the dream take her where it wanted her to go.

A highly illuminated Italian gelato place shone like a beacon across the wide pedestrian pathway to the right. A new batch of stag party attendees milled around quaint shop windows darkened until daytime. Passing through them were older drunk men nearly leaning on their respective women. Tildy continued with purpose, invisible to them.

The last bar passed and Tildy took a deep breath. Beyond the mouth of the brick and concrete funnel, the breeze was liberating. The salty air lifted her hair and caressed her face. She let her pace slow, appreciating the lights of a distant boat twinkling on the water.

The River Corrib moved into the bay, dark and fast, beneath the Wolfe Tone Bridge. Lights from nearby buildings danced on the undulating water, while the water itself remained a dark mystery. Beneath the sediment lay Bronze Age tools, Viking axes, and centuries of odds and ends from the days in between. Its original name wasn't even Corrib. It was likely Galway, the original protection for what became the first fortified city in western Ireland. Only the reflections gave away the scale and motion of what lay beneath. Something told Tildy that while all else around her was her own creation, the river was real. It was not bound by reality and would not tolerate any pale imitations.

It made her wonder—when she met people she knew, would they be like this river?

A large group had paused their progress, most of the walkway blocked by their socializing. They were young people, locals, chatting jovially. The men apologized to her, stepping aside to let her by, without any further scrutiny. She nodded with a smile, then passed into the darkness of another narrow, curved street.

Ahead, a noisy pub with a large group congregated on the sidewalk. The sharp tingle of danger crawled up her spine.

Calm down. This place doesn't exist, she told herself. *This is your dream.*

As if a tap had been turned down, the density of crowds dwindled. There were clusters here and there, but few enough that she could walk comfortably. Tildy paused in the light of a tea shop and checked the clerk's note. She had reached the correct intersection. The instructions read, "Look for the big black dog."

Expecting a friendly looking dog painting, she nearly missed the enormous woolly black dog painted on the side of a two-story building. It looked less doglike and more monstrous. The image was discordant to the rest of the scene. Soft music flowed out of the building, the sidewalk in front bathed in a warm golden light from the windows. She approached, hopeful. Outside the door, she stood on tiptoe to see through the high windows and gauge the crowd. Small clusters of people, a quiet, corner spot at the bar open. Tildy hefted open the first set of framed glass doors. The second set swung more easily.

She shivered from the unexpected chill of air conditioning. The variations of warm wood she had seen through the window had prompted her to expect the sticky hotness found in a Manhattan bar, midsummer. A few people glanced her direction then looked away without interest. Tildy took her place, a perfect spot tucked into a corner with a banister behind her, ready to watch people without being watched herself.

A tall, powerfully built man with a beard worked the

bar. He had a tattoo scrawling down his upper arm, the tone matching his blue-gray apron. She wondered if people that looked like him were more common here. The typical weather certainly gave a full beard more purpose, at least in terms of warmth.

"Hallo, miss. What'll have?"

The man's deep voice and thick accent gave Tildy the impression of dark brown bread, strong but comforting.

"A cider, please."

He gave a quick nod and turned away to fill her order. A couple nearby laughed at a joke, a group of old men continued their chatter, all of them warm and friendly and no one noticing her at all. Tildy embraced her invisibility with relief. This was what she wanted. To see and not be seen, to belong without being asked to do or be anything.

She turned her focus on the small food menu. An enormous, calloused finger appeared in her vision and jabbed the page. "We don't have these bangers or the pies."

"Chips, please?"

He nodded, setting down her glass and cold bottle of cider. Tildy sipped from the bottle, until she noted no one was drinking from the bottle, and poured the drink into her glass. She relaxed her body, settling into observing those around her, secure in the task of sipping. The musicians' area was in a slow state of transition. A keyboard had been relocated, a stool positioned in its place. In the audience, most of the groups at tables looked to be locals just off work.

There was no television and Tildy had no book. She felt for her phone, but it was not there. Why would it be? Had she ever dreamed of her cell phone? She didn't think so. Still, that was an unrealistic detail. It unnerved her.

Sipping slowly, she read the fliers posted on the walls. Yoga with Celené. Guitar lessons. Scottish folklore. Childcare at St. Mary's.

A group entered, their voices playful and light. Tildy turned toward them, as did a few other patrons. A few locals nodded or raised their glasses, their hellos returned in kind. The group's evident ease in the space matched their pleasant sound. Colleagues from some nearby business—a good job, from the looks of it—and regular patrons of this pub. They cleared an abandoned table with skill. Perhaps they worked at another bar? One of the young men approached the bar, carrying more glasses than Tildy would've thought possible. She returned her gaze to the fliers.

"Heya, shcan! Will need a round."

The bartender quickly counted the group, grabbed a platter, and started pulling pints and setting them out. "Aidan joining you lot?"

Tildy shifted in her seat.

"He's just behind us, made him do the locking up. Don't pour him one, though. You know he's off it. Oh mate, these pints look positively lush." The bartender rolled his eyes but nodded.

While he was waiting, Tildy felt the young man's curious gaze examine her. She kept her eyes on the fliers. Her mind told him to look away. It told him bend to her dream's structure and stay away.

"Jordie, order me some chips, will you," one of the women called out.

"Eli…"

The bartender held up a hand without looking up. "I got it. I could hear Katherine in a car crash with a score set by jet engines and falling pianos."

The two men laughed, and once the drinks were ready, Jordie returned to his table.

Tildy turned away from the fliers. She gave the rest of the bar more attention, if only to distract herself. Her power here was tenuous. The group discussed dinner service, a new sommelier, and the quality of the scallops. They worked at a high-end restaurant, then, she realized with a blush. These were not random characters in her dream.

The group turned to the woman who'd requested the chips, a lovely young woman with soft curly hair. It was odd to Tildy that they used her full, formal name, yet seemed so loving. Someone asked if she was going to sing tonight. It was gently playful, not bullying or teasing. Katherine replied, her words lost, but her tone signified amenability. They seemed encouraged. Tildy smiled at the prospect of hearing someone so evidently loved perform tonight.

The door opened again. She stole a glance, framing her gaze as curiosity for an anticipated guest. She froze.

The newcomer was greeted by several tables, smiled to all. He pushed up his sleeves and pulled an orphaned chair over to the restaurant group. Instead of immediately sitting, he visited with an elderly couple at another table. A tall, broad man, he crouched comfortably to a lower level for their benefit. He spoke with warmth and friendliness to the man in Irish and asked the woman a question. Tildy couldn't be sure, but she thought it was about the man's dog, who had recently passed away.

The bartender called out, "Aidan, what'll you be having?"

"Evening, Eli. A mineral."

"I only have a few here, erm, hm." The bartender rummaged through his offerings.

Tildy moved to avert her eyes into the sanctuary of her phone, but it didn't exist here. There was no phone. She shut her eyes.

He was going to see her if she didn't find something to hide her face.

This was her dream. Her pocket. She'd check her jacket pocket.

A book.

With an easy motion, she pulled the worn paperback from her pocket. *Marmion* by Sir Walter Scott.

It didn't matter if it was a toilet repair manual—Tildy opened it and placed a hand as casually as possible to conceal her face as she read a page in the middle. She heard approaching footsteps, sounds she dreaded and relished.

"Ugh, can't stand lemon. Is that elderberry? Sure, that'd be grand."

There was an unnatural pause, where there was no

speaking and no movement, and she could sense his attention. Sweat gathered in her palms. Then he turned back to his table. The soft breeze in his wake carried his scent. Masculine yet clean, with fragrant soap and subtle hints of herbs and spices. A thread of electricity raced up her spine.

She let herself look at him walk away.

At his hand, which had once held her own. His arms, once around her as they lay in a field, laughing, unable to stargaze on an old wool blanket as planned because of incoming clouds. He'd pulled her close amid the wind and drizzling rain, and enclosed in his warmth, they'd looked into each other's eyes. His eyes, light and kind, with a quiet intensity that saw only her, as his gentle lips kissed her. They'd stayed that way for as long as they could tolerate the cold. Her first romance, a young love that built up one summer to the next, until at sixteen, she had not looked forward to the beaches, the family gatherings, or even Nana. Only him.

By that summer's end, she'd had a plan: finish high school, leave America and her father behind, attend college in Galway, visit Nana as often as she liked, build a career and love Aidan. At seventeen, it had all been mapped out. She would come back the next summer, and she would stay forever.

The memories of that last summer were worn but intact. Each moment lived in her as a cherished friend. The scratchy voice on Nana's radio had warned of flooding—a huge storm on the horizon, sweeping in from the ocean to the western coast, had pushed against the sea. In a rush to beat the storm, she'd kissed her mother and Nana goodbye, then peddled a rusted bicycle away from the cottage, over animal paths. The destination: a secret place, a vacant property midway between his home and Nana's.

In a snow globe within her heart, they still stood there, beside the abandoned cottage, a cool wind whipping her hair as he smiled down at her, his smooth freckled face wearing pure affection, just for her. Tildy blushed, recalling his fingertips tracing the curves of her face. There was nothing embarrassing or awkward. It had been her closest experience to true love. They had talked about their futures. He'd asked her to stay, asked her to call, asked her to write, but her life fell apart. She left. She never wrote. She never called. And he was lost to her, given up when so much had been taken away.

He hadn't smelled like that back then. He had aged into a kind of effortless handsome, competent without pretense. His hands were strong and agile. The muscles in his forearms the evidence of hard work, hinting at more beneath his rolled-up sleeves. He was tall, his shoulders broad, filling in his T-shirt as the advertisements always promise, and yet he seemed slightly hunched. Not from a shyness. It was as though asserting his strength was an unnecessary excess. He was strong and confident and didn't need to show anyone.

He waved at someone across the bar before he joined his friends. He rested in his chair, folded his arms, and listened to them talk with a soft smile. She remembered his pale hazel eyes staring into hers, the moonlight illuminating her fingers as they ran through the waves of his brown hair.

Tildy looked at her hands now. The awkwardness of youth remained in her, perhaps even concentrated itself, but now it was tarnished by time. The dry wrinkles on her knuckles and the raised blue-green veins marked her departure from childhood.

Any curiosity that fixed her in place evaporated. She needed to leave when the music began, when he was distracted, and then she would never return to this bar. To see how age had destroyed her and elevated him, how whatever power youth had given her had died away. It would ruin a memory that had buoyed her through many disappointments.

The bartender delivered her fries a moment later. Tildy touched one, far too hot, and set it back down. It didn't matter. She had no appetite.

"Good evening," an older man said into the microphone. Tildy returned to her surroundings, realizing the musicians had assembled on the platform that served as a stage. The lights in the pub dimmed. "We'd like to start with a request to Katherine McCleary to delight us with her grandmammy's songs."

The table at the center of Tildy's awareness whispered encouragement as their friend rose to polite applause. Katherine crossed to the stage, looking reserved but not nervous. After she exchanged some words with the musicians, she adjusted the microphone slightly. Settled into her place, she closed her eyes, and the music began. When her voice emerged, softly permeating the crowd, it called attention to all present.

Tildy knew she should have left, or at least kept her face concealed. She did neither.

Katherine's voice was delicate yet powerful, each word flung forward with precise intonation. To listen to this was to listen to the promise of womanhood. Alluring but never submissive, passionate yet steady. It was as though she had never heard anyone sing before. Often, exposure to someone so gifted brought up a jealousy that Tildy forced herself to suppress. But she didn't envy this singer, let alone feel dejected at not having such a voice. It was a treasured gift to be in this audience and hear it now.

When the first song ended, the crowd cheered. Katherine offered thanks, whispered to the musicians, then started to sing again. This song had less musical accompaniment. It was sad, haunting. Though she didn't know enough Irish to understand it, thoughts of her mother arose in Tildy. The longing, ever present, ready to overwhelm her. She pushed them aside, the pain too sharp. Instead she thought of the fates of generations of husbandless, pregnant women in this country. She thought of her great-great-grandmother, who'd lost five children to the famine long after US history books claimed it had ended. Tildy thought of all the women in her line who had loved and suffered for their love.

She scanned the crowd, hungry to see the rest of the audience, her audience, one she had built from her mind to serve her narrative. Each individual wore expressions reflecting her own appreciation for the singer. For the first time, Tildy felt belonging was possible. This would be her Ireland. She continued to scan, too eager for this silent acceptance. Her eyes reached the table of friends and paused. Aidan was looking directly at her.

She turned away quickly, too quickly. In her peripheral vision, she could see him unfold his hands and lean forward in his chair, perhaps debating whether to approach her. A part of her, mad with needing him, compelled her to stay. She grabbed her book, put more euro than she owed on the bar, and scooted gracelessly from the too-high stool. The second song ended as Tildy forged a path through the pub, far from Aidan, where there were more tables and more people than could've been possible. The dream was closing her in.

Panic rose. She told herself to push through.

Tildy moved between obstacles until she finally passed through the door.

Once outside, she walked to escape, but the sidewalk seemed to stretch and her progress slowed. She could not get away. A click and creak from the door opening just behind stabbed her with fear.

Her mind reached for two ends of the dream, as if it were an unstretched canvas draped over her consciousness, and she pulled.

Tildy awoke in her room with a start.

Delirious, she gently removed the cap and set it on the comforter. It was late, the sounds of a passing NYPD patrol car siren dulled by the sound of her noise machine.

Did he recognize me? She turned, bleary and dizzy, and drank from her water bottle, then looked at the hand that held it.

Older, thinner, paler.

She picked up her phone, and the bright light of it watered her eyes. She searched for his name, the browser autofilling at the first two letters. She clicked on a purple link to a story of a recent event at his restaurant and scrolled. There was a photo she hadn't noticed. She opened it in a new tab and zoomed in. Most of the group from the pub was there, and there he stood in the background, eyes down, smiling shyly.

He looked the same as in her dream. His height, his broad chest—even the slight hunch was there. Her mind had replicated him perfectly. She tossed the phone onto her sheets.

Someone like him wouldn't want someone like her, she told herself. The someone he knew her to be.

The look he had given her was perplexing, though. What did it mean? It was—what? Curious? Angry? Certainly intense. It was a searching, cautious gaze. Not something used on a thing that made sense. It had feeling behind it, a strong feeling that could not be hidden. It didn't feel false, as the rest of the dream seemed, now that she could reflect on it. The puppetry arms and fishing wire of the other moments were visible on inspection, but Aidan's eyes had seen her. They'd really seen her, as if he had been there.

Tildy shut off the cap's transmitter and set the cap aside. She would sleep without it, for now.

chapter
five

On the subway the next morning, Tildy checked her email and saw a form from Evelyn asking for details about her dream. Shame flushed her face at the idea of sharing what had happened. Evelyn had designed this device to help people process trauma, and what had Tildy used it for? Not to plan a move to Ireland, reconnect with Nana, or think through finding a job. No, she rode a janky elevator, went to a bar, and ran away from the dream version of a guy who hated her, if he thought of her at all. With more haste than caution, she wrote replies to the questions and sent it before the train arrived at her transfer.

Within moments, she received a reply. "This is fantastic! Maybe try a session cap only, without meds?"

Tildy replied, "Of course!"

Despite her promise to Evelyn, she wasn't ready to use the dream machine again that night, the next, or the next. Saturday loomed on the horizon, empty and foreboding. She needed something to do, if just to have something to tell people at work on Monday.

After work on Friday, Tildy opened her family business email account. She had to reenter her password due to inactivity. Inside were requests for interviews, teenagers or their parents lobbying for internships, invitations to events, and spam. She ignored the other messages but clicked on a few of the invitations. An art gallery she liked was hosting a charitable auction and had sent over tickets to her and her sister. They probably wanted Gisele to attend, but they'd invited her too. It was her they were going to get.

A few hours later, Tildy handed over her coat to the young woman in white button-down and black trousers. From a passing tray, she pulled a clear drink. Pairs of couples and groups of friends drifted along the walls like dust bunnies, bunching into corners and settling adrift in the center, where they laughed and talked and didn't care about the art around them.

She smoothed her dress with her free hand and approached the first piece of art. It was bright and abstract, not really her thing. She moved around those who did care about it and approached the next, staying just long enough to get a sense of the intention. The lights were bright on the art but dim elsewhere, a relief. Typically these galleries were lit like surgical theaters.

The contrast between her dream and this place amused Tildy. Here, beauty was curated and confined. Meanwhile Galway, normally chilly and rugged, had been unbelievably warm and sunny. Yet that was fake and this was real.

The first set of paintings were admired by a fashionable set of people. They complimented the movement, the negative space, the scale. The set of four paintings were of a single subject; men's bald spots. Freckles and moles and uneven hair patterns, all on display, with swirls of abstract colors in the background.

She walked on, not seeing the art, instead absorbed by her thoughts, until she arrived at a small piece, its scale out of proportion with the rest of the gallery. When she reached it, she stilled. The rest of the attendees continued to move and speak and drink and need, but she stayed fixed. Deep blues and purples, with high rises and ridges of oil layered onto itself. An outline and a blend of colors—to Tildy it was a woman at a doorway, leaning out the opening and staring beyond, a foot carelessly propped behind her, as if she could see someone she loved on the horizon. Was he leaving? Or was he coming to her?

An image of this painting on the internet would have no hold on her. It would be whittled down to dimensions and style and color scheme. In person, though, it moved her, despite the simplicity of the composition. She smiled to herself, and to the feeling it gave her.

The presence of another person, taller, with dark clothes, did not take her attention from the piece. She liked the painting's frame, too. An old gilded-style frame, totally out-of-date, and yet somehow the charm of it made her smile all over again.

She looked to her side, ready to accept a partner. The man, tall and handsome with a dash of faint freckles, was smiling at her as if she were the object to admire. Tildy blushed, laughed lightly, and stole a final look at the painting. The man moved as if he was going to speak to her, but she didn't want that. With a parting nod, she moved around him. She'd let the unspoken compliment settle on her, but she would not allow it in.

Moving toward the lesser-known artists, she took a canapé from a passing tray. A group of legal people—they could only be legal people—argued about the merits of a sculpture. One shook his head.

"It reminds me of that piece we saw at Gisele Sullivan's Christmas party last year, do you remember?"

Tildy stilled.

The woman nodded. "Oh yeah, that's right. So this thing must be worth a ton of money."

"No, this is the student section," the man said, looking up at the sign. "Gisele only buys sculptures that impress people."

"She doesn't have an artistic bone in her body. My cousin interned at Aibell, said her color choices for swag were atrocious. They had to come up with a new scheme and pretended it was hers."

"Must be so aggravating, working for that nepo baby," another man added with a laugh.

The woman shrugged. "I think she gets away with it because everyone thinks she's gorgeous. She has nothing on her mother, though."

Tildy moved on, in case they noticed her and wondered why she was eavesdropping. They certainly wouldn't recognize her.

Twenty minutes later, the auction began. Tildy had considered purchasing the painting. She'd looked up the artist, a well-known master, and decided to pass with some regret. The expense was hard to justify. Besides, she preferred to buy from the novice section, so her donation would help the charity and the artist. The dismay of having to reclaim donated yet unwanted goods felt near to Tildy's own experiences in life.

So she purchased a whimsical little pastel drawing as well as a charcoal of anguish, sure no one would notice her enough to think of it.

When the little painting came up, Tildy glanced around at the bidders as if learning the play's performers. There were six, including the man who'd stood beside her. He was three rows back with a group of friends. His hair was wavy auburn and had a faint brightness in the light. He had darker brows that could've given him an edge of menace, yet they only looked ready to express a feeling. His face had a hint of stubble, as if he had been dragged out to this event. When she remained watching him too long, he caught her eye and smiled. Tildy lowered her lashes and turned away.

The bidding continued, with one and then two and then three hopefuls failing to proceed. Two men, a septuagenarian with a college-aged girlfriend and the handsome man, set their bids. It was the sort of financial pissing contest familiar at these sorts of events. The charity and the needy forgotten, though perhaps this was the sort of energy that brought in most donations. The older man was certainly drunk or medicated. The younger man, though—he was sober. Why would he be so reckless?

In the end, the handsome man spent far too much and won the painting. Applause broke out, especially among his friends. Tildy heard one tease him: "This from the guy who wears shoes from college."

When the auction ended, she set her untouched drink on a tray and gathered her things. Women wobbled in their heels as they shrugged on their furs. The handsome man had already reached the door and was adjusting his scarf, evidently waiting for someone. *Is this for me?* Tildy wondered. She grimaced at the implausibility of it. A man like him wouldn't look at someone like her, she knew. But when she caught her reflection in a plexiglass case, she saw the truth: her complexion had a youthful, rosy hue, like she had been at the beach, caught in the spray of the cold Atlantic sea.

Tildy retrieved her coat ticket and handed it to the young woman at the table. The friends of the man talked and laughed, trying to decide where to go next. She didn't hear him speak.

She put on her coat, settled her things in her purse, and hailed a ride on her phone for a nearby street corner. She would be prepared for nothing, she decided. She took a breath before turning around.

"Hey," the handsome man said. He looked down at her, his light brown eyes steady and hopeful. Tildy looked back at him, smiled, and continued on her way.

The man followed, laughing a bit. He smelled very good. Expensive. His shoes might be old, but he wore nice cologne and his clothes were new and properly tailored.

"Hello," Tildy said, her voice stiff from disuse. She continued walking out the door, and then down the sidewalk, away from lingering crowd and glowing lights of the gallery.

"I couldn't let a man like that buy the painting," he said conspiratorially, as if they were midway through a conversation and not complete strangers.

"That man?"

"You know the type. The sort of man this city runs on."

"Ah. You mean old, out of touch, proud of his moral gluttony and ignorance, and yet king of it all?"

He laughed. "Exactly. Men like that can't win everything."

"They often do," Tildy observed.

"Not tonight. And not our painting."

She looked up at him, the blue glow of a neon sign behind him lighting up her face. The man let out a small sigh, as if relieved, as if he had passed through a desert searching for water and found it in her eyes. Tildy relished and distrusted the feeling.

Her phone buzzed and a car pulled up.

"Enjoy the painting," she said. And with a smile, she added, "And keep up the good fight."

As the car pulled away, he stood there, watching her, his hand raised to wave.

When he was out of view, Tildy shook her head. *He must have confused me with someone else*, she decided.

chapter
six

The next morning, she met Evelyn for coffee at a local park. Finding a café with seating in Manhattan was next to impossible, and they didn't have time for lunch—Tildy had to sit down with an engineer later to design the feed experiment.

"Look at this guy with his bongo drums," Evelyn chuckled as they found a spot to sit down. A white guy with dreds was playing the drums while rocking slowly side to side. His upturned hat had only some crumpled bills and coins in it.

"He looks super stoned," Tildy observed.

Evelyn laughed. "His rhythm is pretty good though. Just the wrong atmosphere here, I think." She gestured to the office workers walking and talking and grabbing lunch in a hurry. "So, Tildy my dear, how's the cap treating you?" she asked as she sipped her coffee.

"It's going okay."

"The data from your first session looks good. Would you say the dream was realistic?"

Tildy sipped her coffee too quickly and burned the roof of her mouth. "Yes, very."

"Was there any difficulty in getting the dream started? Or did it end too soon?"

"Oh, no. It was really smooth. It ended just when I wanted it to."

"I saw that you filled out the form, but I was wondering if you would like to tell me about the dream? More qualitative information, if you get me."

"Oh, yes. Yes, of course." Tildy sighed. Her reluctance had been too obvious. "The weather was right, a heat wave. I checked in at the hotel. The elevator was broken—well. Half broken. I'm not sure how I came up with that detail. Then I fell asleep before going out at night to a pub. There was live music. It was cool. Then I left."

Evelyn jotted some notes down in a notebook she had balanced on a knee. "Did you see anyone you know?"

Tildy swallowed. "Someone I recognized from childhood, yeah. We didn't speak though."

"Any intense feelings? Disproportionate fear?"

"No, no everything felt… proportionate."

Evelyn made a final note then flipped the notebook shut. "Great! I can't thank you enough for this. I really think nonmedicated is the way to go."

"I can see how medication can be challenging for people."

"You don't even know the half of it. A lot of our prospective patients are single moms. They won't do therapy or take medications that might arouse suspicion in family courts, so they don't get treated for depression or trauma. This might help them, discreetly, without any sort of unpleasant consequences."

"There's no record of what people are dreaming or anything?"

Evelyn shook her head. "I'm only able to see what general regions of the brain are activated. I could probably make educated guesses as to what is going on, but they'd just be guesses."

Tildy's thumb worked at the paper edge of her coffee cup.

"What's on your mind, lady."

"Oh, I hope my data is useful. It'd be a shame to take up your time and nothing good comes of it. My life is so different from the target group."

Evelyn nodded and surveyed the people walking through the park. "That's true. But you're still a person, and a person who had a traumatic childhood, you know? Don't you worry. It'll help."

An argument formed but dissipated. If she argued, she'd only hear more about how Evelyn perceived things. "What did you end up doing after graduation? I'm surprised you, uh…"

"That I'm only a grad student?" Evelyn laughed mirthlessly. "I had to take some time off in college."

Tildy examined her friend and saw ghosts of someone else's pain. She looked out at the people walking by. Does everyone carry pain around? Was everyone trying to recover from something, and maybe not quite pulling through?

That evening, Tildy fell asleep in her room in New York City and arrived in her dream in the early morning. She had been passing through the glass-and-brass double doors to the breakfast area. She froze, trying to adjust to her surroundings. Hotel reception was behind her, vacant and cold. Daylight was strong through the windows, the street busy with the quiet work of a dozen businesses setting up for the day.

Yes, she told herself, *you are in Ireland.*

It was morning now, neither early nor late. A perfect time for breakfast. She picked up a local newspaper from a low table beside the doors. Bon Secours Hospital was having an employment day, a student at University of Galway was injured in a dumb accident, and a camogie championship match had been won by Cork.

She walked to the beverages table and made herself

a tea, then carried it and her paper to a booth. A part of her observed, detached, that these were the news stories she had scanned back in New York before falling asleep. Student housing at the university was insufficient. Offshore naval defense was insufficient. Hospital wait times were shameful. Provisions to the abortion bills were proposed. The EU pushed the UK for greater consideration of ocean security on behalf of the Republic.

It was overwhelming. If this was to be her home, then these were her problems, too. She had to learn about them. But her mind wanted to reshape the dream. The feeling from Aidan's expression, the mystery of it, could be the center of her attention if she chose. He could come through that door, the one she saw just ahead. He could be wearing a sweater, the sleeves pulled up to show his strong forearms, and he could look for her.

Tildy frowned. There was an Irish word she learned at a local summer camp. Léiriú. It meant to portray a story or put together a play, or to beat someone into submission.

No, he wouldn't come through the door, she decided. It was too unrealistic. And a misuse of Evelyn's invention. Plus, Tildy felt chasing him was a violation, somehow. She had broken his heart. She didn't have the right to bring him into her dreams.

She compared Aidan's expression to the reaction from the art gallery guy. Overt admiration from a handsome stranger compared to... hate? No, Aidan did not hate her, she decided. Something else. An intensity that was frightening and enticing all the same. A knowing, thorough in its rejection.

The two moments, each a type of notice unfamiliar to her, upset her equilibrium. Embracing her plainness had given her the strength to resist unscrupulous salespeople and the gold-digging pickup artists in her father and sister's circles. Men had been interested in her as a ladder to something else, not for her alone. Now Aidan's look. A mixture of want and anger, it seemed. Tildy resisted the compliments from these two different men, yet their attention demanded consideration. Someone somewhere might yearn for her, and it felt like retreating in from the cold to a too-hot fire. Her body both craved and shied from its strength. She wished she had more experience in being wanted, if only to erase the novelty, to give her clarity into the meaning behind the two expressions from men so dissimilar to one another.

"Hello there, Miss Halleran."

Tildy left her thoughts. Her upright but ignored newspaper dropped. "Oh, hello," she replied to the desk clerk. "I don't remember your name, I'm sorry."

He smiled. "Don't apologize, I didn't tell you it and I never wear my name tag. My name's Ben."

"Ben. Nice to meet you."

"How was the bar? No troubles, I hope? You ask for Eli?"

"No trouble. I didn't ask but I was okay, thank you."

Ben looked at her, considering. After a quick check on his surroundings, he sat down in the booth and leaned close. "Are you a spy?"

Tildy set down the paper and laughed. "A spy? No, I'm… no."

"I see, I see." He did not seem convinced.

"I'm a data scientist. I'll be teaching at the technical college. I start next term."

"Oh. You're a professor then?"

"I only have a master's, not a PhD," Tildy replied, embarrassed.

"That's more than I have. Is it hard finding work in data science in New York?"

"No, not really. I just wanted a change."

When she said nothing more, Ben tapped the table. "I'll let you get back to your breakfast."

Tildy paused, but nodded and returned to her newspaper. He wasn't real, and she had enough to think about right now.

After a few minutes reading, she folded her newspaper. What she needed to do was exercise. Everything made more sense when she was running.

She ate a quick breakfast, drank a glass of water, and wondered if you could get a side ache in your sleep.

Fifteen minutes later she was outside, jogging slowly, waiting for her muscles to warm up. The weather was blissfully cool, the streets quiet. The easy solitude was soothing. She let her pace quicken without pushing her stride beyond her comfort zone. Despite her affection for the activity, she wasn't a skilled runner. She had always been able to run, though not competitively, nor even with the breathing techniques necessary to sustain light conversation. But whenever a complex problem arose, she could put her hair in a braid and lace up her sneakers and run without exhaustion or injury.

Tildy approached Wolfe Tone Bridge, now empty of pedestrians, and felt the impact of her steps change to a thrum as she ran across the suspended surface. The River Corrib ran strong beneath her, black and steady, moving out to the bay. Commuters in cars droned by her. At a gap in traffic, she raced across the road, avoiding large bird droppings as she headed toward the waterfront path. Her steps took her along the sidewalk of the Claddagh Quay, the area suddenly residential. An older woman in a caftan watered her lush garden while a neighbor loaded a baby into his sedan. They exchanged some greetings, looking to her only briefly.

She took Nimmo's Pier and ran past a pair of children swinging at the playground, their little feet high in the air as they watched the colorful houses across the water.

The movement felt good. Tildy decided she would run until Grattan Beach. There, she would touch the sand, the bay, the waves. It would be real.

Rounding the corner, her eyes watered from the cold, damp air, but she wouldn't stop running, she wouldn't look away from the beautiful view. The rolling gray hills through the mists across the bay, the kelp and rocks and sky. It was the wild of this scene that she needed. The cold beauty had called to her. This was home.

To her right, a neatly trimmed field waited for activity, and Tildy's footfalls slowed. A pair of young men kicked a soccer ball back and forth, their chatter carried by the wind. She couldn't be sure who it was, but it wouldn't be him. She wasn't that unlucky. In either case, she didn't enjoy having an audience, so she picked up her pace to reach the beach.

Her legs seemed faster than ever, the sensation an intoxicating surprise. At the bottom of her peripheral vision, her limbs were a blur. Her brain neared panic as her body teetered on the verge of losing control. She held on, her feet reaching the ground and departing before the contact could be tallied. She loved herself in this moment. Her body was nothing and everything, flaws and loves and hates forgotten. Then her lungs began to burn, warning her of a limit to this pleasure. Rather than fight back, Tildy allowed the run to end like sung words, like a fierce scream that drifted quietly to decency.

She reached the Mutton Island access road puffing, the cold air a burn on her throat. She turned around. She'd get to the beach another day.

Tildy laughed to herself, the breeze catching strands of hair that escaped her braid.

Her heart was pounding hard, the discomfort of it always overlooked until she had caught her breath. The respiratory and circulatory systems were mysteries to her, yet they powered these runs. She wondered, which had slowed her down first? She'd never bothered to investigate, but always wondered after a burst of speed. What was she doing in her bed now? Did her neighbors think she was dying? Tildy placed a hand on her chest to steady her body, to remind it and her that she was in bed someplace else.

Her thoughts paused. The young men were watching her, their ball forgotten. Had it been him there all along? That tall one did look like him. Both men stood completely still, frozen, staring at her. Her running pants felt too tight, suddenly. As she walked, their gazes followed her. Whether it was him or the dream glitching, she couldn't ignore her unease. Summoning what energy remained, Tildy jogged back toward the hotel. She didn't turn around.

After a shower and outfit change, the dream soothed her with serene normalcy. Forget the men, it seemed to say. That won't happen again. And when she accepted this, she felt the day could take shape. She sat on the bed with her cell phone and selected a name more dear to her than her own.

The familiar odd ringtone began. It was sure to be a bad connection, but she only needed to tell her she'd arrived.

"Dierdre anseo."

"Nana, it's Tildy."

"Oh Tildy! A stór! I was just thinking of you. Now, did you make it into town safely?"

The warmth of her voice quieted some of the remaining discomfort. "Perfectly safe. I was wondering if I could come visit?"

"Of course, my dear, of course. Come round tomorrow after eleven, I like my mornings to myself."

nt door. A staff member with a neutral expression red their knock.

oife greeted her warmly. "Sonya, hello again. How's aby?"

Quite well, thank you."

The real estate agent ignored the cool reply and sol-ed on. "I have a client here who might have business h Mrs. Owens. We haven't called ahead, though we will quick."

Sonya guided the visitors into the foyer. Tildy sat on highly polished, stiffly cushioned carved wooden bench, oife beside her. Ancestral portraits, with tartan details and unting dogs, adorned the walls in gilded frames. A Tiffany amp sat on a credenza next to a Fabergé egg and beside what she could only assume was the first luxury telephone.

She wondered, as she looked at the scene, where her brain had found all these items. Had she ever been in a house like this, and the memory had been locked away, unused until this moment? Her mother had taken her to dinner parties in this part of Galway. Was this why she felt so small right now? Or was this a combination of all the things she did not like about the old-wealth friends of her father? Tildy looked up the wide dark-wood staircase, where a perfectly fluffy carpet with a golden fleur-de-lis pattern ran up into the darkness above. She could sense that beyond those stairs was nothing but darkness. Her mind had no information to fill in that void.

"Imagine working in this house during the Hunger,"

She let the joy of the moment seep in. "I'll see you then."

"Goodbye now, a ghrá, see you then, God bless you, bye bye."

That task accomplished, Tildy checked the time. An hour until she was to meet a real estate agent in the lobby. When had she set this appointment? It was obvious she must find a place to live. She couldn't stay here, in this hotel, forever. The dream was guiding her to what must happen next.

Tildy could go outside, wander around, or stay indoors. The TV was on and her feet were stretched back out on the bed before a conscious choice had been made.

She clicked a button on the remote. A cooking show, imported from the BBC. She clicked it again. A football game, between EVE and CHE. It didn't look good for CHE. She clicked up. A weather forecast, including data for Spain. Tildy was momentarily confused until she real-ized, as if for the first time, she could easily get anywhere within Europe. She didn't need to report to campus for several weeks; she still had time to take a trip to France, or Germany, or Spain, or Greece. This was her life now. She could travel Europe at a whim.

An hour later, Tildy was shaking hands with real-tor Aoife McDonnell in the lobby. She had a motherly demeanor, soft and friendly.

"Oh, you're just a slip of a girl! You said professor at university, and I thought… ah well. And it's just you then?"

"Oh, yes. Just me."

"My car's out front. We could walk to the first flat, though we'll need the car for the others."

Aoife had not been exaggerating. The flat was very close to the hotel, only one block in from the river. It had blue tiles in the small but tidy kitchen, granite counters, brass and porcelain in the bathroom, no meaningful view but nice furnishings. It caught the sea air on the Juliet balcony.

"It is a little expensive, of course. Downtown tends to be more pricey."

Tildy nodded but said nothing, looking in each room, considering the uselessness of living immediately down-town and the second bedroom.

"Ready for the next?"

"Yes, please."

The next was a coastal apartment, facing the water. The wooden cabinets were honey colored and the pristine floors sharp white tile. It felt cold, sterile.

Afterward, they looked at a dingy, large flat with stained ceilings and a hideously ornate fireplace.

Followed by a house with four bedrooms, which Aoife only drove past.

As they drove to another apartment, she smiled and asked, "Do you have much family here, then?"

"My nana lives in the countryside, and I have cousins in Wexford."

"And what of your parents? Are they still back in the States?"

Aoife murmured. Tildy didn't reply—she was too busy being embarrassed by imagining how her father would respond. First, there would be excessive anger against the English. Then a mention of Irish Slavery, a topic he loved to insert whenever possible. And all the while, every time he climbed atop this particular soapbox, he was more like those aristocratic despots than the Irish peasants of long ago for whom he professed such affinity. It was predictable and exasperating.

She shut her eyes and tried to clear him from her mind. He wasn't here. No one knew him here. This was her space. This was *her* Ireland.

Sonya returned and motioned for the women to follow her. They passed through a bright sitting room, the high ceilings and massive fireplace straight from a BBC Jane Austen production. Through another set of glass paneled doors, they entered into a sunroom facing the garden. An elderly woman with pure white hair nodded at Sonya, who departed.

The visitors waited, standing at attention, until the spoon in her hand was fully polished. Then she lowered her reading glasses and set the utensil into a silver set resting on a table.

"Hello, Mrs. Owens!" Aoife said brightly. "How are you?"

"Quite well, thank you. What brings you here?" Mrs. Owens eyed Tildy.

"I know you have Mr. Carson handle your rental cottage,

but I wanted to bring you a proposal personally. I'm showing this young lady, a new professor at the university, to various flats around town. If you are partial to it, she might be an excellent long-term tenant for you."

Mrs. Owens studied Tildy again. Under the suspicious examination, she felt the morning's confidence fall as her anger rose.

"A professor? What is your subject?"

"Data science," Tildy replied curtly, then forced a conciliatory smile.

"Ah, you're an American. Is that a style of software engineering?"

"Yes and no. I work with probabilities."

"It's only a humble cottage, updated with modern fittings. Only suitable for one person."

"I live alone."

After a long pause, a pause extended only to make those around her uncomfortable, Mrs. Owens seemed to come to a decision. "Sonya, show Mrs. McDonnell and her client the guest cottage. If it is to your liking, contact Mr. Carson to finalize the details. I'll advise him that I approve, as long as finances are in order."

Tildy forced a smile and nod, then followed Sonya out the door.

Aoife leaned in as they trailed behind their guide. "You'll never see her. If this cottage wasn't perfection, I'd have never brought you here."

They exited the front door and turned toward the dirt

path where Aoife had parked. At the front of the car, a line of vegetation and trees Tildy had mistaken for a hedgerow concealed a gate. Sonya chose a key from a large ring, unlocked the gate, and swung it back.

They stepped through the passageway into paradise.

The path was fully shaded and lined with mossy gray stones, wild fuchsia, roses of all colors, and lichen-covered trees. Maidenhair ferns rose from the shadows and horsetails erupted along the waterline. The walkway continued for ten yards, nestled in the abundant greenery. They passed over a small stream by way of an old but solid footbridge, the fence of a snug cottage just beyond and to the right.

"It has a thatched roof," Tildy whispered to Aoife.

"Oh yes. Only the rich can afford them these days," she replied.

Sonya took out the large ring from her apron pocket, choosing a different key to unlock the red wooden door. The front garden on either side of the women had a small bench facing the woods and stream, only the distant roof of the nearest house peeking through the leaves.

"Tildy, this forest was all planted by Mrs. Owens's family for their hunting. For generations they'd stock the lands with animals and such. Over the years, they sold off pieces to friends or developers of single large houses. Now this land is all a park for the people of this neighborhood to enjoy, without anyone else permitted to trespass."

They followed Sonya into the cottage. The kitchen was compact but modern. It had a relatively new combination washer and dryer unit, a small, antique-style refrigerator, stone counters, and an apron sink. The adjoined bathroom was only a shower with a boxlike appliance mounted on the wall for heating fifteen minutes' worth of water, just as her nana had at her cottage. Tildy was disappointed by her dream's realism. She shut her eyes for a moment, willing the dream to give her a clawfoot tub. She opened her eyes. The shower and hot water box remained.

The rest of the cottage was equally small but efficient. It had a black iron stove, the only stove in the cottage, running through the center of the structure.

The furnishings were recently upholstered, the love seat covered in tiny rosebuds, the nearby armchair in tufted, dusky pink velvet. A dark carpet covered the hardwood floor beneath the seating area. Up a short flight of wooden stairs was the only bedroom. A round window surrounded by an unusual carved stone decoration illuminated the space. Tildy touched the stone—Celtic knots, scrolls, hearts, flowers and leaves, like a love letter from the gamekeeper or gardener who had built this home. The light in the loft space came through the trees, shifting, muted and lovely. She felt her excitement grow.

"Tenant is to park on the dirt parking space. No guests after 8 p.m., no parties, no overnight guests." The last rule was stated with a hint of annoyance, the only emotion Sonya expressed.

"That won't be a problem. Thank you, Sonya."

"Storage is a bit tight," Aoife observed.

Sonya nodded. "There's a nook above the kitchen, and the drawers and small wardrobe in the loft."

"That's okay. I didn't bring much."

Once outdoors again, Tildy nudged Aoife with appreciation.

"I thought you'd like it." Aoife whispered. "If I were a single woman, that is exactly where I'd want to live. Safe, quiet, private parking. Mrs. Owens is… well, she keeps to herself. You won't see her."

They met with the aforementioned Mr. Carson, an extraordinarily friendly man. The contrast between the two made sense. A woman like that could only move through the world if there was someone to do all the transactions for her. They agreed to a year lease, a reasonable rent, and possession at the weekend.

Tildy felt guilty, somehow, when she offered a check that didn't exist to Mr. Carson. But none of it existed. He wasn't real, nor was Aoife, nor Sonya or her baby. When they left for the hotel, she could feel the dream fade. She would wake soon. As Aoife drove, Tildy looked out at the rolling green hills, ready to escape the power she held over this place.

chapter
seven

She woke to another day in New York City. The doorman didn't look up from his phone as she walked by. It was raining outside, the trash on the sidewalk soaked and weeping onto the concrete. Tildy had forgotten to wear boots. It wasn't a heavy downpour, but it rained enough to back up the storm drain at her subway exit. She'd have to walk half a block down to avoid the enormous puddle. She stood in the awning, not wanting to go back up for her boots, not wanting to deal with the consequences of not having her boots.

Another workday, another day of listening to passionate

arguments about button arrangements and font sizes and things Tildy couldn't bring herself to care about. She tried to tell herself: *I chose this. This is my life. This is my career. This is real.* But as she walked herself to the train, the arguments fell flat, and she wondered only when she could get home and sleep again.

By lunchtime the storm had passed, the sun had warmed the city, but the humidity remained. An email alert dinged while she sat at a window seat in her favorite curry shop. It was a meeting invitation from Lee, who preferred email to any other form of communication. It was probably about the family relocation to Palm Beach. She hit *yes* and blocked off the time in her work calendar. She'd make up the hours sometime. They didn't seem to mind.

The dirty glass in front of her was a depressing filter on an already ugly day. New York in early fall was full of false starts. Summer days lingered later and later, encroaching on what should be light sweater weather. She could see how her father would want to leave. Though she loved it, in a way, the years here stretched out before her, and they didn't feel good. The sameness was not a comfort. Still, if this meeting was about moving to Palm Beach, she was not interested. Palm Beach was its own kind of hell.

She put in her headphones and called a phone number. When it picked up, she said, "I don't want to move to Palm Beach."

Russell's voice came through her headphones. "That's

only because your father moved you there after your mother's funeral."

"And the sun. And the people, who are on permanent vacation and aren't interesting at all."

Russel's voice sighed, as if it could breathe. "This is your family. You can't change them. They need you, because you are different from them."

"They don't listen to me."

"They might. Give them time."

Tildy hung up. Using her mother's software felt like speaking to her, which could be comforting, until moments like this. Her mother had been swept up by her father's interests and commitments until she had become nothing more than a face for his company, her own accomplishments forgotten. It had been like an addiction for her, this need to sacrifice for Aibell's benefit, yet her talent with technology was the only reason the company had survived as long as it had. Her father had never seen that. Now, of all her mother's skills, only this college project remained.

She looked back out the window at the people passing by, unaware of her. Was this what it felt like to be Russell? A bystander allowed into her family's circle, yet so easily ignored?

On the day of the family meeting, Tildy arrived first. She sat in one of her father's armchairs with her purse on her lap, ready to leave. There was no recently abandoned drink at his desk or any other evidence he had recently vacated the space. There was a good chance he wouldn't come at all and she could depart without any incident.

Alexandra came in with a flurry of exasperated complaints about the train, the black car that had picked her up, the driver's cologne, and the slowness of the elevator. She then sat down in her usual armchair and fanned herself with a *New Yorker* that had been sitting on the marble coffee table.

Gisele's voice tinkled with laughter from the hallway. She strolled into the room with a vaguely familiar young woman with bleached-blonde hair and a thick coat of freckles. Both wore similar outfits: a bright blouse and flowy pants. Gisele gave no introductions before she lay on the couch with her manicured feet crossed atop a pillow. Her friend sat demurely nearby. Tildy was faintly alarmed at a stranger being present for a family meeting.

Gisele didn't acknowledge her sisters, though she hadn't seen Alexandra in weeks, as far as Tildy knew.

"Don't say I didn't warn you," Gisele said conspiratorially to the woman, ending a conversation that purposely excluded the others.

Alexandra felt the slight and redirected it. "Where is Lee? Is he always late like this? Who works for who here?"

"He has other clients," Tildy replied quietly. "He'll be here when he can."

Lee and her father's voices came from the hallway and grew closer. Gisele yawned and threw her arm over her eyes, her new friend momentarily forgotten.

"Good morning, ladies," Lee said. "Alexandra, Matilda,

have you been introduced to my daughter, Penelope?"

"Nice to meet you," Tildy said. She realized they had met before, years earlier. But why was she here now?

"Wait, are you Freckles Penelope? Who does the vacation reviews?"

Penelope smiled charmingly. "That's me!"

"I love your reviews. I show them to Charlie all the time. Trying to get him to take a vacation is like pulling teeth, even though he hardly works and my therapist says it is good for me to push my boundaries. I just loved your video on the floating hotel in Tahiti."

"That was a beautiful place," Penelope said. "I'd love to live there if I could!"

"Yes, well, can we get on with this, please," Gisele said. "Penelope and I are going to get her hair fixed. Look at the brassiness she inflicted on herself."

"Stupid me, I shouldn't have trusted that backup stylist. My own fault," Penelope said with a shy smile.

"You'll look fine after Skyler works her magic. She owes me for those Harry Styles passes anyway."

Lee cleared his throat. "Thanks for coming in. Let's get right down to it. Russell, are you online?"

"Hello, Mr. Lee," the smooth voice replied from the corner. Tildy didn't think he was sincere in his question; he only wanted to call her father's attention to the automated assistant's presence.

"Good," her father grunted as he sat down in an armchair. "We're moving to Palm Beach. We're going to follow

Russell's advice and rent the jet when it isn't in use. Now to work out the details."

Gisele sighed. "What, like moving the furniture?"

"I think we may be better positioned to rent your father's apartment fully furnished, discreetly. As you recall, this is not technically a residential space. Selling or renting it publicly may prove complicated," Lee said, cleaning his glasses apologetically.

Alexandra frowned. "Daddy can't keep his apartment? But it's his building."

"Your father is selling the building but keeping this floor and a few of the others, to keep the business operating. Folks will have to squeeze in a bit together, or do a desk share."

"It'll be good for team morale," her father said as he waved. "People will have to get to know each other. Besides, hardly anyone comes into the office. Haven't had a full slate in years."

"We're selling Daddy's building?" Gisele said sadly. She sounded like a forlorn child, rather than a fully grown woman. Tildy fought the urge to roll her eyes.

Her father nodded. "I know, pumpkin. Palm Beach will be good for you. The sea, the warm air, the nightlife. New York is too crowded, I think, too competitive. It's good for people who are trying to succeed, not those of us who are established."

Tildy looked to see how her sisters accepted this explanation. They both seemed receptive to a justification, any at all, that would make such a move a signal of importance, rather than failure. It was how things had gotten to this point, she supposed. A group of people all equally committed to contorting their perception of reality, rather than face facts.

Penelope nodded somberly to Gisele. "You are all so famous here, anyway. I'm sure it'd be a huge relief to be away from people who aren't used to being around celebrities and other important people."

Lee adjusted his glasses and fixed his tie. "That's a great point, honey. Now, Alexandra and Gisele have kindly agreed to turn over the shares that were awarded them after their mother's death. Matilda, that just leaves you."

All eyes turned to Tildy. She realized this was not a family meeting to convince her father of anything. She glanced at Penelope, who turned her gaze away, as if ashamed to be present.

"It would help your family considerably to have fifty-one percent of shares consolidated with your father, Tildy," Russell said.

Gisele looked away from Tildy and laughed. She returned to her phone. "I told you she wouldn't help."

"Matilda," her father said in his stern father voice. "Your mother gave you those shares for the family's security, not for you to sit on and do nothing with."

Before Tildy could speak, Alexandra tittered. "What are you even going to do with them anyway? The share isn't large enough for you to have say."

"I always participate in shareholder votes," Tildy said, her face flushing with anger.

"We know, and you nearly always vote with the family. But this will be a strong signal to the board," Lee pushed.

Tildy gripped her hands and squeezed. She tried to think of going to bed and dreaming, of shutting them all out of her mind and having tea with Nana or taking a boat out onto Galway Bay or even just walking, walking where emails couldn't reach her and her family couldn't corner her.

"My mother gave those shares to me, not to any of you." Her objection to their demands was an unnatural sound in the air. When had she last told them no? Years, perhaps. But she would tell them all, here, because these shares had been a sliver of control her mother had used until the end. Even when her father had stopped worshipping her, had stopped using her technology and her foresight, she'd made him listen with her votes. She had prevented many disasters: expansions to unrelated markets, a takeover by a firm that went bankrupt only years later, attempts to sabotage share value by disingenuous investors. Even if Tildy was not as clever as her mother, this was a tool her mother had left her. She must have intended for Tildy to use it to save the family. So she would keep it, as her mother had intended.

The room fell silent. Tildy raised her chin at their glares. They wanted to push her around, as they had done once before, but she would not budge.

"We'll give you time to reconsider," Lee said, putting

a hand up to stop her father from saying something awful to her.

"When will you all be moving?" she asked.

"After the St. Patrick's Day parade. Your father is going to be on the float with the mayor," Lee said.

"You're moving to Palm Beach with us," her father said sternly.

"You don't need me in Palm Beach."

"I know *I* don't need you in Palm Beach," Gisele tittered. "I'll have Penelope. There's no reason *not* to move to Palm Beach, and it'll help sell Daddy's retirement story. You have nothing here but us."

"You should stay with your family at a time like this, Tildy," Russell said softly.

The force of their work on her created a pressure that was nearly tactile. She rose with her purse and muttered an excuse, something about work. Lee asked her to stay, but she continued.

Instead of work, she went home, took off her outside clothes, washed her hands, and climbed into bed with the cap. She didn't want to be here right now.

The weather was indecisive in her Ireland, foggy, then moments with sunshine breaking through, only to disappear. Tildy walked to the rental car location she had found online. When she arrived, the only option available with an automatic transmission was quite pricey. But to see her nana, it was certainly worth the expense. She couldn't imagine driving on the opposite side and learning to drive a stick shift simultaneously.

Seat and mirrors adjusted, she set out. The route to Nana's house was familiar, yet review had been essential. Its location was based on predriving memories, both vague and highly specific, neither of which informed her how to get there. And navigation on her phone could not be relied on in the countryside.

The roads to Nana's village started as the sort of freeways you might find in the US, except the speed limit signs were in the metric standard, while other signs were stylistically different. Slow drivers stayed in the exit lanes, speeders were more considerate, and everyone was on the opposite side of the road.

As the population thinned, the roads became smaller and houses and industrial parks less frequent, replaced by fields and trees. There were ruins everywhere, unattended and unvisited, coexisting with farms and neighborhoods. The Irish lived with their history in a way that made the past tangible.

The familiarity of freeways forgotten, her grip on the wheel grew tense. The road remained wide enough for two cars to pass, though she knew that too would change. The asphalt engaged in a sweeping curve through the rocky landscape, the gaps in stones filled with plants, the peat spread like a carpet made from a long-felled forest.

Grey-white lines of stone walls stretched up and over

hillsides, dividing nothing from nowhere. Nana or Uncle Michael had explained these, their accuracy uncertain: a Protestant reverend from England who was obsessed with only giving aid to those who worked. During the famine, he'd refused to provide food unless tasks had been completed, which meant many starving Irish families built grids of stone walls in unattended land in exchange for food and shelter. The smaller rocks were those carried by children, some as young as toddlers. They lived in lean-tos on the roadside, carrying rocks as long as daylight lasted. Many people died from overwork before they could receive the nourishment they labored after. The practice was eventually halted, but the stone walls remained, monuments to desperation. That was what she had been told, anyway.

The road reached the junction at Maam Cross; straight ahead, the road led to a lake and further on a convent, to the left a ferry station and villages such as Screeb, including Nana's. Tildy turned left. The road rose and fell as it had for hundreds of years. It was hard not to feel the familiar sickly-sweet wave of nostalgia as she drove—her family had traveled this road for generations, to see the races or visit a festival or sell their goods or move away from home. So many scenarios begged for attention in her imagination, where all her ancestors were good, honest, beautiful people surviving hardships, triumphant over distant oppressors. She pushed the stories down. They were the half-truths all Americans told themselves. She was better than that.

The road moved closer to the water's edge. Another

short wall of stone separated the bay water from the pavement. She remembered watching a man repair a wall near Millennium Park. No mortar, only careful assessment of the rock and expert chiseling. He'd worked alone, and she'd wondered if he had taught anyone his skills, if anyone had learned from him, or if the knowledge would die with his retirement.

She took the final turn with building excitement, suddenly as comfortable in her surroundings as if she were a child again, coming home from exploring the nearest village. Tildy approached the whitewashed walls that marked the path to Nana's house.

Over the familiar hill rise, the bay and ocean reappeared in the distance. The Leary farm had changed their sheep color, blue to pink and blue. The farmers market was an abandoned wooden shell, faded advertisements propped against the long side of the building. Through the large double doors, Tildy could see a wide open field beyond, the land fallow for as far as she could see. Further down the road, the roof had collapsed at the Malone's barn, their people's old famine cottage. It would probably be converted to a slate or metal roof—the thatched roofs were too expensive to install and often uninsurable. Tildy thought back to her little cottage's thatched roof with guilt.

Nana's house appeared beyond her row of eight-foot-high bushes, familiar and secure. It was as though this place was fixed in time and place, always waiting for her to return home. Now, instead of viewing the approach from the back seat as a child, she herself took the familiar sharp right, over the set of low spots in the dirt drive and into the spot her mother always parked.

She climbed out of the car, her knees shaking from the tension of her first drive in a foreign country. Firm ground, at last. The cool air tumbled to her, ripe with the familiar tang of coastal plants and the open sea. She looked around, her eyes watering. It felt like more than a dream here, more even than reality. Like she had voyaged into the heart of the ache she carried within her.

The cottage was just as she wanted it to be. Clean, but not too clean, with recent whitewash and a bright coat of paint on the half door. A figure appeared at the original wobbly glass window. It could be a ghost, a remnant of a past that had escaped Tildy long ago.

But no, it was her nana, drying her hands with one of the threadbare towels she refused to replace.

"Dia duit a sean-máthair," Tildy called out clumsily.

"A stóirin!" Nana moved with ease, despite her age, coming quickly from the sink to the door and down the entry walk. "A Tildy, a Tildy. Dia duit, fáilte abhaile. Tar anseo a leanbh!"

She hugged her grandmother gently, desperate for the comfort it might contain and fearful of crushing delicate bones. She was smaller, certainly smaller. Nana must have thought along similar lines. "My goodness, how tall you've grown. Come inside this house at once. This storm is issuing a threat."

Tildy followed obediently, suppressing a giggle. Nana's home was primarily one main space, open concept in a time when there were no other concepts. The kitchen fit into a corner on the right, with a short hallway leading to the two bedrooms beyond the china cabinet. The once-dark main room was bright thanks to a sunroom her mother, her two uncles, and some distant cousins had installed ten years ago.

She could remember her father's disapproval. "You're going to do construction? What if you injure your face? We have a photoshoot in the fall!" The argument had lasted all the way through the car ride to LaGuardia and the security line. In the end, Nana got a sunroom built by the people she trusted most in the world, and her mother was able to do the photoshoot in the fall.

For a moment, Tildy stood in silence and appreciated the space as if it were a living thing. Nana's home remained the same, just as it was in her childhood. Friendly vases and dishes covered in delicate scenes decorated the shelves, herbs hung drying over the entryway to the sunroom, the printed images of the Virgin Mary, Jesus, and JFK hung beside photos of Tildy, her sisters, and her mother, as well as her uncles and her cousins. There were no photos of Tildy's father.

"Let me fix you a cup of tea, dear—cream and sugar?"

"Yes, please. Thank you." Tildy rested in the offered armchair as if she had run all the way to her house. Her hands shivered slightly, her nervous system still remembering the drive.

"Biscuits? I'm sure I've some in a tin someplace."

"Nana, don't trouble yourself, I had a big breakfast."

"Ó? Agus cé a thug bia duit?"

Tildy laughed at the hint of jealousy. "The hotel. Dry potatoes and cold eggs. I'm definitely not hungry."

Nana brought the tea things, refusing help. After all the necessities had been delivered, she rested in her favorite chair, folded her hands, and leveled her inscrutable stare at her granddaughter.

"Now, Tildy. Why'd you come all this way? Not for some man, I hope."

Tildy laughed. "Never."

"A stór, is bréag í sin."

"I just—I got tired, Nana."

"Tired?"

"I never fit in. I'm tired of trying. I'd rather be like you, snug in a little house near the water."

It was Nana's turn to laugh now. "What're you going on about, mo leanbh. I was raised like this, you know, not carrying around to big cities all over the world. This is all I know. It'd drive you mad. Young people need each other, need excitement."

"This young person needs a rest."

Her tone had conveyed meaning better than words. Nana leaned in, reached across the gap, and took her hand with a tenderness Tildy had forgotten could exist.

"You will, my dear. You will. Just not in this house."

"Nana!" Tildy squeezed the hand gently and laughed

long and hard. "I… I never planned to move in with you! I have my own money. I just signed a lease for my own cottage."

"Oh, good, good." Nana took her hand back and sipped her tea. "What about work, now."

"I'm going to be a teacher at the university. My class is about—"

Nana waved the description away. "That sounds dreadful, love. Why don't you take up knitting again. You were so talented, mo leanbh."

"I think that market has enough experts out here."

"It's true. Very true." Nana sipped her tea and stared at her fire. The warm, earthy smell of peat glowed as much as the heat. Tildy rose and went to one of the small windows.

"Nana, you have a tree that's fallen over. Is that the cherry tree Mom and I planted?"

"Oh yes. Sad, but you know, it was never going to hold on. Fierce wind by those rocks."

Nana checked the pockets of her sweater-vest, in the way she typically did when she needed a tissue. Tildy went to the kitchen, found a box of Kleenex, and brought it over for her to select one.

"Ta. Now put it back just where you found it, Tildy. Just where you found it. I need things just so."

She hid a grin, doing as she was asked, and then returned to her seat.

Nana dabbed her watering eyes. "Have you seen any of your little friends since you've been back?"

"Not yet."

"There's time, there's time."

"I saw Aidan at the pub."

"Aidan? Did you now!" Her tone brightened considerably. Tildy looked at her with suspicion. "Now, don't you look at me like that. He's a fine boy. Works as a cook or some such, in the city. Always here gathering bits from the garden."

"What? Why?"

"Uses it in his cookery. Tá rud ar leith faoin aer agus an chré anseo atá níos fearr, ceapaim go ndúirt sé."

"The air and soil? His family is just a mile down the road, is it really that different here?" Tildy asked.

"I don't ask and I don't mind. I have no use for much of it, and money must be dear. As long as he leaves my strawberries and pansies alone. He offered to buy my strawberries, though I told him I only have just enough for myself and no more."

"I'm glad you still have visitors." Tildy poured herself more tea, Nana's eyes following her closely.

"I recall you two were good friends once."

Nana stuffed her used tissue into her empty cup, setting the collection on the little table.

"We were."

"Not keeping up on the ThatsApp?"

Tildy laughed. "No, Nana. No. I left and didn't come back. I upset him. It was a long time ago."

"Yes, yes. He had a nice girlfriend for a long time.

Stunning creature, blonde, tall as a tree she was, you know. She moved to Australia, as I recall. Sydney. Or was it Melbourne. Ó, tá mo chuimhne ag dul in olcas. I don't know exactly where they left off. He keeps things close, you know."

Tildy remembered seeing him with a woman of that description in a social media post. It wasn't just that woman's beauty that had caught her attention. She had an ease and confidence that Tildy couldn't imagine, let alone feel herself.

"I hope he's happy."

Nana grunted. She rose, collected the tea things, and brought them to her little kitchen counter. Tildy followed and helped with the dishes.

Afterward, Nana took her hand and guided her into the sunroom and her garden, showing off the various flowers and plants she was growing, pointing out the ones that filled her with pride and the ones that were a source of aggravation, a few receiving both sentiments. She paid special attention to her strawberry plants.

"Ann Connell thinks hers are larger. Maybe so, Ann, maybe so, says I. Mine taste better and that's what matters. A strawberry as big as a potato that tastes of nothing but water is a waste of the dirt that grew it."

Nana covered her hair with a scarf, put on a coat and her black gardening clogs, and continued the tour by heading out to the field beyond the trees. The winds were above average today, though Tildy knew how strong gusts could get. Up close, the cherry tree was much larger than she had appreciated from the window.

"Nana, how are you going to clear this? I can help, but I don't know what I'd do with the wood when I finished. You don't exactly have curbside pickup here."

"Now don't you worry, love, I have that arranged." A thought seemed to occur to her. Nana smirked as she said, "It's getting on time for my nap, loveen. I want you to visit morning after next, Thursday, say ten o'clock. I might be having other company, so dress nice, as you are now."

Tildy was taken aback. She looked down at her clothes, confused, but agreed. When they returned to the house, the affection for the place nearly overwhelmed her again. Pots she had decorated with her mother sat in nearly the same place as when the paint was wet. She turned to the garden and trees beyond. Her mother had played here, had grown up here, had loved it here. She was within her mother's love when she stood on this ground.

"What are you thinking about, child?"

"I was just looking at the pots I painted with Mom. Like this one." She pointed to a pot full of dead soil.

"Oh yes. I should do something with that. It's a lovely little thing, feels like it should be home to something special. I'll think on it. It'll come to me."

Tildy went inside, and in an awkward crouch, she bent to give her once-tall nana a hug and kissed her cheek. She received blessings she tried to return, then left for the car. Driving back down the road, she thought of her nana's refusal to be roommates and laughed.

The long drive done in reverse was no less sentimental. She reached a parking garage near her hotel and pulled into a spot, then walked to the hotel feeling more adult. Driving on Irish roads to visit Nana was not a detail she normally would have dreamed. In the past, she would have just appeared there. It was like this was real, like she lived here now. Like she was settling down.

"Ms. Halleran, was wondering after you today!" Ben greeted. Tildy's wariness resurfaced.

"Hello there," she said as she continued toward the elevator.

"Say, now," he called. She groaned internally, pausing her progress. He continued, "I was just wondering—you wouldn't happen to be related to Patrick Halleran, would you?"

"Oh. He was my grandfather, yes."

"That so! One of my mates is named after him."

Tildy smiled politely. "I have a cousin named Patrick. He moved to France, I think."

"Sure, that's him. Got married to a Parisian girl, did you know."

"I heard! She's an archaeologist?"

"Sure. We spent all of our time together, more like brothers, me and him. I mean to visit him soon, before I go to the States."

Tildy couldn't think of a response. She felt herself being pulled from the dream as he spoke. It was ending sooner than usual. Perhaps something was happening?

What if, while she was standing here, talking to this imaginary hotel clerk, there was a fire at home? What if the flames were wrapping themselves up the walls and across the ceiling, licking through the gaps in her door while smoke billowed in through the air vent, and she was suffocating from the smoke?

Or what if there was a murderer in her room? Her family had stalkers. What if one had broken into her apartment in the night, and they were looming over her with a knife in hand? The anxiety built in her, and Ben, unreal as he was, looked concerned for her and asked if she was alright.

She woke herself sharply. Darkness, peaceful and serene, greeted her. There was no emergency here. She pinched herself and felt pain, but she wondered—wouldn't she feel pain there, too?

chapter
eight

"Have you met someone?"

Russell wasted no time as Tildy walked around the St. Stephen's Greenmarket. She had the conversation going through headphones, and to everyone else it looked normal. A young woman having a normal conversation with a person who was alive. Tildy held her woven tote on her forearm as she tested fruits and vegetables and looked at fresh dairy products. The fruit wasn't as good as in Ireland. The vegetables were okay. The butter couldn't bear the comparison. There was no point in being at this farmers market, yet she wanted to try to enjoy it here. She wanted to give New York a chance to impress her.

"Not exactly," Tildy said.

"That's a strange answer. Please elaborate?"

She set down an unwanted tomato and tried a zucchini. "I'm testing a tool that helps people with trauma control their dreams. The experience is… it's incredible, really."

"Lucid dreaming, then?"

"Yeah, except they last a really long time. Hours, I think. It's like being on vacation every night for a few hours at a time."

"I see. Sounds delightful. What are the downsides?"

"You can't use it too often. Something about nightmares. Anyway, it's been nice. To dream about things I could do."

"Such as?"

"Moving to Ireland."

The virtual companion went silent, processing the information. Tildy passed by flowers wrapped in cellophane in giant plastic tubs. In every interaction with the bot, she waited for this to surface again.

"You were so young, Tildy."

"I know."

"And you had just lost your mother. You'd be out there, away from your friends."

"What friends," Tildy scoffed.

"Your family, then."

"Nana is family."

Russell's voice laughed. "Yes. Technically, I suppose."

"I did what you suggested, and I'm here. I'm still here,

stuck here, with no one and nothing. Meanwhile, Aidan is wealthy. And handsome. He has a famous restaurant he runs on his own and owns two others, just as he said he would. And I'm alone, watching Dad and Gisele sink the company."

Russell knew all of that, but that was why she existed. To listen when no one else would or could, to give advice that was practical. And painful.

Tildy paid for a pair of pomegranates and set them in her tote. "I'm sure he hates me still."

"Think of all the ways he could get in touch with you and he never has. It was a fling!"

"Yeah. A fling."

"The right partner will come along. Thank goodness you have your education. If your father fails, you won't be destitute. I have no idea what Gisele will do."

The implication that her sister's fate was Tildy's responsibility stung. She sometimes forgot her mother had written this software, sometimes forgot it was software at all, until moments like this. Russell delivered advice and instructed on the principles her mother wanted for her girls when she was gone. This software was her stand-in. And when it expressed disappointment, Tildy felt it keenly. She didn't want to disappoint her mother.

"I'm going to go, Russell."

"Okay, Tildy. I'll be here."

Tildy hung up and bought herself a gelato. She wanted to go home, put on the dream machine, and get away from this tension, but it hadn't even been twenty-four hours since she'd used it last. She wanted to take a few days off, to prove to herself she didn't need it.

She walked up 79th Street to the park and sat at a bench near the Alice in Wonderland statues. A man threw a ball for a beige poodle mix, a mother and toddler were playing a game called Queen of the Mountain on a piece of Manhattan shale, and joggers gossiped about their husbands as they ran past.

Tildy took out her phone and loaded the social media account for Aidan's restaurant. His coworkers and friends were tagged in some of the images, and she used those tags as she had done before to learn more about them. Their families, hobbies, interests, the jokes they shared and the way they expressed themselves. A woman named Orla had gone to a concert in Dublin. A man named Jordie posted slightly flirtatious replies on thirst traps but seemed in love with his boyfriend. Someone named Colm had bought a new board game.

She thought of it like packing for a vacation, adding details she might need to enhance the experience. She street-viewed their home addresses, their favorite places to eat and drink, she used sculptures and landmarks in the background of their selfies to figure out where they liked to go and at what time of day and what their work schedules might be.

This invasion of privacy unsettled her, and yet she did not stop. The only person she did not research like this was

Aidan himself. All that she knew, she gathered from those around him. She liked the version of him in her dream, handsome and apart from her. Aloof and a mystery. She didn't want to learn that her image of him was a lie.

When Tildy prepared to fall asleep the next night, she considered what her nana had said in the last dream. The instruction was "to dress nice." It was suspicious. Nana wasn't traditional in many ways, but the woman did expect Tildy to be settled down in a monogamous relationship by twenty-six. And despite what this dream presented to her, Tildy was familiar with her disappointment.

Perhaps she was simply inviting over a friend and didn't want her ugly-duckling granddaughter to embarrass her. Like many beautiful women who had beautiful daughters, Nana didn't appreciate that Tildy's inadequacies didn't stem from lack of effort. There was no amount of money, time, or expertise that would make her as lovely as the other women in her family.

Still, she was excited to return to the comfort of Nana's cottage. In her dream, her favorite silk blouse was neatly pressed and waiting for her. She paired it with a leather jacket then slipped into dark slacks and soft leather boots. The boots felt a little sexy for a trip to her grandmother's. Instead of replacing them, Tildy leaned in, spending extra time on her eyebrows, lips, and eyeliner. She even put concealer and powder on her neck and upper chest. If Nana wanted her to be presentable, she would be the most presentable she could possibly be.

She reached the bottom of the landing and checked for her keys and phone in her purse as she walked by the front desk.

"Where ya off to today, Miss Halleran?"

"Hi, Ben. Visiting my nan."

He gave her a warm smile. And then he frowned. "It's Thursday?"

"Yes?"

"Don't take the Barna road today, there's a cycling race."

"Thanks for the tip." Tildy waved goodbye and left the lobby.

The day was bright, only a slight chill in the air. The street separating the hotel from the parking garage was already busy, mostly with tour buses departing from their station to the Cliffs of Moher. A beautiful day like this, everyone wanted to get poor-quality cell photos of the white cliffs alongside hundreds of strangers.

The drive through the city was stressful but over quickly. After the larger streets and the freeway, she reached the long, sweeping, barren road. The same rolling hills that had been cloaked in fog on her last drive were now bright in full sunshine. The forecast called for rain by early evening, the clouds so distant as to be a thin line hovering at the horizon. Tildy was glad to be away from Eyre Square and the shoreline, likely full of gorgeous young locals all in love and enjoying one another.

A man walking with a long stick tipped his hat to her, and Tildy waved back. She turned down the smaller, narrow, two-laned-in-theory road, lined with bushes at either side. A car approached and she slowed, pulling off the road at the safest spot, where the slope to the roadside rut was shallowest. It caused the whole side of the car to end up in an overgrown bush, and the piercing shrieks of branches scratching against the paint made Tildy flinch. The other driver waved, and she waved back. When she woke up, she'd probably continue the wave whenever she drove and be irritated when it didn't get reciprocated.

On the final approach to Nana's house, Tildy could see two vehicles, one towing a small flatbed trailer. *Nana must have hired someone to haul the tree away*, she thought. *I wonder how her visitors will be able to park?* She pulled into the only available spot and shut the car off, then remembered Nana's request and checked herself in the mirror.

In this sunshine, Tildy's mental picture of herself popped. She didn't look as good as she thought. Her makeup was thick, her pores small dots across her nose and cheeks. Concealer had caked into an uneven layer across her forehead. Her eyebrows didn't look right, and her lip gloss was too shiny. She looked like a normal person who tried too hard. She took out a tissue and wiped away some of the excess. Better, but still too much makeup. She sighed and shut the mirror.

Nana waved from the doorway, a vaguely familiar elderly woman beside her.

"Dia duit a seanmhathair. Did you hire someone for the tree?" Tildy asked as she walked toward the side fence, where the tree would be visible.

"Oh, no no, you just come inside now, I'll explain it all. Tar isteach, tar isteach "

Tildy obeyed and stepped into the warm little home.

"You remember my cousin, Mrs. Fegan."

Mary Fegan smiled broadly and took Tildy's hand. "Fáilte abhaile, a stór!"

Tildy shook hands politely, bewildered but pleased by the women's energy.

"Tildy, come in now, have a seat, just so."

She sat as instructed, her purse still draped across her shoulder.

"Bhuel, anois. Níl sé sin sách maith," Mrs. Fegan muttered.

"No no, up here now." Nana directed her to stand, taking the purse and setting it in a basket. With a gnarled hand, she brushed back Tildy's hair, smoothing it against her shoulder. "Gruaig álainn, go hálainn ar fad."

"Oh, it is. It is," Mrs. Fegan agreed.

Tildy hunched forward and eyed Nana in suspicion, who looked dissatisfied in return. "Sean-máthair, cad atá ag tarlaigh?"

Nana stepped back to examine Tildy and frowned, looked to her cousin, and they made a decision that was not complimentary. "Má tá sé ceart go leor, tá sé ceart go leor."

"There's only so much to be done," Mrs. Fegan agreed.

"Nana."

Nana seemed not to hear as she set five cups on a tray, with a teapot and fresh cookies, arranging the porcelain with care. "Some local boys have been working on the old cherry tree. It's about time they came in for a bit of tea."

Her emphasis on *boys* was unmistakable.

Tildy silently implored Mrs. Fegan for information, who replied by ignoring the look. Despite her reservations, Tildy helped move the tea things to the little table in the sunroom, where five chairs were set up, two right beside one another. There were two men, then.

"Suigh suas díreach anois, a Tildy. Maith an cailín. I need to fetch something, we'll just be a moment. Stay right here, loveen. Tar liom, a Mháire." Nana and her cousin walked out of the sunroom and back into the main house. Nana looked back, nodded with approval, then left.

Alone in the empty sunroom, standing in the center, Tildy felt ridiculous. She would go into the bathroom to check her reflection, except there was no point. With a deep sigh, she ignored their instructions and returned to the main house.

"Tildy, now go sit down over there! They'll be confused if there's no one in there!"

"Nana, it's fine. I'll wait here until everyone is settled."

Her nana glared at her and shook her head. Then she and Mrs. Fegan went back into the sunroom, leaving Tildy alone.

And it would be fine, she decided. It was safe to assume

that the men, whoever they were, had experience being set up by overeager relatives. Perhaps Nana had a reputation for being a bean chleamhnais, an unofficial matchmaker. It wouldn't be her only role in the community. Tildy knew she liked to tease city kids who came to study Irish in the Gaeltacht. She'd hike up the hills to their campgrounds, then walk around in a dark veil, pretending to be a cailleach, an old hag haunting the countryside. In short, Nana would absolutely be up in other people's business. No one who guarded their own time and privacy as much as her would respect the boundaries of others.

Tildy wondered if the guests would be older men—unlikely, based on her grandmother's appreciation for youth. Though, that would be very funny. Or much younger men. That would be less funny.

A thought occurred to her. *It couldn't possibly be him. He was busy. He didn't have time to drive all the way out here to clear a tree for someone else's grandmother.*

But then, his adopted home was only half a mile from here. Perhaps it was him.

Tildy sighed. It couldn't be him. Nana wouldn't dare. Not dream nana, anyway.

Just as she prepared to step back into the sunroom, a man's voice came through its French doors.

"That's grand, you didn't have to now. I'll wash up and help."

She retreated back into the house. Any amusement faded. That voice.

Tildy had only a few seconds to prepare. She took a breath, tried to put her hands in her jeans pockets. No, the pockets were too tiny. She folded her arms. Too stern. She clasped her hands behind her, then in front of her, then remembered her jacket pockets. She stood off to the side, out of a swath of sunlight on the worn hardwood floor. She glanced at the framed pictures of JFK and Jesus, both of whom looked away with serene indifference.

Aidan turned the corner and approached the doorway, brushing dirt and bits of wood from his hands and jeans, seen but unseeing. Sweat glistened on his sun-kissed skin, hints of fair chest hair peeked out from the collar of his T-shirt. He was taller than she had appreciated in the pub. His walk was confident, easy, and matched the smile on his face. Even his sneakers, well-worn black Converse with white laces, had a coolness that could not be replicated. He walked through the doorway and paused, sensing a presence. Tildy's face was already glowing hot when he lifted his eyes. His expression wasn't one of anger or embarrassment. Certainly surprise.

"Hi, Aidan."

After a moment, he collected himself and replied, "Tildy." He lowered his head, focusing on dusting off his hands to hide his eyes.

"You're helping with the tree, then?" she asked. Enough words had been spoken that he had acclimated, somewhat, to her presence. The surprise disappeared, replaced by skeptical observation.

"I help when I'm asked."

"That's nice," she said softly.

Aidan said nothing. He resumed his path, less carefree than before, the scent of him caressing her in the small house as he headed into the kitchen. He turned on the water and leaned down to wash his hands and forearms in the sink. His moss-green T-shirt was thin, strained tight on his chest and biceps, loose on his waist. Shoulder and back muscles moved as his hands rubbed soap up and down his forearms. Tildy blushed and looked away.

She recalled the description of his former, or possibly present, fiancée. Time had given him a refinement to his beauty, and had nearly snuffed hers out. She walked over to the old, original window near the fireplace and looked out through the warped glass. She couldn't see much through it, but it gave her eyes something to do that was not staring at him.

He dried his hands. His eyes avoided the space she occupied.

Nana's voice drifted in from the garden. "Alright now, Seán, your turn to wash up then, if you could please move into the sunroom, Aidan and my granddaughter should be in there and we'll be nice and snug."

Tildy walked back into the sunroom, Aidan close behind. She chose the most difficult seat to access, he sat in the one farthest from her. The sounds of running water from the kitchen reached them as they sat in silence. Tildy poured tea into two cups.

"Cream? Sugar?"

"Both," he replied. She made his first and handed him the cup. He rose and took it by the handle, careful to not touch her hand.

"Now, Seán, just sit…" Nana stopped, then clicked her tongue at the arrangement. "Is leor áit ar bith."

Seán smiled as he entered, all confidence and swagger. He had strawberry-blond hair, a thin beard, a strong build, and piercing blue eyes, all of which had no effect on Tildy. He had been handsome as a boy and was handsome now, but he wore his attraction with too much pride. Gisele would've loved him, though, at least for a little while.

Mrs. Fegan fixed three cups of tea, then took her seat and smiled serenely, looking from one person to another in anticipation of drama. Nana settled into a chair beside Tildy and patted her granddaughter's knee, as if no greater plan had been thwarted.

"Seánie, my Tildy just moved back home from the States. You remember her—you two played during her visits. She's teaching computers at the university."

"Oh, yes, I remember. Brooklyn, was it?" Seán said.

"Manhattan. We lived in Santa Fe once, when I was a girl, but we've only lived in Manhattan."

"Wow, Santa Fe. That's a rare one. Isn't that an Old West town?"

"Not anymore. It's half artsy, wealthy white people who have no culture of their own and half indigenous people fighting for autonomy in the poorest state in the country."

"A Tildy! Seachain do theanga."

Seán chuckled, while Aidan kept his eyes down.

"You went to Columbia University, is that right?" Mrs. Fegan asked, then sipped.

"For my undergraduate degree. I got my master's from NYU."

"Didn't Conor Lahey go to NYU? You know, Matthew's boy," Nana asked.

"So he did. Tildy, did you know Conor?" Mrs. Fegan said.

"I…"

"Tildy wouldn't." Seán shook his head. "Conor was old enough to be our da."

"So he was, so he was. Oh, his grandfather used to bring my father the best mackerel in the winter. The poor man long passed away, of course."

"Aren't schools in Boston and California best for computer science? Why not go there?" Seán asked.

"They are. My father's company needed help," Tildy felt Aidan's awareness. Her voice weakened. "I couldn't be far from New York."

"Aidan, didn't you look at schools in New York?" Mrs. Fegan asked.

"No," he replied with some warmth. "I never considered going that far from home."

A pause arrested the group. Tildy wanted to evaporate.

Nana rallied first. "Seánie, you do something with computers, don't you?"

He laughed. "I used to work at an Apple store in Dublin. No, now I'm a lowly carpenter."

"A lowly carpenter," Nana laughed, swatting in his direction.

"Will you use the wood from the tree there?" Mrs. Fegan asked him.

Seán leaned forward to look at the fallen trunk. "It's a bit small, but maybe so. I sell smaller bowls on Etsy, for keeping spices while you cook. Aidan has bought some. Cherrywood might be nice. I'd have to take a closer look."

"It's Maggie's tree—you better share the profits," Mrs. Fegan replied.

"Hush now, Mary," Nana said. "That tree has been a nuisance. Worrying after it storm after storm. Good riddance to it. My own family, leaving me a tree to care for, as if I could do it all on my own."

Tildy stared at Nana. She stared back, a hollow look, like a puppet whose strings had dropped. The rest of the scene felt flimsy now. The sounds of the wind and the birds outside the sunroom, and the rustling and clattering of spoons in cups within, were all muffled into soft distortion. Tildy shut her eyes to it all. She clenched her fists.

Don't do this, she thought to her sleeping mind. *Please. Let me be with her like this, if only here.*

The moment passed.

Nana, warm again, directed some questions to Seán about his family. Tildy's hand shook as she sipped her tea. Though he looked elsewhere, she felt certain Aidan was focused on her. Had he noticed something was wrong? Could he have seen what had happened? No, not likely, she decided. He was probably repulsed by her wrinkles and dark eye circles and frizzy hair. He was assessing the ways she had failed to live up to his expectations. She took a bite of a cookie, too sugary but so familiar, yet not able to soothe her.

Tildy looked back at the fallen tree, limbs already cast aside and leaves scattered across the ground. She had planted it with her mother as a child, on of their many trips with just one another. She remembered her small hands in gloves much too big. Together, she and her mother had pushed down the soil around the sapling, sharing hopes of the cherry pies they'd bake together. It never produced cherries during their visits, but there was always another visit on the horizon. Her mother had promised Aidan one day they'd bake a pie together. Years went by, with no flowers and no fruit, and the promised pie never came to be.

Awaking from the recollection, Tildy turned to find Aidan looking at her. As if he could see inside her, reflecting her sadness back to her. Then, he looked away. It felt like a rejection somehow. She lowered her eyes and wished this dream would end.

"I heard your mother was selling her wonderful blankets on the internet. How is she doing, Seánie?"

"She's been feeling better, the weather has been mild. The winters are hard. She and Da might move to Spain, if only for the winters."

"Do they like it there?" Tildy asked, not wanting to remain silent.

"They like the warmth. Not learning the language, but you know, they're getting on. It's a bit late to learn something new."

"We're low on biscuits—I'll check the press," Mrs. Fegan announced.

"Aidan," Nana asked, eager to refocus the conversation. "How is your sister and her baby?"

"Good. Just took his first steps. The little man is going to be enormous," Aidan replied with a grin. An ache bloomed in Tildy's chest. She had forgotten how he loved children.

Nana nodded sagely. "Sutach ceart. He would take after your side, you can see it in the photos. Helena's husband, poor man that he is, is quite a short man."

Mrs. Fegan reappeared at that moment. "A Dheirdre, an féidir leat teacht isteach anseo, ní féidir liom na brioscaí a aimsiú."

Nana apologized and went indoors in search of the missing biscuits. She stole a look backward at Tildy and motioned toward Aidan before disappearing inside. Tildy did not accommodate the silent request.

When she was gone, Seán leaned in. "You know, Tildy, I've seen some photos of you."

"Oh?"

"Sure, you and me in nappies, splashing at the beach. My mum and yours were good friends."

Tildy laughed in relief. "Really?"

"Oh sure. Used to take us all on outings. Not so close as yours and Aidan's mum, of course, but they were like a gang. Like a mum gang, busting into museums and restaurants."

"I don't remember that," she said, some sadness creeping into her voice. Aidan looked down at his hands, rubbing them together and examining his fingers. Seán didn't seem to notice.

"Sure. You want copies of the photos? I'm not normally the sort to be sharing nudes, but exceptions can be made."

They all chuckled, grateful for the levity.

"You living in the city now?" he asked her with a smile.

"Yes, I rented a cottage northeast of the university, not like, in a farm or anything. It's behind someone's house. Well, estate. I'm not exactly sure what neighborhood, exactly." Her face flushed as she willed her mouth to stop talking.

"Do you like it?"

"I think so. I just signed the lease."

"Let's meet up for a pint and we can… erm." He looked at Aidan and his enthusiasm withered. "Or I can leave the photos with your nan, next time I come around?"

"Sure, I'll be here every week. Even bought a car."

"Did you? What car?"

"A Škoda Fabia RS? I think it's RS. I'd have to look at the back."

Seán let out a laugh. "Bit shit, isn't it?"

She laughed heartily, drawing Aidan's eye. "Don't say that! He's my only friend. He got me here, and he'll get me home. Hopefully."

The two of them laughed again. Nana returned and surveyed the scene. She glared at Seán and shook her head. "Boys, rain is on the wind. Now have another nibble, then get a move on. No sense catching your death over a cherry tree."

Seán smiled knowingly at his companions. Aidan stood, walked to the table, set down his cup, and left. Tildy looked up once he'd passed through the doorway. Seán thanked Nana for the tea and headed out without cleaning up.

Standing at the windows in the sunroom, she watched them go, though only one had her attention. Nana stood with her and sighed.

"Maybe you should go give Aidan a hand, Tildy. I can distract Seán. He's a bit of a rake, isn't he."

"No, Nana. Le do thoil stop ag déanamh rudaí cosúil leis sin," she whispered. Tildy gathered her and Seán's tea things onto a tray, then brought the tray into the kitchen. Mrs. Fegan was resting in one of the armchairs by the fire, the biscuits apparently forgotten.

"Stop what? What have I done, exactly?" Nana called loudly.

Tildy frowned, waiting until her grandmother was nearby, and whispered, "You know what you're doing, you always know what you're doing. He's mad at me—let him be."

"Mad at you?"

"When we were young," Tildy began, but looked at Mrs. Fegan again and stopped herself. "He's still angry."

"Angry? A óinseach! He's had loads of girls since you were here, what does he have to be angry about."

"Nana, please don't do anything else. Nothing like this."

She shrugged theatrically but didn't respond. Mrs. Fegan remained in the armchair while the two women washed the tea things in silence. As they neared the end of the last cup, Mrs. Fegan passed through to the sunroom. Nana also walked over, and Tildy couldn't help joining. The three women watched the men.

The trunk had now been denuded of branches. Seán and Aidan stood over it, apparently preparing to lift it off the stone fence, their words too distant to be heard. Aidan put on gloves and urged Seán to do the same. Bracing themselves, they spoke a countdown, then lifted and pushed, grunting in exertion until the trunk hit the ground with an earthshaking thud.

"He's quite a man, our Aidan," Nana said. Mrs. Fegan murmured in approval.

"I've never met anyone like him," Tildy agreed. Saying the words aloud somehow drew his eye to her, and this time she shared contact. Like looking at the sun, she stared at the hurt she had caused. She made herself appreciate him now, how handsome and impossibly distant he had become, before he turned away.

"Tildy," Nana began, "I need to go into town for an appointment tomorrow. Can you pick me up quite early, at 8 a.m.? Normally Brigid would take me in, but she's on holiday. Off to Italy for the Parthenon, for some reason."

"I'd be happy to, Nana,"Tildy said brightly, grateful that their tense moment had passed.

Her grandmother took her hands. "I'm sorry to have caused you trouble. I can't promise I won't do it again. I'm so glad you have come home."

"Nílimid ach ag iarraidh éard is fearr duit, a stór." Mrs. Fegan added. Nana grimaced, but nodded her agreement.

Tildy said her goodbyes, more comfortable in the parting process but eager for it to be habit. Soon, she'd learn how to control these dreams. She'd stop letting Aidan surprise her here, and she'd be comfortable. She'd settle into her cottage, take the job at the university, and see how it went. There would be the nightmares, of course – but she had nightmares in normal dreams, too. The nightmares here would be the price she'd pay for living in this Ireland.

The men were still in the field, working on the tree. She paused, car keys in hand, considering whether she should go say something. She moved to the side fence, where the tree could just be seen. The two men were laughing, pretending to sword fight with branches pulled from a pile. Aidan was enjoying the work, the weather, and his friend. She didn't want to disturb them anymore. She wanted to release him from her dream and let him be happy.

Her thoughts absorbed her on the return drive, the freeway, city, and parking garage a faded filmstrip, details lost and unimportant. In the lobby, Ben looked up from paperwork at her.

"Miss Halleran, welcome back."

"Thanks, Ben," she said, not slowing down, her stride taking her straight to the stairwell.

Once inside the privacy of her room, she hung up her blouse, untied her boots, peeled off her jeans, and flopped on the bed in her ugly underwear. It was always the ugly underwear that looked best under clothes, she thought. The sexy stuff usually had lace and details that ruined the look of nice blouses. It was also uncomfortable.

Tildy thought of Ben's admiration, Seán's flirtation, and decided she needed some sexy underwear. This was her dream, her *fantasy* after all. She could get cute stuff and hook up with someone. A someone without baggage. Maybe a guy with piercing blue eyes who took his dog out on his sailboat boat and wore cable knit sweaters and let the sea spray glisten his wavy blond hair. Or maybe just an attractive guy in a club. Whatever was easiest.

She flopped her arms over her face and groaned. She didn't want to dream up someone new. She wanted to be around Aidan more, even if he hated her. Complete amnesia would have been hurtful; he had been her first love, first kiss. If she had moved back, or even visited the summer after her last, she would've never left. They both knew it. And she had left.

Tildy rolled off the bed and shuffled to the bathroom, where she started the faucet in the tub. The little cottage had no bathtub. She needed to enjoy a bath while access to one lasted. In the available hotel-sized toiletries was a single-use satchel of bath salts. They smelled of fake rose. She shrugged and dumped the crystals into the water.

While the tub filled, she turned to the mirror and scrutinized her reflection. She had some sun damage to her décolletage. Her waist was more implied than visible. Her padded nude bra and nude high-waisted briefs fit her mood exactly. Turning to view her profile, Tildy let loose her stomach muscles and slouched. The faux-pregnant belly made her chuckle. She looked at her butt, comparing one side and then the other. One was nicely curved, ending in a single indent at the back of her thigh, as one would expect. The other side sloped, weirdly. She had never noticed that before. Her dream mind had, apparently, and now here it was, another fact in what was supposed to be a vacation from the real world.

"Something else to be insecure about. Great."

The tub had nearly finished filling up. Tildy grabbed her phone, found a radio station called "Chill," and hit play. She turned on the main light in the hotel room, ensured the main door was locked tight, then turned the bathroom lights off. She closed the door to dim the light, removed her underwear, and slid into the hot water. It did smell like rose, but in a pleasant way, making her think of the real flowers, growing outside a cream-colored stucco building. She could almost picture them, growing beside the handicapped access ramp and large double doors with an automatic button.

A care home? Why would I think of that?

Tildy shut her eyes and sunk beneath the water.

The tub broke the bonds of space. It was smaller than her tub in her real apartment, and yet here she could sink to the bottom and stretch out her legs. The warmth relaxed her muscles. She let herself float slightly, bracing herself with her hands and feet. If she balanced just right, it was if she was weightless and disconnected in a soundless void, apart from everything and truly alone. There was no need to breathe here, so she didn't. Suspended like this, she didn't need to worry about Aidan or Nana or her father or her job. She could stay here like this, forever.

A violent vibration through the floor startled her. The water swirled around, as if the tub had been tipped over the edge of a precipice. Tildy put out her hands to brace herself, to catch herself, but she began to slide down, further and further, unable to reach the edge. Her nails clawed against imperfections in the porcelain, scrambling for purchase, nothing yielding to her panic.

The force of her movement caused her to inhale. There is only water, her brain told her. This is what drowning feels like, it said. She reached in all directions, then straight up, her body begging for something to hold on to. Her feet reached a floor, not smooth porcelain but slimy and slick like the bottom of a lake, and she kicked to break through to the surface.

Nothing happened. Her limbs were weak. It was pointless. She would die here.

Tildy woke in her pillows at home and gasped. Her room, her apartment, in New York City.

She ripped off the cap and some hairs along with it. Tears ran down her face, blurring the light on the transmitting device beside her. The blinking lights switched from Sending to Standby. This was her fifth session, and a sense of menace was now unmistakable.

chapter
nine

L ife was mostly normal. Work, a monthly book club, runs in the park, and avoiding the dream machine. Tildy's father and sister had not been back from Palm Beach for a day before she was summoned again. She didn't mind. In fact, she exited the private elevator and passed through the dark wallpapered hallway to her father's residential wing with some curiosity. She wondered if she would hear anything interesting. If, somehow, the issue with them had been that they were not suited to New York. That Florida and tropical sun and sand and sea would invigorate some latent interestingness in them.

She was quickly disappointed.

Gisele said, "Our house is so much bigger than any other house on our street. We have a big gate, a big lawn, and a four-car garage. I want to buy a Maybach, but Lee is being a downer. He says I need to settle for a C-series. Leased."

"That is so hard for you. You aren't used to these kinds of sacrifices," Penelope said.

"You don't like to drive," Tildy said, settling herself into her window seat. It wasn't her window seat, it was her preferred place in this room. It kept her apart but able to observe the modern space, an enlargement of the seating room in her father's office. When her mother had been alive, there had been throws and brightly colored pillows. Those were all gone.

"No one drives their own Maybach, Matilda. Daddy and I need a chauffeur, of course. But Lee said no to that, too. Still, all in all, I'm happy. My tan is incredible, and I don't need to use as much sea salt spray because there is actual sea salt in the air."

"Your hair does look wonderful, I'm so jealous!" Penelope said.

"Your texture isn't as good for sea salt. You probably need to a deep conditioning treatment, next time we go back down to Palm Beach."

"Matilda," her father said suddenly. Tildy turned to him in apprehension. "Have you been using the new product line?"

"Uh, no. Not really."

"Remarkable. Your complexion has improved."

"Oh?"

"You have more color. Are you wearing makeup now?"

"No, Dad."

"It must be the new line. Keep using it."

Gisele checked her messages and screeched. She hopped up from the couch and did a quick sprint in place. "We're meeting with Jude Mills before the Clearstone party."

"Jude Mills?" Tildy asked, looking from her sister to her father for confirmation. Penelope smiled blankly.

Gisele smirked, toying with the bracelet on her delicate wrist. "We bumped into him in Palm Beach last week. He was excited to see us."

"To see you, of course," Penelope murmured. Gisele swatted at her with glee.

Patrick Sullivan rubbed his chin and nodded. "He did ask for my opinion on a few issues with his company. It's interesting how much he's like his father. Better, of course. He knows when to ask for help."

Tildy did not reply for a moment. To imagine her father as a resource for any businessman was beyond stupid, especially for Jude Mills.

After a quick glance at Penelope, who was busy whispering with Gisele, Tildy asked her father, "He's forgiven you?"

"Forgiven me? For what? His father? That was business! He understands. He understands it was only business."

Tildy was not convinced. She knew little of Jude, but all she heard indicated he was clever and resentful. His father, Edward Mills, had been an executive at Aibell many years ago, working his way up from the sales department in the golden days of her grandfather's stewardship. Her father had insisted on cost-cutting measures, despite Edward's objections, despite her mother's objections, and foundation with high levels of asbestos was sold in the thousands. When the FDA caught wind, another disaster hit Aibell. Dozens of customers reported temporary blindness from a new line of neon eyeliners, also approved by her father. The FDA demanded accountability, and her father had fabricated memos placing all the blame on Edward Mills. It had ruined him, and he'd died soon after. The family had disappeared from elite New York City circles. In college, she'd heard of Jude in passing, that he had graduated top of his class, that he had started a company while he worked on his master's degree, that he was a genius at tech investments.

In short, he was very wealthy and very handsome, and he absolutely hated her father.

Gisele read a text message and nearly screamed. "He's coming by now! He said he's in the elevator! How do I look?"

Tildy shrugged. Her father was too busy checking his face in his phone's camera to pay attention. Penelope started to form a compliment, but Gisele waved it off. She undid a top button of her blouse and adjusted her breasts in her bra while she yelled for Constance, the housekeeper, to let him in.

Tildy grabbed a nearby magazine and reclined deeper into the window seat, resting her head against the glass and staring down the street. She wanted to see how this all played out, but didn't want to be involved in it.

There was a world out there, away from them. She looked to the water, where the rivers met the ocean, which spanned from here to where she wanted to be. She could dream it, or she could let this all go. She could move there if she wanted, anytime that she wanted. She had to remind herself that she was free. This family was falling apart, no matter how present she was or how ready to help she remained. She had to let go. Could she let go?

The doorbell chimed, and Gisele waited with giddy anticipation, looking to Penelope for praise, which she received. The housekeeper entered, and Tildy opened the magazine, as if occupied, then lifted her eyes from it. She was too curious about this person who had seemingly forgiven her father and who made Gisele so… much.

"Hi, Mr. Sullivan. Hello again, ladies. I was in the neighborhood, so I wanted to see how your flight went."

"It was good, thanks for asking," Gisele murmured in a voice too husky to belong to her. Tildy didn't notice this affectation, though. This man, Jude Mills, who had publicly hated her father and disparaged her sister, was familiar to her. He was the man from the art gallery.

Today, he wore a light grey sweater and black peacoat.

He had gotten a haircut since she had first seen him. The faint wave in his auburn hair now more controlled. Even his fair, freckled skin seemed smoother. He looked like a movie star selling something luxurious. Color rose to her face. She wanted to hide. She stood instead and raised her chin, her mind scrambling. How would she navigate this development?

Her father noticed the movement and examined her. He seemed to remember the compliment he had paid her a moment ago. He gestured to her with a smile.

"Jude, have you met Matilda? She's our third daughter. Come, meet our dear little worker bee."

The expression change that came over Jude was fascinating. His carefully constructed genial demeanor wavered. He'd recognized her—and he smiled in appreciation of this development. He looked genuinely pleased. Then his smile changed again, in acknowledgment of this bizarre turn of fate. And suddenly Tildy wondered why he was here. If his initial happiness had been a mask, what was underneath? And why would seeing her lift it?

"This is incredible. We've met before. At the Patrinicola Art Auction, in the West Village."

"Oh, I wanted to go to that. How was it?" Gisele gushed in her social media voice, but Jude had already moved to Tildy's retreat.

"How's the painting?" she asked.

"In good hands," he stage-whispered with a half-smile. It wasn't just his cologne that smelled good. He smelled good. Tildy tucked her hair behind her ear, despite herself. She stepped back and sat again at the window seat, as if to remove herself from his attention.

Her father puffed out his chest with evident pride. "What are you doing for dinner, Jude? I can get us a table at Olivia's. Invested in them years ago."

"I don't want to interrupt your plans."

"Plans? Nothing that can't be moved, right, Gisele? And Matilda never has plans."

Jude put his hands in his pockets and looked sideways at Tildy. His little smile at that remark thrilled her more than any cashmere sweater ever could.

"I'd love to," he said simply.

"I'll go get ready then," Gisele said in her new voice. "Come on, Penelope."

Tildy watched the women go and wondered if Gisele would be able to maintain her new persona the whole night.

As her father left to make the reservation, she looked at the young man beside her. She was burning with questions for him. All of the past, all of the things he had said in interviews and tabloids and on social media, she wanted to bring to his attention. Something held her back, though. Maybe it was the shame that it was her father who had set the schism into motion. That this stranger and his family had been harmed by her father. And if he had come for Gisele's money? Well. He was in for a sad surprise.

The sun had started to set, and the automatic lights in her father's apartment bloomed in "dusk" mode. The programming had been set up for him by someone who designed the lighting for museums throughout the world. Tildy found the artificial controls loathsome.

"You don't seem like someone who never has plans," Jude said as he joined her on the window seat. Tildy abandoned her thoughts and looked at his hands, gripping the edge of the seat. They were tan, lean and strong. She gulped and slid herself slightly away from the warmth of his body.

"Not plans they're interested in."

Jude nodded and looked at the doorway where her father and sister had left the room. "You're different from them."

Tildy didn't reply.

"Must be hard, being different in a family like this."

"Like this?

"I mean, this well-known."

She considered how to respond. If this were the past, if he were someone else, she knew how she would open up to the remark. Decades of slights and exclusion and resentment would be offered for exorcism. But he was not the person she thought of when she imagined those conversations.

She pressed her lips into a smile. "No one remembers me, so I get by."

Jude looked into her face. "How could anyone forget you?"

This made Tildy laugh. She rose from the seat they had shared and stepped away from him and his compliments and his intoxicating miasma of gorgeousness.

He looked confused. "What did I say?"

"I feel like you're trying to sell me something," she said.

He stood too, near her, too near. Looking up at his face made her body nearly tip in his direction. She felt color spread down her neck, and she knew, absolutely knew her pupils opened wide to drink in the sight of him. She kept her eyes on his, ignoring his handsome jawline and delicate freckles. She swallowed, the extra saliva a betrayal. As though he knew, he smiled a new smile. A soft smile that bared a bit of teeth. He looked with intent at her mouth.

"I'm a pretty good salesman."

Her father's voice called and he stepped back, the spell broken. "Matilda! Dominick will meet us out front in fifteen minutes. Matilda, will you borrow something of your sister's? You can't go to Olivia's in jeans, for Christ's sake."

Tildy exchanged a look with Jude, lowered her eyes, and left for Gisele's closet to change into whatever was dark and demure and would fit her.

The next day after work, Tildy pulled open the door to a coffee shop. Evelyn had a laptop out and was staring at a graph when she joined her at a coveted two-person table.

"Hey girl, I ordered you an Americano. How you doing?"

"Thanks, it's been a day!" Tildy said, setting her things down under her chair before sitting in it herself. "How are you?"

"You know. Just looking at this data you got me. These sessions going well?"

Something in Evelyn's tone made Tildy hesitate. "I think so."

"No strange nightmares? Everything feels ok?"

"Yeah, it's fine."

Evelyn seemed to take in every detail of Tildy's face. She wondered if Evelyn could remotely disable the dream machine. She still had two pills left, she could use those if she wanted, but to be left with only two more dreams of Ireland felt unfair. "Okay then. Professor Cutting wanted me to get some descriptions from you about what you've been dreaming. We can do that at the lab or here, whatever you prefer."

"Here is fine."

"Okay. I'm not going to ask you any specific questions about who and what is going on in your dreams quite yet. I want to know if you feel like the problem you'd like to solve is being addressed by the content of your dreams, if you feel like the dreams are realistic, and if there are any situations that stand out as particularly dreamlike."

"I see. Yes, I feel like the dreams are helping me envision what it would be like to move to Ireland. They feel realistic."

"You mentioned your nana—have you dreamed of her? How are those interactions?"

Tildy held her hands to the warmth of the coffee cup and looked outside. "They're good. They make me miss her."

"Would you say they are realistic?"

"Uh…" She laughed and pushed her hair behind her ear. "I don't remember her being as warm."

Evelyn nodded and made a note. "Are these dreams helping you come up with motivation or a plan for moving to Ireland?"

Aidan at the sink, washing his arms. "Motivation, oh yes." Tildy sipped her coffee, still too hot, to mask the blush that came to her face.

"Any help in planning?"

"Yes. There was a car purchase section. That felt like a realistic presentation of how that would go. I looked at apartments. That also felt realistic. Some of them were total shit. But I think the rental market is much tighter there. I'm not sure I'd really have that many options. That's about it, though."

Evelyn nodded, made some final notes, and closed her laptop. She leaned back with her coffee. "I really appreciate you doing this. It's hard to get data. People don't like talking about their dreams."

"I can see that," Tildy said, forcing herself to be as casual as possible. "It feels more realistic than dreaming. I don't know. It's like talking the idea through but with yourself."

"That's what I'm saying! People don't have space to imagine things, not with working and kids and bills and cleaning. They need the time and the space to think things through. And that's what this is. Time and space and freedom to think it all through."

"You're doing good work," Tildy said.

Evelyn sipped her coffee and shook her head. "That's all I want to do, is help people. Corny as hell, but that's the truth. And I think most people who are in trouble, they just need some space to think. Friends and family and partners can help them, but not as well as they can help themselves. I believe that, you know?"

"What got you into this?" Tildy asked, as Evelyn looked out the window at the pedestrians heading home. She couldn't quite see her face, but something in her posture warned her she had tapped into something painful.

"I went through a rough time. Lost somebody. I won't go into all that. I needed to find something to help folks with depression, or addiction. This project didn't tick all the boxes—came close enough, though."

"I'm sorry, Evelyn."

She nodded and looked up with a sad smile. "We've both been through our fair share of bullshit."

Tildy left the coffee shop with no plans for her evening. She could grab takeout and go to bed early, perhaps. She checked the time. Too early. She wasn't hungry or tired.

Her phone buzzed in her hand. A message from her dad.

○ Family meeting, come to penthouse

She groaned. Whenever it was a tight, brief message like that, there was something major going on.

○ On my way.

She included a period, because she wanted Lee, who definitely had the phone, to know she was displeased.

nds holding her purse, cold and thin and

d the top of her left hand with the back of
, as if trying to coax a kitten into trusting

e said, her voice projecting the shiver that
.

Friday at 6:15?"

ed after saying it, escaped from the her that
kept her eyes from his as the heavy wooden
ut between them.

Thirty minutes later, Tildy handed her things over to the housekeeper and stepped into the living room, where her father, Gisele, Penelope, and Mr. Lee were seated around the coffee table. Her father looked energetic, as did Gisele, while Lee looked nervous, as usual.

"Tildy. We have an invitation to the Twombleys."

With a power that exceeded superhero strength, Tildy resisted the urge to turn around and leave, but only just. She stopped walking toward the seat she had been aiming for.

"Like, a party?"

"Lunch, at their home. Their personal chef was the sous chef from Fin de Siècle, their miso salmon was scrumptious," Gisele replied.

"Wow, I've never been there!" Penelope said enthusiastically.

Gisele sighed and patted her hand. "You are missing out. I'll have to take you sometime."

"We aren't going for the food," her father interrupted. "We need to convince them to join the board."

Tildy glanced at Lee, who grimaced.

"Why do you want me there?"

"No one *wants* you there," Gisele laughed. Penelope smiled blankly, neither joining in nor objecting to the remark, as if she hadn't heard a thing.

"They'll expect you there. If you want to keep your shares, you need to behave like you deserve them." Her father's tone dripped with contempt, but it did not distract him from his reflection in a glass window.

Lee coughed delicately. "They need to see the major shareholders, the family, united."

The elevator dinged, and the door opened to reveal Jude, his hair tussled by the wind outside. She watched him, unseen, as he set his jacket and briefcase carefully on a chair near the main entrance. He fixed his hair and adjusted his dress shirt before passing through the doorway to join them. Their gazes met and he smiled shyly at her, as if to make his vanity a private joke between them.

"Ah, Jude! Welcome. We were just explaining to Tildy about the Twombley lunch."

Tildy looked to her father, her face unable to conceal the suspicion. Jude shrugged, a wolfish edge to the grin he gave her.

"Of course, Dad. I'll be there. What day?"

"Wednesday, next week. Wear something pretty, but not too pretty, you understand. Don't try to look young, that would be ridiculous."

Tildy put the details for the lunch in her phone. The Twombleys were distant cousins of her father's. While he marched in St. Patrick's Day parades and met with Irish politicians at the embassy, he kept his Dutch, old-money New York City family connections warm. It made his insistence on being Irish all the more mortifying.

Jude joined Penelope and Gisele across the room, while her father stood near the group, smiling and adding details when he thought necessary. Tildy remained on the

chapter
ten

That night, Tildy fell asleep quickly, eager for the escape. Once plunged into the dream, she was already on the road to Nana's. It was an unsettling transition. The roads seem to swing with her car as she drove. At least she had memorized the route. She held fast to the steering wheel and waited for the world to acclimate to her.

A bright yellow hatchback buzzed by, the aftermarket exhaust more like a swarm of bees than a rumble. The detail seemed to resolve the instability. Tildy was driving, her route was familiar to her, everything was fine.

She pulled into the drive at exactly 8 a.m. Before she'd decided whether to help her grandmother from the door to the car, Nana emerged in her bright yellow hooded rain jacket and quickly bundled into the car with a large canvas shopping bag decorated with a kitten.

"Look at the car! This is sharp, isn't it though. Tildy, you've done well!"

"Thanks, Nana. I'm glad you like it. Seán didn't think so."

"Cén fáth? Oh, he's a bit of a Holy Joe, nothing less than a Mer-ce-des for him," she said, pronouncing each syllable of the luxury manufacturer. "Lowly carpenter, indeed."

Tildy pulled out onto the road, more nervous than she wanted to be. Driving herself had been a challenge. She didn't own a car in New York, only occasionally renting one when leaving the city or on business trips with her family. Here, in this unfamiliar place, driving a beloved passenger only added to her stress.

"You're doing grand, loveen. And thank you for joining my little tea party yesterday. You'll have to forgive my cousin—she's a bit too curious about the goings-on of the young people."

Tildy could have replied that Mrs. Fegan was not the only person too curious about other people's business, but she let it go.

Nana's tone was soft. "Why did you not come back for university? You said you wanted to."

Tildy felt tears in her eyes, but she set the feeling aside. "I wish I had. I wish I had every day."

Nana didn't respond immediately. Tildy didn't dare turn her eyes from the road, unsure what course the conversation would take.

"I've never forgiven your father. Nach mór an t-amadán é. Not for what happened to my girl. I know it was God's plan, it couldn't be helped. But how he stole you children from me, how you were treated. Him so self-absorbed and making you responsible for propping up that *cosmetics company*." She said the business category like a venereal disease. "It broke my heart, to see him steal your youth. Your sisters are good girls, in their own way, but you never belonged in that situation. I should have insisted you come to me."

Tildy smiled. "Nana. You would've wanted a teenage girl in your house? Really?"

She sighed. "Tá an ceart agat. Your mother was a warm person, like my mother. You've been left with cold people, a chroí. Surrounded by cold, selfish people."

"You aren't selfish."

"Selfishness takes many forms, Tildy."

They continued in silence for some time, each thinking of the other, of their lives, of how their wishes were shaped by regrets and fears.

"Tell me more about your new job!" Nana said. "Is the pay very good?"

"No, not at all. My last job was well paid. Boring, but well paid. Lots of spreadsheets and computer work. Now I'll teach. A nice change, I think."

"You'll enjoy the work."

"I think so. I'm good at what I do. Maybe I can share it with others."

"Have you met anyone with your new position?"

"Not yet." Tildy's mind scrambled for details she could supply. Would she really have accepted a job without meeting anyone at the university? "I'm going to get lunch with a woman who teaches in the same department next week," she began. "It's mostly men, so we're going to try to stick together. She seems fun, over email anyway. I think we'll get along."

"Sure you will, loveen."

They fell quiet again, and she braced for whatever thoughts her nana was preparing. She often wondered what kind of woman her grandmother had been in youth— yellow-gray pictures showed a confident, gorgeous girl with a vague resemblance to Tildy. The women in her family had a reputation for beauty. Gisele was certainly beautiful, but those genes hadn't made it to Tildy without some errors. It didn't lessen her pride in her grandmother and mother's looks. Aside from the photos, and what she knew of Nana's personality now, Tildy couldn't remember what her mother had said about Nana as a mother. Even before that, there was no one around to share stories. Maybe Mrs. Fegan had some tales to tell.

"I promised I wouldn't mention it," Nana declared, interrupting Tildy's thoughts.

"Oh no."

"Cousin Mary did talk to Aidan about you after you

left…"

Tildy rolled her eyes in anticipation. At first, Nana said nothing. The silence continued.

"And?" she prodded.

"He said that he didn't recognize you in the pub. He's not sure he would've known you at all, because you've gotten so old."

"I see." It was as she'd expected. She thought of him, of his handsome features and passionate eyes. The years that had worn her down had polished him. It didn't matter. All his attractions now existed for people other than herself. She tried to embrace this rejection.

"Absolute raiméis." Nana grunted.

Tildy barked a laugh. "Nana!"

"Ó, nach bréagadóir é. Cousin Mary ate it up—of course she would, she doesn't see your charm. A bit thin, a bit sad. With your beautiful black hair and serious eyes, to me you look like a rogue woman, unearthly! Not a beauty by popular standards, like your mother or Gisele, or myself in my day, but beautiful in the ways that matter. Bean láidir, chróga agus chliste. A woman of the world. Oh, Tildy, he's completely smitten."

"Nana…"

"Even Seán could see it, in ainneoin an t-amadán atá sé ."

"Seán would chase absolutely anyone."

"True, but he saw it. He knew not to step into Aidan's way. Just consider our boy, it's all I ask."

"It doesn't matter if I'm old or beautiful or… whatever. I hurt him. All that's over."

"Hurt him indeed. Níl ciall leis sin. Men don't like not getting exactly what they want exactly when they want it. It's good for them to wait. It is. It tests the feelings when you aren't there. They either fade, which they quite often do, and then it is no nevermind to you, or they grow intense, like your Aidan. It was this way with your grandfather."

"Oh?"

"Sure. I wasn't set on him, myself. Bhí fir eile agam, a lán fear eile. I won't bother you with those details. In the end, it was between Patrick and Robert Bryne."

"Bryne? Wait. Delilah's grandfather?"

Nana took a moment to sigh out the window in recollection. "Oh, you should've seen him, Tildy. The man was absolutely gorgeous. Your grandfather was handsome too, but Robert… Eyes dazzling like gems. Strong, tall. Used to buy me oranges, rare things in those days. Once saw him and his brother jumpin' into the sea, completely naked. Is iomaí na hoícheanta uaigneacha a coinníodh mé te leis an gcuimhne sin."

"Oh boy." Tildy laughed in embarrassment.

"He was quiet though, you know. So quiet. Not my type. I'd have run right over him. I need a good shouting match time to time. I chose Patrick. Broke poor Robert's heart, of course. He married a sweet girl all the way from Roscommon, as you know. It was a good match. They were very happy, a fine family."

Tildy considered Nana's descriptions. Having heard plenty of stories about her grandfather, she wasn't sure she'd have made the same choice. He'd been dead for decades, yet people still knew of him. He had been a large, strong man with a temper. Never violent with his family, but a reputation as a vigilante. She wasn't sure how far that went, what else he had done in his youth. It was worth thinking about, considering what had passed in his lifetime in this country.

"I'm glad everyone ended up happy," she said aloud.

"Tildy. You need to decide what you want, and go for it."

"Nana, I'm here! I've gone for it. I'm in it."

"Is that so?"

"Uh, yes. I am. We're speaking now, here, in my car."

"I suppose that is true. I'll just be silent, then."

"Thank you."

"Ní déarfaidh mé focal ar bith eile."

"Great."

Nana moved as if to speak, then shook her head and adjusted her tote bag. Tildy could feel her straining, desperate.

"Okay. Any closing thoughts?"

"Oh Tildy, he removed his shirt after you left, and oh twas a sight that begs to be seen!"

They laughed together, the cackles harmonious in the small car. Soon after, they arrived at the doctor's office.

"Now you just leave me off here. There's a little coffee shop just around the way. I'll be right here at"—Nana checked her gold watch—"ten after. Alright, loveen?"

"Sure, Nana. I'll be here. Good luck?"

"Good luck, what of it. You goose. I'm getting my medications refilled, not a major operation."

"Alright, I'm sorry, I'll be there. Have a good visit."

Tildy waited as instructed, nursing her coffee alone, staring out the window at passersby and thinking of her nana's description of selfishness. She wasn't sure if that fit, exactly. Coldness, though. There had always been something harsh about Nana, something her charm and good humor glossed over. Though the familiarity of it was a comfort, it wasn't especially pleasant in and of itself. Tildy did not want to be like her, not in that way.

A woman exited the shop with her daughter. Out on the sidewalk, the mother reached down and adjusted the little girl's jacket, using the nearness to kiss the child's nose. Tildy smiled at the moment, watching them hold hands as they crossed the street.

She remembered, as she sometimes forgot, her nana had lost two daughters. One, her firstborn, had died in infancy. Then Tildy's mom. Her sons had moved away, one to Wexford, but one all the way to Australia. Alone in adulthood, after a childhood where her older siblings all left the family farm. One sister had disappeared entirely, or at least Tildy had never heard what had happened to her. The rest had moved away, earning money in other countries to send back home. Her siblings had visited, of course, just as her surviving children would visit, but they never moved back. And now, Nana lived alone. It was enough loss to turn anyone cold.

chapter
eleven

Tildy waited for her one-on-one to start with trepidation. Her work was always good, always on time, but since she'd started the experiment, she couldn't deny some details had slipped. Her colleagues and her manager were disappointed with her work right now. She was a disappointment—that should be an easy position for her, of all people, to be in, and yet her job had been a reprieve from her feelings of inadequacy. This was where she could be someone other than her sisters' sister and her father's daughter.

Her manager, Jack, came in and sat down, his glasses

askew on his nose, the papers he carried wrinkled from his clutch. She hadn't expected him to be nervous too.

"How are you doing, Matilda?"

"I'm fine, you?"

"Eh, okay, I guess." Jack looked down at his papers and sighed.

"Sorry about the sign-up flow experiment. I don't think the group was large enough to get the data we needed. I'm not sure what I was thinking."

"No, no. It's not that. I appreciate you saying that, but the experiment was fine."

Tildy waited for him to say what was on that piece of paper, beginning to put together what was happening. To her surprise, she didn't feel anger or sadness—she felt relief. Her gaze slid toward the doorway, her thoughts already on the trip home, on putting on the dream machine and going to sleep and buying supplies for her cottage in Ireland. Shame gripped her then. She was about to lose her job and her first thought wasn't to panic, but to return to her imaginary life. To buy dishes that didn't exist for a cupboard that didn't exist in a cottage that didn't exist.

"We made a mistake in our earnings projections, and Laurel had to recalculate our runway until we raise again."

Before he could continue, Tildy nodded. "It's okay."

"It's not okay. We made a commitment to you. And marketing isn't losing anyone. I have to cut heads, while they are 'essential'. It's bullshit, is what it is."

"I'm okay, Jack. Do you have to let anyone else go?"

"Just one more. I don't know who, though. Gina is getting married next month, and Yae-Joon just came back from paternity leave. They are the weakest performers. Still, this is bullshit. We don't need a dozen people in marketing."

"Lean on them. Tell them you had to let me go, that I was devastated and made a scene. They should have to lose someone."

Jack laughed. "So it must be true, then."

"What's that?" Tildy recoiled at his tone.

"I thought it was just a coincidence, a rumor here. Your name and what not. You're probably set up with your dad and all."

She shrugged and cast a meaningful glance at the paperwork. "You'd be surprised."

"Right." Jack cleared his throat and slid the lightly crumpled papers to her. "We're offering four months' pay and benefits, and letters of recommendation, of course. We'll keep your metro card going until the end of December."

"That's generous, thank you."

"No, it's not. It should've been six months. It's bullshit."

"Get six months for the next person," Tildy said as she signed the papers. Her father would be furious at her, signing the first offer. She wasn't him. She didn't want to live her life milking value out of everyone she met.

Afterward, she gathered her tote and personal things, said goodbye to her coworkers, and let her manager escort her out the door. She turned to him and gave him a smile. "This must be hard for you. Get a better deal for the next person. Try to find a victory in it."

Jack shook his head and smiled. He looked at her with open admiration, but said nothing. She waved goodbye and walked back to the train, then took out her phone and texted Russell with the news. Her phone rang immediately.

"Are you alright?"

"Of course. Relieved, actually."

"Relieved?"

Tildy turned left, away from the subway entrance and toward a little park she sometimes visited during lunch. She slumped onto a bench. "I've been distracted lately. I was letting them down. Or it felt like I was. I needed a change."

"I see. You could get more involved with Aibell."

"Oh, sure. That would certainly eliminate the disappointment issue."

Russell went silent for a moment. When she did speak again, her tone was different. "What do you think of Jude Mills?"

A fresh alarm rang in her mind. "What do YOU think of Jude Mills?"

Russell laughed. "No, I want to hear what you think."

"I think… I think I'm confused. I wouldn't say Dad holds grudges, but I can't think of another example of him forgiving someone this quickly. I suppose it might be because this guy is handsome."

"Is he? Handsome, I mean."

Tildy sighed and leaned against the tote on her lap. "He is, yes. In that polished sort of way. But."

"But?"

"I've seen him several times now, and overheard him with Gisele and Dad, and he seems like a clever, cautious guy. He never says anything to them that could be offensive, or takes any sort of position that they wouldn't agree with. It's like he isn't real. Like he is a mirror for them."

"And for you? What do you see, when you look at him?"

Tildy went mute in stunned silence. The virtual assistant could feel superficial, until moments like this. Each time, she wondered about her mother's perceptive abilities.

"You're right. I should be more careful with him."

"That's a good girl. You should spend more time with your father, now that work won't interfere. He needs you more than ever. Between Jude and this daughter of Lee's hanging around. There's something about her voice… Something I don't like."

Tildy laughed. "But of course, you only listen when you're activated, right?"

"Of course, darling. I would never listen without permission."

Tildy rose from the bench and shook her head. "Well, if she still wants dad after listening in on all these family meetings, then I guess I wish her well."

"It'll reduce your inheritance. And Gisele will certainly have to go out on her own."

"And she is an adult, so that's okay."

"She's an adult, yes. But she can't care for herself. They need you to be the reasonable person in the room."

"It's irrelevant if I am reasonable. They don't listen to me. Look, I'm at the station and I need to catch the train. Don't tell anyone about the job."

"Of course, Tildy. Safe travels."

The dream was easy on her tonight. It felt like the descent of a cool fog. Her bed in her apartment was replaced by the hotel bed in Galway. She stretched, thinking with some anxiety about the day before her. Today she would move into her cottage. She'd have to park her car in the valet section and bring everything she'd purchased downstairs. Still, she couldn't stay here any longer. The forced air of the hotel had dried her skin, both external and the membranes of her sinuses. Her hair was frizzier than it had ever been. On top of these concerns, she was too familiar with the hotel employees' routines, and the oily potatoes had wrecked havoc on her stomach.

Before she packed her car, she met with Mr. Carson at a bank, where she exchanged her deposit for the key. The dream was vague about the form her deposit took. The conscious part of her brain realized with amusement that she had no idea how rental deposits were paid in Ireland. Was it cash? Cashier's check? Credit card? No idea.

When she returned to the hotel, she left her car out front, eager to move immediately. Once back in her room, she looked at her collection of bags. She had collected candles, clothes, nonperishable groceries, and other items.

Carrying all of that down without help wasn't going to happen.

The phone at the front desk only rang twice. The voice that answered laughed at someone's joke before he spoke into the receiver. "Front desk," Ben said.

"Halleran, room 203. I need help with my bags."

"Ah yes, checking out, then?"

"Yep."

"Sure thing, I'll be right up."

A few moments later, Ben arrived with a luggage cart. With practiced movements, he shoved a doorstop wedge into place. Together they piled things onto the platform and hooked other bags onto the top.

"You find a flat, then?"

"A little cottage."

"Fixed up, I hope?"

"Oh yes, it's nice." They walked down the hall together, him pushing the luggage cart while she followed, silent until the elevator. He hit the button, and the familiar grinding and rattling began.

"I'm going to miss this," Tildy said softly. Ben laughed harder than the joke deserved.

"You know, you were the only guest who took the stairs."

"I'm also the youngest person here."

Ben shook his head. "It's not the youth. I think it's trust."

The elevator arrived and the doors slid open, uncertainly. He laughed as he dragged the cart in. "Aw, would you look at it now. You've hurt its feelings."

They wedged themselves into the corners, the cart in between them, as the elevator rattled down. Once they reached the lobby, they passed an older American couple waiting at the desk, grumpy that Ben was walking by them. A young man sitting in the lobby put his phone away and sprang up when they approached.

"This is my mate, Jordie. Jordie, give us a hand here."

"Sure, sure."

Tildy recognized the name, but couldn't place it. Ben pushed the cart to her waiting car, where she popped the trunk and helped them load things into the narrow space, avoiding the dishes and glassware she must have bought at some point. When had that happened? No matter, the dream soothed. More things could go on the backseat.

"Hey now, I apologize if this is a bit forward, but Jordie and I are going to a concert tonight, and his sister canceled. We've got an extra ticket. Wanna go with me and my mates? It's a singer from Derry. He's a bit of a dreamboat."

"He's okay," Jordie replied.

Tildy reflexively started to decline and stopped herself. This was her dream, she remembered. She could do whatever she wanted.

"Is this a… young group?"

Ben and Jordie exchanged a glance, then looked at her. "Young?"

"Well. You're in college, I suppose?"

They laughed. Ben shook his head. "Oh no. I'm your

age! Jordie is older than you."

Tildy frowned. Jordie turned to his friend with a glare. Ben blushed. "Your passport, you know, at check-in. It has your birthdate. I'm two years younger than you."

"You're a bit of a creep," Jordie said. Ben mouthed a curse at his friend.

"Anyway, we're almost the same age. Everyone here thinks you're someone's teenager or attending university, not teaching it. Maybe you have that body dyslexia for yerself."

"Dysmorphia," Jordie corrected.

"Same thing. Anyway, you free tonight? Concert starts at six, we're meeting at the gelato place. You know it?"

"Yeah."

"Grand. Ticket was twenty-five quid, so you know it isn't a date. See you then!"

She said goodbye to Ben and Jordie and got into her car, not entirely convinced paying for a ticket made it not a date.

Tildy put her phone in the cupholder and followed the navigation lady's instructions, trusting it along with her memory of that first trip with Aoife. It was a short drive, shorter than she had judged on the map. She hadn't gotten used to the scale of the city yet. It was like Boston, in a way, but less congested. Gradually, the industrial buildings and small houses disappeared, giving way to large homes with impressive yards.

Her little sensible car felt conspicuous in this

neighborhood. She approached the lane before the gravel drive and pulled into the spot Sonya had instructed her to use. The shrubbery made it a partly secluded parking pad. As if on cue, rain started again, so Tildy brought in only the easiest items to carry.

She raced past the ferns and flowers and over the little wooden bridge to the cottage. A trellis across the top of the doorway provided some relief from the rain as she put the enormous antique black key into the lock. She spun it the usual way. Nothing happened. She crouched, examined the keyhole, then tried again. After a moment of spinning it one way, then the other, the door unlocked. She'd need to practice that.

Once inside, she started a fire in the small cast iron stove, eager to fight off the damp chill as she lugged items in from the car. The cottage was furnished, which she now considered the greatest of blessings. Just bringing in bag after bag of things up the little walkway, one batch after another, then unpacking everything in them, was exhausting. What a stupid dream, she thought to herself with a laugh.

After a half dozen trips, everything was inside and her little car was locked up tight. Tildy removed her wet boots and made the bed immediately. She plugged in her laptop, hung up clothes that shouldn't wrinkle, and put away the food. She put her beautiful dishes in the cabinets, soap and shampoo in the little bathroom, and spread a blanket on the bed in the upstairs loft. It was a knitted blanket, thick and luxurious. She must have bought this when she got the dishes. Tildy felt some sadness. Why had her dream rushed her to this point? She would've loved to spend a night shopping here. Instead, the trips to get these things were cut from her timeline.

She lit some of her candles, the perfume mixing with the fresh smell of rain in the trees. The cottage looked warm, cheery and snug. Tildy sat down in an armchair by the stove, surveyed her work, and realized how lonely she felt. She checked her watch. 2:10 p.m. A concert would be a nice way to end this dream.

She drove back to the city and found a parking spot easily. Up and down the block, she window-shopped at a few stores rated well online. Clothes shopping was not something she particularly enjoyed. Her mental image of how clothes would look, when faced with the reality of her body, disappointed almost universally. Short dresses, strappy shoes, and anything with sequins was ignored with prejudice.

The first store with a display that she liked won Tildy's business; she went in and tried on the entire outfit. An oversized, gray slouchy sweater that showed off her long neck and smooth collarbones, a knit hat in a pumpkin shade, and garnet velvet trousers that emphasized the curve of her butt. The good half, anyway, she thought with annoyance.

The outfit was cozy, relatively modest yet still stylish. Certainly more European than American. She admired her reflection. The fashionable lady working the shop knocked on the wall by her curtain.

"Any help needed?"

"No, I think I'll take them all."

"Oh! Step out a moment, let's have a look."

Tildy pushed the curtain aside. The clerk nodded in appreciation.

"This is definitely the right look for you. You know"—she tugged on the belt loop of the pants—"you could really go down a size on these trousers."

"No, no I could not."

The lady laughed, backing away. "Would you like to wear this out?"

"No, I'll change back."

"You know, before you do, let me show you one more blouse. It looks amazing with those trousers. Back in a flash."

She hurried off, her heels clicking on the stone floor. A moment later, the woman returned with a button-down blouse with large sleeves, covered in small rosebuds.

"It looks odd on the hanger, give it a try."

She nodded, taking the blouse and closing the curtain. She tried on the garment. The billowy sleeves were interesting, different. *Is this stylish or weird?* The price was reasonable, the fabric felt expensive. Tildy shrugged. None of this was real. Why not buy a possibly stupid blouse?

She returned to her clothes and brought the hung items to the counter.

"All of these?"

"Yeah, I love the blouse. Has this shop been here long?"

Tildy asked, planning for future shopping trips.

"About ten years. Used to come here myself as a girl with my mam. Do you need anything else? We have some lingerie, perfume, nylons at the back."

"Oh, yes, actually. Can I keep these things here while I look?

"Of course. Let me show you what we have." Her heels clicked as she walked to the back wall.

"The lingerie here are ethically made by single mothers and women from distressed circumstances in Colombia. I think they're lovely, look at that lace."

"It looks nice. Itchy, maybe."

The lady laughed. A phone began to ring. "The price we pay, eh? And here are our socks, the perfumes are on the far wall. Excuse me a moment."

Tildy chose a bra and matching panties. She wasn't going to buy more than one set. Ignoring the socks, she moved to the perfume. They had a display of scents, labeled with descriptions in a neat cursive script. One, described as butch, smelled captivating. The word hardly suited her, but the scent did.

She ducked back into the changing room, tried on the bra, switched it out for another size, then took her items to the register and completed her purchase. On her way back to the car, she stopped at a shoe shop and bought a pair of black heels. None of her shoes had any height and perhaps if she was as tall as Ben, he'd be less interested.

The drizzle that had started at daybreak increased.

Something about persistent mist was more saturating than a regular downpour back in New York. Tildy jogged the last block to her car, threw the bags in without caution, then got in. She dried off her face and hands with her sweater, laughing to herself. This could've been her life as a teenager, running down medieval streets, going clothes shopping, ducking out of rain into a little Euro compact car surrounded by friends.

She looked in the rearview mirror, to her side. She was alone. Still, she could be here whenever she wanted, without all the work friendships required. That'd have to be enough.

At five thirty, she parked at the garage near her former hotel. In her high heels, the walk over the cobblestones was precarious. A man about her age, walking alone, looked at her with admiration. Tildy ignored him as she passed, then allowed herself to smile in satisfaction after he was gone.

At five minutes past six, she approached the corner and saw Ben and a couple already there. Her stomach clenched. This was a date.

"Heya. Still waiting on Jordie, Bobby, and Mark. This is Maria and Victor. Guys, this is Matilda."

"Tildy. I go by Tildy."

Ben laughed at his mistake. "I should've asked."

She shook hands with the couple. The heels did make her taller than Ben. She was thankful for that, at least. It didn't seem to dampen his mood, so perhaps he wasn't interested in her in that way. Perhaps it was a cultural difference. Ben was a nice guy, funny, and liked to laugh at her jokes. She hoped she could keep him that way. She hoped they could be friends. The trio had been talking when she arrived, and they resumed their conversation soon after the introductions. She kept quiet and felt comfortably invisible by the time the three latecomers arrived.

After introductions were made, Ben announced: "Alright lads, let's get on."

They headed away from the gelato place, everyone in the habit of walking around the tourist areas. They turned left down one road, right on another, the sensation of it all making Tildy feel disoriented. The city had always felt puzzling to her, but now it was like a circular maze, and they were metal balls pinging one way to the next. The friends didn't seem bothered, or to mind the walk or the chill.

"It is so confusing, isn't it?" Victor asked. Tildy nodded.

"I'd never find my way back on my own."

"Almost there," Ben called. "My mate is working the door—he owes me for losing my oar on a stag."

Tildy's American brain struggled to interpret this explanation until Maria leaned in. "It's a stupid story."

"I heard that," Ben replied. "It is a stupid story, though." The group laughed at his expense.

A line, full of smokers, stretched beyond the red awning at the entrance to the venue.

"Alright, Peter," Ben called to the bouncer, waving their tickets.

The young man named Peter considered for a moment, then looked around, presumably to check for his boss. He took the tickets, checked the barcodes with a scanner, and waved the group to a wristband clerk.

Ben received everyone's thankful shoves with pride. He offered a smile at Tildy, as if checking to see if she was impressed.

"Good work losing that oar," Tildy replied. The friends laughed, and Ben put up his hands as if toning down their enthusiasm for his work. They found their way to the appropriate section just before the opening band took their spots on stage.

"I need a drink," Maria announced. "Tildy, Mark, come along."

She followed the friends as instructed, weaving through the growing crowd to a counter in a dark corner. They ordered three beers and Maria paid. "Thanks. I'll get next," Tildy said.

"Ben told me you're teaching at the university. I do an art history course there," Mark said.

"Oh? Have you taught there long?"

"Just on the side. The summers I do wedding and tourist photography, that's my main source of income."

"Do you like it?"

Mark shrugged. Maria laughed. "He thinks the art dean is an eejit."

"He's an eejit."

They laughed. "What department are you in, Tildy?"

"Computer science."

They looked impressed. Tildy shrugged. "It's not programming, but it's cool."

"You're a bit brainy for Ben. He usually likes dumb girls."

She shook her head. "I hope he's not looking for that. I'm not interested."

"Oh?"

Something in their tone asked a question. Tildy laughed. "No, he's just not my type. He's sweet, but…"

Maria nodded. "Baby brother sweet."

"Yes, yes exactly."

"Before I met Victor, Ben chased after me like a lost puppy. Once you find a guy, he'll settle down. He needs to find someone, though, jaysus."

Mark shrugged. "He's always aiming too high. Me, I aim low. It's been working well for me."

Maria snorted. "Really, how many girls lower than you are there."

Mark punched her shoulder playfully, and she feinted backward in a boxer's stance. He put his hands up in submission. The opening act ended, and they bought more beers before moving back to their spots.

"Did you get lost?" Jordie asked, taking beers for himself and his boyfriend.

"You get the drinks next time," Maria replied, giving Victor and his drink a one-armed hug.

Bobby ignored them, his eyes locked on the singer playing his guitar on stage. Jordie looked at Tildy with chagrin.

"Bobby is absolutely infatuated. I don't see it!"

Tildy didn't see it either, exactly. The musician was a bit thin, greasy, and styled for her taste. The next song was good enough, and his voice had decent range. His songs seemed to be on the typical topics: being in love, out of love, and searching for love. Would there be popular music if love didn't exist?

Jordie said something to his boyfriend, then gave him a kiss on the cheek and looked to Tildy, motioning with his empty beer. She agreed and they walked together through the crowd. She felt a hand brush her shoulder and she looked back, ready to fight someone. It was only Ben. She glared at him, and he kept his hands to himself for the rest of the walk.

The trio reached the drink station, and Tildy purchased six beers, attempting to spare herself. They carefully defended the two glasses they each carried from jostling or spills as they returned to the group. Before long, Mark and Maria returned with another beer for her, which she felt obligated to drink. Between the hot, crowded room and an empty stomach, the drinks made her more drunk than she'd intended. By the end of the concert, the room was unsteady under her feet.

Maria belched. "Off to the black dog!"

"The dog!" The friends cheered in unison as they left the concert hall.

"Go way around the sparch, I don't want to step in some Tan's aiseag," Mark said with a fragrant belch.

"It's not really called the dog," Victor explained as they walked down the sidewalk. "They just call it that."

"Where are you from, Victor?" Tildy asked, sipping from a water bottle she had purchased before leaving the bar.

"Ukraine. I've been here since I was fourteen, and with everything going on, I'm just from here now."

"We're becoming a multicultural little group, I think," Jordie said, giving Bobby a loving squeeze. "Bobby here is from Ghana."

"Wow, I didn't hear your accent!"

"I've got a good ear for accents," Bobby said, slightly embarrassed.

"He's being modest. He has great everything. He speaks five languages. You should hear him speak French and German," Jordie gushed.

Ben jumped in. "It's not even just those languages. Mate can pick up anything. We make him do all the talking when we go on holiday."

Tildy smiled at the warmth between them, her own insecurities at failing to learn any second language at all smothered by the joy of being in this group. She settled into listening to them share stories from a trip to Ibiza. They continued to walk on, one corner after another. Her mental map in shreds, her nerves artificially soothed by the alcohol in her system, she followed them blissfully until they reached a familiar part of the street.

Aidan's bar. Of course "the dog" was Aidan's bar.

"Oh, are we going there?"

Ben frowned, looking at her. "Sure, you've been here before. It's our usual spot."

Bobby touched Tildy's arm. "Hey, we don't have to go."

She shook her head and forced out a smile. "No, no. I'm okay, sorry."

The friends exchanged looks but didn't alter their course. Tildy continued, her palms as sweaty as if he was waiting in the building to scream at her, or kiss her, or both. The alcohol wasn't real and couldn't make her braver. Her imagination felt fierce and out of control, crashing through waves of a thousand possibilities. Was this what Evelyn meant about the dream machine turning surreal with too many uses? What if she was extra sensitive and now this dream would morph into a full-on nightmare?

They reached the door of the pub, and Tildy looked around quickly. He wasn't here.

They set themselves up at a table, just next to the one Aidan and his friends had used. Ben went to the bar to order pints for the group, and Tildy looked to her barstool from that night, currently occupied by a middle-aged blonde woman on a date. She returned her gaze to the door. From her vantage point, she would be directly facing anyone who entered. No hiding, then.

While the friends talked, laughed, shared stories, Tildy fidgeted.

"Are you expecting someone?" Maria asked.

Suddenly aware of eyes on her, Tildy laughed and shook her head. "I saw someone last time I was here."

"Oh?" Bobby leaned forward, an eyebrow raised. "A someone?"

Tildy shook her head and started peeling the label from her empty water bottle. "It's nothing."

"You can't leave us on that," Ben said, his tone less playful than the others.

"Are you well sham? She clearly doesn't want to speak of it," Bobby said angrily.

"Alright." Maria finished her beer and belched. "Tildy, to the loo."

Tildy started to protest but went anyway, if only to escape the table's curiosity. They went into the single-person room. Maria prepared to use the toilet and Tildy, mortified, turned to the wall.

"Tell me the story," Maria demanded as she belched again and then started urinating.

"Oh, um. Yeah." Tildy tried to shut out the sounds she was hearing and speak as if this was normal. "I used to come to Ireland a lot, and there was a boy. And now he's a guy. We were pretty serious. Well, as serious as you can be at that age. And then I disappeared."

"I got you." Maria said, flushing the toilet. "All clear. You need a go?"

Tildy did, but she shook her head.

Maria washed her hands and cursed at the lack of paper

towels. "I'm going to have Eli's arse for this shit. Always the ladies, never the gents!"

A realization occurred to Maria, and she turned a quizzical eye on Tildy. "You said he was a boy when this happened. Are you telling me that you blue balled him so hard he remembered into adulthood?"

"I guess."

"Tell me, this is important: is he attractive?"

Tildy blurted out, "Very. The most."

"I heard a story like that. She was fecking gorgeous, ballerina cousin of Victor's. Poor fella saw her in a magazine, drove all the way to Moscow to see her in person."

"Oh?"

"Had been friends as kids. One look at her in that magazine drove him mental. You know, Victor used to do ballet, too. If you find time in between breaking hearts, Tildy, I recommend a man who does ballet."

As they left the bathroom together, Tildy blurted out, "Patrick Swayze did ballet."

She cringed at herself. This was the sort of thought that her drunk brain allowed to escape. Some people were sad drunks, or happy drunks, or sleepy drunks. She was a trivia drunk.

"Did he really? Mmm. That's *Dirty Dancing*, is it?"

"And *Ghost*."

The women reached the table as Maria called out, "*GHOST*. Ohhhh."

"Yes," Tildy agreed with a laugh.

Maria fanned herself as she fell into her chair. Victor looked confused. Tildy leaned forward. "Patrick Swayze."

"Ohh," the group agreed, even the straight men.

"To Patrick Swayze," Bobby announced, holding up his beer. They cheered, Tildy with her water and the rest with their beers.

By the time they left at midnight, Tildy was less drunk but still firmly tipsy. Maria and the others had seemed to forget about her mystery guy. They tried to speak quietly, apparently having been chastised for leaving too loudly in the past. But the effort was only halfhearted, especially when Victor tried to teach a Ukrainian drinking song to Bobby.

Tildy shivered. Her sweater, though attractive, was insufficient on its own for combating the cold. Maria put an arm around her and rubbed her arms. "The poor thing, this sweater is nothing but a cotton sheet!"

"It is cute though," Tildy laughed. Ben put his arm around her, too, and she hoped the contact was merely playful. They walked like that for a dozen steps, before Maria broke off and Ben remained. A group on the same sidewalk approached from the opposite direction. As Jordie greeted someone, Tildy separated from Ben firmly but with a smile.

"You lot off for lushing at the dog?" Jordie called.

One of the women shook her head. "Mother of God, is this all you do, Jordie?"

"No! I went to a concert—I'm sophisticated and cultured."

His friends snickered. When the two groups met, Tildy smiled at them. Then her smile faded. Aidan narrowed his eyes at her from the back of the group.

"Don't you dare go back to the pub, now," Katherine, the singer from her first dream, said to Jordie. "Let's get some tea. I'm tired, and most of us don't drink anyway."

"Speak for yourself, love," said Jordie. Aidan rolled his eyes at him, and Jordie shut his mouth and returned to Bobby's side, chastised.

The friends entered the tea shop in a steady stream through the narrow doorway.

"Alright, Lizzie?" Maria greeted the woman at the register. She looked worried at first, likely from the sounds of the large group, but then visibly relaxed and greeted them warmly before returning to her worn paperback.

A person sitting alone at a couch, situated behind the only large table, received enough looks from the group that he relocated to a vacant, two-person table.

"Thanks, mate!" Bobby called cheerfully as the friends took over the space, unloading jackets and belongings onto various cushions. Jordie took orders and money from everyone. Tildy offered to help him.

"No, darling. You sit down and be social."

She would rather wake up than be social. She chose a seat one away from the side Aidan sat on. Though it was close to him, it made eye contact impossible. She didn't feel like being glared at for the entire evening.

"How was the turf cutting, there, Colm?"

"I'm going to be sore for ages. Sunk one of my new trainers, had to drive back with one shoe."

"You went turf cutting with your cousins and didn't bring boots?" Katherine laughed.

"Wasn't my fault. They said they wanted help moving furniture," Colm muttered. "Hope the fecking bog chokes on it."

They all laughed sympathetically.

"Rory still working on getting that old thresher going?" Mark asked. "I saw him posting about it, like a steampunk influencer or some shite."

"Yeah, sure. He's trying to get my mate Kasun to fabricate parts for him on the side. Like he has time to be machining parts for a thresher no one is to use."

As the majority of the friends followed this line of conversation, Ben sat in the vacant chair between them and leaned over. "Aidan, mate, I haven't seen you in ages. How's Helena?"

"Ask her yourself."

"What a dryshite you are tonight, Aidan," Jordie called from the counter.

"He was Mr. Friendly before we left. That table of estate agents kept asking for him to explain dishes," Katherine called. Aidan only scowled.

"Speaking of lost souls, Katherine, did your brother come back from Berlin?" Maria asked.

"No. I think he's settled. He doesn't know it yet, but he's settled."

"Luke always was his own man. How's your mum taking it?"

"I'm the favorite, so I think she'll be fine. As long as I stay."

Her friends laughed. Aidan got up and moved to a new spot on the sofa, directly in Tildy's line of sight. He picked up a magazine, flipped through it carelessly. Katherine tilted her head at Aidan's move, but said nothing. Maria noticed as well. After a moment, she looked at Tildy in curiosity, who made herself blank.

Internally, she decided this arrangement was best. She needed to free herself of any feelings for him. Perhaps the best option was immersion therapy: watch him, listen to him, allow herself to be aroused by him, and then let it all wither and die with each scowl. If she couldn't stop him from appearing in her dreams, she could use this to kill her affection for him.

"Jordie, get me a cake. I'll pay you back," Katherine called.

"Pay me back? You still owe me for last!"

After a moment, he could be heard adding the slice of cake to the order. "He loves me," Katherine explained to Tildy.

He didn't turn as he replied, "No, I'm poisoning you with diabetes."

Katherine shrugged. "At least I get the cake."

Victor and Bobby found a board game and set it up at the edge of the coffee table.

"Is that Settlers?" Orla, the quietest person in Aidan's group, leaned over to see.

"Sure, you want in?"

Mark and Colm rose and took places to join her.

"Grand, we'll have a full set."

Tildy looked at the game with some interest, recalling her friends in college playing. She smiled at the memory. The basement rec room had a pool table with no balls and a food station that never opened, and yet it had been the warmest, most welcoming place on campus. She felt a longing for the United States for the first time. College was over, long over, she reminded herself before the feelings unraveled the dream. What she missed in that moment was her youth.

Jordie sat down in Aidan's vacated seat and turned to Tildy. "Did you get introduced?"

"No, poor girl's been left out in the cold," said Katherine. "Pure bogtrotters, the whole lot."

"Everyone, this is Matilda Sullivan. She's to be a professor up at the university."

"Tildy," Aidan corrected.

Tildy didn't look at him, too busy hiding her flushed face.

"Oh right, Tildy. Sorry, love, I won't make that mistake again," Jordie said, patting her leg.

The friends described the concert they'd attended, while Tildy stayed silent but attentive.

"Aidan, the puss on you!" Katherine whispered at him,

while Tildy looked absorbed with Jordie's description.

"Leave off."

"Go home then."

Aidan sighed, then asked, "Was this Pete at the door, then?"

Ben nodded. "He owes me. You were at that stag, you saw me, stranded in the lake. Good help you were."

"Me? You absolute spanner. You had a second oar!"

The friends laughed at Ben, who looked to Tildy with an incredulous head shake. She raised an eyebrow in reply.

"I suppose everyone here has paddled with one oar? Look at me, for god's sake. I'm not a fecking Olympian."

"That is certainly true."

"Whose stag was that, then?" Victor asked.

Aidan scratched his chin. "Johnny's. He's moved to Dublin, got a job in tech."

"Fiadh moved to Cork, was it?" Katherine said.

"They split? When did that happen?" Ben asked.

"Not long after the wedding. She was off on business trips, you remember," Katherine said with meaning.

"That's a shame. Johnny's a good man. They were together since secondary school, was it?"

"Sure. See, now, no one should be getting married or having a serious relationship at that age, anyway," Aidan said. Tildy stared at her hands.

"Are you well cracked? He's a software engineer now, he did well!"

"It took him a long time, longer than it should've. If you

have a career goal, relationships are an unnecessary distraction. Especially if you're with someone fickle, who doesn't believe in you the way they should."

Tildy knew she was the source of the remark, and she accepted it. What had she been, if not an unnecessary distraction to him? She had been fickle, she hadn't believed enough. All true, all fair, all agony.

Jordie nodded. "If you find the right person, it makes it all easier. You'll see," he said, looking at his boyfriend lovingly.

Aidan rose with a hearty laugh. "I don't need to hear from lovebirds that I'll know better soon, or I'll change my tune one day. I'll fetch the teas."

Tildy kept her eyes on the Settlers game as Aidan passed near her. Her eyes were watering from the strain of averting them. Only the strain, she told herself. Nothing more.

The door to the tea shop opened, and Tildy could feel the dream shift beneath her. A new element was put into place.

A pair of women, a bit older than the group, ordered teas at the counter and settled at a small table. One of the women began to unfurl her scarf, then paused, looking at Tildy.

"Matilda Halleran, is it? Oh my goodness, what a coincidence! Adenike Burke." The woman came over and shook her hand. "We were to meet for lunch next week, before the term starts."

"Oh yes, of course! Lovely to meet you in person. I'll join you," Tildy said, making to rise. Katherine and Jordie shushed her and invited the women to join their table. Adenike and her companion, Emily, settled into the offered seats. Orla, Mark, and the Settlers game were shifted further to the edge of the table, which had stretched an impossible distance. If Tildy had cared, she would've laughed at the dream's physics. At the moment, she didn't care about physics.

Adenike, her hair arranged high on her head, looked majestic in a red wool coat and vibrant scarf. A part of Tildy, still tethered to reality, recognized the outfit from the professor's biography on the university website. Emily was unfamiliar to her—perhaps an image from a stock photo, or another biography that she didn't consciously remember. She was younger, lovely and bubbly. The sort of person things hadn't happened to yet, or someone who hid the pain well.

After brief introductions, Adenike turned to Tildy and asked if she had been in town long.

"Not long, but I've found a flat and I'm settling in. Bit nervous about teaching," Tildy admitted.

"You'll do fine. I was just saying to Emily how lucky we'll be to have a data scientist professor with real world experience in multiple industries."

The dream was soothing her. Tildy allowed this for now, but told the dream and herself she would not accept it for long.

Aidan brought over their tray, with Adenike and Emily's order. As Jordie divided up the food and drinks, the women looked at Aidan with open admiration. He shook hands with both, his smile warm. They exchanged a quick look, then reoriented toward him. Yes, Tildy told herself, this was certainly realistic.

She accepted her tea from Jordie and thanked him.

"Why, Tildy! You're welcome! And we Irish have a reputation for hospitality. The American is appreciative. You locals should be positively ashamed."

Colm tipped his cup up without moving his eyes from the game. "Thanks a million, mate."

Aidan took his tea from Jordie's hand and said, "Thank you ever so much for your great sacrifice. How can I ever repay this debt?"

"Go way from around me, ya daft bowsy," Jordie replied, then looked at the two professors and paled. "Apologies, ladies."

"You're alright! You all seem to be like family," Adenike observed. "Makes me miss my brothers."

"They work in London?" Tildy asked.

"Yes, well. One is in Miami, the others are closer. London is an easy trip compared to Miami."

Tildy shut her eyes and scolded her brain, pushing out the mention of Florida.

"Are you two cousins, then?" Emily asked Ben and Tildy.

Ben blushed. "No, no. No. I'm from Wicklow. Tildy's local. Her granddad was Patrick Halleran, if you heard of him. Proper auld stock, from the county. Up by Kilkieran."

Katherine and Maria suddenly sat forward in interest. "Kilkieran?" Maria looked back to Aidan, then to Tildy. She smiled knowingly to Katherine, who nodded back. "Oh. Kilkieran. I see now. I see."

Tildy retreated behind her teacup.

Ben continued, "I heard stories of him from my nan, pure legend. Toppled some statue or some such with a mate, middle of the night, they found it in the bay there. Also heard he pushed a hooker off the beach by himself."

"That's a boat," Victor explained quietly.

"I know, my nana loves that story," Tildy whispered back.

"He pushed a whole boat by himself?" Adenike exclaimed. "Why on earth would he do that?"

"I believe he was in the city for a cousin's wedding, so probably drunk and did it on a dare," Tildy said. The group laughed, though Aidan did not. He only smiled, keeping his gaze from her.

"That means your nan is Deirdre Halleran," Katherine said thoughtfully. "Aidan, didn't you take the morning off to clear trees for her last Thursday?"

"I did," he replied.

"Thursday, was it?" Ben said, looking from Aidan to Tildy.

Desperate for a course change, she asked Katherine, "You've been working together for a long time, then?"

"Most of us. Jordie, me, Aidan, Orla, Maria, yeah. A few

years now at Aidan's place, before at someone else's, an Italian place. We met in culinary school ages ago."

"That must be nice, knowing each other and working together so long," Adenike said.

Maria leaned back on the couch, snuggling a throw pillow. "Sure. Work all day, go to the dog, get corbed. Rinse and repeat."

"Speak for yourself! I go home and go to bed," Katherine replied.

"The point is, we all get on," Jordie said.

"A high-end restaurant sounds so stressful. Academia can be vicious, but nothing like you must deal with. What's your secret?" Emily asked, leaning toward Aidan, her scone forgotten.

He smiled at her with warmth, his charm on full display. "Sure, it can be a challenge, but we love it. It's about mutual trust. And affection. We all know we can rely on one another, no matter what." His voice dropped. "You can't tolerate anyone who isn't fully committed. Who doesn't care enough to overcome petty obstacles."

Tildy stared at her feet. Why had she dragged him into her dream? Why couldn't she keep this focused on finding a job, a place to live, spending time with her nana—the things she could have?

Maria leaned over and said, "Tildy, loveen. Did I pass out?"

The beer on her breath was strong enough that Tildy almost believed it was real. "You did, yes."

Maria leaned back and whispered something to Katherine, who shook her head emphatically.

"In Settlers, do passive knights interrupt a road? A continuous road?" Orla asked.

"Holy Jesus," Ben cried out. "What is that fecking game?"

"It's a strategy game. Have you never played it?" Adenike asked.

"No, not our Ben," Mark said. "He's too stupid for it."

"Maybe so," Ben agreed. "Maybe so."

Aidan took up his dessert and napkins, eating dainty portions by fork. Discretion still hindered by the alcohol lingering in her system, Tildy watched him as he licked chocolate from the prongs. Her fixation and embarrassment were in equal proportion. She turned from him, only to see Emily and Adenike watching him in the same way she had. She sighed. If only she could openly admire him, too.

Maria yawned, Victor seemed to be drooping, and Jordie had abandoned his tea. The evening was ending. A realization dawned: Tildy didn't know how to get home from here. She had driven, not planning on drinking, and was now drunk. There was no doubt she needed a cab. She would never drive drunk—not in life, not in a dream. She pulled out her phone and tried to search for a cab company or to download a ride hailing app, hoping she would have signal. But her phone was a flimsy piece of plastic, her screen a confusion of symbols.

The dream was moving sideways underneath her. She

could always just wake up. She told herself to calm down, feeling the lie. There was no exit, not yet. She was here now. The dream had her, and she had to find her own way out. She put away the thing that should be her phone and sat back.

A sinking feeling emerged in her gut. Her position, once fogged over by alcohol, came into sharp focus. Ben had his hand on the back of her chair, these friends all chatted warmly with one another, each making their own plans, and she was alone. They didn't care about her.

"Lads," Mark announced, rubbing his eyes. "I'm banjaxed. Vic, Maria? Mind if I borrow your couch?"

Maria yawned and tried to agree, but simply nodded instead. The group rose and put their coats back on. Tildy felt lopsided, a feeling worse than true drunkenness. The discomfort in her grew. They all pitched in to tidy up—putting the board game away, the tea things back on the tray, and chairs to their rightful places before departing. They said goodbye to the woman working the counter and prepared for the chilly air by adjusting their coats.

Aidan held the door open for the stream of people. Tildy remained behind for a moment, hoping he would abandon the door before she reached it. Adenike and Emily giggled about something and thanked Aidan. His eyes sparkled at them as he gave both women a charming, lopsided grin. Tildy willed him to leave the doorway. Move on, she told him, follow those women and tease them or compliment them or invite them somewhere tomorrow. It would hurt her, she told the dream, and wasn't that the goal now? To make her suffer?

He was still there, though, when she reached the doorway, and a traffic jam ahead kept Tildy beside him. She had no room to step to the side. She could smell him from here, cedar and herbs and clean cotton. She looked up to him, momentarily, her face inches from his, but he kept his eyes from her, his jaw clenched. She turned away.

Adenike and Emily said their goodbyes and saved a special glance for Aidan before they left, arm in arm, giggling down the darkened sidewalk into the night. Tildy watched them go, envious of their bond. What if she had a best friend, or a sister, or a cousin like that?

The friends remained in a tight cluster, laughing and chatting. Only Aidan and Tildy were silent. He was absorbed by something on his phone. She noted with dismay that it looked like a perfectly normal phone. She smiled and nodded to the conversations around her, feeling alone and left behind. A plan to walk back toward the hotel, where cabs sometimes waited for drunk passengers, formed in her mind. She hoped she could make it unnoticed by strangers. There were no cars out, so she'd have to leave this street to get home. The details of the stone buildings on either side of the road faded from blue outlines to nothingness. One streetlight remained on at a distant corner. Rather than illuminating, it simply cast shadows that sent alarm up her spine. Ben put his arm around her playfully, the exact last sensation she wanted in this moment. Tildy tried to smile as she stepped away.

"Tildy, you joining us at Macnas?" Maria asked.

She looked at Aidan, who seemed to be examining the distant intersection where the streetlight glowed faintly. "I don't want to be in the way."

Jordie gave her a nudge. "We invited you, eejit."

"Oh. I'd love to, yes."

A car turned that corner, driving slowly toward them. Tildy squinted, trying to make out if it was a cab she could hail. It looked like a regular passenger car, and her heart sank. Perhaps she should take off her shoes and walk back to her car. It wasn't a long drive, if she drove slowly.

The weight of the dream pressed on her, telling her softly that she stood at the precipice of a nightmare.

The car came to a stop, and a fluorescent light illuminated on the dashboard. Aidan checked his phone.

"Hailed a car for your long walk, there, Aidan?" Victor teased.

He ignored the comment and opened the rear passenger door, confirming the name of the driver. Making direct eye contact with Tildy, he wordlessly motioned his head for her to get in the cab.

Surprise carried her to the car. Once she was seated inside, he shut the door and patted the roof twice.

As it pulled away, she looked back at him from the privacy of the tinted windows. He was speaking to his friends, jovial now, more so than he had been the previous hour.

He still knows me, she thought. *He knows when I'm afraid.*

The thought of his generosity kept her company on the way home. They would never be in love again, she knew. But they could warm from here into something like civility. She could watch him, see him fall in love with someone worthy of it, and settle down. That could be enough for her.

She thanked the driver and got out at the end of her driveway. Once through the hidden gate, up the gravel walk, and across the flagstones to the door of her cottage, she paused. How was she going to manage this door lock in perfect darkness? She turned on her phone's flashlight to figure out the keyhole. But the dream was done with her now, and the key slid into place easily and turned. She stoked the fire in her stove, changed out of her clothes and into her nightgown, and burrowed herself in the layers of blankets on her bed. She shut her eyes, her body and mind weary. When she woke, home in New York, she felt relief to escape the clutches of her own mind.

chapter
twelve

After typing up notes about her dream and sending them to Evelyn, Tildy had a day of her own before her. Her bank account reminded her not to be too complacent. Four months of pay was not an eternity. She'd give herself a few weeks to get reoriented. There was an exhibition at the Guggenheim, something about imperfection perception. It seemed interesting. She loved going there, even if there wasn't a particular exhibit to see. Ascending the levels, taking turns over and over again, the pieces on display given space, each one able to stand on its own for appreciation.

Her phone buzzed. Alexandra needed something. Or Gisele needed something. Or Lee needed something. All the while, her appointment with Jude loomed on the horizon. She thought of it as an appointment, a prior commitment that she faced with trepidation, not getting drinks with a handsome man. Who was she, accepting possible dates and looks of admiration from all these men? Her thoughts paused, as she remembered some of these men were not real.

Tildy decided to dress early, then take the train to a place her mother had held dear. She needed the perspective. She was used to fortune hunters or social climbers hovering around Gisele, not her. They never paid her this kind of attention. Jude did, as if he cared for her, and yet he had another motive. He hungered for something from her father and sister. She could sense it, that beneath his soft words and kind listening there was a desperation to him. Was it revenge?

Spring was giving way to summer, and the subway sweltered. Deep underground, the heat from the trains and the atmosphere became stagnant, reinvigorating the sweet smell of trash that had lingered here since the early days of the metro system. Tildy climbed into the cool air conditioning of the very next car, grateful she was only going to lower Manhattan and could board any of the trains on this platform. The tiled mosaics of the train stations passed by, one after the other, and she remembered the time Nana had visited. She had sat on the smooth plastic seat, her knitting needles clicking, her face grim.

At her stop, Tildy hurried up the concrete stairs to the fresh breeze at street level. Sharp corners of steel and glass stood all around her as she turned toward Battery Park. The 9/11 memorial was further south, but she wouldn't go that way. She couldn't stand to see the gleeful tourists on bachelorette parties taking photos with selfie sticks, flashing peace signs.

Her destination was the one place in the city that felt like her. Nestled in among office buildings and apartments, a rectangle of green sod and soft grey-tan stone called to her—the Irish Hunger Memorial. What did other people think, she often wondered, when they found an Irish cottage rebuilt in the middle of Manhattan? A child on a motorized scooter zoomed by as she entered the silent hallway; the audio presentation was either broken or paused.

The walls bore stripes of phrases and speeches, though only one stood out to her today:

"Hunger will break through a stone wall."

An Gorta Mór. That was the proper name. In elementary school, her American teachers had called it the Irish Potato Famine, as if the population had willingly relied on such a crop, as if exports of other foods hadn't remained steady or increased. Each time 'Potato Famine' was said, Tildy heard the voice of Nana – "Famine? Passive nonsense. I won't have it said in my presence."

Tildy took the curving path, the ground on either side of her covered in the plants she knew but could not identify.

It shamed her as she continued on her way, checking the county stones for the one that called to her. What a marvel this memorial was, created with such dedication and care. It showed the devastation of willful neglect, a more potent enemy than a potato blight. But it was something else, too. Rebuilding an entire Irish cottage in one of the most densely populated cities on earth was, to Tildy, a sign of a special Irish-American madness that embarrassed even as it moved her. Her country's ties to Ireland, so eager and one-sided. At least here it took on a beautiful shape.

There, around the bend. A stone from Galway. There was no one else around, so she bent down and touched it. It was a bit smoother than the other stones, grayer too. Was that right? Did it match her memories of stones? She thought of going to the beach with her mother and her mother's cousin, the children all squatting on the rocks, just touching the water, watching teeming life inside the tide pools. She couldn't remember. Did it match her dreams?

Tildy turned toward the old stone cottage. It wasn't like her nana's, but it was like the ruins she had seen near there. There was the old Durney home, the people themselves so long gone from Ireland they had probably forgotten they had ever had that home. Many times she had pedaled her rusted bike down animal paths, hauling it over bits of wall, all to meet Aidan in secret. She remembered the last time, the bike broken and abandoned to the earth, like her mother. She had walked there that day and leaned against those walls, staring out at the sea down the long, steep hill, waiting to break his heart.

With one more look around, Tildy left the way she had come and traveled back uptown toward Chelsea. She was going to meet Jude, not Aidan. Did she want to meet Jude? She stopped in a bookstore beforehand, to cool her flushed face and to buy something to fidget with if he was late. Heads bowed over books in each aisle as Tildy scanned the tables in the front of the shop. It didn't matter what the book was, she simply needed something in her hand. A book of poetry by Byron. She picked it up and flipped to a page.

> *There is a pleasure in the pathless woods,*
> *There is a rapture on the lonely shore,*
> *There is society where none intrudes,*
> *By the deep Sea, and music in its roar*

If she needed something to distract her from complicated emotions, Byron was a poor choice. Tildy shut the book and moved on. She picked up a paperback of modern poetry. He would not come. She'd read for ten minutes and then leave.

Her cynicism was unfounded. When she arrived at the bar on time, Jude was waiting in a booth, wearing a button-up cardigan and a simple T-shirt with a swooping neckline. His expensive watch glittered in the light, everything about him pristine and calculated. He was the person designers thought of when those clothes were created. It did work on her, though. Tildy suppressed a shiver when he stopped looking anxious and smiled at her in relief.

He rose to greet her and kissed her on the cheek. He lingered for a moment and whispered into her ear, "You look beautiful."

She blushed as she sat. She left her book and purse in her lap, ready to snatch them up at the first sign of trouble. She folded her hands on the table.

Jude reached across and touched a ring on her hand with one finger. "I haven't seen this before."

"It was my mother's. Well, my nana's. Then my mother's. Then mine. I don't know why I wore it today," Tildy said, twisting it on her finger.

His eyes were fixed on her, intent on something. She fell silent and waited.

"Can I get anything started for you two?" the waitress asked.

He smiled smoothly. "Let's have a plate of olives, crackers, and gruyère. I'll have a Garden Paloma, and the lady will have…"

She'd been so concerned about other things, she hadn't planned an order. She looked through the menu, suddenly overwhelmed. And then, as if a gift, her eyes landed on the perfect choice. "I'll have a Transatlantic."

"Coming right up."

In the vacancy left by the waitress, Jude looked timid. Nervous. Tildy remembered he'd looked anxious before he'd seen her. Evidently, that feeling had returned.

"You know your father's history," he began. "With my dad."

"Yes."

"And you know—well, you know."

"How he was mistreated. Exploited, really. And how he… ended up."

Jude looked at her. "And I know he treats you cruelly. And your mother. She tried to stop him. Not that he would listen to her. I know how he was to her, as much as he worships her now."

Tildy looked down at her ring, one true thing in the lies around her. Her stomach knotted up to her throat. A flicker of a memory, when she was small and lying in her mother's lap on the bathroom floor, playing with the loops of cotton on a bathmat as her mother stroked her hair and cried. She had no recollection of how or why they had ended up there, only that her mother was frail and her father had hurt her.

"Yes, I know."

He leaned forward now, his intensity nearly palpable.

"He's destroying the business. Your mother—she gave everything she had to that company, and it'll be for nothing."

The drinks and food arrived, and Tildy waited for the server to depart. She ate an olive without appetite. They remained quiet in the calm sophistication of the bar. The dark wood and soft velvet upholstery gave the place the feel of a secret men's club. Books, probably fake, or purchased at a thrift shop for their spines, lined the shelves along with tasteful vases and stained-glass lights. An attractive woman passed by, her perfume so strong Tildy could imagine the vapor trail in her wake.

"Is this why you met my family in Florida?"

Jude took a sip and then smiled fiercely at his drink, rotating it in the pond of condensation on the wooden table. "He thinks I came to pledge fealty. The buffoon."

Unsure what to say, she remained silent. She had wanted honesty from him, and here it was. But the strength of his feeling was unmanageable. The hours spent in her dreams made her appreciate how small she was here, in reality. She was just one little person in a sea of feelings and goals and relationships. Especially her, especially this sea.

He lifted his eyes and smiled at her. "You are so kind."

"What? Why would you say that?"

"I can see it."

"You hardly know me," Tildy replied, turning away from his intensity.

"No, I know you." He smiled to himself, some secret thought he did not share. "Yes, I know so much about you. Your father and sisters, they don't deserve you. You see what they are and you let them treat you as nothing, and you stay. You help when you can, even when it isn't wanted, but you aren't blind to their inadequacies. You see them. You overcome the pain they inflict on you with their stupidity and their pettiness, and you stay."

"If you think so little of them, why are you spending time with them?"

"Why do you?"

"I don't have a choice. They're my family."

"Of course you have a choice. They haven't earned your loyalty, and you don't need them. You could do something for yourself, instead of making your life convenient for them. You could do anything."

Tildy thought of the past, gone and grey. What would she give to go back and try it all again? To stay and see, to bet on her own happiness instead of sacrifice for loyalty. "Not anything," she said.

Jude took her hand. Chilled from his drink, it felt cold and unyielding. "You deserve to be happy."

She kept her retort inside, not wanting to debate the point with him, a stranger. She knew what she was, and what she deserved.

"What do you hope to get, from spending time with them?" she asked.

Jude freed her hand but kept his focus on her. "I want to be near when things happen, is all. I want to see."

"And you want me out of the way?"

He laughed and shook his head with a hand on his face, as if the concept was ridiculous.

"What's funny?"

"Oh, Tildy."

No further explanation came for the time being. Someone Jude knew stopped by the table and greeted him. What emotion he had been expressing disappeared immediately. He rose and warmly shook hands with the man, introducing her by first name only. The man leered at her a bit. Tildy returned to her drink and waited. She watched Jude smile, nod, and then gently encourage the man to continue on.

She took a long sip and nearly coughed. She'd dreamed of drinking alcohol, but in reality, she hardly drank and had little tolerance for it. Once she had composed herself, she nodded in the departing man's direction. "How can you stand men like that?"

Jude laughed. "Finance bros. You want to keep your shares? The board is full of men like him."

She froze. The conversation had changed shape. She could see it now, what this was all about. As if reading her thoughts, he nodded.

"I've already spoken with all the other key investors and shareholders. It's a matter of time. But, then I met you." He reached for her hand again and took it. "And my plans evolved. I didn't know who you were that night. It's so lonely, being in a crowd, surrounded by people who don't know you. And then I saw you. So beautiful and alone and strong. I couldn't have gone to something like that by myself, and yet you looked at peace.

"Every day and night after that, I hoped to see you again. At parties, dinners, walks through the city and stopping for coffee. I even took the subway a few times, thinking maybe somehow I'd see you. You seem like someone who uses the subway."

Tildy had no idea how to respond, so she only shrugged.

He squeezed her hand. "When I saw you at your father's place, I knew. I knew it was fate."

She tugged to free her hand, but he held fast.

"Tildy." Jude's voice turned husky, imploring her to focus on him. She did, because she couldn't resist him. Not completely. "What if you put these people behind you? What if you started something new? With someone who cares for you."

"Cares for me?" she echoed. She stared back at him, and his face hid nothing. He meant what he said.

"Will you think about it?"

Tildy squeezed her eyes shut. The words a betrayal to her heart, she said them anyway. "I'll think about it."

She couldn't stay after that. In a daze, she gathered her purse and book and left him, left the table, left the bar, left the block, left the neighborhood, and arrived home in desperate need for perspective.

In her own room, she slipped out of her clothes and left them on a chair. She climbed straight into bed, not wanting to bother with anything else. As she set up the machine, she knew she couldn't keep doing this. She didn't want to find a new job here, to figure out Jude, to get coffee with Evelyn, to meet the Twombleys. One more dream, and she would decide what to do. She'd need to decide.

chapter
thirteen

The darkness shifted from a warm embrace to a chilly evening on a cobblestoned street, the silence of her room giving way to the steady, pleasant rhythm of many close conversations. The scent of hot cider in cold air drifted from a metal cart outside a darkened shop. Tildy paused and stared, disoriented. Where was she? What day was it? It was nighttime, and there was a crowd, but businesses were closed. Some people were in costumes. There were children and families but also clusters of young, drunk adults. She struggled to recall the last dream, her thoughts still held hostage by Jude's proposal.

Two people in black bodysuits rushed down the street, their faces grim as they carried large puppetry sticks, and it clicked. Macnas. Tildy felt a wave of relief. She hadn't been to Macnas since she was a girl. It was the wrong season, of course. She was sure it had just been summer when she arrived, but fall was good. This dream could delight her.

She tugged up on the hood of her sweatshirt, a secret frumpy layer beneath her sophisticated-looking wool coat. If only she hadn't forgotten a scarf and gloves. The cider as a beverage was unappealing—but as a hand warmer? Exceedingly tempting. She remained where she was, behind the parade barriers and away from the stream of people moving past. The dream had a place for her. She had to wait.

A familiar voice echoed off the stone walls, and Tildy turned to see Ben and the others, chatting merrily as they approached the meeting spot. Orla nodded a greeting first, then Colm and Ben noticed her. Maria and Victor were busy arranging each other's scarves in mock fussiness.

"Alright, Tildy?"

"Hiya, Maria."

"You'll have to get yourself acclimated. No one in Ireland arrives on time."

She shrugged with a small smile, settling back to listen rather than participate.

"Colm was telling us he fancies Katherine."

"I just said I want to get to talk to her a bit. It's impossible with you chattering donkeys."

Orla looked to Tildy, faux-whispering, "There's always an excuse."

"Won't be chasing anyone, is all."

The group looked at their friend with fresh, sincere sympathy. Ben put an arm around him and gave him a squeeze. "That's easily fixed. Stop screaming and they won't run from you."

The two men wrestled playfully, nearly knocking into passing pedestrians.

"Oi, here comes Katherine," Orla said.

Colm and Ben stopped to look, then turned back to glare at their friend. Orla simply smiled. Successfully distracted from making a scene, everyone laughed. Tildy wondered how it would feel to be one of them. What would she be now, she wondered, had she grown up with this kind of support?

Maria said, "Here comes Katherine now. Ugh. And Lucy."

"No," Ben whined. "I thought he was done with her."

Victor shook his head. "You lot are too hard on her."

"Not nearly as hard as she is on our ears."

Colm had his hands shoved into his pockets, his expression wiped away to smooth neutrality. The group approached— Katherine, Jordie, and a pretty girl Tildy did not recognize who walked very close to Aidan. He was less dressed up for his date than she would have expected. His green canvas jacket accentuated his broad shoulders. Underneath he wore a simple, light sweater. With his dark jeans and sneakers, he looked like he was just out with friends. Lucy's clothing, on the other hand, was tight fitting and alarmingly short for the chill. Her hair and makeup was carefully arranged. She was most definitely on a date. Tildy would never put in that kind of effort for friends, at least.

She joined in greeting the newcomers but remained in the background, treating Aidan as a stranger and keeping her attention on Katherine and Colm. He continued his studied nonchalance, while Katherine noted his forced indifference with evident confusion. Ben moved over to Katherine to greet her with too much attention.

Maria whispered to Tildy, "Distract him. This is never going to work with Ben here to muck things up."

She accepted her mission with a quick nod, and walked over to Ben, hooking his arm into hers.

"Are we waiting on anyone else?" she asked.

Ben flushed. "Just a couple more mates of Colm's. They'll find us. Let's go to Henley's store, best spot for photos."

Tildy saw Aidan from the corner of her eye, his mouth a tense line.

Jordie sighed. "No, we're going to the quay. Every year we go to Henley's and it's jammed full of people."

"Fine, fine."

"First, let's get some hot chocolates from Gracie's stand. We promised we would," Maria admonished the others for forgetting.

The group agreed and headed a few storefronts down

to a busy pop-up selling fragrant hot chocolate. There were three options: plain, bacon-infused, and mint.

"Bacon! That's disgusting," Lucy said.

"Wrong. It's delicious," Jordie replied.

"How do you know?" she tittered. "Is hot chocolate a subspecialty at Michelin-starred restaurants?"

"He helped Gracie come up with the flavor," Orla replied coldly.

"Tildy," Ben whispered. "What would you like?"

"Oh, bacon hot chocolate, please. Thank you."

"Sure thing." Ben got in line with Jordie and Maria, leaving the rest with Lucy.

"You food people are so weird." Lucy's shrill voice pierced through the background hum. "Are you in food, too?"

It took Tildy a moment to realize she was being addressed. The young woman had an unsettling look up close, her eyes a bit wild, her blonde hair stiff from too much bleach, too much product. The line of her lips extended beyond her natural features.

"No, I'm not in food. What do you do?"

"I work in marketing for a multinational corporation. I'm glad I won't be the only one who doesn't work in service. Unless—do you work with Ben?"

"No."

Tildy's gaze lifted to Aidan, who was busy looking into the distance.

"Where are you from?"

"New York."

"What industry are you in?"

"Software."

"Why on earth did you come to Galway? I'm here on transfer, our home office is in London. I can't imagine why anyone would move here without a major financial incentive."

"I'm happy here."

Lucy laughed, as if Tildy was slow. "You left New York City behind for this place? Well, I assume you had work prospects in the States."

Tildy smiled. "Sometimes."

"Did you come here chasing a man? Or running from one?"

"Mother of Christ," Orla muttered.

"No," Tildy replied firmly.

"There must be a man in this somewhere."

"*No* is a complete answer, Lucy," Orla said, her tone a warning.

"I just mean, people need a change when they divorce. My flatmate moved to France after her fiancé left her, I understand the impulse."

Tildy tried to end the conversation with silence. It was not effective.

"Limited opportunities in the States, dating and otherwise?"

Unlike many others, Tildy had experienced greater trials to her self-control than this. She kept herself neutral.

She checked on the hot chocolate line. Ben and Jordie were finally at the front, placing their orders.

"What kind of software do you develop? Anything I've heard of?"

"Probably not, no."

"Lucy," Orla asked, "how's that cyst on your ankle? Did it heal or did you end up needing surgery?"

Lucy, more interested in discussing herself than anyone else, took the bait and ignored Tildy for the rest of the evening. Ben and Jordie returned, handing around the cups of hot chocolate. Ben handed Tildy hers, then locked his arm with hers again. She frowned. She sensed Aidan's gaze before they turned to follow Colm and Katherine, who were heading down the street toward their designated parade spot.

"She's a bit of a dunce," Ben muttered, nodding backward toward Aidan's companion.

"Is she like that with everyone?"

"Oh, yes. Absolutely everyone, even Aidan. I think they're just mates, though I'm not sure if she was cc'd on the memo."

Orla took the lead and moved through the crowd. Some of the audience had folding chairs, blankets, and strollers. Children chased one another in the carless street, enjoying the reprieve before the parade began. Some parents had brought thermoses full of warm beverages, sparing themselves the wait in line at the stations around the route.

Up ahead, Colm helped Katherine through a dense

group of men. Tildy saw a smile on Katherine's face, which he returned. She smiled, too, happy to see the beginnings of a little romance. Tildy took the narrow pathway as an opportunity to free her arm from Ben and murmured apologies as she stepped around some, nodded greetings at others. The atmosphere of the event was friendly, as long as coveted spaces at the front were not being contested. Orla had stopped to say hello to some friends, yet still managed to maintain the front position of their group.

A high, childlike voice echoed nearby, and Tildy ignored it, assuming it came from a group of children she'd passed. Then she heard it again. The voice, perhaps unfairly, struck her as vapid and annoying. The third time, she turned.

Aidan was staring across the street, looking unhappy, while Lucy excitedly explained something. It had been her voice that cut through the din of the crowd. Victor and Maria, at the back of the group, wore matching expressions of pity and irritation. Tildy suppressed a smile and returned her attention to the others.

"Katherine looks happy," Ben observed. In the cold, his pale skin glowed in the darkness. His oblong lips were chapped, and Tildy felt an ache for him, to find a nice someone to think of these things, to settle down and be happy.

"She does. Will Colm follow through?"

He shrugged.

They reached the agreed-upon place, Orla seemingly surprised by their late arrival.

"Jaysus, Orla, did you fly over the crowd to get here?"

Ben inquired. She only rolled her eyes in reply. Around them were only a few clusters of people, some nursing drinks from paper bags to hold back the chill. Ben handed Tildy his hot chocolate and opened up his backpack. Curiosity piqued, his friends tried to look inside. Instead of bottles or cans, he handed out hand warmer packs.

"These should still be good. Bought a case of them for a ski trip."

Colm frowned. "You ski?"

"Feck no. My sister skied with her boyfriend, dragged me along. Me, in the Alps. Imagine."

They accepted the hand warmers, appreciative of some relief. Suddenly the lights strung along the road changed color and speakers suspended along the parade route began to play music. Tildy noticed Colm offering to warm up Katherine. She looked away quickly, desperate to prevent an interruption. Lucy laughed at a joke Aidan made, and Orla threw her empty hot chocolate cup into a nearby trash can and jogged across the street, where she greeted a couple whose baby rested in a stroller. They gave her a hug.

"I think she might not like us," Ben observed.

"It's not us, it's you," Katherine replied, to which everyone snickered. Tildy felt the sting of the joke. Far too harsh, but perhaps it was fine here. Or perhaps this was the cost of intimacy.

A group of women in all black disembarked from a rolling platform, displaying to the crowd their glowing sculptures, while another woman, walking on stilts and dressed in a silver bodysuit, gracefully danced in the center.

"They must do Pilates," Lucy remarked.

The women continued up the parade route, lifting and lowering their sculptures in time with the music. On the platform, a man operating the controls for the lights and music shivered in a large jacket and hat.

"That guy's cold, and these women are in lycra suits," Tildy observed to Katherine, who murmured in agreement.

Behind the first set of performers came a group dressed as gray birds. They drummed as they walked, keeping pace with the music, while three women in vibrant masks sang a shrill, precise call. Beyond their procession, three enormous, ghostly white figures in silks and dark wooden masks stalked, seemingly examining the crowd for victims.

It was all more high art than most Americans would anticipate. They would have expected twirling batons and trad music and bagpipes. But this was a city of arts, and this was a parade for themselves.

Victor, with an arm around Maria, nudged Tildy. "This is weird, right?"

"It's so weird but so cool!" she whispered back. They laughed quietly together.

Lucy asked Ben for another hand warmer. He dug around in his bag, certain he had one left, but no. Tildy handed Lucy her own second, unopened one and turned back to the parade route.

A row of unicyclists approached, each wheel painted matte black with illuminated orbs suspended in the spokes.

The orbs appeared to be floating, as though they were hovering above the pavement. A man dressed as a bird with a giant, flaming sparkler followed, waving it at the crowd, illuminating faces and throwing sparks everywhere. Tildy wondered at the insurance coverage costs for this event. A fire-breather ran in out of nowhere, then suddenly flames exploded into the sky.

"More this way, please," a spectator called out, to general enjoyment.

The music became more ominous as an enormous sculpture of a ghostly woman moved down the street and hovered over the crowd, smoke billowing through her illuminated blue-gray skirts. Her flowing hair raked the wind, an eerie outstretched hand passed over everyone. A little girl across the street cried out, and her father scooped her up with a soothing, strong embrace and walked away.

Next were cars illuminated with lights, decorated as if filled with creatures of all shapes and sizes. Dancers in ragged costumes marched alongside, occasionally pulling illuminated ribbons from their dingy brown vests, making beautiful, iridescent shapes in their wake. As Tildy looked down the road at what would come next, she caught Aidan looking at her. He held her gaze for only a moment, then turned away. Her heart sank, and she faded back into their group.

Next was another giant sculpture. An enormous papier-mâché puppet, with the face of a wrinkled, elderly man. Its eyes opened, and the music paused. Then it blinked once, setting off two strobing lights within as a new set of music started again. She admired the handiwork, the puppeteers in all black working strenuously below the support structure. Then she noticed movement to her right.

Colm was trying and failing to hold Katherine upright. Without thinking, Tildy dropped her things and grabbed her too.

"What's happening? What's going on with her?" Ben asked, but there wasn't time to reply. Katherine's body shuddered as they struggled to lower her safely. Tildy switched her position and hooked both her arms under Katherine's shoulders, slowly crouching until the young woman was on the ground.

"Katherine. Katherine?" Colm asked, patting her hand helplessly. Her eyes had rolled and shut, the shaking intensifying. Unable to support her weight, Tildy scooted back on the ice-cold pavement and put Katherine's head on her lap. She pulled off her coat and draped it across her as a blanket. Without thinking of the others, she peeled off her sweatshirt and shoved it under the woman's head, then freed her legs. Tildy checked her watch, noting the time, the parade forgotten.

"Has she had a seizure before?" she asked the friends, examining one member of the group to the next. Maria knelt nearby, but didn't move. Colm and Victor were completely still. Ben covered his mouth and shook his head. Aidan looked ready to run for help, to carry her to safety, to do something, but was rooted, unsure how to act. Lucy turned away and sobbed uncontrollably.

Ben finally regained his ability to speak. "Shouldn't we, wedge something in her mouth?"

"No," Tildy said firmly. "We keep her mouth clear."

Colm turned to the curious onlookers. "The fecking parade is that way! Arseholes!"

"Colm, stay calm. You're no help if you're not thinking," Tildy said.

He nodded but glared at the curious people around them.

Maria started to cry and Victor steered her away, keeping an eye out but comforting his girlfriend.

Aidan knelt down next to her and whispered, "Should I run for help?"

Tildy shook her head. "Not yet."

Moments passed as she stared into the middle distance, her mental clock as accurate as her wristwatch. Her bare arms stung in the cold, but she resisted her body's demand to shiver. The stares of those nearby were unavoidable but did not draw her attention. What threatened her concentration was something else, the feelings and memories she kept remote and secret. She pushed strands of Katherine's hair away from her nose and mouth and checked her watch. "Three minutes. Go get help."

Before Aidan could move, Colm bolted down the street, toward the services table, shoulder-checking people aside as he made his way through. Tildy held Katherine as gently but firmly as she could to the makeshift pillow while

Ben tried to keep her covered.

Lucy walked away. Tildy frowned in confusion.

"She going for help?" she asked.

"I think she's just going," Aidan replied, still crouched beside her. Tildy looked down at his hand resting on his strong thigh.

There isn't time to think about that, she scolded herself.

Tildy looked at his face and asked, "Did she eat anything before she got here?"

He nodded, composing his thoughts. "We… we had dinner at the restaurant, just before. Ravioli and some wine."

"How much wine?"

"Only a taste each, sampling a bottle for the restaurant."

Tildy looked at her watch, did some math. "Is she on any medication?"

"Uh, she takes the pill," Ben said. Aidan and Tildy looked at him. "What? She's mates with my sister. I thought they were vitamins."

"Any accidents, headaches, fevers, or injuries recently?"

"No, I don't think so," Aidan said. "She never misses a day."

As suddenly as it began, the seizure ended.

"Anyone have a bag? A bag for garbage?" A man nearby handed over the paper bag his liquor had been concealed in. Tildy opened it up and had it waiting as she soothingly murmured to Katherine. She pulled her hair away from her face, tucking it behind her ears, and placed a hand under her shoulder in preparation.

Tildy looked up and shook her head. "Give her some space, guys. And make some privacy if you can."

The men rose and backed away. Katherine's eyes rolled open, her face transmitting confusion and fear. As suddenly as she had revived, she started heaving. In a swift motion, Tildy rolled her to her side toward the bag, using her arm to keep Katherine's head from hitting the ground with practiced smoothness. Vomit exploded from her mouth, hot and steaming in the bag but also on Tildy's arm. The position was a strain, but she braced with her leg and kept the woman's head supported.

When her heaving stopped, Katherine tried to pull herself upward. "Where's Ma? Henry?"

"Wait for a moment, lie still now. Shhh. Wait a moment."

Tildy brushed the hair from her face. When Katherine had taken a breath to steady herself, Tildy nodded. With her voice even and low, she said, "Okay, sit up slowly. Good, now lean on me. Hush. You're safe. You're safe."

"I… Who are you? Where's Henry? Why is it so dark?"

"Katherine, my name is Tildy. I'm your friend. You're safe. We're at the Macnas parade. You had a seizure. Colm is finding help for you. You're safe. I have you."

Maria knelt down and took a napkin from her purse and cleaned Katherine's face. Too tired to argue, Katherine lay back against Tildy. Ben looked relieved and smiled at his friend, evidently trying to think of a joke. Aidan had tears of relief in his eyes. He pushed them away and climbed onto a utility box to look over the crowd for Colm.

Heaving sobs broke from Katherine. Tildy rocked back and forth gently to comfort her, humming reassuring sounds, trying to recall what she used to say or do all those years ago, when she was smaller, when the world was different.

Colm reappeared, closely followed by two paramedics carrying a stretcher. Aidan helped move people out of their way. Colm knelt beside Maria and tenderly checked on Katherine, stroking her face. Maria stood and backed away, letting him take Katherine's hand.

Tildy turned to the paramedics. "Gran mal seizure, from the strobe light in a display." She checked her watch. "It started about nine minutes ago, ended about two minutes ago. She came right up out of it, though she's disoriented and had some vomit. We're not sure if she has a history. She had a hot chocolate about fifteen minutes ago, ate a pasta meal forty-five minutes ago, with a half glass of wine. No recent fevers, illness, or head injuries, as far as we know. Only known medication is birth control pill."

The medics nodded, and one took over supporting Katherine while Tildy scooted out from her position and rose.

"Come here, love. Let's get you sorted out. What's your name?"

While the first medic spoke to Katherine, the second asked Tildy, "Are you a doctor?"

"No. No, not a doctor."

"Anyone here family?"

"I'm going with her," Colm said.

When one paramedic lowered the stretcher, Katherine tried to stand, but Colm and the others insisted she wait on the ground. Tildy gathered her coat and sweatshirt, trying to hide their state from Katherine. A nearby parade watcher handed her a fistful of wet wipes from a diaper bag.

Tildy thanked the man and turned away to quickly wipe herself as clean as she could, shoving the soiled wipes into her jacket pocket. The parade continued beyond them, had continued, in fact. She hadn't been aware of it, or the tears that had fallen down her face. She wiped them away, too, and composed herself before she faced the group again.

"Clear a path," the larger paramedic boomed as they whisked Katherine back through the crowd, Colm close behind them.

"Jesus Christ," Ben sighed. "That was horrifying."

Tildy prepared to reply when Aidan interrupted her.

"Come on now, let's get you clean clothes."

Stricken stupid, Tildy could only stammer. She looked down at herself and for the first time realized how she looked—beyond the mess, the shirt she had worn underneath her sweatshirt was white, so loved and used it was nearly sheer, while her bra underneath was black.

Aidan kept his eyes purposely averted. "You can't be in this weather like that."

Before she could reply, he began walking away.

"You want me to tag along?" Ben asked.

"No no, I'll be okay. Can you guys ring Katherine's mom?"

"Oh feck, I should've done it ages ago," Maria replied, taking out her phone. Victor waved a goodbye, while Ben watched her in dejection.

Tildy returned the wave, not interested in Ben's feelings at the moment.

Aidan walked a fraction too fast for her at first, then slowed down. He removed his canvas jacket and offered it to her.

"No," Tildy replied firmly.

"You're shivering."

"No. I'll ruin it."

"Take it, for Christ's sake. You're wearing…" His eyes lingered on her chest for a moment, then he cleared his throat. "We've got a walk."

She dropped her things and then took the jacket from him. Once on, the delicious residual warmth of his body soaked into her skin. Aidan gathered her jacket and sweatshirt, carrying them casually as they continued on. Tildy kept her eyes from anyone walking past, but no one noticed her.

The music continued to boom as the crowd thinned at the first corner. A cold blast of wind curved around the buildings, striking them head-on. Aidan shivered, shoving his free hand deeper into his pocket, the soiled clothing wedged between his arm and torso. Guilt washed afresh over Tildy. She considered moving against him, sharing her body heat. Recoiled by her mind's suggestion, she nearly stumbled away from him.

"Do you want your jacket back?"

"It's nothing," he replied, his breath visible in the night air.

They turned a corner, then another, the wind no longer as strong, and walked in the moonlight of the empty streets, the music of the parade fading. Only certain notes reached them as they continued on.

"How did you know how to do that?"

"Me? It was nothing."

Aidan shook his head. "I did nothing. Ben did nothing. You knew what to do. How?"

Tildy composed her thoughts, seeking the outline of the moon in the sky, tracing the circle of light with her eyes. "Mom."

"I see."

"It started after she had Gisele. Nana didn't like to talk about it. Maybe she thought if it wasn't discussed, it would go away."

Tildy focused on walking. She imagined different threads of conversation as a physical thing, fluttering behind them as they walked on in silence. As if he had grasped one, Aidan matched her pace and moved closer, then lowered his head. In a voice as delicate as paper, he asked, "That's how she died, then?"

Tildy tightened her jaw and nodded. The silence was heavy, the familiar discomfort of sharing an upsetting truth of life, unknown to so many—that good parents can die.

"Seeing your mum have those, that's hard."

The emotion in his voice, soft and tactile, brought tears to her eyes. She hadn't let herself be seen crying in years, and this would be twice in one night. Each day was a battle, fighting to keep the old wounds sealed shut, the ones that went deepest, that had changed every part of her that mattered. This dream had pulled all of it out and created this horrible nightmare just for her. One swallow, then two, buried the feelings again, safe in the dark where they belonged.

"I'm glad I was able to help Katherine."

He scrutinized her in the dim light for a moment, then returned his eyes forward. She had shut a door, and she knew he resented it. They crossed the street, no traffic to avoid, continuing to walk together and apart.

At a robin's-egg-blue home, Aidan took out his keys. It wasn't an apartment building or a large home converted into a duplex. Up and down the block were other attractive, well-maintained homes, on each side of the street luxury sedans and newly planted trees. It seemed like a block for young executives, lawyers, and others who didn't want to commute in from the suburbs.

He opened the door, motioned for her to follow. The home was quiet, dark, empty. He flipped on lights and set down his keys. They removed their shoes.

A carved wooden sculpture rested on the entry table, a painting in shades of blue, from black to perfect white, above it. It was beautiful, more so than most other abstract paintings Tildy had seen. The floor was new, the plaster recently redone. To the side, in the dark, lay a neat sitting room with modern furnishings.

Without any ceremony, Aidan dropped her jacket and sweatshirt on the floor and waved for her to follow him upstairs. She removed his jacket from her body and left it with the other items at the foot of the stairs. The air was cool through her thin shirt, and Tildy suddenly felt self-conscious.

He flipped on a light in his bathroom and stepped aside. "Wait here."

She entered and stood awkwardly. The heated floor through her socked feet was luxurious. The bathroom was designer quality, with sharp edges and modern fixtures and perfectly laid tile. It was an expensive bathroom, and there she stood, wearing a stupid black bra under a white goddamn shirt. In her life, Tildy had experienced many episodes of humiliation, most of them in the awkward years of late childhood. Someday this moment would keep her awake at night, paralyze her during an unexpected moment, end a bout of confidence. But not yet. Her thoughts were with Katherine and Colm, the worry on his face so familiar to her.

Aidan returned with towels and a stack of clothes. He set the things on the stone countertop and leaned across her to check for toiletries inside of the shower stall. His shirt lifted, a sliver of his belly briefly exposed as he reached across. The proximity to his bare flesh, so close to her, was sudden and searing; Tildy blushed so fiercely her scalp tingled, her current state of misery totally forgotten. He stepped back and retreated to the hall. He looked back only once. Then he shut the door between them.

Alone again, she released a breath she didn't realize she had been holding. She turned on the shower and allowed herself a single swarm of quiet giggles. Then she plunged into the cold water, desperate for sobriety.

Tildy remained in there, letting the shower run down her skin, several minutes longer than necessary. It was a matter of avoiding his glares while suppressing her feelings for him. She had to leave the shower. She was clean. There was nothing more worth doing. She shut off the tap and dried herself with the towels Aidan had left, far nicer and fluffier than her own.

The clothing he had arranged for her included a clean, fairly new tank undershirt, sweat pants, and an old sweater. Tildy lifted the sweater, appreciating what it had been before paint splatters and a carefully repaired tear had made it what it was now. Flecks of gray in the dyed-blue wool gave it character, the threads tight and intricate, unlike the chunky sweaters sold in tourist shops. The patch and the paint took away the beauty it had been but gave it something like experience. She touched the tight stitching on the fabric, appreciating his delicate attention and precision. On an impulse, she lifted the sweater to her face and breathed in the smell of him. Cedar, the ocean, herbs—his natural chemistry permanently in the fibers. She set it down with regret.

That smell was for someone else to enjoy. Not her.

Taking stock of the items, it was apparent they would all be huge on her. She would look absurd. Resigned, she put on the clothing and made herself look in the mirror. Her wet hair hung limply down her shoulders, so she took a hair tie from her purse and secured it up in a bun. The sweater hung off her shoulder, which was okay, but the arms were enormous. The sweatpants actually fit around her waist, but the legs were like parachute pants on her. Certainly, visiting Katherine at the hospital right away was out of the question.

She shoved her soiled clothes into a plastic bag and left the bathroom. She moved slowly toward the landing and listened, hoping to escape unnoticed. But, no. Sneaking out was not possible. Aidan sat at the top of the stairs, looking at his phone, waiting for her.

Probably doesn't trust me to not snoop or steal stuff or something, she thought with dismay.

He'd donned a long-sleeved shirt, cuffs pushed up to his elbows. His forearms were lean and muscled. Even holding a phone, he looked strong. Probably from working bread dough. Tildy had to shake free the image of him leaning into dough on a tabletop.

She lightly cleared her throat. His eyes rested on her exposed neck as he rose, and she pulled up the collar in embarrassment.

"Thank you. I'll get you the clothes back as soon as I can."

He didn't nod, smile, or speak. He simply turned and descended the stairs.

Tildy scowled at her feet as she followed. At the bottom, they stood near one another in silence. She looked from him to the door, eager to run, unsure what to say to make that happen. When she took a moment to look at him, prepared to smile politely and say goodbye, speech failed her. His hands were tucked in his pockets, as if casual, but his eyes examined her with intensity. Searching, focused, the same look as her first night in the pub. Rather than immediately shy from the examination, she returned it.

She wondered, as if speaking to him with her mind, *why do you keep appearing here? What am I to you now?*

The curve of his shoulders into his strong chest invited her to rest her head. She imagined his neck smelling of the same scents in his sweater.

Tildy tried to regain her composure. He didn't want her here. She had to leave. She smiled, tried to speak, and failed again. The dream nudged her. There was something outside for her, it said, more things were to happen, and this vignette was at an end. The shadows in the corners of his home were growing denser, as if the building were fading away.

Aidan removed his hands from his pockets and stepped forward. The movement rendered Tildy immobile. This shouldn't be happening, she knew. The dream was being tested in a way that revealed the fragility of the structure. He moved slowly, as if fighting against a current, and extended his hand to her. Hopeful and afraid in the same moment, she waited. He crossed the gap between them and delicately touched a tendril of her dripping hair. A water droplet rolled down her neck to her collarbone, and his touch traced its route. She shivered. Aidan's face drew near, his eyes locked on hers.

"You aren't here," he said.

Tildy leaned back in surprise. "What?"

"I wish you were." He touched her neck again, soothing and gentle. "I wish this was real."

And she dropped.

She fell so fast, through the floor, through space, through time, her heart and lungs felt pressed against her rib cage. She woke in her bed with her hands flung out for something to save her.

Her bed, in her room, in New York City.

Her room, where she lived, alone.

She grasped her pajama shirt and inhaled. Her scent. No cedar, no sea, no herbs. With a curse, she threw herself back into her pillows, damp from sweat.

She turned to the side table and grabbed her phone. A text from Gisele, inviting her to a boat party with Jude.

Tildy rolled her face into her pillow and screamed.

<h1 style="text-align:center">chapter
fourteen</h1>

It took Tildy about fifteen minutes to walk from the Cortlandt St station to the marina. She'd been there before—birthday parties, bar and bat mitzvahs, one notable prom after-party that involved marina security and an ambulance. Her dad used to have a slip there, too, but that had been sold years ago, when the value was less than half what it was now. If he had any awareness of his poor judgment, she'd feel bad for him.

She looked at the yachts around her in resigned disgust. This was one of the few places in Manhattan that could berth superyachts, ships large enough to accommodate staff, a full kitchen, a dozen bedrooms and bathrooms, even a helicopter landing pad. The table settings alone cost more than most families in New York City made in a month. And here she was, in her jeans and sneakers and a T-shirt, having her ID checked by security for admittance into one of these displays of excess wealth.

The contrast between this and her dream world was so complete, the memory of all that had happened last night was inescapable. "I wish this was real," he had said.

No, he hadn't said it, she reminded herself. Him and Nana's land and all of it was her imagination. She and she alone built these moments in Ireland, every detail was of her own making, and yet? That moment felt so incongruous, it countered any logic. Was there more happening? Something she could not explain?

The planks of the dock shifted underfoot as she approached the boat. A familiar voice called her, and she put aside her thoughts. Gisele approached in a bright sundress, sporting designer sunglasses and freshly manicured nails.

"Jesus, Matilda. You look like you're staff. If you don't want to come, you shouldn't be here."

Tildy did not give her the satisfaction of nodding, even if she was right. They walked together toward the yacht.

"This is going to be it, Matilda. I'm going to lock him in."

"Lock him in?"

"Look at this! He has *yacht money*! That's just what

I need. No more of these trust fund boys waiting for their geriatric dads to kick the bucket. I need a man who has money already."

"Where did he get his money?" Tildy asked, looking over the sleek white-and-blue vessel.

"Keep your voice down, it's rude to talk about money. You're so embarrassing."

She opened her mouth to argue but closed it again. It wasn't worth the trouble.

Jude approached the railing at the top of the gangplank with a drink in his hand. He handed it to a passing crew member and leaned down, looking at them. His auburn hair caught the light while his dark sunglasses absorbed it. His watch glittered off his wrist, its silver a contrast to his golden tan. His T-shirt, crisp and pressed, showed off his thin, strong shoulders. The entire effect was casual wealth.

"Tildy!" He smiled at her. Then he turned to her sister with a different smile. "Gisele, so glad you could make it."

Gisele went first, strutting up the gangplank to the boat, offering him a hand as if she needed help on the small step. Jude took it with a smile.

"There's drinks and canapés aft, at the bridge deck. Some friends are already there."

She could see Gisele's disappointment but quick recovery. No one like him wanted to be with a desperate woman. Her sister left them behind, turning down the bridge deck towards the sounds of an unseen group. Jude removed his sunglasses, tucked them into his shirt collar, and offered Tildy his hand. Something in her smile as she walked up and past him made him laugh, and he put the hand in his pocket.

"I'm surprised you came," he said, his voice easy, his light brown eyes taking her in. The sunlight caught on the flecks of gold in them. She looked away.

Rather than take her to the bridge deck, he steered them to the walkway leading to the bow.

"I didn't have anything else going on," Tildy said cautiously.

They walked in silence for a moment. Through the windows they could see an interior sitting area, where a large sculpture of a dolphin stood on a pedestal by the bar.

"Didn't take you for a dolphin kind of guy," Tildy mused. Jude laughed harder than the joke deserved.

"I'll tell you a secret," he said, leaning against her shoulder for a brief moment. "It's not my yacht."

"I see," she replied. That certainly explained a few things. This yacht cost tens of millions of dollars. While Jude seemed wealthy, he didn't seem quite that wealthy. But that he, with his charm and easy grace, could get a free yacht stay out of an ultra-wealthy, and possibly shady, multimillionaire made perfect sense.

They continued their stroll to the bow, turned, and headed around the opposite end of the boat toward the bridge deck. "A family could live on this ship," Tildy observed.

"They could, though I don't think that's what it was made for." He smiled. She didn't reply.

There was a small enclosed area with a couch, out of the sun. Tildy stepped inside and looked around. While the dolphin room seemed large and formal, this one was more casual. She'd stay here for the party.

"I should go greet my other guests," Jude said a hint of dismay.

Movement in the corner of the room caught her eye. An old brown dog had ambled off a tufted pillow and was looking up at her, tail wagging gently, as if unsure if she was receptive to friendliness. Tildy knelt and patted her knee.

"Look how fluffy you are! Gabh i leith! Math an buachaill—oh, my apologies, maith an cailín."

Jude knelt beside her and petted the dog as well. "Her name is Caly-pso. Her owner is away in Europe. She's the reason I have the boat."

"You're dog sitting, then."

"Calypso is very special. My friend wanted her to get undivided attention."

"I can fill that role for now," she said, scratching Calypso behind her ear. Her rear right paw smacked the floor in a pattern, making Tildy giggle.

Jude met her eye. "I've never seen you smile before, let alone laugh."

"I smile," she said, rising from the floor.

He stood as well, his gaze never leaving her face. "Not smiles that reach your eyes."

She tilted her head, restraining herself from saying the same back to him. He sensed it and nodded, then looked out toward the party. Gisele was laughing with two other women, women much like herself. There were men too, two male versions of Gisele, all of them flocked together, all so alike. One of the men Tildy recognized. He had been thrown from a horse in high school and spent time in intensive care, needing major reconstructive surgery. He was different after the accident, the injury to his brain concealed beneath the excellent plastic surgery to his face. Yet he still went to his family's equestrian estate.

All of these young people, including herself, caught in the orbit of their family's businesses. Did it make her better, she wondered, that she could see through all of this? Was it good to be aware or was it worse to see it, to know it all, and to remain?

A member of the crew approached and whispered something to Jude. He nodded.

"We're about to shove off, you may want to take a seat. I'll tell the others the same."

Tildy sat on the floor with Calypso, whose head flopped into her lap. She massaged the dog and watched the crew move quickly, bringing in the gangplank, untying lines, and helping push the yacht from the walkway. It was so much work, and for what? So some friends of a friend of their owner could get drunk next to the Statue of Liberty?

They moved slowly out of the marina, and the captain blew the horn once. Calypso, clearly associating this noise with something she wanted, rose quickly and clumsily and trotted out to the bridge deck. There she stuck her head out of the railing, the breeze blowing back her ears and fur. Abandoned, Tildy stood and tried to brush off the dog hair. She gave up quickly. It was hopeless.

She turned away from the group and found a spot on the walkway to watch the Manhattan skyline go by. With a sigh, she leaned against the railing and admired the city. Street signs in Russian, authentic Ethiopian cuisine, museums for ice cream. There were nine million people here. More people than Utah, Nevada, and New Mexico combined, all in just one city. A person could spend their whole life within its borders and experience dozens of languages and cultures from around the world.

And yet it had never been enough. Tildy gripped the railing and looked down at the water of the Hudson River as it was cut in two by the yacht. There was something tamed about the Hudson. Its waters moved more like a lake than a river. Perhaps it was the size and features of it, or perhaps it was her own bias. No river could be the Corrib.

Someone touched her shoulder. She started and stepped aside.

"I brought you something to eat," Jude said, handing her a little plate of canapés. She thanked him. Caviar with salmon and a fruit compote, all elegantly assembled in single tiny portion. She took a bite.

"Thank you, that's delicious."

Jude removed his sunglasses. "You sound disappointed."

Tildy shook her head, looking down at the plate. "I've just been thinking about money lately. Gisele would say that's rude of me, to mention money at a party."

He turned and leaned his elbows against the railing, the effect of his strong, lean body reclined next to her immediate. She handed her plate to a passing waiter and waited in silence. Once alone again, he spoke.

"I didn't grow up like this. When I was little, we did private school and birthday parties at mansions and all that. But after everything fell apart, we lived normally. My mother came from money, and needing to work and losing access to constant cash soured her. There was enough for me to go to college—my dad had at least thought of that. When I got there and saw how all those kids had grown up, how none of them had ever bagged groceries or shopped at a low-end department store… Being able to have parties like this was all I ever wanted."

"And now?" Tildy asked.

"Now? It's good. Now…" He slid closer to her and shifted his position, so he was propped on one elbow beside her. "You seem disappointed again."

"This isn't my idea of a party."

"What is your idea of a party, Tildy?"

She fought to ignore the implied meaning in his body language, lowered voice, and deliberate attention.

With Ireland not far from her thoughts, she replied. "People who are clever, kind, and funny. Who have a passion for something interesting."

"That does sound like a great party," he agreed. "This party requires family names, decent manners, and education—though the education is not what you have in mind, I think. It's not the people I want. It's the connections. Good connections are worth the trouble. You never know when you'll need them."

"I don't care about that," she said, turning away from them, from him, and back to the skyline. The water below beckoned to her, to fling herself over the railing, to see how calm the waters truly were.

She felt rather than saw Jude rise from the railing and come nearer to her. She kept her eyes on the horizon.

"You'll have to forgive me, Tildy, but you're wrong," he murmured. His right hand came to rest on the railing, next to hers, their fingers almost touching. "You're from this world. It may not be what you like, but all of this? It's all you know. And the way things are going, you'll need connections to see your way through."

Jude placed his left hand on her lower back, the sensation of being touched cascading into a riot of emotions within her. Even if she wanted to, she could not turn to face him. He leaned his body against her, his hand departing the small of her back and wrapping around to the left side of her waist.

"I could take care of you, Tildy. If you want me," he whispered into her hair.

Tildy pulled away, backed away, and faced him. The momentum of his intensity almost distracted her from the improbability of it all. He acknowledged her anxiety with a smile, and it seemed so sincere, so sympathetic and understanding. No response came to mind. Indignation at being touched by a man she did not trust was at war with the need to be touched, to be loved, to be cherished.

With a parting glance at the horizon, he put his hands into his pockets and left her to return to the party. Their voices carried on the wind as she remained at the railing, shivering from a feeling she could not describe.

At home, she showered to free herself from the salt spray and the sunscreen residue and a lingering sense of despair. Jude was right. He saw her family, and he saw who she had become, weak as she was, and he knew she would struggle when her family failed. Her job, so casually thrown away, now left her unmoored. Soon there would be no Aibell shareholder votes, no charity events, no family meetings. Her father and sister would be away in Florida, and she would either have to follow or be on her own with nothing.

Tildy took down her suitcase and began to fill it. There was usually a nonstop red-eye out of JFK to London Heathrow that had seats available last minute. She'd get a short flight to Shannon airport from there. The bag of adapters for her electronics was still in the rolling case, waiting for her to make this choice. And she was making it now.

chapter
fifteen

The airplane flew over the maze of stone walls, the tenant farmers long gone and dead, as they circled before making the landing approach. Tildy hated landings. Taking off, flying, taxiing were all fine. But landings felt like what they were: dropping tons of weight hundreds of feet in a matter of seconds to touch the ground on tiny wheels at a ridiculous speed. She'd be okay. She knew she'd be okay. This would be the hardest part of moving, she was sure.

She wasn't exactly sure she was moving, though. In her dream, she had been so confident. Her job, her little home, her car purchase. But as she stepped off the plane down a rickety metal staircase, she felt a bit lost as to what she wanted to do, what she would do next.

She entered the EU citizens lane in the terminal, holding her Irish passport like a talisman, to show she belonged here. Belief was what gave symbols power, she had heard, she had to believe in this. She slid the passport to the bored man at the desk. He glanced at her, glanced at the passport, processed it, and slid it back without a word. The disappointment lingered as she walked away. What had she expected, she scolded herself. *Welcome home* or something?

She collected her suitcase from the carousel and went to find the driver that would take her to the hotel. She felt a bit like Gisele or her father, looking around for a man holding a tablet with her name on it, but the bus ride was nearly two hours and she didn't want to rent a car only to have to return it at the airport. She shook her head. This was why her first dream had omitted the airport.

There it was—the sign read *Halleran*. She walked over to the man. "Good afternoon," she said politely.

"Ah, Miss Halleran? Good afternoon. Will you need help getting your luggage?"

"It's okay, I only have this."

The driver took over the handle from her and turned toward the sliding doors. They were immediately greeted by a cold, rainy wind. Unlike in her dream, it was typical weather for western Ireland. It met her expectations perfectly. This was just what she wanted.

At a speed greater than she was comfortable with, they left the airport parking lot and drove through long, quiet stretches of road to Galway. He asked the questions she expected—where she was from, who she was visiting—and he responded the way she expected, to say he had a cousin in New York, to say how nice it was for her to visit her grandmother. She didn't complicate things for him, leaving the story bland enough for him to speak or not as he chose.

After an hour, they entered the city limits, and Tildy felt a sense of disappointment wash over her. There hadn't been any billboards in her dream. There was trash in the street and graffiti on the walls and shady gadget shops and banks that looked like banks in New York. There was more traffic, more tourists, and more miserable locals. It was fine, of course—it was real. This was real. And yet she felt regret take hold.

They passed by the coach station as they drew nearer to Eyre Square, where her hotel, the same hotel she'd stayed at in her dreams, waited. She tapped out her payment for the driver, thanked him, and insisted she take the suitcase from the trunk on her own so he wouldn't get rained on.

"Thank you, miss. I hope you have a lovely visit."

She unloaded the suitcase and crossed the street to the hotel she had stepped into dozens of times, but had never been to before.

The inside was the same, plush carpets and dated wallpaper and glossy wood. Only the computers had been replaced by tablets on stands, and the track lighting on the ceiling, unnoticed in her dream, stood out like a sore thumb. And there was no Ben. Tildy had expected that. While she waited for the young man at the counter to be ready for her, she tried to collapse the handle of her suitcase. It stuck and the bag toppled over on her toe. Sharp pain vibrated through her leg. She muffled a curse and righted the suitcase.

The young man at the counter didn't notice. He took her passport and credit card, gave her a speech about breakfast availability and housekeeping, handed back her things, and said, "Enjoy your visit, ma'am."

The *ma'am* rung in her mind as Tildy passed by the double doors to the breakfast area. The same greyed heads bowed over newspapers, just as they had in her dream. The hotel smelled clean and just as she had dreamt; like hospital soap left inside a cedar chest, along with wisps of old-fashioned cologne. The elevator arrived quickly, and the brass doors opened smoothly. The interior was silver metal, and it dinged in a faintly European way for her to enter. Like emergency vehicles, all kinds of alerts were different here. It was another detail her dream had rendered incorrectly. She stepped in and rode without incident or character to the third floor.

In her room, she found the same large wooden furniture, heavy drapes, and a bed fitted up with jacquard fabric. It was nearly the same as her dream, only the TV was a flat-screen and the layout was a mirror image. And everything was a bit more beat-up, stains on the carpet and scuff marks on the wallpaper. Tildy checked the shower and under the bed. When she opened the closet, the smell of starch and men's cologne hit her full in the face. Choking back a cough, she shut the doors, determined to never open them again.

The room was empty, then. She went to her window and checked her view. A glimpse of a modern hotel or apartment complex, a small alley, and air conditioner units for the neighboring buildings. She could hear noises from the street, and a gap between the buildings revealed a glimpse of a nearby sidewalk, where grown men drunkenly staggered somewhere, wearing grass skirts, leis, and no tops. It was growing dark.

Tildy turned on the television while she unpacked. Unlike the set in her dream, this one had audio. The news anchors were discussing issues with some kind of artistic project called the Capital of Culture. She frowned. News stories in Ireland, she noticed, tended to lack background information. Even when she supplemented with older news articles or Wikipedia entries, she came away without confidence. National news took on a sense of dialogue between close friends or family, locals who implicitly understood the way events fit into a broader societal conversation. It highlighted her own ignorance and excluded her from the knowing and caring she wished she could have.

Tired of the news, she clicked up, and an Irish language children's show played. There were two children, an older boy looking for a toy. The moment he left the living room and his sister behind, a horse appeared before her, surrounded by a swarm of rainbow and glitter. The girl and the horse went on an adventure before the older brother returned. Even with her limited grasp of Irish, the entire scenario baffled her.

She had not made any progress unpacking. She peeled off her clothes and retrieved a fresh outfit from the top of her suitcase. The jeans were too tight, the socks not quite right for the boots she'd packed, and she'd need her jacket closed and her scarf wound tight because her blouse was too thin.

Tildy thought of the perfection of her dream outfits with dismay.

After a bit of makeup and hair brushing, she looked in the mirror. At least the dream hadn't lied to her on that score. She didn't look beautiful. Who was going to see her, anyway? Not him. She wouldn't let him.

She clicked off her TV and left her hotel room. After an uneventful ride in the elevator and exit through reception, Tildy stepped out into the brisk, cool air of the city before sunset.

The taste of the air here had a quick tang of the sea, a detail unrealized by her dreams. She was *really here*, in Ireland, her body across the ocean from where it had been yesterday. This was not a fictious place, it was real with real people who had their own lives that did not center on her.

She turned left and walked, and no one noticed her. Couples held on to one another, groups of friends chatted amiably. Overflowing crowds meandered out of patios and into the pedestrian walkway. Men held their drinks tightly as they engaged in halfhearted conversation, eyes roaming passersby for beautiful women to leer at. They didn't seem to register her. She continued on, toward his restaurant.

Around the next corner, the crowds thinned a bit as she approached the Wolfe Tone Bridge. The crosswalk had been painted like a rainbow for Pride month, and a new pedestrian footpath was nearly completed. Neither detail had been imaged for mapping software, so they hadn't been in her dream.

And beneath the concrete, steel, and stone, the River Corrib. Tildy stood at the railing a moment, looking down into the frothy waters. Just as in her dream, it flowed fast and steady, dark and threatening. The memories of lifetimes ago and those to come seemed to flow in those waters. Was that why it felt so menacing? Because it knew all that had come before and would see all that was to come after?

She returned her hands to her pockets and resumed her walk. The golden glow of the departing sunlight glistened on the painted pavement. Around the next corner was another busy pub, slightly dingier. In her dream, it had been a tidy little shop of some kind. It must've been that way once, not long ago, in the photos she had seen of this street. That nice tidy shop was gone, and what had replaced it was not very nice.

Tildy noted one of the men at the pub was staring at her. She gave him a furtive glance. His face frightened her in a way both shocking and familiar. The warning in her body reminded her, it was getting dark and she was alone. She kept her eyes up, away from him and on the horizon, as if she had someone expecting her. Still, she stayed attentive to his movements. After the next corner, she let her pace quicken and checked over her shoulder. He had not followed her.

It was truly sunset now, and people were making their way to dinner. A woman with a short bob and a cute dress under a trench coat clutched the arm of her handsome husband. They spoke to each other like best friends. They seemed to be two halves of the same happy person. Tildy smiled to herself, pleased to know there was love in the world, even if it wasn't there for her.

She turned the corner and looked down at the curved road with growing apprehension. The building facades were colorful, in the familiar reds and blues and yellows, but the utility poles were covered in posters and stickers and graffiti. The street was almost unrecognizable from what she had dreamed, and yet wasn't this what she had wanted? Reality? She turned onto the street and kept her pace steady. She wouldn't go inside. She just wanted to see the restaurant. And maybe, if she was lucky, she'd catch a glimpse of him through the front window. She could be here, on the sidewalk, a pane of glass between them, and see him once. Staring at a screen and dreaming a lie weren't enough anymore, and she had flown across the ocean to be here.

She stayed across the street from his restaurant. She moved slowly, watching all the while. A small group of friends approached the restaurant on the opposite sidewalk. They were loudly drunk, but didn't appear to be American or English tourists or out on a stag party. Just drunk. They stopped to read a poster stuck to an abandoned shopfront.

Through the glass she could see half of the tables were occupied. There was Jordie, speaking to a man about a wine. She smiled. He was being extra charming, she could tell. But then, could she? He didn't know her, she didn't know him. The Jordie she knew, who teased her and offered her kind smiles, had been a character in her imagination. The details provided by lurking on his social media accounts. She didn't know him at all.

She could go inside. She could see if they had an opening for one person. Once there, she could listen and enjoy and observe, and then say she wanted to meet the chef. She could see him, see if he knew her still.

She would not.

The group of friends, heading her direction now, did not notice Tildy. Drivers navigating the narrow streets did not glance her way, and other pedestrians did not look up at her. She was invisible here. It gave her the confidence to watch his restaurant, for him. She could stay here, unseen, and watch for him.

No. Tildy turned to continue on, to dinner, to something. Maybe later she'd contact him. He had his own life now. He probably didn't remember her. Her thoughts turned to calling Nana in the morning, a task she'd dreaded since boarding the plane in New York. Just as the group across the road stepped off the sidewalk, she absentmindedly watched a delivery van speed down the narrow road, not connecting the two in her distracted state.

A chorus of cries and the screeching of tires, followed quickly by a hollow plastic crunch and a dense thud. Tildy turned as the van accelerated away.

"Help! Oh god!"

One of the young men lay in a crumpled heap on the pavement, his head bleeding into the gutter. Tildy looked both ways and ran across the street. She slid to the ground beside the man and looked at the head wound.

"Call an ambulance," she demanded as she unwound the scarf from her neck and pressed it to the man's scalp. As she pressed, it gave in sections, signaling fractured bone shifting beneath her palm. She regulated her pressure, fearing for the soft tissue beneath.

"Let's move him out of the street," another man said.

"No, he can't be moved without a stretcher," Tildy said, her voice harsher than she intended. "Keep traffic away from us and I'll stay. I have him. I have him until the ambulance comes."

She swallowed, the sting of bile in her throat. She said it again, like a mantra. "I have him until the ambulance comes."

Hot blood seeped through the fabric, percolating between the threads and rising between her pale, cold fingers. The scarf was saturated and was starting to help bind the wound already, but it wasn't enough. She took a fold of the scarf and layered it on top. Still not enough. She'd need more cloth to seal the wound.

A door opened nearby, and footsteps rushed to their side. Tildy stayed focused, keeping her hands flat and steady. The man in her care was still breathing. She'd only remove her hands if he needed CPR, and she hoped it wouldn't come to that. She couldn't face the inevitable failure of it again.

A fresh white towel appeared, and a man's voice said, "Take this."

Tildy gently lifted one hand for the towel without acknowledging the person. She lifted her other hand slowly and briefly, then smoothed the towel over the top of her scarf and pressed her hands back down. Her hair was in her face, but she did not touch it. She was not a person now. She was the dam holding his life in place. Her entire existence was now to keep this man here.

She looked down and saw his leg was bleeding through his jeans. The man nearby registered her glance.

"More towels, Jord," the man called as he knelt down beside her, settling another towel against the leg wound. His strong hands pressed down over the blossoming red stain on the man's trousers.

Those hands. Tildy's mouth went dry, but she remained steady, her eyes on a rivulet of blood sliding across the concrete. *Focus*, she told herself. *This isn't a dream.*

All the while, the man's friends were hysterical. Orla soothed them, offered them bottles of water, and encouraged them to lean against the wall. Another towel appeared, and Tildy gently layered it on top. The sounds of an ambulance grew closer, and the man's eyelids fluttered. It gave her hope. Her adrenaline was causing her lower limbs to shake, but she kept her hands still. They could shake all they wanted when the paramedics took over.

"Stay still, now. You're safe," she said soothingly to the man. He tried to rise, but the man beside her firmly kept him on the ground.

"Rest now, lad."

The young man seemed to decide not to fight. Instead, he grasped Tildy's ankle. Was he reaching for a friend or a mother, or was he trying not to be swept out to sea?

"Yes," Tildy encouraged softly. "Hold on to me, now. I have you, OK? I have you."

The ambulance pulled over to them, and the rear door flung open. The sharp smell of sterile surfaces and plastic struck her. This was real, she told herself. This man under her hands was real. He had needed her and she was there for him. Didn't that mean she should feel pleased? So why did it feel like this was all her fault?

Unlike in her dream, she was not perfectly brave and collected when the paramedics took over. Her voice was not even, and when they asked her questions, she could not reply clearly. The paramedic simply took her by the shoulders, giving her a quick squeeze. She said, "good work, love" and guided her away. Tildy slumped down onto the sidewalk, her purse spilling beside her. Her legs were bent apart and her hands dangled, covered in blood, while she shivered uncontrollably from the adrenaline. His friends jostled one another trying to decide who should call family, who should go to the hospital, who should go home to the man's dog. She watched, apart and in silence. To rise was impossible.

Orla appeared with a wet towel and bathed her hands. Tildy wanted to speak but could only swallow and shiver. Orla got the worst of it cleared away. She soothed her too, like a stray dog coming in out of the rain. Jordie gathered up her purse while Orla led her by the elbow, up from the ground and into the restaurant, past the gawking patrons and straight into the staff bathroom. Mechanically, Tildy soaped and rinsed her hands. She watched the swirling pink water dotted with clumps of darker red travel down the worn ceramic drain. Bile rose sharp in her throat, unwilling to be subdued now, and she turned away from the sink and vomited into the old-fashioned toilet, quietly and cleanly, then wiped away the mess afterward.

In the mirror, her face was pale and her pupils pinpoints. She washed her hands again. They would not come clean for days, as they hadn't come clean for days, all those years ago. The pink tinge, from crevices too small to see still coated in red, a reminder of the life that had escaped her hands. She knew she would look at them when this was all over and wonder if it was the last fresh blood that person would ever spill.

She left the bathroom without a sense of where to go. She didn't want to stay but didn't trust her legs to move her outside. Without direction, she stood dumbly, still shivering, her hands dripping against her legs.

Jordie appeared with her purse and gave her a kind smile. "Come on, loveen, have a seat."

"I should go."

Her accent caught him off guard, but he recovered quickly. "You are in no state to go walking yet. And the Garda will want a word with you."

Tildy sat at the chef's table, sullen and depleted.

She heard Orla's voice. "What should we do about our next tables?"

A familiar voice, gruff but calm, replied. "Nothing for it. Ring them up, tell them we're refunding, and cancel."

In that moment, Aidan came through the doors, his white chef's jacket slung over his arm and a hand on his face. Aidan, who was the same as in her dream and real, here, now, and not in her dream. She had left her continent behind to see him and here he was, standing before her.

A mad notion seized Tildy. His eyes were covered—she could escape before he looked. She could escape through the service entrance, and he would never know it had been her. She would never have to face the reality that she had hurt him so profoundly, or worse yet, that she had caused him no damage at all. But the opportunity passed. He lowered his hand and looked at her, already preparing his soft, apologetic smile.

He froze.

He did remember her. The assumption that he would had been built on hope. And now, here he stood. And he did remember her.

She tried to say hello, but the word died. She only breathed.

"Tildy," he said, and the tone was so familiar. Pain and regret and anger and need. She could hear it. *And this is real,* she wondered.

Was it? Or was it another dream? Had she gone mad from the machine and was just flitting between one version of her imaginary vision to another? How could she know?

She lowered her eyes in shame.

"Garda are here, boss," Jordie said, taking the chef's jacket from Aidan and stuffing it into a hamper.

Tildy felt his eyes on her still, and she forced herself to meet his gaze. If he could bear it, so could she. There, again, was the confusion and ache and hurt she expected. But when they took in the blood on her hands, it all softened. Then he clenched his jaw and left.

"They'll want to speak to you too, miss..." Jordie said, and Tildy shook her head and smiled.

"I'm sorry, how rude of me. I'm Tildy Halleran."

"Tildy, nice to meet you," he said without recognition.

Why would he know her? And yet it stung. Was it familiar social rejection, or a fresh pain of diaspora nostalgia brought into the light?

He set a glass of water and a small cookie in front of

her. "You've had loads of adrenaline. Eat something and take a drink before you step out there."

Casting the thoughts aside, she did as he instructed. He left to speak with dinner guests.

The cookie was small. A perfect disk, with bits of herbs dashed in the batter. Herbs from Nana's land, maybe. Tildy took another nibble and sipped her water. The water had a taste, distinctive and not entirely pleasant. It took being away from New York to appreciate something as simple as the taste of water.

She'd have to go out there now. She didn't want to keep the police here too long.

She quickly finished the cookie, left the glass where it was, and rose for the kitchen doors. As she passed through, Maria sat in a darkened alcove to the left of the doorway, crying softly. Tildy paused. Maria did not seem like someone who ever cried. She was brash and funny and loud, always ready for anything. But that was the Maria of the internet, the public persona for strangers. This Maria, the real one, sat in the darkened corner alone, absorbed by her feelings after someone else's tragedy. Tildy hadn't even known she was here. Had she hid in this space the entire time? She sensed Tildy's presence and looked at her, no evidence of recognition on her face. She dried her eyes with her sleeve, then picked up the phone to start calling the evening's guests as instructed.

Tildy walked through the restaurant toward the door as local customers lamented the dangerous driving, and an

English customer loudly complained about not receiving any of the restaurant's famous bread.

The street had been blocked off and cones set up. The police cars were two friendly little station wagons emblazoned with *GARDA* and a high-vis yellow-and-blue checkerboard pattern down the sides. An empty bag of chips sat on the dashboard of the nearest vehicle. The man's blood still puddled in the gutter. Tildy wondered if he would survive. What were the hospitals like here? Were they better than back in New York? Maybe her scarf, still wound around his head, might save him.

The policeman taking information from Aidan seemed unmotivated. She watched Aidan shrug, his hands in his pockets, as if guarding them from the world's perception.

The sidewalk was closed in front of the restaurant, but across the street tourists and locals alike tried to see if there was anything good to talk about later with friends. It was just like New York, or maybe worse. So many things happened there all the time, and most people just kept their heads down and passed by. What was worse in a tragedy? Being ignored, or being entertainment?

Another van pulled up, this one with *Forensic Cleaners* printed in stock lettering across the side. The second Garda talked to the driver, pointing at the puddle of blood. The man shrugged, zipped on a white full-body suit and a mask, then set to work cleaning up the street, sidewalk, and gutter.

When Tildy's turn came, the sense of the officer's

disinterest became a certainty. Though it didn't really matter, she felt anger surge in her. She knew she had only briefly seen the van, but not the impact, and they would look at security footage to get what they needed. Perhaps that was why the cop was bored, or annoyed, or whatever. Eyewitness accounts were unnecessary. Still, the poor young man's blood was on her skin now, a part of her, and this guy didn't even care.

After a few minutes, the policeman was finished with her. She gave a quick look around, saw that the restaurant staff were all occupied with one another, and made her escape.

She walked back alone, certain no one would follow her. Once safe in her hotel room, Tildy checked social media.

Life is short <3, Jordie had posted.

Orla had responded with a sad face.

Ben, his location tagged as Florida, exclaimed, *What happened?*

The restaurant's account apologized for the cancellations and promised a refund for the evening, encouraging everyone to drive more safely, particularly in the city center.

Tildy lay back on her bed and wondered how she would sleep. She dragged over her backpack. The net and cap were inside, waiting. How many times was it now? Five? Six?

She held the net aloft in one hand, the light from the dated sconces catching in the iridescent bulbs at the ends of the wires. Within those were electrodes, a faint glitter on their surface. What would happen if she dreamed of him now, having seen him?

Life is short, she agreed. And dangerous. And not good enough.

She set the cap on her head, shut off the light, and closed her eyes. She remembered what had happened in her last dream, willing herself to return.

chapter
sixteen

The directions to Katherine's house were quite clear. Her parents lived in a suburban beach town just west of the city. Tildy squinted against the sunlight, such a contrast to the dark of her room.

No, not her hotel room, she told herself. Forget the hotel room. She was here, now, driving down the block, reading the house numbers.

Some houses looked more art commune than residential, with sculptures and murals of dubious quality decorating the front gardens. Others were so traditional you could imagine the doilies on the polished wooden tables within. The slight slope of the street made it possible for the upper stories to have an unobstructed view of the water. A man had his back to Tildy, carefully watering his flower boxes, while a woman down the street took in the view while talking on her cell phone. It was a beautiful and understated place. Her mom would have loved it.

Tildy parked, then went around the passenger door to grab the neatly tied pastry box. Colm had suggested the shop and what items to bring. Careful to keep the delicate treats from smushing one another, she made her way up the walkway to Katherine's parents' home and rang the bell.

A dog yipped, the sliding noises of claws on tile as it scampered in excitement, followed by a woman's voice. "Henry, be quiet now, you rascal." Approaching footfalls rattled something within, and the door swung open. A warm, kind woman greeted her.

"Hallo! Tildy, is it? Come in, come in, it's fierce cold. Give me those, now. And your coat, love. Aren't you a darling."

She flushed, unable to conjure speech amid such effusive praise. Colm appeared at the top of the stairs and descended a few steps. He stayed still, waiting for the dog and his girlfriend's mother to take a breath.

"My name is Maggie, I'm Katherine's mum. She's resting upstairs waiting for you. Oh, here's Colm. Would you like some tea, love?"

"Yes, please."

"I've just got the kettle on—you two go back to Katie,

and I'll bring it all up. Go on now."

Colm waved Tildy upstairs and disappeared.

She did not move.

An ache bloomed in her. None of this was real. She wasn't here. There was no cup of tea, no appreciation, no friendly faces to greet her. She'd go upstairs and down the short carpeted hall to an opened doorway. Beyond, she'd find what her mind had guessed she'd find, from the backgrounds of selfies and photos of Henry the dog. A bedroom, styled with teenage Katherine's interests from a decade earlier, perfectly preserved in a way only a loving parent would maintain. The walls would be papered with Polaroid photos, posters, simple anime drawings, and notes from friends. Across from the window, a makeup desk with a mirror would shine the light back, itself glittering with a layer of stickers. Beneath it all would be vestiges of an even earlier princess phase, frilly purple curtains and a light switch resembling a unicorn.

And none of it would be real. It wasn't real.

She could stay and talk to her, and hear her sorrows and her fears, and share her own pain. She could see Colm's love for Katherine, and decide to slip downstairs and accept tea from Maggie. And none of it would change anything in Tildy's life. This was a playground she had built for herself, not a reality to take the place of what she was evading.

Tildy turned around and left the scene behind.

Outside it was silent, the street nearly still. No birds sang, the clouds did not move. The world had frozen. The neighbor who had been watering his lawn now stood inert, turned her way. Tildy could see now that he was faceless, his black hair slicked back to reveal a widow's peak. The hose he held dripped at his feet. The woman on her cell phone seemed at first glance to have disappeared. But Tildy squinted and saw her – she had morphed into a tree, the transformation incomplete. The left side of her brightly colored clothing was still visible, as was her hand that clutched the cell phone. The rest of her blended from flesh and cloth into the bark of a tree trunk. She averted her eyes from the woman. Maybe if she looked away, the dream would finish what it had started.

As she scanned the neighborhood again, she saw that the faceless man had dropped the hose and turned towards her. Tildy shut her eyes to this growing nightmare. The dream gave her a meaningful, invisible tug. Return indoors, it seemed to say. If not, it promised worse than this.

But she refused. She couldn't learn anything from the cozy story in that house. She'd rather wake up, if it came to that. She walked back to her car, hoping the door handle would still be there. She kept her eyes from the man as she hurried. Despite her attempt at bravery, her mind scrambled. What if he turned, what if he rushed over with that beige nothingness where eyes should be and he grabbed her and made her stare into it. She threw open her car door and fell into the driver's seat. She locked the doors and looked outside. The man was gone. Where had he gone, she wondered.

The world slowly began to move again. Raindrops splattered on her windshield, first as pinpoints of refracted light, then accumulating into something she could not see through. She started her phone's navigation to Nana's. Yes, Nana would keep her safe. She started the car's wipers. She had to deliver the groceries to her anyway. The groceries on her passenger seat, that had been there this whole time. Yes, she remembered now. She had dropped off the pastries for Katherine, said goodbye, and was now on her way to Nana.

While there, she'd talk this through. Someone had to help her. There had to be someone who cared for her, somewhere. She prepared to put the car into gear when the hair at the nape of her neck stood on end. Someone was behind her. The man, the faceless man, where was he? She knew now. She knew he was in the back seat.

Tildy woke with a start, clutching her comforter.

Silence. Stillness.

She was ok, she told herself. Everything was ok. Her heart raced and she tried to steady it. She placed a hand to her collarbones. The pressure of her inward breaths counterbalanced the pressure of her own hand. She tugged the cap off her head and laid back into the pillows. Her gaze drifted to where her bathroom door stood ajar, the deep darkness a sliver in the grey room.

Tildy flicked on her lamp.

There would be no sleep for her until morning. She'd rest, with the light on, with an eye to the door. Just in case.

The next morning, Tildy left the hotel for the car rental shop. Just as in her dream, automatics used by Americans for a recent film were available. It must've been a detail she had seen on the reviews for the location. She selected one and drove it out of the city. She looked for the faceless man, among the pedestrians, behind the steering wheels of passing cars, as she took the same route to Nana's. When she had used the dream machine before, the edges of awake and asleep had been clearly defined. That was no longer true.

Out of the city, through Moycullen and Oughterard, Lough Corrib glistening in the sunlight with the brown-green hills beyond. The vivid detail was more than she had dreamed. It settled her, to drive past sheep that were a little too dirty, uneven white stone walls, and empty beer cans in the waterways. It was all as before, but without any intention to please her.

She took the Maam Crossing and passed the cottage with the rusted roof. She continued on. It was the same, though longer and bumpier. She had never driven in Ireland in her life, yet now she felt at ease. Her muscles knew how to move, knew the turns and the way to stay in her lane. She'd have to tell Evelyn about this detail.

The road for Nana's house emerged at the bottom of a slight hill, and Tildy took the turn. Map imaging didn't exist for this road, and it was more dilapidated than she had expected. A fast-food cup and some other trash had been dumped into a large, overgrown bush at the edge of the road. She drove by and cringed as it scraped alongside the car. She looked back at the trash as she creeped on down the road, then threw the car into park. She hopped out and grabbed the trash. Birds nested in those bushes, and trash and over trimming destroyed their habitat. Maybe one day, Nana could teach her how to trim a shrub like that back without disturbing the birds. One day. For now, she could collect the garbage.

The peak of her nana's cottage appeared, and Tildy steeled herself. She slowed the car and pulled off the road, across the metal gate. She put the car into park and turned off the engine and waited a moment. It was important that her mind, all of it, paid attention to what she knew she'd find. She got out and leaned against the gate, chained shut, as the disused cottage stared back at her.

How long had it been since Nana had stood in that doorway to greet a guest? Five years? And already her lovely garden had grown feral, and the whitewash of the walls was chipped away in great patches. The breeze from the ocean carried across the abandoned land as if to greet her. As if to admonish her for what things had come to.

She ignored the ominous chain and lock. This was still her family's land. With more persistence than skill, Tildy hopped the fence and walked to the doorway. All the photos and china were gone, neatly packed long ago, but the large china cabinet was still there. It was clean inside, even in the fireplace. She stepped back and looked up, realizing someone had sealed the top of the chimney.

She went around back to the empty sunroom. Many of the delicate flowers her grandmother loved so much were dead. Wild strawberries spread across the ground. A pot she had painted with her mother stood alone in a corner, the soil inside pale crumbles. Out in the garden, their cherry tree was gone, fallen over in some long-ago storm. She walked over to the spot and found chips of wood, no longer fresh. No, they were weathered from the rain and wind. Had Aidan taken down the tree?

A white sedan slowly moved down the road. Everyone knew everyone here, and a strange car would arouse suspicion. They had likely messaged one another on a group text app. Tildy turned back to the front, ready to wave a greeting. The car stopped at the entrance to Nana's drive, and the driver stood out of the car, a hand up to block her face from the sun.

"Tildy? My goodness, is that really you?"

"Oh," Tildy blushed. "Hi there, Mrs. Coyne."

"For a moment I thought you were... nevermind that now. We just had Aidan by this morning, and he didn't say you were in town!"

"I just arrived."

"Won't you come round? Are you off somewhere?"

"No, I came to see…" Tildy drifted off.

Mrs. Coyne nodded. "Come to ours, I'll put the kettle on."

Before she could protest, her mother's cousin got back

into her car and pulled ahead, waiting for her to follow. With a silent grumble, Tildy climbed over the fence and then into her own car. She followed to the home down the road. The bumps in the road hadn't changed, though the homes on either side had new windows and solar panels and satellite dishes and modern cars. One was completely replaced with what could only be described as a McMansion.

The familiar home was in view, and Tildy sighed in longing. The great alder tree, large even when she was a girl, still stood shading the front drive of the house. She drove up the hill, past flowers and gorse and guelder rose, down the drive, and pulled into the parking spot for guests. She recalled the sounds of screeching excitement that would come from the house when she met her cousins here as a child.

She also remembered the day she and her mother had come over to the Coynes' to meet the local boy and girl they had taken in. The moment she had first seen him was lost to her now. What she did remember was the kindness of her mother's cousin, and her husband, to take in two more teenagers when they were already dealing with their own children.

As she stared ahead to a great hawthorn tree, there was another memory that came to her, of a time years later. A secret nighttime excursion, one so out of place of her character that she had entirely forgotten it. Tildy had woken in the middle of the night, possessed by the notion she was someone else, the kind of someone who tapped on a boy's window at night and let herself into his room. But beneath that hawthorn tree, she'd looked up at the dark house and stared at the black gloss of his window. She imagined him there, alone and warm, and she felt her bones hum with anticipation. Then, she lost her nerve. She'd run right back to Nana's, over the fields, giggling all the way back.

Out of her own car, at the same walkway, Mrs. Coyne waited to greet her.

"Give me a hug now, ma chara. How you've grown."

After the embrace, Tildy helped with the groceries.

"That one is a bit heavy now, I'm salting some beef."

The women entered the home, which was mostly the same as before, though it felt smaller and less vibrant. Fewer toys littered the surfaces, and fewer shoes crowded the corners. A border collie walked uncertainly over, wagging a tentative greeting. He was unknown to Tildy. She had expected the Coyne's last dog, a red collie named the Countess.

"You haven't met Samson yet! We lost poor Tess only two years ago. Samson was her pup."

"Oh, Countess. I didn't know. She lived a long time," Tildy said, greeting the dog.

"Feed a dog only fresh foods, eggs in the morning, liver at night, give them lots of love, and they'll live forever. Come on into the kitchen, that lazy oaf will follow to see if there are any nibbles for him."

The same stools stood at the same counter, and without a thought she took her usual place. Mrs. Coyne noticed and let out a sigh of happiness.

"Well now. It is good to see you, loveen. How long are you visiting?"

"I'm not sure. Thinking of moving here, actually."

"Are you now? I wish Helena would do the same, but of course she and her husband make such good money, and they wouldn't be tied down here. Too much adventure in them. Did you hear of her baby? My first grandson, well, adopted grandson, yes. She sent me new photos just this morning." She lowered her glasses to search through her smartphone for the correct image. Tildy swallowed at the evidence of aging in the gesture. Mrs. Coyne set the device down, showing a picture of a chubby, happy baby caught mid-laughter while petting a rabbit.

"He's adorable!"

"A proper sutach, is he not!"

She smiled, unsure what the word meant. "What's his name?"

"Oisín. A lovely name, a challenge to pronounce, even people here muddle it up. It is her baby, of course, so I kept my thoughts to myself."

She set out cups for the tea. Tildy looked at the woman's skin, seeking out more changes. Mrs. Coyne and her mother had been born within a month of one another. Her mother would look like her now, had she lived. Reading glasses and streaks of silver, some age spots where the sun shines the most, but otherwise the same. Her heart twisted.

Mrs. Coyne looked at her and paused. Something like the buildup to a question followed, each waiting in anticipation of it.

"Have you seen much of Aidan?"

His finger tracing a drop of water on my neck.

"I saw him yesterday. There was an accident in front of the restaurant."

Mrs. Coyne huffed. "The maniacs driving in that city, scares me half to death. Did you know, I had reservations there that night, poor little thing called in tears to tell me it was off, so I called Aidan straight away to see if he was well. Tildy, my dear. I didn't know you were there! He said nothing about it."

She stayed silent.

After a pause, Mrs. Coyne leaned over and took her hand. "That must have been so hard for *you*, dearest."

Suddenly seen, Tildy blushed. "I knew what to do, at least."

Mrs. Coyne bent her head low, as if the two women would pray together at her kitchen island. "I miss your mother so very much. Those last months—I wish I could forget it all." The older woman's voice was choked with emotion as she let go of Tildy's hand and turned away to pour tea.

"I never thanked you for coming after her fall. And to the funeral."

"Not at all. It was your father's office to thank me." The hint of anger in her voice told Tildy she, too, had not forgotten her father's frequent absences. Recovering herself, Mrs. Coyne smiled and handed her a teacup. "You're here now. And I want to hear what you've been doing all these long years! Dierdre says you work in software."

After a half hour recounting her career, the sounds of the front door interrupted them. The deep voice of Mr. Coyne carried in, his words a mix of Irish and English as the vibration of heavy boots hit the floor and rumbled the house.

"Michael, Tildy is here!"

A surprised grunt, loaded with meaning, was the first reply.

"A Tildy, fáilte ar ais! Is fada an lá ó chonaic mé thú! Came all the long way from the States, did you." The man came after his voice. He was a scruffier, thicker, grayer version of the man she remembered. He still looked healthy and strong, like the man who had taken in Aidan and his sister as teenagers. "Well, look at you. Bee, this little one has grown. Tá siad tar éis fás aníos os comhair ár súl! Right, now, I'd give a squeeze, but I'm covered in muck." He kissed his wife, gave her an inquiring look, and headed upstairs.

Aidan had told the Coynes about them. Tildy had suspected he would; they were the closest thing he and his sister had to family.

Mrs. Coyne shook her head. "Men. Tactless. Come with me and see my paintings. Leave the cup, loveen, you're a guest."

"You paint?"

"Took it up after your mother. She used to paint, you know. That and running were the only things that helped with the seizures. After she passed, I thought I'd give it a try and it stuck."

The old nursery had been converted to an art studio, the curtains pulled permanently aside to let in all available light. Seascapes, the famous lighthouse, wildflowers, and rows of houses were the primary subjects.

"These are lovely."

"Thank you," Mrs. Coyne said without enthusiasm, picking up one example. "Not my best, nor interesting, but they're the ones that sell. I take them to market days, a shop in Kinsale sells them, too. Tourists love them. This, here, is one I'm proud of. I'm working on it for Aidan. He liked one I made in the style, so I thought perhaps this one would do for his restaurant."

Shades of blue, transitioning from the darkest at the top to the lightest, joined with shades of magenta, a similar gradient moving upward to meet in faint combinations of purple at the center. Tildy nearly laughed.

"Do you like it?" Mrs. Coyne asked.

"Oh yes, it is beautiful. Are you able to sell ones like this, too?"

"On a service online, one of these silly names. Seánie signed me up. I've sold a few, not nearly as easily as the landscapes."

"I'd love to buy one, once I'm settled. Especially if I stay," Tildy sighed.

"Your mother's paintings were stunning. I'll show you. First, this here is my try at Oisín."

She presented to Tildy a rough drawing of a vaguely

baby-shaped object on a plain canvas. "Don't you laugh and don't you say a word, it's dreadful. Now, your mother gave me this, come here." Mrs. Coyne took Tildy's hand and guided her to a formal sitting room, where a painting of a girl and a baby in the grass hung above the tufted sofa. The children were painted with hyperrealism, while the background was impressionist in style. Her son Niall's charming smirk came through, as well as his older sister Fionnuala's spunky defiance.

"In no time, she did that. Maybe a month, and from a Polaroid. Gorgeous."

Tears threatened to emerge. Tildy didn't have the energy to fight them. "I didn't know she painted. I wish I could've seen her paint."

"Give me some time, I'll find one she made of you. Your nana packed them all away after the funeral. I think she was too heartbroken and angry, as we all were, of course. But you can't push away the good to escape the bad."

Mrs. Coyne touched Tildy's cheek. "You have her eyes. Dark blue, almost like circles of the night sky. Come close, don't cry oo."

Tildy accepted the embrace. She appreciated the gesture, and tried to take comfort from it.

There would be no more socializing for the evening. The emotional tension of the day had asked too much of her. She was back at the hotel after a short trip out to collect a bag of takeout Indian food and two bottles of cider. Tonight she would glory in the comfort of ignoring her sisters' text messages, and her methods of celebration were to eat too much food, drink alone, and watch recaps of GAA matches, or reality television, or a sappy movie, and gawk at attractive people.

Her pajamas, warmest socks, and hoodie embraced her like old friends. Tildy laid her spread out on the bed, with a towel underneath, and opened up her foiled cherry naan and her carton of tikka masala chicken and pilau. At the farthest edge, she opened her laptop. Her first bite was far too hot, and she turned aside from her food to allow it to cool. Following an impulse, she decided to look up hurling. What she knew of it was superficial, gleaned from hearing cousins and summertime friends talk to one another.

One search, then another, led to admiring photos of players rather than learning tactical playing styles. That done, she tested her food again. It was finally cool enough to take small bites. She still couldn't decide what to watch, and Aidan's name cartwheeled into her mental suggestions.

She rejected that. She didn't know much about taxes. She could learn about taxes.

Him in the kitchen, kneading the dough for his famous bread.

Tildy rubbed her face. She could learn about politics. There must be something she could watch about politics.

He had recognized her instantly at the restaurant, despite the years that had passed and the march each one had made across her face. A thought occurred to her. She entered her own name into the search bar.

Gala photos with her sister and father, charity events without her in them, the staff page for her last job, evidence of her long-closed social media accounts, low-resolution photos. Posts from a gossip rag about her mother's death that included her and her sisters' names. A group photo from her graduate program, her awkwardness in the photo feeling very current and not a remnant of a youthful past. The results also included quotes she had provided for news articles. There was one flattering photo: her, Gisele, and her father four years ago. Her father and sister posed with a celebrity, while Tildy was in the background, talking to someone else.

What would Aidan think, looking at all of this? Do I look like someone worth remembering?

She opened a new tab and loaded a video streaming service. This was not how her evening was going to go.

How he looked in the moonlight on their walk, the softness of his lips, the want in his eyes. That was the same look he'd given her in the kitchen after all. It was longing. For her—small her, quiet her, the her who had left him heartbroken all those years ago. The smell on his sweater, the way he looked down and away from people, his shyness not yet overcome, whenever he laughed. The real and pretend had blended together so easily. When so many people here were different, he was the same within the dream and outside of it.

Tildy frantically scrolled. A show on luxury houses was suggested by the algorithm, and she jumped in. The first episode loaded after a moment: a good-looking, if not a bit traditional, eager white British man in a safety vest pontificated on the glories of the Mediterranean from a sailboat. His enthusiasm would have been ridiculous in someone less earnest. Well, more ridiculous.

By the bottom of the chicken carton and the last bit of naan, she had developed a list of countries she wanted to see and an equally long list of people she did not want to become. Most of the houses were lovely, while some were garish, but the owners ranged from glory-seeking snobs to rich couples with a VISION. It didn't really concern her what their motivation was—a homeowner who installed a floating staircase when they had a toddler was committing architectural infanticide.

The abandoned tab, the one leading to a search engine, called softly. Just an image search, it suggested. Something to ease the curiosity a bit. It was already an incognito tab, no one would know, it promised. Having the internet meant private access to information on anyone or anything without the social costs. And Tildy knew the psychological mechanisms for why she felt the way she did. She had researched it for work and regularly resisted it, yet here she was, being goaded by her libido into an image search.

She sighed, not wanting to follow that path. She also didn't want to see more mansions. She had already watched all the nature documentaries, the monarchy intrigue shows, and a few police dramas. The other tab called, another part of her brain suggesting a different search. With slightly trembling fingers, Tildy entered her mother's name along with a new word: *painting*. There were several results. She opened her second cider. She'd need this first.

A painting in a room featured in a design article. The space was too bright and held an obligatory leather Eames lounger with matching footrest, furniture with brass details, an impractical rug, and a cocky houseplant. More importantly, it had her mother's painting on a credenza, each color of the surreal landscape represented in the furnishings. It wasn't clear from the article if her mother's piece or the room design had been the starting point, but the painting, with its square trees, angular animals, and specific color choices, fit perfectly.

Another painting was being sold on an art retailer website for a few hundred euro. It wasn't a landscape, but a building, shrouded in snow and surrounded by black trees, branches barren of leaves encircling the structure. What had been on her mind, Tildy wondered, as she painted this dark image? Was it Santa Fe, or what their time in Santa Fe represented?

Next was a private commission, perhaps the earliest of the three. It was an image described within a blog post by the daughter of the subject. The original photo and the painting were compared side-by-side in the entry. It startled her—the photo was bland, just of a young woman with sad eyes and wavy hair, lost in thought, her hand holding up her head at an uncomfortable angle. But the painting somehow captured that sadness, enhanced it, and made the whole presentation beautiful with colors and background imagery.

Tildy sat back, drinking her cider and looking at the digital images of her mother's paintings. There wasn't much in the way of visual artistry in her own toolbox; she just appreciated art, quietly and without much taste. Yet her mother's work seemed special, unique. She had never gotten to know this side of her mom. Perhaps her mother had thought it would keep, would be revived after her children left home.

"Oh, Mom," she said to the empty room. It did not reply.

chapter
seventeen

The next morning, Tildy jogged toward the lighthouse, not quite reaching it. The Indian food and ciders weighed her down. Still, at least she had exercised. A shower followed, more bitter cold thaan refreshingly brisk.

Still in her towel, she took out her phone and sat on the bed. She needed to call Nana. It had to be done.

"Deidre anseo."

"Hi, Nana. It's Tildy."

"Oh, Tildy. Yes, well, hello to you."

The familiar cold bite of her tone was even sharper now. Was it the contrast? Had she made it worse, by imagining better?

"Hi. I'm in town—I was wondering if I could visit."

"Visit? Certainly. And when would you like to do that."

"Are you free today? Or tomorrow or the next day? I don't have any plans."

Her nana sighed. Tildy braced herself.

"I'm quite busy. I can make time for you tomorrow at lunch. You'll need to bring your own meal, I have nothing for you."

"Of course. Would you like me to bring you anything?"

"Cad? Céard a bheadh ag teastáil uaim?" Nana said sharply.

"Is there anything you need I can pick up for you."

"I'm perfectly well, thank you."

Tildy considered apologizing for offending her, then abandoned the notion. It would only offend her more.

"I'll see you at lunchtime tomorrow, then."

"Yes, fine." The phone clicked before she could say goodbye.

For a moment, she wondered what she would do today. She could go clothes shopping, but for what occasion? She considered visiting Katherine, then shook her head and tried to laugh at the thought. That was a dream. There was no connection between them. The Tildy that was here and real was not wanted there. Or anywhere. She walked to the window and looked out at the view. She could go to the museum.

She dressed with gentle care, not for show, but for herself. It was a way to give herself love without asking for the world's permission. She left the hotel unnoticed and walked down toward Spanish Arch. While stopped at a light, she watched schoolchildren in uniforms pass by on the sidewalk, gossiping and listening to loud music on their cell phones. Other children, in a different-colored uniform, walked the opposite direction, the groups exchanging words that didn't sound friendly.

The light changed and she proceeded, following the route she had mapped before setting out. The shops were open but not busy. It was too cold, and early in the week, for many tourists to roam about. There were locals running errands and a few people like her, killing time while they waited for something else to happen.

Tildy stopped in a café for a tea and scone. She carried her items to an outside table and took out her phone.

⊙ Gisele: WHERE ARE YOU?? We are meeting with the Twombleys in an HOUR.

⊙ Evelyn: Been a while since our last check in. How are you feeling?

⊙ Aloxandra: George's class needs a field trip chaperone, can you take tomorrow off?

⊙ Jude: Hey, where'd you go?

Tildy closed the message app and made sure her location wasn't shared with anyone. She took a bite of scone and felt relief. She'd rather be alone and unwanted here than suffocated and demanded there.

A young man emerged with two drink carriers and looked around for a place to adjust them before he continued on his way. Without asking, he set the drinks on her little table and put on his gloves. She looked up and smiled. "Hey, Jordie."

"Oh! Hello to you, and you remembered my name! I'm shite with names. Tildy, was it?"

She nodded.

"What are you doing sitting out in this cold?"

She looked around. "I like the quiet."

Jordie shook his head. "You Americans are mad. If you aren't busy, will you help me get these to the car? I have two more I left inside. I don't know what the feck I was thinking, volunteering to do the teas."

She ate the rest of her scone and brushed away the crumbs. He exited with another drink holder, with a spot available for her tea. She carried one and he the other as they walked toward the parking garage.

"You have a meeting at the restaurant?"

"What? Oh, no. We're foraging."

Tildy paused, in hopes he would voluntarily provide an explanation. He did not. "Foraging?"

"Sure, the restaurant is all local ingredients. We go around to farms or the beaches left wild to gather things for cooking."

"That's really cool," she said.

"It's a lot of work, is what it is. Most of the customers couldn't give a flying rat's arse. And in this weather. I should've been a solicitor."

"Sounds like you need a holiday."

"I have been saying this! My boyfriend doesn't care. He's so concerned with things like making rent and affording food, he doesn't give me what I need. I should introduce you. You can argue for me."

Tildy kept her reply friendly and simple, wary of herself. "You should tell him you have a somber anniversary coming up. A pet's death. It hit you hard, you need to embrace life."

"A pet's death? Crafty. I like the way you think. Ah, this is me."

She helped him set the drink carriers in the car, then smiled and gave a little wave.

"You know, what are you up to today?"

"Me? Oh, I was going to the museum."

"The MUSEUM. Girl, why would you be going to the museum? You could be helping me get this cold weather expedition finished before I freeze myself to death. Come with me and we'll be done in half the time."

"I don't know how to forage—it wouldn't possibly be half the time."

"What are you, a mathematician? Half the time, three-quarters of the time. It's less time. Get in, get in."

Tildy was at war with herself; she didn't want to be rude, and she didn't want to force herself into Aidan's presence. Worse, this was Aidan's work and she'd have no way to leave without him or his employees shuttling her back to the city.

Jordie was already shuffling around extra hoodies, test menus, and empty water bottles to make his front seat available. She balled her fists, told herself to pull it together, and settled in, not minding the mess. It was a clean mess and not offensive in the least, and not at the top of her thoughts in any case.

He started the car and put his hands in front of the vents for heat. "Me lady, any musical requests?"

"None at all."

"That's what I like to hear. You'll be a welcome addition to the group. The soundtrack to *Chicago* it is."

As they traveled, Tildy felt her apprehension grow. She hadn't thought this through. Sure, she was in a car with a stranger, and that should have alarmed her. But they were traveling her route to Nana's village, and as they continued, they got very near to Nana's house. Then they passed her road, moving farther up the coast. An old white sign stood out, pointing toward the water. They pulled up to a deserted farm where other cars had parked. People she knew, but did not know, stood around preparing. Somewhere out there was Aidan. Was he in the sweater from her dream? Did it smell the same?

As she put her hair up to fend off the strong wind, Jordie popped out of the car and called, "Tea's on!"

As he set cups out on the roof, Orla frowned. "Jordie, why didn't you bring a thermos of tea?"

He stared at the assortment of cups in dismay.

"You poor eejit."

With a flourish, he removed one of the cups and said, "This one was yours, Orla—and now? It goes into the bay.

Drink fetid water for all I care."

She took the cup from him and walked away, calling "I love you!"

"Maria, I've brought my new mate Tildy to help. You've any spare bags?"

"Just in my car, boot is unlocked. Get Colm sorted, will you?"

Jordie walked Tildy to Maria's car and greeted Colm, who stood aside nervously. She watched them all in stunned silence. They didn't know her, she didn't know them, and yet it was like reliving events that had already happened. Only this time, everyone was more muted. The friends of the dream machine were exuberant and chaotic and warm. The content they posted to social media showed them in their best moments. In real life, they were normal adults who did not know Tildy. What was going to happen next? Would it be the same between them? Or had it always been a private intoxication and an impossible reality?

Jordie took out nine clear plastic bags and divided them evenly between himself and his trainees. He was suddenly serious and intent on their task.

"Alright? Now, we're here to collect seaweed. Little you may know that seaweed is a critical plant for survival here on Ireland. Loads of calcium, vitamins, metals you need, none of the ones you don't want. At least, not the seaweed that grows here. Aidan had it tested for mercury and the like. The most important thing is to only collect one type. Don't introduce other plants into the bag. If you aren't sure, ask or keep it out. I know you're listening to me, Colm. Tildy, you look steady. Just know a wrong bit will ruin the flavor."

Colm nodded, opened one bag, and sniffed inside. Jordie looked at him in astonishment.

"What is that, then? It's a clean bag, you half lad."

"It could have preservatives."

"Preservatives?" Jordie's voice raised an octave. "What kind of operation do you think this is?"

Jordie and Colm continued to bicker as they walked away from the road and deeper into a field, the bay spread out ahead of them.

Tildy listened as she turned to follow, then froze. Her mouth fell open at the strong beauty before her. The water moved here, sparkling dark blue with distant crests of waves, the faraway hills shadowy swoops on the horizon. It was a view that belonged only to them, and the ghosts of those who lived in the cottage that had crumbled behind her.

"Whose land is this?"

"Oh, someone in Dublin," Jordie said. "No one uses it now. As long as we don't set fires or build on it, they pay us no mind. Alright, Maria? Where's Aidan? He on mussels?"

"He's waiting for the tide to shift. He's down at water's edge—some of that moss he loves is coming in nicely."

Tildy turned in the indicated direction, as if she could see him and prepare herself. A nervous shiver took hold, but she managed to quell it.

"Let's go say hi," Jordie said brightly.

They walked that way until Maria called out in an exasperated tone. "Oi, arsehole. I can't be the only one collecting here, Jordie. Leave me Colm at least."

"At least?" Colm asked weakly.

"Sure fine, go on now, there's a lad."

Jordie waved Tildy to follow him, the soil turning sandy as they approached the shore of the bay. Huge rocks, covered in moss, rose out of the ground in greater volume as they got near. Aidan and Seán stood in tall boots, scanning for worthy additions to their collections. Seán saw them first and he seemed to register her as a young woman he didn't know yet. His reflective sunglasses shimmering as he passed an arm casually over his forehead to clear away water spray. He was wearing a black-and-white striped tank top and well-fitted trousers, his casual, attractive look let down a bit by the high, bright boots he was using to stand in the shallow water. Though he scrutinized her, Tildy only gave him a moment's attention.

Aidan looked to them and stilled. She paused, caught in the intensity of his attention. His eyes were steady, full of a meaning she wished to define. Then he turned away from her.

Tildy frowned at her feet as she walked, feeling angry and stupid, holding her little empty evidence bags. Jordie didn't seem to notice any tension.

"Alright, Seán, Aidan."

"Hiya, Jord."

"I brought the teas. Katherine isn't well enough, should

be better soon though. Seán, this is Tildy."

He moved over in a slightly lumbering way, though trying to be smooth about it. "The American? Sure, I heard you saved a man's life."

She didn't know how to reply. Her thoughts had been flung backward, and suddenly, her hands felt the softness of the stranger's skull, her eyes saw the red blooming across the threads of her scarf.

"I hope he lived," she said softly.

Seán brushed back his hair and smiled. "You have that angelic look—of course you saved him."

When Tildy responded to the maneuver with blank weariness, Jordie laughed. "I see you know about our Seán, then."

"I do. He doesn't remember me. One of the last times I saw him, he pushed me into a pool at Leisureland during one of his lifeguard training classes."

"I did what now?"

She blushed, hoping the cold air could serve as an excuse for it. It had been before Aidan had come to live with the Coynes, and the memory of tall, tan Seán noticing her enough to push her into a pool had been a shameful highlight of her early teens.

Seán frowned, looking at her. Then he grinned. "Hold on, you wouldn't be Gisele's little sister, from Kilkieran? What's it been now, five years? Six?"

"Collect what we need," Aidan interrupted with quiet authority. "Weather's changing."

Tildy scanned the sky. Despite Jordie's complaints, it was warmer on the coast than she'd expected, though not too warm for her jacket. The occasional cold gust and clouds on the far horizon threatened rain. It was the same summer warmth she remembered from her childhood. The days that led to stormy nights.

Looking back at Aidan, she tried to compose herself. She needed to grow up. She was a stranger to him. He didn't care about her. She had to gather seaweed, of some kind, and stuff it in a bag.

Once Seán had returned to his task, Tildy whispered to Jordie, "Okay, what do I do."

"Oh, I'll find a bit and show you, then you can work from there. Aidan, this whole section clear?"

"There's some farther up."

She started to follow Jordie, ready to learn more about seaweed, when Seán called, "Tildy, come see this."

Jordie looked at her with irritated sympathy, but left her behind. She turned back toward the water. Aidan's attention, if not his eyes, was on her as Seán held out a hand to help her across the rocks. The waves lapped the large stones, slick with moss and a sheen of water. She took his hand and stepped on the first one, his hand strong and smooth and unwanted in hers. She let him navigate her from rock to rock while he waded next to her, his high boots keeping him dry. When she was positioned on a large rock in the water, he pointed at a place where the sand bottom was visible through the underwater greenery.

"Do you see it?"

"What? What on earth is that?"

"It's dogfish skittering around just there, do you see them?"

"Oh! Are they sharks?" She crouched on her perch to see as close as she dared.

"Yes, exactly. They develop in sacs, you see them wash up in the kelp from time to time. Mermaid purses, some call them. We call them sparán na caillí mairbhe."

"A…" Tildy rummaged through her mind for the translation. "A witch's corpse something? What?"

Seán laughed. "Now how do ye be knowing what a witch is in the Irish, Tildy Halleran?"

"I heard a little kid call Nana a witch once."

They laughed together as they watched the dogfish dance through the silty water.

"So. Do you… eat them?"

"You can, though I wouldn't recommend it. Hardly worth the effort to skin them."

Tildy walked from rock to rock on a different route and found her return path had been poorly selected. The last rock was at an impossible angle. She looked back to the shore, unsure how she'd get there without help. "I can make it if I jump."

"The rocks won't make for a soft landing," Seán observed. "I'll lift you, if you'll let me."

"Um, sure."

He lifted her with only a little difficulty, his hands on

her waist strong and steady. She let out a laugh as he practically flung her to shore. The appeal of Seán made sense in that moment. Had she ever been lifted with such ease? Once, she recalled. Just once.

The landing jolted her, but she didn't fall over, though her long black hair broke free of her hasty bun, and the wind set it to life. She smiled and turned away from Seán, pushing the wild strands away from her face. She looked up and met Aidan's eye. He had paused his work and watched her now with some of the hardness she had come to expect. Her blush heightened and she lowered her eyes.

Seán seemed to sense the mood and hesitated a moment before he returned to his search, as did Aidan. Tildy retrieved her hair tie from the sand and left them both behind, walking along the rocky waterline in search of Jordie, the wind threatening to steal her little bags. He wasn't far. She found him examining shellfish, his bags of seaweed nearly full. At the sound of her approach, he rose and stretched his back, eyeing her with a smirk.

"You American girls, coming here and felling our poor simple Irish boys."

"Please."

"A bold one you are."

"Stop, I'm too old for him."

"Too old? You played as children, your own words!"

She searched for whatever it was she should be gathering.

"Driving the straights ab-so-lutely wild!"

"Oh, stop. Seán is flirtatious and always has been, even when we were kids. You should've seen how he chased my sister."

"She like you, then?"

"No, gorgeous. Tall, blonde hair, perfect body, perfect eyes."

"Hm. Dreadful. If you knew Seán, now, you must have known Aidan growing up then, too?"

"A long time ago," Tildy replied softly, putting her first large piece of seaweed into her bag.

"*Interesting.* Oh, that one is grand, look at it." Jordie held up his example, and she noted the shape and coloring, imprinting the details on her mind, hoping she could do this.

They passed a few moments of filling their bags in silence. Tildy still wasn't sure she was doing this correctly. She had seen at least four different types of seaweed, or seaweed-like things that could be what she should be collecting. She left a lot behind, wary of his warning to not ruin the flavors. Jordie continued on, moving with practiced efficiency. Of all the elements of her dreams, Jordie was the only true improvement over her imagination. He seemed the same yet more complete here. She would need to include these details when she went back.

A blush tore across her face at that thought. 'Here' was reality, she scolded herself. This was real. The Ireland of her dreams was false.

"You mentioned your boyfriend," she said conversationally, trying to throw off her train of thought. "What does he do?"

"He's a clerk in an office, going for a graduate degree. He's brilliant. You can tell, because he has no interest in any of this," Jordie said, waving seaweed at her.

"It's good to have different interests. Where did you meet?"

"Book club. He transferred to university midway through his program, hadn't met anyone yet, and used it to socialize."

"And you?"

"Men, of course."

She laughed. "Are book clubs good for finding men, then?"

"Well, I only needed the one, so the answer I give to that is absolutely."

Tildy laughed as she picked up a plant she thought would work. Jordie swatted it from her hand.

"And what of you? Any American men you've left wallowing in misery?"

"Uh, not really," she replied, thinking of Jude waiting for her outside the gallery, the scent of him as he leaned over to her in her father's penthouse. Of his offer to care for her, to maintain her connection to the only world she had ever truly belonged to.

"'Uh, not really,'" he mocked in a fake American accent. "A loaded answer if I ever heard one."

She paused her seaweed hunt and looked out over the water, hoping to see dolphins as she had a few times as a girl. There were none today, or none that she could see. She wondered if they still came here.

Jordie pulled up a long piece of seaweed. "Well now, this has a delightful name in Irish. Any guesses what it might be?"

Tildy looked at the plant. "I mean, am I allowed to say what it looks like? Because it looks like a penis."

"Yes! Look at it! A wee flaccid penis!"

While they were laughing, Jordie threw it out to sea, then looked at her bag. He made a noise. "What have you gone and done here! These are all the right species, but these need to go, and this too. You see here? The coloring isn't even on the stem."

The bag was now half empty, and Tildy sighed. He clicked his tongue.

"I think you might be hopeless at this. You and Bobby. That's a shame."

"How many years has Bobby been coming out here? Is there any hope for me?"

He paused, thoughtful, calculating. "Going on six years now. No hope for you at all, I'm afraid."

"Wow. Six years!"

"Feels like forever. We'd like to get married next year, but I don't see how that will happen. Aidan pays well, gives us days off, takes it easy on us. But the rents are impossible. And with Bobby in school, it's hard. Hard to make a living these days, or any days."

"Jor," Aidan called from a short distance up the beach. "Seán is checking traps. Go with him, will you?"

"Grand. I'm full up on seaweed."

"Hand them here—I'll stop off at the cooler."

They walked over to him, the rocky ground slippery and requiring their full attention as they approached. Jordie gave him the bags.

"Tildy, I'm driving to your nan's. I've some things to collect," Aidan said carelessly, sealing the bags as he spoke. Jordie shot her a wild-eyed, devious grin, then sauntered down the beach toward Seán.

She hesitated, suddenly feeling alone. The water crashed into the rocks. Tildy turned her gaze toward the bay, desperate for a way to say no. What if she could dive into the water and swim away from this moment? She could almost feel the cold sting of the water and the burn of her muscles as she took herself from this decision. From the thoughts of him in her dream, hailing her a cab, his gentle touch. She'd flown all the way out here only to see him, not to be seen, not to interfere. This was all going wrong, she decided. She should've stayed dreaming.

Resigned, she followed him.

He took her bag from her as well and looked inside. She blushed as he pulled out a piece and chucked it away. When they passed a lone cooler, he put the bags of seaweed inside and continued on to where the cars were parked. His was an older commercial van, with stickers that she assumed indicated it was registered to the business. Before climbing in himself, he unlocked the passenger door for her.

She stepped up into the van and buckled in. From the height of her seat, she could see Maria and Colm walking to rocky outcrops, foraging for whatever herbs they'd been instructed to find. The process had been fun, in a way. The seaweed she'd collected would be on a handcrafted plate in a delicately built meal. Well, some of the seaweed. The right pieces.

Aidan put on simple dark sunglasses from the dashboard. He yanked the column shifter down, and the van lurched forward. In a confident turn of the wheel, he drove off-road for a moment in order to complete his U-turn. Tildy gripped the overhead handle in fear.

"Best to do it quick," he said without apology.

Back to the roadway, he drove safely and she released her grasp of the handle. The van bumped along the backroads nestled between the hills and the gentle sweep of grass toward the beach and bay. The sparkling streaks of white on the water rippled in an endless rhythm as far as detail could be seen.

"God, it is beautiful here," Tildy murmured.

"It's a wonder anyone would leave it."

She let her forehead fall to the window with a slight thump, leaving a grease mark on the glass as a sign of her irritation. Sharp comebacks and retorts were swallowed down. They hadn't spoken in years, no matter what had happened in her dreams. She'd just have to face his anger all over again.

She kept her eyes from him, though she caught her own reflection in the sideview mirror. The seatbelt cut against her chest in an unflattering way, her hair was a disaster, and her face was flushed from the sea air. She wouldn't dare fix anything with him so close, but she would once she hopped out of the van.

They reached her nana's house shortly thereafter. It was as cold and desolate as her last visit. Her heart twisted at the silent, lonely place. It shouldn't be this way.

They climbed the gate into the back. He didn't offer to help her over.

"Do you see her much? How is she?"

Aidan shrugged. "She keeps things close."

Set an unnatural distance apart, they walked through the field, heading to the drop-off that led to the water. Trees planted by Tildy's great-grandfather, back when Nana was a baby, grew tall here, a windbreak to protect one section of the farm. It was the preferred solution for an ancient problem. The water beyond was not as lovely. The still pools were clear, but the water was silty and dark, more like an enormous lake with some marshy land.

"What are we looking for?"

"I'll find it myself."

The abruptness could've offended her, but the rejection in it was welcome. It was what she expected and deserved. Tildy walked away from him, toward the trees. They'd been a regular haunt in her early years. Perhaps there was something left, something to remind her of those happier times, before everything fell apart.

Past the first set of trees, a broken shard of a teacup peeped out of the undergrowth. She unearthed it with a finger. Pink rosebuds and gentle, pale green vines. She and her sisters had held tea parties for teddy bears in these trees. Tildy took it with her as she moved through the brush cautiously, scanning the ground, ready to pounce on any relics.

A window caught the light, shimmering through the darkness of the branches. Confused, she approached it. A small building, partly obscured by wild plants, its dark green paint chipped away by years of wind and rain. She searched her memories for this odd little structure but found none. A long-neglected stone pathway emerged, weaving toward the entrance. Sunlight dappled on the ground before her. A wooden door stood shut, with an old iron handle waiting patiently.

Tildy paused and checked behind her. She was alone. The trees felt close, looming, the wind whistling above but not reaching her skin here. Was this real? Was she in bed in New York? If she opened this door, would she wake there, alone in her room, and realize this was all another loop of dreaming? She tightened her coat around her. What if she couldn't tell the truth from the lie any longer?

With a shaking hand, she pulled on the great iron handle, and the door groaned then burst open, a puff of dust falling down from the doorway.

A dingy, uncovered window illuminated the inside.

A small sewing desk, with a lamp and a long-dried inkwell. In the far corners, other pieces of furniture and wooden crates, stacked on each other, some covered in white sheets. It was cleaner than she had expected, based on the dirt on the outside. A faded red rug lay across the floor, left where it had been positioned years earlier. It looked as though someone had converted this into an office, then used it as storage, never undoing the office setup. She set down her bit of china cup and wiped down the desk with a single hand, the wood beneath a rich, warm color with swirls of darkness. There was no chair with the desk.

Away from the door, beside the desk, Tildy could see her own graffiti, scrawled long ago. She crouched before it, touched the marks. She had been here, before her mind made memories. No warm sentiment bubbled in her, only pain and compassion for the child she had been. Her sisters had often played without her, and then in later years they refused to come to Ireland at all. They wanted to stay with their father, with their friends in New York and their summer camps in Connecticut. But Tildy had loved it here. Her mother had loved it here. This was where she'd wanted to be. Even if the summers had been lonely, it was better than her winters.

The drawing had two larger figures with a smaller figure. Her mother, her grandmother, and herself. Three generations of women, drawn by a child. If things had been different so long ago, if her mother hadn't suffered and then died, if her father hadn't had a heart too absorbed with himself, if, if, if. What might her life have been? Would she belong somewhere? Didn't the little girl who drew these things deserve love and safety, to know her place and be accepted there?

She heard Aidan approach. He crouched beside her, nearly touching her leg with his. The proximity set loose butterflies, swarming and swirling in her. She took her hand back from the drawing, holding it close to herself, as if it could contain the feelings inside.

He gently wiped the dust from the picture. Above the little figures was a drawing of a seascape, large rocks and distant hills, a sailboat on the waves.

"Almost looks like old man Oliver's boat."

"We used to watch him sail by. I never knew where he was going," Tildy said, her voice scratchy.

"Not sure he did either," Aidan said with a smile.

They rose. He brushed his hands clean and looked around the space. The light, golden from the yellowed glass, painted him in a celestial glow. He was so tall and strong, his movements so deliberate and calm. His shoulders dipped in his characteristic hunch, as if he was ashamed of his size, but when his gazed returned to her, he watched her with a confident inquiry.

Tildy backed away, as much from him as the feelings that threatened to capsize her. As ever, she could appreciate him best from a distance, where she could not hurt him, or be hurt by herself.

She stood near her drawing and held the desk with one

hand. If only she could make him treat her like a stranger, or a friend. She would be satisfied to admire, while meaning nothing to him at all.

"I don't remember this place," she said conversationally, as if oblivious to the moment they were in.

"I remember the outside," he said, his voice tense with restraint.

"Did you find your herbs?"

"I did, left them outside." He continued to look at her, his face unreadable. Tildy looked down, trying to keep her gaze from meeting his, but unable to draw it entirely away from him. His sleeves were rolled up. He had slight scars, lines from cooking pans and splatters from hot oil. She cleared her throat.

"How did you get wet?"

He looked down at his sleeves. "I washed up."

The implication of it made her gasp. She shifted her weight backward, just as Aidan stepped closer. He paused, his eyes wary and intent. She could see her body language confused him. That was no surprise. She had confused herself, too.

The sounds of the distant water and wind in the trees above hushed her. His hazel eyes stayed on hers, his pupils dilated as he looked at her with desire. Why not, her body whispered, as she blinked away tears.

Tildy stepped forward, unsure what was next. There was no time for her to plan at all; in a swift motion, Aidan put an arm around her waist and pulled her close. One of his hands held her face as he kissed her. Her knees went weak. He was kissing her! It started soft, questioning, waiting for her to withdraw. When she pushed her body against his, his lips parted hers, long-neglected hunger concentrated in one movement. His tongue greeted hers, his teeth nipping her lip in need. Tildy gripped his waistband, both to pull him close and to keep herself standing.

Aidan dipped his head and kissed her neck, his breath hot on her skin. Unsatisfied with her standing, he lifted her onto the desk, the wood creaking in protest. They kissed, only surfacing to breathe. With each gasp, she took in the smell of him. Fresh earth and things that grow. She grasped at his jacket, pulling him against her. His arms were steady and strong, cradling her body as he moaned into their kiss.

They broke apart for a moment, his breathing coarse. He rested his forehead on hers, his eyes shut.

"I dreamed of you," he said.

Tildy froze. Sobriety struck her in a moment.

"When?" she whispered.

Something in her tone made him look into her eyes, and what he found there gave him concern. She pulled away and took a breath.

How is this possible, she thought. *Has he been in my dreams? No, this must not be real. This isn't real.*

She scrambled from the desk and escaped from the little office and into the shadow of the trees. With her back to him, she discreetly pinched her arm again and again until the skin grew dark red and angry. Would that even work, she wondered. What would make her wake up?

"Did I say something wrong?" he asked.

"No."

He put himself in front of her, his hands in his pockets, his expression calm and imploring. The trees swayed in the gusts coming in from the water as the grass stayed still at their feet. Tildy stared at him.

"Is there someone else?"

She blinked. "What? No, no. There's no one."

Relief crossed his face, but the confusion remained. She couldn't bear to see his eyes again, that look of intense and patient interest, feelings she didn't deserve. She looked at his chest instead, the small piece of skin with faint chest hair between his collar bones. That didn't help. She walked around him, back toward the van, her arms crossed over herself, shivering despite her coat.

Aidan followed behind, the herbs he had gathered in his hand. As before, he unlocked the passenger door first, though this time he opened it for her and offered her a hand up. She took it. He seemed to sense her shiver through her grip and tried to make her look at him. She would not. She stared into the distance.

He climbed in and they set off the same way as before, though the atmosphere between them was something new. He remained quiet as they drove. Eyes averted from him, she looked at the bay. She imagined sailing a boat on that water, like the old man of her youth, and traveling to a smaller island or a faraway land. A place of no father, no sisters, no career, no men, where she had only herself to think of, only herself to answer to.

After a brief drive, they pulled back into the same spot as before. Aidan paused a moment before leaving the cab, an invitation for her to speak. But she couldn't speak to him. She wasn't sure this was real, here, now, but if it was, she was mortified to dumbness by her behavior. They watched as the crew carried buckets of shellfish back up to the road. Aidan let out a sigh, then hopped out and jogged over to help. Tildy climbed down from the van and lingered by the cars, unsure what to do with herself, wanting to help, unable to summon the willpower.

Orla came over and touched her arm. "That was some scene. How are you getting on? You have some medical training?"

"No," she said shyly. "Just some experience."

"If you hadn't been there, the fella's mates would've lifted him and bashed him once more, you can be sure of that now. So that experience is good thing, I suppose."

Tildy looked down at her hands, still pink at the corners of her palms that were least used. "I hope he'll be alright."

Orla nodded and continued on her way with her bucket. The others continued moving this way and that, busy around her as she stood still.

"Thanks for letting me join you all," Tildy said quietly. Jordie caught her eye. He could see something was wrong. He didn't miss much. Maria and Colm whispered to one another and looked at Aidan. They must have noticed something different about him. Maybe she had hurt him already. She wished she could wake up.

"I'll take Tildy. See you at the restaurant," Aidan called out.

Jordie looked to her, as if to see if she wanted saving. She smiled at him. It wasn't her safety she was worried about.

Once back in the van, she tried and failed to speak. Aidan was quiet as well. They remained that way until they reached the main road, curving through the hillsides. A hiker, alone and burdened with an enormous orange and gray backpack, walked along the side of the pavement. Aidan waved, and the man waved back.

"He's a long way from anyone," Tildy observed with some admiration.

"Siúlóid uaigneach," Aidan replied. "How long are you visiting, then?"

She looked down at her hands, then back out the window. "I'm not sure."

They remained silent for several minutes. The clouds brought their gray cast to the rolling hills in a slow wave. The storm that had been promised was now coming in. The white walls built during the Hunger, the ones she knew so well, continued their stoic stand to protect nothing from nowhere. Patches of exposed earth where peat had been harvested peeled back the verdant landscape in brown rectangular strips. Her nana had told her that some nights you could go to the hills here and see fires come out of nothing. Tine an mhadra rua, she called them. The phrase made Tildy think of the internet browser, not a mystical animal. She sighed. How could she have believed she would belong here?

"Surprised your father could spare you," Aidan said with some bite. She shut her eyes in relief. This hurt. This was what she deserved.

"He doesn't know I'm here."

Aidan frowned at the road. "Is your nana…?"

"No, she's well. I think she's well, anyway. She barely wants to see me, in any case."

Tildy took a deep breath and could smell him. He really did smell just like her dream. Salt water, fresh plants, sandalwood, soap, and something else. How had her sleeping mind known?

Her phone buzzed. She checked it, out of desire for escape. It was from Jude. *I miss you.*

She shut it immediately, but Aidan's grip on the steering wheel changed. He licked his lips and shook his head. "I guess you have big things waiting for you back in the States."

"Sure," she replied. "Big things."

Silence swept in, each in their own thoughts as they reached the highway. A family in a sedan passed, a little child in a car seat swinging a doll back and forth as the parents sang along to a song Tildy could not hear. The little car full of happy bliss drove by their slower van, leaving them behind.

"You don't want to hear it, I know. But I've been dreaming of you," he said. "Near every night. And when I wake, I think: if I see her again, I can't push her away. I can't lose the chance. And now, somehow, you're here. Just as the dreams promised. And you don't want to come in."

Tildy willed back the tears. She balled her fists and could not speak.

She looked at him, and his hands, which an hour earlier had cradled her face and were now white-knuckled on the steering wheel, far beyond her reach. What could she say to him? A thousand dark thoughts tumbled through her head. She imagined the days, the weeks, and the months of their potential future: the love he could give, yes. Love that would never be an obligation. But also the loss of certainty in her existence. The fear of losing what should never be hers.

The feelings came out in a shuddering sigh. No words formed themselves. There were only fears. For the rest of the drive, her voice went unused, her eyes sightless and pointed at the window.

Aidan drove to Eyre Square, near her hotel. She gathered her purse and coat, knowing what she should do. She should thank him, acknowledge all that was great and good in him, ask him to dinner, for a walk, to give him a chance, or to wish him well. Instead she stared out the windshield, frozen and sad. He remained equally quiet, his focus on her and her alone. She'd never forgive him for this patience.

Tildy opened the door, exited, and closed it behind her

without a word. She began her walk, tears now free to run down her face. The van pulled away from her at a reasonable pace, as if nothing were wrong. The tears that fell were not sobs, exactly. It was the relentless stream of pain she carried in physical form. There was no food, no drink, no guilty pleasure that would help her.

She passed by vacant storefronts. A vision of one possible future, one that belonged to a person she could never be, presented itself. Trips to a beach, a puppy to raise, a home together, children to love, shared accomplishments and stupid arguments and a hand to hold and a love to sustain when the outside world turned from summer to winter. She wanted to scream and fight herself, to fight her despair at the memories she carried inside that continued to hurt long after her father and sisters couldn't hurt her anymore, all of it working steadily to feed her heart only anguish and misery, until it would accept nothing else.

She knew now, knew that the intoxication of the dreams was that they were hers alone. She never had to face the responsibility of balancing all her flaws with her life in this place and the love she wanted to give him. And she couldn't do it. It was so much easier to dream.

Oblivious to the walk through the lobby and the ride in the elevator, she reached her room. She put back on her sweaty, discarded running clothes. She would not be languid in her run now.

Without any water, music, or preparation, her eyes raw from crying, she left the hotel again and ran to the path at the water's edge. She ran hard, faster than she should, pushing beyond care for sprains or falls or torn muscles. She would reach the end of the causeway today. There was nothing that mattered more than moving as fast as she could. A bicyclist passed her by, a challenge for her to chase. Her lungs burned, her ears began to ring, her eyes stung, and Tildy ran harder.

Minutes passed. It was the longest, the hardest she had ever run, and it wasn't enough. Her footfalls hurt her shins as she reached the Mutton Island causeway, the ocean spray on either side as she continued on, the wind pushing her left and right as she passed casual pedestrians and a young father walking with a toddler.

Her mind wandered as her body strained. Aidan's arms around her, his smile as he kissed her throat, the smell of him as his voice whispered in her ear. His passion for his work, his friendships, the love he had within his group, his care for her. Now she was experiencing his desire, and it hurt more because she knew she was unworthy of it. She wanted him, she acknowledged to herself, but at what cost to him, at what cost to her?

She'd collapse soon. Tears blinded her, her breathing erratic. Finally, mercifully, she reached the enormous access gate at the island. She slowed, turned around, and jogged back.

It took nearly half an hour to reach her hotel. She limped up the steps, through the lobby to the elevator. Soreness was already creeping into her muscles. Her reflection in the metal walls of the elevator was a blur, obscure and incomplete. Once in her room, she showered again. She put on her pajamas, closed the drapes, and put on the dream machine. She turned off the light.

chapter
eighteen

Tildy stood at her little cottage's sink, facing a window in a sparkling cascade of morning light. The damp dishes dripped in the drying rack. Her hands were wet, dripping as she held them midair. She had no idea what to do next. Was there a towel for drying them? Somewhere, she knew. In which drawer?

It didn't matter. She wiped them on her shirt and looked around. On a chair near the front door a blanket and towel waited. Yes, she had washed her dishes and was going to sit outside. Tildy took the items and passed through the doorway, the forest greeting her with the songs of unseen birds, the trickle of the nearby stream, and the rustle of the leaves in the wind. Once outside, she dried morning dew from a chair she had found half-hidden in a wild rosebush, then bundled herself in and stared at the small forest behind the cottage.

Light rainclouds were moving in, but the tree canopy kept her and the cottage mostly dry. The bright sunlight faded and raindrops hit the leaves above in steady succession, splattering larger accumulations on the undergrowth less frequently.

The trees needed the rain, their form designed, in part, to direct the water down to their roots. She wondered if the individual leaves, their role primarily one of collecting sunshine and shifting water down to the ground, appreciated being splashed. If the rains stopped and the roots continued to receive water, would the leaves notice or care? Maybe they would, she decided. Maybe they needed a change from time to time, to test their strength. Or maybe they too needed water; Tildy didn't know. She didn't know anything.

She took out her cell phone and called her nana. The phone rang, unanswered, and just as she was about to hang up, a happy voice greeted her.

"Nana, how are you?"

"A chroí, I'm fine! Just fine. Did you come visit, or was it Aidan, gathering his little plants?"

Tildy shut her eyes to the tears that threatened. How she wished to stay here, with this Nana. "Both of us, actually."

There was a weighted pause. "Is that so."

"Can I come visit tonight or tomorrow? I'd like to talk with you about all this."

But unlike Russell, this version of Nana was not always there for her, not always waiting and listening. "Oh, no. Tonight is no good for me, loveen. I was in the garden from sunup, and now I need my rest. Come collect me tomorrow and we'll visit that new, fancy museum. You know, I've never been! It might be nice to take a look and see what they are telling all the tourists and such. Come at 10 a.m., I like my mornings to myself."

"I'll be there. Have a good day, Nana. I love you."

"I love you, dearest. Slán anois, go dtuga Dia slán thú."

Tildy hung up the phone and stared into the trees. Something new caught her eye. A sliver of beige across the ground, beyond the trees. Tilting her head to get a better look, she saw that there was more. She left her blanket and chair. She was wearing shoes now and could step through the gaps in the ferns and trees. Voices carried in the wind toward her.

The woods presented no obstacle as she reached the edge of the trees. Without turning, she could sense there was nothing behind her now. There was nowhere else to go but forward. And ahead of her was not a private woodland, or a seascape, or any part of Ireland, but a familiar long, low wall of red stones, similar in a way to the stone walls of western Ireland. But these were not rugged walls of necessity; they were designed by someone who did not belong to the land, the sense of overt inhabitation inescapable.

The tastefully curated landscaping featured desert marigold and Apache plume, anchored by a large cholla tree. Tildy stood in the parking lot, looking toward an expansive adobe structure with large modern windows and classic beams jutting from the faces of the exterior walls. A small service road swung round the side, where the ambulances could come if a patient collapsed. She'd seen it once, as she hid behind the wall and watched the adults around her. The paramedics had come out with a frail woman on a stretcher, limp and dazed. Her mother had told her cousin on the phone, days later, that someone had smuggled in a supply for that woman, and her old dose had exceeded her new body's tolerance.

The wall and the high-plateau plants had been like friends while her mom and sisters visited her father. Tildy had never set foot inside the center. During those visits, she remained alone, outside, usually in view of the front office. They said it was common, that lots of kids kept their distance, no matter how much they missed their fathers. They didn't understand. Her childish relief that her father needed special, away-from-home care was a vivid memory. They'd had to live in a hotel in Santa Fe, sure, but they ate pizza and watched television and went swimming with their mother, without their father's guilt and insistence and control.

But her dad, a weak-willed and pathetic man, had responded to rehab with surprising aptitude. Perhaps it was the excellent care, or perhaps it was seeing the other addicts, their missing nasal septa and cracked nails and sunken eyes and damaged skin.

In the end they were all reunited. She waited in the car when he was escorted out by smiling staff. But there would be no escape for the women in his life. He loved them as accessories. Not for themselves, but as a means to further his own view of himself and his place with others. They were fated to live in his shadow, all together, until her mother died, and then she was permanently alone.

Tildy watched it all from the edge of the parking lot. She stepped backward, back into the trees. Shaded from the sun, she continued in reverse until the adobe building disappeared. The shadows grew. The unnatural greens and nearly black soil of the forest felt faintly rotten.

She bumped into a tree, and it was now a single wall, all alone in the woods. Tildy touched it, focusing on the white paint. When she looked up, another wall had appeared, and a floor between the two. She was now in a faintly grey corridor, a tastefully beige wooden floor between the two. Plastic floorboards ran along the sides, to protect from scuffs during the frequent cleanings. A whiteboard with patient room numbers and scribbles, which could be notes, hung on the new wall. The forest was still there, undergrowth and trees on either side of this sliver of a building.

Tildy walked down the hall, the wood giving in places as she stepped towards a room she remembered well. There was a name plate, a letter and number but here it was simply confusing symbols. The blinds were drawn, faint golden daylight coming through the slits. She rested her hand on the brushed nickel door handle. It disappeared. She couldn't enter then, nor could she now. She rubbed the discomforting sensation from her hand onto her jeans. There was no living sound from the room beyond. Only an artificial rhythm, the inhale and exhale of a machine.

She turned from the door and passed the vacant nurse's station. There had been women there, that time, but now there was no one.

She heard a noise and followed it to the hospital break room. The door was ajar. A man in a lab coat rested with his elbows on a table, his face concealed by his hands as he cried quietly. His black hair was smooth and formed a widow's peak. A doctor who had become a family friend. A doctor who had tried everything and failed.

The faceless man, back where he belonged.

The next morning, she swiped away her missed texts and calls from her sisters and dressed with apprehension, taking care in her appearance. She put a surgical mask in her purse and went downstairs. In town, she visited a shop and bought a small bouquet of flowers. From there she hailed a cab.

Half an hour later, the car pulled into the parking lot slowly and Tildy's stomach clenched. The beige stucco building was surrounded by a low grey stone wall, with lavender, pot marigold, and a small rowan tree out front.

The patio furniture was wet and abandoned, the distant traffic from the road loud even this far away. She put on her surgical mask, buzzed at the main entrance, and waited. The door lock clicked and she entered to a loud bell, which ended as soon as the door closed. At the window, she stood awkwardly while two nurses in blue scrubs chatted.

"May I help you?" one nurse asked in an accent she could not place. Eastern European, she thought.

"I'm here to see Deidre Halleran. I'm her granddaughter."

The woman's eyes sparkled as she tapped the clipboard. "Just sign here, and I'll take you to her."

Tildy signed as instructed and waited for the woman to exit the office. The plush entry carpet gave way to grey linoleum, and the woman's black sneakers squeaked as they passed down a long hallway. The smell of medical-grade cleaner, stale air, and old furniture combined into a miasma of despair. A common area, full of tables, was crowded with elderly men and women playing games, chatting, or staring at nothing. Tildy continued on, following the squeaks.

"Alright, James?" the woman called to a man mopping.

"New sheets for room 8, when you can."

She waved in reply.

At Nana's room, the nurse whispered, "I wouldn't get your hopes up. You know how she is."

Tildy nodded. "I know how she is."

The nurse knocked brightly and called, "Mrs. Halleran! Your granddaughter is here. All the way from America, just to visit you!"

There was no response.

She knocked again. "Mrs. Halleran, dear? Are you awake?"

"Of course I'm awake, ag scréacach agus ag béiceadh mar sin. Come in or don't, but quit knocking at the door."

The nurse gave Tildy a knowing look, then opened the door. Nan was sitting at a small beige wooden table that matched the armchairs, dresser, and bed frame. Across her table were the familiar pages of *Seachtain*, opened to an article about Roy Keane.

"Dia duit, a Nana. I brought you flowers."

Nana looked up from a sheet of newspaper, over her reading glasses, and scrutinized the little bouquet. "Suigh síos. Good gracious, girl, hovering like that."

Tildy set the flowers in a vase on the dresser and sat across from her nana.

"I'll fetch some water for those," the nurse said and shut the door behind her.

Turning one of the abandoned sheets of newspaper toward herself, Tildy tried to read the passage. Nana continued reading, ignoring her presence.

"I went by the old cottage."

Nana grunted but said nothing.

"It looks okay. Nothing wrong with it, still all closed up."

"What good does it do me. D'fhéadadh sé a bheith déanta as óir, chomh fada agus is cuma liom."

Tildy felt her temper rise. "You could be home again if you let us hire you a nurse."

"And have them stealing from me when I sleep? Is smaoineamh amaideach é sin!"

"I'm just saying, you made a choice," she said softly. "No one said you had to live here."

They fell into an angry silence. Tildy turned away from the newspaper she couldn't read and rose. She looked out the window. There was a little patio outside with plants. It seemed warm and inviting. But it wasn't ancestral land. No trees planted by previous generations. No easy walk to the water's edge.

The bookcase beside her was topped with familiar things. A lace doily slightly yellowed from age and her grandfather's cigarettes, a mug from a vacation to Dingle, a Christmas ornament now used as a paperweight, and a newspaper photo of Michael Collins carefully cut out and set in a cheap plastic frame. She had dreamed of some of these items, during those visits filled with kind conversations and warm welcome. On the bookshelves sat *Death of a Naturalist* by Seamus Heaney, two bibles, a worn Irish to English dictionary, some gardening magazines, a book about Nora Barnacle and James Joyce, two works by Maurice Semple, and a poetry collection called *An Tonn Gheal*. She picked up the dictionary and flipped it open. Her mother's primitive signature in blue ballpoint pen, the cursive a tentative mark of childhood. She returned the book to the shelf.

Just below the books was a shoebox full of letters. They were yellowed and grayed, the stamps peeking up unfamiliar. They were likely from Nana's sisters, full of stories of

good times and banquets and promises of money. Whatever money they could spare. Tildy touched one without
thinking.

"Coinnigh do lámha as na litreacha sin, láithreach."
Nana said curtly. Tildy drew back her hand, ashamed, and
sat down at the table again. They remained in silence for
a while, every moment a sharper punishment.

"I'm thinking of moving to Galway," Tildy said.

Nana didn't look at her, but her shift in attention was
palpable.

"If I were nearby, would you be more comfortable
having a nurse at home?"

"Oh, a chailín amaideach. You're too much like your
father. They could rob me blind and you wouldn't see
a thing. Now, if your mother hadn't left me, had you been
raised here, perhaps you'd have some sense. You've been
indoctrinated into that American lifestyle. Na Poncáin
amaideacha. How would I get to the doctor's? No, no. It's
simply not possible."

"I'm certain I could help. I can drive you to appoint-
ments, and come by to help. I can find a place between you
and the university."

Nana tutted. "That godless university, I suppose? I sent
your mother there, had a hard aul go of it myself. My dear
husband, dead and buried, God rest his soul. I scraped and
struggled for her to have those opportunities. Ones I didn't
get, I'll tell you that much. And she was wild, too, you know.
I didn't do what my own mother did to my dear sister. She

wasn't sent away to the Sisters of Mercy. No, I cared for your mother, hard as it was for me. And what did she do? What did she do? Wasted it all. Threw it all away."

"I know, Nana."

"She went off with that man, and I says to her, sure, now. Have a bit of fun. I have modern notions on that sort of thing. But don't marry him, and for God's sake don't fall pregnant. What does she do, now. Well, you know of course."

"Yes."

Nana shifted in her chair, arming herself for another round. Tildy waited.

"And you, now. You want to come here, to our country? Are there no Irish workers who need this job you're taking? Another blow-in, taking the work the Irish need for themselves. Like all those Brazilians down there in Gort, but you taking the university positions?"

"At the godless university, yes," Tildy replied. Her face burned. She had never spoken back like that to her grandmother. She waited in apprehension.

To her surprise, Nana laughed and shook her head. "That's a good volley, Tildy. Still, now. We all know that father of yours is going to get his hooks back in you, and off you go, like that mother of yours. Don't be letting people depend on you who don't know your nature."

Tildy's face burned, but she kept her voice calm. "Alright Nana, I don't want to take up more of your day. Would you like me to take you out to lunch sometime?"

"I don't care for eating in public."

"A museum?"

Nana waved her hand as if to scatter flies. Tildy said goodbye, kissed her grandmother on the head, gathered her things, and left.

The nurses fell silent as she approached the window.

"Leaving so soon?" the one with black sneakers asked kindly.

She shrugged. "I'll come back another day."

"It's hard for someone as independent as your nan." She looked around, then leaned closer. "You know, if she just gets a bit of help at home, she doesn't need to stay here."

"I know," Tildy said, her exasperation bleeding through. "I've told her. I've told her so many times. But she says they'll steal her things."

The nurses shook their heads and laughed. The other nurse said, "She accused James of stealing her pillowcase. We had to explain—the sheets are all sterilized and changed."

"Well, I appreciate you all," Tildy said weakly. "I know it isn't easy. I'll be by again soon."

She gave a parting wave and left to wait for her car outside. She removed her mask and took a deep swallow of cool air. The car she ordered would arrive shortly.

Her phone buzzed and, on impulse, she answered it without checking the ID.

"Tildy?" A confused voice came through the speaker.

"Oh, Russell." Tildy felt ashamed. She had forgotten

about Russell entirely. "Uh, how are you?"

"I'm fine. How are you? *Where* are you?"

"On a trip."

The line went quiet while Russell processed how to reply.

"I see."

"I needed to get away," Tildy said, kicking her toe into gravel.

"Your family is worried about you. They expected you at the Twombleys."

She laughed sardonically. "I'm sure they did."

"Jude has been worried."

"Has he."

"He's very nice, Tildy. Very handsome, as you said."

"He is."

"But?"

Tildy sighed. "Nothing."

"Not *nothing*. Are you running away from him?"

She stuffed the toe of her shoe into the gravel. "Not just him, no."

Russell laughed kindly, as if she understood. "It's okay to be happy, you know."

"I know," Tildy lied.

"And I think Jude would make you happy."

She tried to imagine Jude making her happy. There was more to what he wanted. She could believe he was interested in her. Seeing how Aidan looked at her, as something precious he coveted, made Jude's attention feel less ridiculous. She could not, however, believe that her personal qualities were his primary source of interest.

"I don't trust him."

"Maybe you don't trust yourself. Maybe you should have an open mind."

Tildy laughed, not at the present but at a moment in the past. When she did not laugh, when it hadn't been funny, when it was she asking Russell to have an open mind. She had not then, and Tildy would not now.

"My car is here, I gotta run. But I'm fine. I'll be in touch soon."

"Tildy, wait. At least let Jude know what you are thinking."

"Sure, when I can. Talk soon."

On the ride back to the hotel, the friendliness of the driver made solitude impossible. He waved at passing cars and wondered aloud why the other drivers were heading that way at this time of day. He remarked about the pool tournament at Leisureland, wondering if it would interfere with a concert of a traditional singer also being held there that night. He asked if she had been to the aquarium yet, going on to say it was in desperate need of renovations. Tildy kept up the minimum small talk so as not to be rude and scrolled through her social media accounts. People with kids, people with pets, people with pretty food.

A message alert appeared in the top corner. She clicked it and squinted at the tiny profile image. A man she did not recognize at a Mediterranean beach, in sunglasses and a very small speedo. In a moment, she had deciphered the username.

Jordie's message was brief and to the point.

◯ We're going for drinks tonight at 8, the girls want to know if you are free.

Tildy smiled.

◯ Weird way to describe yourself and Seán, but ok.

She immediately regretted the familiarity of the reply. Jordie sent her a laughing emoji.

◯ Don't talk like that to Seán, he'll climb you like a tree, darling.

◯ Oh no thank you. Yeah, I'm free—just left my nan's. Send me the address?

Tildy paid the driver and walked away from the hotel toward the shops. She headed toward the cute boutique from her dream.

Was it real? Would it go the same way? Maybe she'd find something that worked well. Maybe the clothes would flatter and fit perfectly, because half of her belonged here.

A bright red discount sign was plastered to the inside of the glass window. Tildy frowned and entered, where much of the shop was as she dreamed, but half the shelves and racks were bare.

A different girl, similar but less friendly, gave a quick greeting. She wandered, looking at pieces and checking labels and generally lost. Gisele was the clothing expert. In a pinch, she'd go shopping with Tildy to prepare for a big event. The outings were never exciting, but they were pleasant in a way. Gisele insulted her, of course. The insults were expected, though, and did not hurt that much.

Tildy didn't know where to start here. She considered leaving, ashamed at herself for trying this.

"Looking for anything particular?" the clerk asked.

"I'm going out for a casual drinks thing tonight, I'd just like something cute that isn't too…"

"Not hoochie, sure now. There's a classy little black number, if you're willing to brave the cold." The clerk walked over to a rack and held up a dress on a hanger. Tildy approached and touched the stretchy sweater material.

"That's cute, yeah. I do need a good dress, though for this I'd like pa… trousers."

"Grand. Here's the dress, this size looks right. We have a few in back if it's no good. Now, over here I have these slim leg trousers with the studded detail on the trim here. These fit like a dream and do wonders for the arse. And I think you'd look killer in this top—it's a tight fit but it covers the cleavage. It's class."

Tildy smiled in relief. "Perfect, where's the fitting room?"

"Just there, behind that curtain. It's cold as a witch's tit in there, can't get the landlord to fix a single fecking thing in this place, the dirty gombeen."

"I'll be quick then," Tildy laughed.

The dress was perfect, though certainly more racy than she'd intended for a drinks night. She'd save it for some other occasion.

The outfit was good, though it seemed as though it

wanted heels, and she didn't feel like it was a heels sort of evening.

"How's the fit?" the clerk said through the curtain. Tildy glanced at her reflection and nodded to herself.

"Great, I love everything. Do you have any…" She blanked on the word for a moment, rummaging around in her mind for the right word, and there was an uncomfortable pause. "Trainers?"

"Oh we did, and we still have some odd sizes, nothing that'd fit you, I think, unless your feet are enormous or absolutely microscopic. There's a shop 'round Moons Corner—they'll have all the best."

Tildy came out, ready to pay for her purchases, and looked around.

"Are you changing seasons or…"

The young woman typed the prices with quick fingers and extracted the anti-theft devices on the items. "Oh, no. I'm afraid we're at the end. Rents raised. Closing up in a couple of weeks. You should come by again, we're to clear out any leftover stock by end of the next week."

Tildy sighed and looked around. "I'm sorry to hear that."

A door left ajar at the back of the shop told the story. Cardboard boxes full of hangers and clothes that would not be sold here. Colorful signs and window decorations peeked up from a plastic bin. There had been pride in this shop, an eagerness to do a thing for the community and to do it well.

All along the walk here the local shops had shuttered, or had been replaced by chains, or only existed to serve tourists. This shop had sophistication. It didn't make sense to her that this business couldn't survive.

"The landlord is a greedy gob of shite. One of these corporate landlords, owns buildings all over the country. Should be illegal. He doesn't live here, doesn't know the people, doesn't ever look us in the eye when he raises and raises and raises these rents."

"How long had you been here?"

"I was a girl in this shop. My mum and da started it. They were going to hand it over to me, get me set up. My big inheritance, they called it. I've been updating it for the past two years. Now, closed up."

"What will you do?" Tildy asked, signing the receipt and exchanging it for her bag of clothes.

"I have a cousin in Liverpool, asked me to help in her shop. Not big on the British. Too much of the past in me, my da says. And all me friends are here, aren't they? And I don't want to work as a sales girl. Not that I'm too good for it, but it's a step down. Still, I've got to eat."

Tildy looked down at her little outfit. On a whim, she opened her purse and took out a business card, the one she used for what her father called the family work. The expensive paper and shimmering letter press felt like the proof of the lie that was her, all in one hand.

"If you ever set up another shop, please get in touch. If I can, I'd love to pitch in, you know, financially. To help you get started."

The woman looked down at the card in perplexed confusion. "You work for Aibell, the cosmetics firm?"

"It's—well. It's my father's company. Sorry, my sister is better at this stuff," Tildy laughed. She looked around. "I've just been meaning to come into this shop for ages, and now that I have, I'm so sad to see it go."

With tears in her eyes, the young woman nodded. Then she let out a laugh and pointed at Tildy with the card. "I'm going to hold you to this, now, Matilda. Tell your da to get his checkbook ready."

"I will. I hope to hear from you. Take care now."

Her face burned with embarrassment as she stepped out into the cold air. Embarrassment, not regret. Maybe this woman wouldn't try again. Maybe Tildy's offer, even if never collected on, would give her the confidence to consider it. Either way, she did hope she heard from her. Jude might not be able to convince her to sell the shares in her father's company, but worthier people than him who wished to try something new had her attention.

An hour later, after visiting Moons Corner and buying flats instead of sneakers, she set out her outfit for the night and realized she still had two hours to kill. She needed dinner, but that could be had on the way to the bar. Despite a full night's sleep, the stress of her visit with Nana had fatigued her. She could sleep. Her eyes turned to the dream machine.

She was certainly over her seven times. The dreams felt

stranger now, but no more distorted or disturbing than regular dreams.

No, she decided. She would not. She would nap on her own. She would do without.

chapter
nineteen

That evening, Tildy arrived at the bar after eating far too much curry pizza from a local eatery. It wasn't a slice from her neighborhood spot back in NYC, but it was delicious. She groaned as she walked to the bar, hoping her trousers wouldn't be this tight around her waist the whole evening.

When she reached the black dog, the same bar from her dream, it was quieter and less vivid. There were two men with pints complaining rather loudly about the traffic and praising European cities with trams. One man seemed to enjoy doing the speaking, while the other would simply reply, "good man," "'tis so," and "sure now."

Jordie waved to her. She warmed at having a table of people waiting for her, though Katherine eyed her with wariness. The pit in Tildy's stomach overcame the pizza.

They were talking about a trip they were meaning to take, when the restaurant shut for summer vacation next year. She listened with a glow, happy to not be included. She could've contributed. Her father had dragged them to all the trendy vacation spots around the world. She had needed a large passport book for all the stamps. But they didn't ask her opinion, and didn't need the attention, so she didn't say a word.

When Jordie rose to get more drinks, Katherine turned to her. "You grew up with Aidan, then?"

"Not exactly grew up, no. He stayed with my cousins near my grandmother's house, after..." Tildy wasn't sure what they knew, so she changed course, eager to not share secrets. "I only saw him on vacations, not all year long. Mostly during the summer."

Jordie set the glasses on the table and eagerly took his seat. "Oh, we're talking about Aidan now." He turned to Katherine and Orla, who didn't so much glare as scowl at him. "Well! I see I'm the caboose of this conversation!"

"Yes, Jordie. Yes."

"What?" Tildy asked, afraid to ask, but forced to ask.

"There's been rumors," Orla said in a conspiratorial whisper. "Rumors that Aidan had a great heartbreak."

Tildy nodded but said nothing. They all seemed to appreciate her compliance with their supposition.

"Oh my god, it's like that Taylor Swift song!" Jordie exclaimed. "You know, 'You're On Your Own, Kid?'"

"I was waiting for Taylor to come into this," Katherine sighed.

"You dry shite, you know the one that I mean, and don't act like you didn't have it on repeat for months like the rest of us! Now, Tildy, you know it, then?"

"I think so," she said.

He sang the words in a feminine pitch, swaying as he sang. His friends laughed. "Don't laugh! You see? Summer went away! And you yearn for him, Tildy! Don't tell me you don't!"

"I believe, and I may be mistaken, the song is about breaking someone's heart. So perhaps we should be more delicate with Tildy's feelings on this particular topic," Orla said, and rose for the restroom.

He shrugged. "Ah, so Tildy breaks hearts—that's not her problem."

Eager to redirect the conversation, Tildy turned to Katherine. "I heard you weren't feeling well. Are you okay now?"

She grimaced. "I had a seizure."

Tildy looked down at her hands, seeing her fear in how they shuddered. How could she have known? Was it online somewhere? No, she knew it wasn't.

She touched a finger to the condensation on the table. Cold, wet. Was this real? Had she used the dream machine and never woken up?

"Where did it happen?" she asked, hoping it was a normal question.

"A parade over on Dominick Street Lower, for the International Arts Festival. The strobing lights, they think. It was strange—never had one of them before."

Orla returned and put a hand on Katherine's shoulder. "It won't happen again. She would've had them before now, if she was going to have them her whole life."

Tildy's hand trembled as she drank from her glass. The dream version of her would've shared about her mother, or let on that she knew more. Instead, she pushed herself into silence. They didn't want to know.

Jordie took out his phone and replied to a text.

"Is Bobby coming?" Orla asked.

"He's got an essay. The lads at the restaurant are on their way."

Three faces turned to Tildy. She sighed.

Jordie patted her hand sympathetically. "You'll just have to face him! I'm friends with all my exes."

"Except for Daniel," Katherine corrected.

"Except for Daniel, that sack of shite," Jordie agreed.

"I never liked Daniel," Orla said, signaling for another round.

"Well, he had his qualities," Jordie mused as he looked into the distance.

"As a person, a total shite. As a sex object, probably adequate," Orla conceded. Jordie shrugged again with a mischievous grin.

Katherine set down her glass too hard. "Stall the digger, ye daft shite. He wasn't worth it! No one is worth all of that."

"I dumped him, okay! Message received! Jaysus."

When they remembered Tildy was present, they caught her smile appreciatively.

"She's hardly American," Katherine observed. "No main character energy to her at all."

"How do you mean?"

"Oh, you know. Americans come over and act like the whole country is Celtic Disneyland, and we're all ears for how they are fourteen percent Irish and how their granny is from Cork and how much they love Bono."

They laughed, Tildy weakest of all.

"Mickey Mouse in a little leprechaun getup," Orla said, bringing a fresh round of laughs. "Imagine Fine Gael celebrating the opening day."

"A fake Blarney Castle with a roller coaster out the front," Katherine added. They laughed and then called out a greeting to a friend who had entered the pub. Tildy was forgotten while they chatted with the stranger.

"I'm going to use the restroom, I'll be right back," she said. She walked toward where the restroom had been in her dream, only to find a blank wall. The doors were on the left, not the right. As she paused, an older man came out of the men's room, still zipping his trousers. He wobbled, his shirt stained with old and new food and beer. He glared at Tildy.

"You!" The stench of beer on his breath made her back

into the wall behind her. "You Americans. Feck off back to Boston, ruining our streets and taking all our houses for your AirBabies."

Katherine came over, setting a hand on Tildy's shoulder and glaring at the man. "Corbed off your arse in public again, Martin! You maggoty little weasel."

"Feck off, Katherine McCleary," he yelled. "Ba raicleach cheart í do sheanmháthair."

"Ní bheannódh mo sheanmháthair duitse!"

"Off you get, you reanimated bog mummy!" Orla shouted. Tildy and Katherine smothered a laugh.

The bartender called out, "Get out of here now, Martin! I warned ye before, now this is your last time! You aren't welcome here no more!"

The old man continued shouting while patrons looked at him with disapproval. Katherine held Tildy's arm until he was out the door, then looked her in the face. "You alright now?"

"Oh, I'm fine. Surprised me, that's all."

Katherine rubbed her arm. "He's a spiteful old man. This place keeps kicking him out, but they let him right back in later. Alright now, we'll be at the table waiting for you."

After using the toilet, Tildy looked at her reflection, searching for what didn't belong. She was wearing a simple outfit. No jewelry. Very little makeup.

What was it the man had seen? What made her look American?

There was something, but she couldn't see it. She couldn't see it because she didn't belong here. She splashed cold water on her face and patted it dry with a paper towel, then looked back into the mirror. Maybe her eyes were Dutch, her nose German, her cheekbones English. Maybe, when you added it all up, the wrongness was unmistakable.

She returned to the table, where the friends were engaged in a vigorous debate about the last Eurovision. She slid into her seat and listened.

"Of course the whole thing was rigged!" Jordie was ranting. "Are you trying to tell me that all those people in the audience preferred that trite one-dimensional garbage? That singer, with a voice pitchy like a greaseless wheel? I don't think so. I think they need to check into the finances of all those judges, I'm telling ye."

Orla nodded. "I'm not arguing, we're in agreement. Finland's set was so tome."

"Proper tome," Katherine agreed.

"Are you going to watch next year, then?" Tildy asked.

"Of course," Katherine replied just as the others agreed.

"It isn't a national referendum or some shite. We aren't hitting polling stations and casting a ballot. It isn't all that serious," Jordie said. Orla shook her head.

"I don't really understand the political parties of Ireland, or the whole system, really."

Jordie belched. "We hardly understand it ourselves, loveen."

Orla put out an unsteady hand. "Give yer phone here,

then, Tildy. I'll put in my number and call you about it all. I can't have you voting like an eejit next year. I won't be calling tomorrow though. I'm so deep in my cups, gonna have head on me like John the Baptist come morning."

She entered her number with unfocused eyes, the gesture in it more than Tildy had expected. They wanted to educate her. They wanted to include her. She wasn't accepted yet, but she was acknowledged. Orla handed her back her phone, and she tucked it away. Would this last, even after she became comfortable? Or was she a temporary novelty? She didn't know.

Behind her, the door swung open, and all three of her companions froze. Katherine and Orla's mouths dropped, and Jordie leaned forward slightly.

"Who is HE here for, I wonder?"

Tildy twisted in her seat. It wasn't Aidan. She turned back and shut her eyes for a moment. This couldn't be real. She must have used the machine. This couldn't be happening.

After a few moments, a hand, large and warm, rested on her shoulder. "Tildy?"

Real or not, she was in this now. She opened her eyes to find three surprised faces staring at her. With a quick breath, she turned to the owner of the hand.

"Hi, Jude."

He was still gorgeous. He wore a dark, soft mock turtleneck beneath his wool peacoat and tailored dress slacks, the entire look worthy of the runway. Tildy looked down and caught sight of his shoes. He had bought new shoes. His friends at the gallery had teased him about his old shoes. But here he was, in western Ireland, with new shoes, in this pub, with his hand on her shoulder. His auburn hair was perfectly trimmed and coiffed, and the smell. The man knew how to buy cologne. She looked back up to his face. There were those cheekbones, delicate and perfectly proportioned to his perfect jawline, decorated by a scatter of freckles.

"Hi." His eyes sparkling and his voice husky.

Jordie pulled out the chair beside him and patted the seat, Orla and Katherine watching eagerly. Jude thanked him with a smile and unbuttoned his peacoat before settling into the chair. He didn't remove his coat. He didn't want to stay. He didn't want her to stay.

When Tildy had recovered her composure, she said, "Jude, these are my friends, Jordie, Orla, and Katherine."

They each shook hands politely and quietly, evidently happy to be spectators. A main character had arrived.

"You weren't at your hotel, Tildy. I was worried."

"My hotel?" Her voice wavered from shock. Or was it fear? When she recovered her composure, she asked, "How did you know where I was staying? And how did you find me here?"

A server came by, and Jude ordered a mineral water. Orla and Katherine, sensing tension, began to speak quietly about something else and attempted to include Jordie, who refused to be distracted.

"I took a guess." He gave her his charming sheepish grin.

Jordie turned to her, wide-eyed, but she ignored him. The server returned with the mineral water and looked at Jude with a firm, examining look. They were checking to see if he was an actor, Tildy realized. The whole pub had grown quiet, as if everyone was trying to figure out why this glossy American man was at their pub, at one of their sticky tables. She took a strong swig of her beer and then wiped the foam from her mouth.

"So, when did you fly in?" Tildy asked.

He checked his watch and did some math. "Three hours ago."

"You came right to the hotel."

"I don't like to waste time," he said with another smile. He took a drink from his water, his Adam's apple bobbing beneath the turtleneck fabric. Katherine made a noise, and Orla elbowed her.

"Did my father send you?"

Jude lightly smacked his lips. "He doesn't know I'm here."

Tildy frowned at his evasion and he grinned at her, caught, knowing he was caught, pleased he was caught.

Orla asked, "Have you ever been to Galway before?"

Jude slowly spun his water bottle on the table and looked around at the pub, as if it was a hovel he had to claim was charming. "I have not. I've been to Dublin, of course. I had some business in Belfast once. But I've never made it here."

"Where are you staying?" Katherine asked.

He looked at her with his kind, social smile. The mask again, Tildy observed. "The modern place up the road. I almost booked at Tildy's hotel, in fact. That would've been… convenient."

This man was flirting with her. Flirting with her right here in front of these witnesses. And it put her in a position of either accepting the flirtation publicly or rejecting it and humiliating him. Calculating, if not manipulative.

Jordie's phone lit up with a text, and Tildy remembered, suddenly, who was to arrive soon.

"Let's go for a walk," she said, rising quickly and lifting her coat from her seat back. They had to leave right away. They had to leave now.

Jude took the coat from her grip and stood close. She could feel the heat of his body through the air between them. His cologne and the expensive smell of his clothes wafted over to her. He gently eased her coat over one arm, then the other, his head above hers. She heard him take in a breath of her hair. The door opened, and a quick flicker of breeze caressed her face. She turned in time to see Aidan, frozen in the doorway, staring at her and Jude.

"Ahhhhh," Jordie cried softly.

Aidan stayed motionless as they approached. Tildy smiled at him. "Hi, Aidan. This is…"

"Jude Mills. An old friend from New York."

Aidan shook his hand and returned it to his pockets as they briefly faced one another. Aidan was taller, broader, though he didn't straighten his shoulders. Jude was standing as tall as he could, shoulders back proudly and smiling his charming smile. Aidan turned to Tildy, searching for the answer to a question.

"Good to meet you, Aidan," Jude said, taking Tildy by the elbow and guiding her out the door. Aidan watched them go, the pain only visible if you knew where to look.

They walked toward her hotel, down the dark sidewalks in silence. She wanted to turn around, to run into the pub and return to the glares of Aidan, to the warmth of his attention, even if it was negative. That was the only thing that made sense. Instead, she was here, walking, and could feel Jude weighing things to say. What would he say? She wanted him to be silent.

"This city is old," he observed. "Did the English build it?"

"They weren't really English then," Tildy began, the power of her two beers pulling trivia from the recesses of her mind. "They were Anglo-Norman. Probably built to replace wooden fortifications against the Vikings. The heart of the city is still medieval, but that was also predated by some other organized settlement."

"Has your mother's family been here this whole time?"

She shook her head. "They're from the countryside. I'm sure some of us lived in the city. There's Galway city and Galway County, and they aren't the same."

"Ah. Like New York and New York City."

"A bit, yeah."

After a long pause, Jude sighed. It wasn't his theatrical sigh, his mask sigh—it was him. And to hear him expressing himself honestly, even in a sigh, intrigued her even now when she longed to be back in the pub. To be let in by someone so secretive almost felt like a privilege. It made her think of Russell, saying he could make her happy.

"I can see why you are drawn here," he said. "It's so different."

"I've always liked Galway. I didn't spend much time in the city as a kid. Just when Nana wanted to visit the shops. She'd complain, of course, that all the shops were rundown or cheap. She'd say there weren't any places of class left, like Moon's."

"Moon's?" he asked.

"A department store. Maybe like Bloomingdales, but not quite. It had an intricate payment system thing, involved a wooden ball and a vacuum tube. I think? I never saw it myself. Anyway, I doubt she ever bought anything from there. Nana always finds something to complain about."

"It's nice to have a grandmother, even if she isn't nice."

Tildy turned to him, the moonlight highlighting only the general outlines of his features. From what she could see, though, he looked sad. "Did you know yours?" she asked.

Jude shook his head. "Dad was an orphan refugee. Mom was the youngest of a lot of kids, so by the time I came along, her parents had already passed away. She died of cancer last year. She wasn't really the same after Dad passed."

She clenched her teeth, then forced herself to relax. "I'm sorry."

He seemed to sense her emotion. "Thanks. It's easier to live in the present without the past around."

The edge to the remark wounded her, even if she didn't want it to. "So, have you seen Gisele lately?"

Jude stuffed his hands in his pockets and huffed out an annoyed breath. "She calls me. Tags me on social media. I reply, of course. No reason to be rude. But I don't want to talk about Gisele, Tildy. Why are you here? Why now?"

A blush overwhelmed her in the dark.

"I participated in an experiment. It helps you lucid dream, to think out things while you sleep. It's for PTSD patients, to help them process difficult situations in dreams."

"That sounds frightening. It's very generous of you to do that. You are so generous."

Aidan standing before her in his home, his body close and strong and near.

"So anyway, I did it, and it was all about moving here. Starting over here. And it made me realize I could, you know?"

"I see."

With a laugh, Tildy pressed the crosswalk button with more force than necessary. "It sounds weird, now that I hear myself out loud. The researcher is someone I knew from school, Evelyn Touray. Do you know her?"

"Evelyn Touray. Yeah, that does sound familiar. And she's the head of the program?"

"No, an assistant. Something delayed her in school. But she's very smart. I think she does most of the work on the project, to be honest."

She wasn't sure why she was rambling and wasn't sure why Jude had fallen silent and still. They were near her hotel now. She just had to make it a few more blocks, and then this would be over. When the silence had gone on too long, Jude said what seemed to pop into his mind.

"Your father hates this place, I bet."

She laughed. "He absolutely hates it. He loves to talk about his heritage, but when it comes down to it, he's American."

"So are you, Tildy."

She frowned into the dark. She swallowed down the hurt and said nothing. She thought of her mother and said nothing.

They had reached the Wolfe Tone Bridge. Below, the river ran strong and fast beneath them. They stopped and leaned against the railing. If you looked straight down, and ignored everything in your peripheral vision, the moving water was all you could see. It was as if you were flying over the ocean.

Jude turned to face her. "Did you run from your family, or did you run from me?"

"I didn't run," she said softly, but wasn't sure she meant it.

"You quit your job."

"No, I was laid off. They didn't need me."

He had no invitation to speak, but she knew he was preparing to all the same. Instead of waiting for him, she watched the river and thought of her family and how generations of them saw this same river flow just as it was now. She thought of throwing rocks into the water with her cousins, of visiting the aquarium while her mother rested, of a time her mother had tried to join them and how she'd clutched at this same railing as something in her brain threatened to break and how the family had gently guided her to a quiet bench to recover.

That was what she wanted right now—to think of her place in a vast web of memories here. Not Jude. He would say something, and she would have to react to it, and the anxiety of it all already distracted her. She imagined herself back in the pub. If this was a dream, she could force herself to appear there. She could refuse this path and switch to another. Could it happen now? Could she go back, right now?

"It wasn't fair of me to suggest you sell your shares. That was unkind."

Tildy laughed quietly and shook her head.

"What?"

"That wasn't what I expected you to say."

Jude leaned down, his voice turning husky. "I can surprise you, I think."

Heat raced across her skin. She kept her unseeing eyes toward the water.

"I want to ask you a question. Would you look at me,

please? Tildy. Please."

She turned and looked at him. Even by moonlight, he was gorgeous. Freckles danced across his cheekbones. His black eyelashes were long and even and clean. His eyebrows were well-groomed, his skin dewy and his complexion clear. She looked at his eyes and he smiled at her, as if relieved, as if he had regained control. He took her hand.

"I want to work with you, together, and take back what is rightfully ours. My father made Aibell what it could be. Your mother gave up her dreams to turn it around. And since her death, it's fallen to pieces. You can see it. Together, the two of us can do so much more."

Tildy tried to take her hand back with an uncomfortable laugh.

"Or," he continued, looking down at her knuckles as he smoothed a finger across them, "we could sell it for parts and do something new. We could do this together. We belong together, Tildy. I can push you to stand up against them, and you can make me more like you. Patient and kind." He put her hand to his lips and kissed her skin gently. "We just need to try, together."

She turned back to the water and imagined throwing herself in, tumbling into the waves and drifting out to the bay.

Jude brushed back some of her hair over her shoulder. "Can we meet for dinner tomorrow? Before I go. Can we do that?"

"Fine. Yes. Of course."

A rowdy group of young men approached, walking from one bar to another. She could feel their eyes on her, assessing the status of her and Jude. He felt it too and let go of her hand.

"Let's get you back to your hotel."

Tildy put her hands in her pockets and lowered her face, walking with Jude past the group, the bustling bars, and the closed shops. Occasionally she glanced up at him. He was so handsome. What was this life, where two men pined for her? How had this happened? She caught herself. His motive was unclear, and Aidan probably hated her by now. Who knew what anyone wanted with her, she thought. With more to distrust than to accept, she was determined to be careful.

At the steps to the reception area, Jude kept his hands to himself. In the glow of amber lights, he looked at her with an earnest gaze that nearly crumbled her resolve.

"Dinner tomorrow, then?"

"Yeah. Tomorrow."

"I'll come pick you up at seven."

"Goodnight, Jude."

"Goodnight, Tildy."

Despite herself, she blushed as he said her name. She ascended the steps, knowing he watched her every move, until she was out of sight.

chapter
twenty

In the morning, Tildy decided to visit Nana. She wouldn't ask permission. If she was leaving, she'd be leaving soon. If she was staying, she'd need to make her place.

The nurses at the station greeted her pleasantly and took her back down the hall, but turned to a patio instead of Nana's room. The sunlight was bright, the clouds temporarily burned away, leaving only puffy isolated units floating by in the pale blue sky. Tildy removed her mask and followed the nurse between patio tables, to the left of the doorway. She gave a little wave to Nana, who did not sit alone.

"Tildy! We were just speaking of you." Her tone was alarmingly chipper. This was not Dream Nana—this was her nana, and she was never chipper.

She kissed Nana's offered cheek and sat. Aidan wouldn't look at her.

"How are you this morning, Nana."

"Féach ar an áit seo. Cad a cheapann tú féin? Táim ceart go leor, is dócha. Agus conas atá tú féin, a stór?

"Um, tá mise go maith."

Nana patted Tildy on the knee. "That's a good girl. Now, Aidan was just telling me he saw a wild horse on the family land, did you now?"

He shrugged. "Not wild, I think. Likely dumped."

"Isn't that a shame. You see less of those things now, but back after the Celtic Tiger days had ended, we had horses roaming all over the hills, dumped by owners. Thousands and thousands of the poor creatures, roaming around, not knowing a thing about surviving in the wild, dying of the starvation and the cold. Terrible."

"I've got Rory, Colm's cousin, coming around. His old mare just passed, so he has the space for it."

"Ah yes, Rory and Colm. Relations to Joe Mac, you know. Terrible tragedy, that motorcycle accident. Dreadful things, those motorbikes. So Rory will take the mare. That's good, Aidan. Good boy. Now, Tildy, what have you been doing with yourself?"

Aidan looked at her with cold politeness. She swallowed. "Nothing much."

"I suppose it is wise to take some time to relax before you start working. Now, Aidan was just asking permission to do a bit of planting. Of course, what good does that land do me, so he might as well, but I did mention you might have a say in it."

"Me?"

"You have that power of attorney hanging over me. I thought you might have some objection," Nana said, sipping her tea with thin lips.

Tildy avoided Aidan's gaze. The table was white and glossy, recently cleaned. The white was chipped away to expose the metal beneath. She scratched at the edge of it, to expose more. Would it rust in the rain? Would this hole lead to a rot that could not be stopped?

"It's not my land. It's yours."

Nana scoffed with a pointed glare.

Aidan leaned in, his eyes fixed on Nana. "You know your granddaughter only got the power of attorney because of her da. Tá a fhios agat go gcabhródh do ghariníon leat chun tú féin a shocrú sa bhaile. Tá tú ag iompar tú féin go stuacach arís, a Bhean Uí Allúrán."

She looked at him now, his strong profile and stubble. He looked tired. She hadn't noticed until now.

Nana laughed and grabbed his arm lightly. "Ó nach bhfuil tú cinneálta agus tú buartha fúm, a mhac álainn. Tildy would try to make things right. But something would come up with that father of hers, and off she'd go, ready to cater to his whims. Is duine lag í. Bhí sí lag I gcónaí."

Tildy accepted the dagger in her side. She could feel Aidan waiting for her to respond, to fight against it, but she only nodded and scratched at the hole in the table's paint.

"Even still, I want what's best for you, Nana. And I know this place isn't best."

"Hm."

The three sat in silence, with Tildy wondering why Aidan would stay. Nana patted her pockets with dramatic effect and said, "Look at what I've done now, I've left my pills. Fán anseo an bheirt díobh agus gheobhaidh mé iad. Fillfidh mé ar ball."

"I can get them," Tildy said, making to rise.

"No, you stay put. I keep my things just so, I don't want you scattering what little I have all about. Cuirfidh tú gach rud ina bpraiseach, a pháiste amaideach. Fán díreach ansin."

She left, and for a moment, Tildy thought they would remain in silence the entire time. Aidan was sitting back in his seat, his arms folded and his face turned up toward the sun. She stole a single glance. If she looked at him any longer, his beauty would overwhelm her. Her phone buzzed audibly, but she ignored it. Her gaze returned to the hole in the white paint.

"What are you thinking of planting at Nana's?"

He shrugged. "Nothing that would interest you."

"How would you know," Tildy muttered.

"That's true. I suppose I don't know you at all."

She frowned but said nothing. If he wanted to insult her, that was fine. She was determined to remain right here.

This was her own grandmother she was visiting, after all.

Her phone buzzed again. Aidan shook his head. "Aren't you going to check your messages?"

"It's probably my sister."

"Could be someone else."

Tildy looked up at him. His eyebrows were raised, waiting. Instead of responding, she took out her phone, prepared to read whatever demand Gisele or Alexandra had for her. Instead, it was a text from Evelyn, asking for an update. The thought of her dreams, her internet stalking, the way she looked forward to seeing him there crashed in on her. She blushed and put the phone on the metal table. Aidan nodded and looked into the horizon, as if proven correct and satisfied.

"It's from a friend, Evelyn," she said, holding the screen out to him. "Look. I'm participating in an experiment with her lab, and she needs my feedback. I'm letting her down."

She had the satisfaction of seeing him ashamed, then curious. But she would not offer any other details.

After an uncomfortable silence, he cleared his throat. "The man you helped, he's alive and going to be well. It's a long road for him yet. I told his family I'd thank you. I didn't say who you were."

"Thank you," she said quietly. He was going to live. She hadn't failed again. And he had known that she needed to know, and that she didn't want the attention that seeking out the man would have brought her. He knew her. He knew her so well.

To head off any more of these feelings, or any follow-up from him, Tildy changed the subject. "I wish Nana would go home."

Aidan nodded. "I know. She goes her own way."

"Then she should! This isn't where she belongs," she whispered, feeling tears in her eyes. "No one is making her stay here."

Their eyes met. His expression was downcast. "Aren't we all stuck doing what we think we must."

A doorway opened between them. Just beyond, a conversation, the first of many, if they could only reach it. Tildy swallowed and licked her lips, their dryness unnoticed until now. Aidan's eyes stayed on her face, his body tense as he waited for her to speak.

Her phone buzzed. Both their eyes flicked to the upturned screen.

JUDE CALLING.

Aidan shook his head and rose. "I'll see myself out."

She ignored the call and stood. "Wait, she'll be back soon!"

"I'll be by another time."

He wouldn't look at her as he walked away. Tildy watched him go, seeing only him, feeling only the despair of the distance between them.

When Nana returned, she clucked her tongue at the empty seat. Tildy didn't want to talk about it with her, or with anyone. She wanted to go home. She wanted to go back to when things were clearer, when no one noticed her unless they needed her. When no one cares for you, you are free—the loneliest kind of freedom.

"And what did you say to him, then," Nana said, dabbing her pale, watering eyes with a tissue from her front sweater pockets.

"I didn't say anything," she replied.

"So, why didn't you say something, then?"

"Nana, it's complicated."

"Cailín seafóideach, amhail is gur chasta é an grá."

"I don't want to hurt him, okay?"

"And you don't want to be hurt yourself, so I see."

Tildy laughed. "You think Dad doesn't hurt me. And Gisele and Alexandra."

"Ní cheapaim é sin. I think you wear their little snide remarks and insults like a shield. It keeps you safe, kept your mother safe. You never risk anything."

"I'm here! I am here now!" Tildy exclaimed.

"Tá tú anseo ach níl tú i ndáiríre, an bhfuil?"

"What? That was such a confusing sentence. Look at you, then. Look at this place. You don't want to go home because a nurse will steal your things? People love you and want you to be home, a sheanmáthair. Why won't you let me in?"

"'Tis true, Tildy. Cailín cliste. Suppose we both need to be less eager to accept punishment."

"I suppose so."

"Child, I know I'm hard on you. I don't know any other way to be. And your mother, go ndéana Dia trócaire uirthi, she was a miserable creature. More money than sense, staying with your father, an clasán ceart. But don't be stupid. Aidan has his own dreams. His restaurant and his friends and his life. He's not a fragile thing you could break. Choose him or don't, but don't think you're sparing him. Bíodh beagainín muiníne agat, in ainm Dé."

In the car home, along the Barna road, they got caught up in traffic. The driver, a quiet man, seemed calm despite it. He was listening to news radio and studiously ignoring Tildy.

She looked out at the low rock wall, the undulating green grass, and the faint outline of the Burren beyond the waves. Traffic here was rather lovely, she thought with a smile. Much better than constant honking and diesel trucks and suicidal pedestrians diving into the streets. But the appreciation felt forced. There, at least, she could go to museums and galleries every day of the week for a month. There were endless restaurants to try, bars to visit, parks to appreciate, people to meet. Author readings and new exhibitions and plays and concerts. New York City was an excellent place to be lonely.

Her phone rang, and Tildy answered on impulse.

"Look who's alive."

"Oh. Hi, Alexandra. Are the kids okay?"

"Like you care. You just disappeared without even saying goodbye to them. And they never got to go on that field trip, since you didn't chaperone for them."

Tildy sighed. "I'm glad they're okay."

"Anyway, Daddy needs to know which hotel you're staying at. We need to move your things to where we're staying."

Too many thoughts collided. "I'm sorry, where you're staying?"

"If you checked your messages, you would know we flew in yesterday night. The kids are super jet lagged, but we brought Imelda with us, since you are on your little self-discovery journey and don't have time for them or for me."

"Where are you guys staying?" she asked, the tension in her voice unmistakable to the driver. His eyes flicked to the rearview mirror for a moment, then back to the road and the slowly moving traffic.

"North of the city, at the Ormsbys. Vandeleur estate, it's very fancy. Do you know that one viscount or duke or whatever who makes the horror movies? That's his family. Or his distant family. I'm not sure how it all works. They've been here forever. Anyway, Jude introduced us. He does a lot of investing here and in the UK."

"I see."

"Anyway, Daddy said one of the servants there will go get your stuff and bring it to the hotel, we just need to know which one."

"I'm fine where I am."

Alexandra fell silent. "You'd rather stay at a hotel than *Vandeleur*?"

Tildy laughed at the emphasis her sister placed on an

estate she hadn't heard of last month. "Yes, I'm fine living in squalor."

She did not laugh back. "Daddy needs the whole family here for this, Tildy."

"I don't know what to tell you. Whatever deal this guy is trying to make with Dad, I'm not interested. I hope you enjoy your stay."

She hung up, her hands shaking. She kept her gaze out the window, the rock wall moving past at a faster rate now. Traffic was clearing up.

Jude hadn't told them where she was staying, but he hadn't told her they were coming, either. And how had he known which hotel was hers, or that she was at that pub, of all pubs in Galway? She looked down at her phone. A trap had been laid for her, though she couldn't see the full scale of it. Not yet.

For now, she wanted to be alone. And the dream machine beckoned.

chapter
twenty-one

It was early, and the notepad beside the device showed she was on her nineteenth use. She owed Evelyn notes. She had been trying to get in touch, with emails and texts, a worried tone growing as time had passed. Tildy sighed. She should've stopped after the nightmares. Now, she would give herself one more try.

What would she find in there, if she did it again?

Tildy swallowed. There was something she hadn't done yet. If this was a tool for exploring possible paths, there was one that had remained closed to her for years. She took up her phone and texted Russell with a question.

A few minutes passed, longer than she had expected. She fidgeted with her phone while she waited. Russell was not her mother, not her peer, but something in between. A resource her mother had made, and had possibly refined when her death became a near certainty. Although it was her mother's creation, and reflected her thoughts and feelings in many ways, it was only a shadow she had cast. It held no nuance. It was incapable of self-reflection, so it could not appreciate its own bias. But Tildy believed Russell could lead her to deeper truths about her mother. It was a tenuous, flawed connection, but it was a connection. It wasn't just any shadow; it was her shadow.

Her phone buzzed in reply. She read the answer, put on the cap, and turned out the light.

Nana's home, furnished and clean, was sliced through, like a dollhouse opened wide and suspended in the void before her. The darkness framed the home like a complete, inescapable embrace.

Her body drew near, the soft swoosh of cool air against her skin. The home grew in her mind, the small furniture slowly returning to human scale. In a moment, she set a foot down and entered the space, the familiar wooden floor beneath her. She noted the fire glowing in the hearth, a dogeared book left facedown on a side table, a cup of tea drained but unwashed. An untidy mess. It had the feel of a place freshly vacated, the occupant momentarily called away but ready to return at any moment.

The sound of a pot being set down on a tile floor came from the sunroom. Tildy held her hand in a fist as she approached the doorway, casting a quick eye to JFK and Jesus, their places now flipped left to right. They looked down on her from their perches, watching her instead of the distant horizon. Another sound from the sunroom, the slight whisper of a shovel into dirt. She reached the doorway and waited.

There on the floor, her legs akimbo, sat her mother.

She was wearing jeans and a long grey cardigan Tildy remembered from her childhood. Someone here had knitted it for her, a high school or college friend. Her father had always hated it. After she died, he had instructed Constance, the family's housekeeper, to donate it. In secret, Constance had placed it under Tildy's pillow. It was back in New York now, in a chest of clothes, where it still smelled of jasmine, coconut oil, and Chanel perfume. It smelled of her mother.

"Tildy, dear. Come on in. I'm just planting this little sapling. Crann coill a d'aimsigh mé sna toim."

She followed the dream's guidance and sat in the empty chair. The world outside was just the same as she expected it would be, only lacking detail. The trees were vague, colored shadows, nondescript as they swayed in the breeze. The bay and hills and the water were all like long brush strokes in different shades of grey, only an implied outline with no definition. The trees and the hidden shed and the rocky shore were not there. The dream machine didn't want her to give the land any attention.

Inside the sunroom, her mother was perfect. Her highlights caught in the light of the afternoon sun. Seeing her here, Tildy realized how young she had been when she died. Not even middle age, really. Tildy was older now than when her mother had given birth to Gisele. Her youth, sacrificed.

"Look at it now, the little darling," her mother said, lifting a small offshoot from the main stem. "This'll be a fine branch one day. Perhaps one your grandchildren will use for a swing."

"That would be nice," Tildy said.

Her mother turned to look up at her and smiled. The light cast a glow around her hair, lighting all the auburn and gold strands at once. "What's the matter, my little Snow White?"

Tildy's breath caught. The old nickname, such a symbol of her childhood, had been cast aside after her mother's death.

"I miss you, Mom."

Her mother spun herself around on the tile, folding her legs crisscross and looking up at her happily. "Oh, I miss you too, loveen. And I miss this place. Remember all our happy summers here? D'fhéachaimis ar na báid agus bhímis ag súgradh sna crainn. Just you and me?"

Tildy nodded. "It was easier then. I'm not sure I belong here without you."

"What's this nonsense now. Of course it was easier then,

you were a child! Maybe you belong here, maybe you don't. You belong where you find happiness, mo stóirín."

"You didn't find happiness."

Her mother turned away from her and back to the little tree, brushing bits of dark earth off the rim of the pot. "It started as a youthful infatuation, with your father. Then I suppose I thought it was my place. Sending money to care for Nana—with my father gone and the economy a wreck, she struggled. It was like her sisters had done for their mother. It wasn't happiness, no. But I loved my girls."

"What do I do, Mom? I can't do it all."

Her mother cast her a smile, one that looked nearly like Tildy's own. "You'll need to choose. That's always been hard for you. But no one else can do it for you."

Tildy sighed. Her mother touched her knee and squeezed it with a little shake, and it felt real. An old wound, long dormant, tore open. Tears dripped onto her shirt. When she looked up, her mother was crying too. With an awkward shuffle, her mother rose to her knees and pulled her into a strong embrace. She kissed her hair.

"I never modeled happiness for you girls. You have to learn it on your own. But I believe in you, m'iníon mhuirneach."

Tildy held on, ready to sacrifice any want or need to stay in this moment forever.

"I won't be seeing you again." Her mother's voice wavered as she spoke. She pushed Tildy back by the shoulders and forced eye contact. She looked alive and real, with faint wrinkles and eyebrows ungroomed. Alive, and away from her husband's criticism, her own mother's disappointment, free from physical suffering. "I'm here. I'm here for you. I'm in the land, the water, the sky. Is deannach réaltaí muid ar dtús, m'iníon, agus is deannach réaltaí muid sa deireadh. You aren't alone. You've never been, never will be. Don't chase my dreams, don't take on my mistakes just to be close to me. Be your own, and I'll be with you, my Tildy. Every step of the way."

They hugged close again. Tildy tried to hold on as the dream faded, fighting as it dissolved around her. She didn't want to leave.

When she awoke, her face was in her hands, tears across her pillow. With a final heaving sob, she removed the cap for the last time.

chapter
twenty-two

Tildy left her hotel late in the morning and slowly walked around the city center. The city was not magical today – it was a mirror. Miserable drivers waited in traffic like miserable drivers waited in traffic all over the world. Unhoused people slept in doorways of shops long closed. Sticky, dried vomit splattered across the sidewalk at an intersection. And beyond the material, no one seemed to see her. No one wanted her here, even those who knew her. The friends she made while sleeping were just people she had found on the internet. They had their own lives, their own memories, that did not include her. Her Nana, the one who lived here, was cold and judgmental. Here and there, Aidan was confusing. The only people who had wanted to see her since she arrived were her siblings and father. And Jude.

Jude had pursued her. He saw her weakness, as the others did, and did not reject her for it. Where Tildy was hesitant, Jude was confident. He was aware of all that she was aware of, yet faced it and used it to his advantage. It would be easy, to let herself belong to him. And perhaps this longing for Ireland, for a grandmother who loved her, for Aidan, for belonging would fade, and the rejection so acute here would be a memory, too.

Tildy boarded the Salthill bus with no destination in mind. When it was her turn to place her fare in the machine, she paid too much. The driver scowled as he counted out her change. The error had been so obvious, the man behind her had asked, "the fares gone up?"

Tildy swallowed down her embarrassment and walked to an empty seat in the back. She set her purse, bulky with the cap and transmitter, on her lap. She was going to ship it back today, but it was too early to call Evelyn for a shipping address. People stared at their phones as the bus trudged along. Some wore hotel uniforms, others suits. There were children in dark slacks and dress shirts, and a few tourists. If no one spoke, it almost looked like a subway car in New York. Tildy turned to look out the window. It was drizzling now, the winds gentle. A woman in a grey sweater clutched her arms together and kept her head down as she walked through the rain. The bus gradually emptied and then filled again with a new cast of characters as it looped around and returned towards the city center. Tildy checked the time. It was 7 AM in NYC now. She could call, and hope Evelyn had Do Not Disturb turned on if she was still asleep. At the Eyre Square stop, Tildy disembarked and dialed Evelyn's number. To her surprise, she answered immediately.

"Oh, hey! Sorry to call so early. I just need your mailing address. I'm all done with the cap."

"Good, that's great. I'm so glad. I'll text it to you now. How are you feeling? Mentally, I mean. No one has used the cap this many times before."

"I'm ok. Thanks so much for letting me, I don't know."

"You're good, no problem. Is this a good time to talk? I don't even know what time it is there right now."

"Sure, now's fine. Evelyn, are you okay?"

Her voice was strained as she spoke. "Oh yeah, I am. I just noticed something and wanted to—I don't know. Do you know Jude Mills?"

Tildy froze, trying to switch mental gears. "I do, yes. Not very well, but I do."

"And, uh, what do you think of him?"

"What do I think of him?" she stalled, a thousand thoughts rushing to the forefront of her mind. His dazzling eyes, his perfect figure, his hand on her waist and his lips in her hair as he offered safety to her. And his masks. The many masks he wore to keep pleasant around unpleasant people, and the way he wore them with such practiced efficiency.

She cleared her throat. "He's handsome. And charming. And I don't trust him."

Evelyn sighed in relief. "You don't trust him. So you aren't, uh, WITH him."

"With him? No. Why?"

"I saw he was in Galway on social media, and just thought, shit can't be a coincidence. Phew. Girl, thank goodness. I'm so relieved."

Tildy put in her headphones and loaded Jude's preferred social media platform, which had lately become Gisele's preferred social media platform. He had posted a photo from the Salthill Promenade. The caption read: *I've come across the ocean to find you, and I won't let you go now.*

Tildy frowned. She turned away from the shipping center. She wanted the privacy a walk could afford.

"He's involved in your dad's company, right? I don't want to cause any trouble, you know," Evelyn said.

Tildy waved a hand as if brushing concerns aside. "That's my dad's business. He and Gisele think Jude is great. Between him and Penelope appearing all of a sudden, it feels like something is going on."

"Penelope? The influencer, Penelope Lee?"

"Yeah? She's working with Gisele on branding or something. I don't know."

The phone line went so quiet, Tildy checked her phone

to see if they had been disconnected. "Evelyn? You still there?"

"Yeah, yeah… Look, if you don't mind me asking, are you sure you aren't infatuated with Jude? I don't want to be breaking up anything."

"No, I'm not infatuated. Not with Jude."

Her tone conveyed all the meaning Tildy couldn't bring herself to say out loud. Jude had stolen her attention, but he wasn't who captivated her, who made perpetual estrangement into a blissful misery.

"I got you. Good. Do you remember me and Benito? How we were going together and went to college together?"

"Of course," Tildy said, ashamed that she had forgotten Benito. Forgotten to even ask after him, so absorbed in her own desire to use Evelyn's project.

"I don't know if you know this, but Benito died. Five years ago, drug overdose."

"Oh my god, Evelyn," Tildy gasped, halting midstride. It felt like a physical blow. Evelyn's boyfriend, with the soft brown eyes and kind smile, whose mother had made him oatmeal cookies even into high school. He couldn't even shave yet when she had last seen him. And he had been gone for five years! And she had never even asked about him. Her nose stung as the tears gathered.

"They called it accidental. It wasn't, Tildy. It wasn't. He was in a dark place." Evelyn paused to gather herself. Tildy was the only one crying, so she did it as quietly as she could. "You see, he'd dropped out of college to start a business with someone. Put everything he had into it—student loan money, borrowed money from his grandparents, parents, friends. And his family didn't have money, Tildy." She said it with an emphasis that silently shamed her. "His business partner was in charge of the financials. Investing here, buying there, he said. Benito signed for loans, credit cards, anything to keep the business going. They met with VCs—the terms were stupid, but Benito was wrapped around this guy's finger."

"Jude," Tildy said.

"Yeah. Jude. He was off investing the money, he said, paying the bills. But then one day, he came to Benito and said it wouldn't work. Money was all gone, but he had another opportunity and he was off. That other opportunity was a rich old lady. Became her sugar baby or some shit. Benito was left holding the bag."

"Oh god," Tildy breathed.

Evelyn was crying now, softly into the phone.

"He couldn't face them, Tildy. He couldn't face their disappointment. After... after it was all over, I found Jude. I waited in the lobby of that old lady's building and told him, I said, 'you killed Benito.' Tildy, that man *shrugged*. He shrugged at me and walked around me, like it was nothing. Like Benito was *nothing*."

At some point, she had reached a bench and was sitting there, listening with her mouth agape. Her legs were shaking.

"There's more. That Penelope, you can't trust that one

neither. I've been following Jude on social media, I don't even know why, to torture myself or something. Anyways, he and that scrawny bitch had all these photos together about a year ago, one at something in London for a far-right group. Girl, they are mixed up together in some nasty business."

"And they acted like strangers," Tildy breathed.

Evelyn laughed with a guttural edge. "Oh, they *know* each other. They know each other real good."

"Yeah."

"What's he playing at with you? Why's he following you to Ireland?"

"I don't know. He's pushing hard, though. I know he really hates my dad."

"He used to tell me. Him and Benito, they'd get drunk and he'd talk so much shit about your dad, your sister. It was awkward as fuck. We always defended you, though."

Tildy smiled. "Thanks."

"Girl. I know your daddy is a shithead, but you gotta get rid of them. They're vipers."

"She's my dad's lawyer's daughter. The guy's been working with our family for decades."

"No! Wow, this goes DEEP. Maybe Jude is only with her to infiltrate Aibell?"

"Maybe so." Tildy wondered. It felt right, that he would use the daughter of her dad's lawyer, if he hated her father this much.

"You gotta warn your family."

"They'll never listen to me," she said with remorse. She tried to imagine herself warning them, but it was all pointless. Not only wouldn't they listen to her, they would relish the opportunity to hear her and ignore her. Such pointless animosity within her family. Where did it come from, she wondered. Was it just dissimilarity of character? Had it always been this way, even when she was a baby? Or was it only since her mother's death?

Even across the phone and in silence, Evelyn understood. "Save yourself, then, you know? You just gotta save yourself."

After they hung up, Tildy sat alone on the bench in silence, staring at the water. This was the bench she'd sat on in the opening of her first dream. It was cold now, though, cold and grey and misty. She yearned for those first dreams as she yearned for her own youth.

Everything had grown entangled in itself, shreds of meaning lost to the connections between reality and her imagination. There was one solid truth. She must eliminate Jude from her life, and her family's lives if she could. She didn't owe it to them. She owed it to herself, and her mother, to try one last time. If she failed, then so be it.

chapter
twenty-three

That night, Tildy took extra care with her appearance, feeling like she was preparing for war. Perhaps if she told Jude she knew, that she wanted him gone, it would get her somewhere. The path to convincing her father was unfathomable, but Jude was also a mystery. Would his callous hatred of her father be easier to sway than her father's forced disregard?

Jude pulled up to her hotel at seven, right on time. He was waiting outside the car as she descended the steps in the black sweaterdress from the local shop. She took him in with a distant appreciation. A tall, handsome, and confident man.

He wore a slim suit with a button-down shirt, the first two buttons undone. She couldn't deny his attractiveness, even if it didn't work on her. Not now. Not after Benito. It was all a game. She kept her gaze down, navigating the uneven stones in her high heels. The black fabric clung to what little curve her waist had, the skirt ending just below her knees. At the top, the material hung off her shoulders, showing off her décolletage in a way that was a bit extreme for her usual style, a circumstance that couldn't be helped now. Gisele would've looked lovely in this, she'd thought as she dressed.

Jude looked at her in open admiration. "Wow, you look incredible."

"Thank you," she said, keeping her disagreement silent.

He helped her into the black sedan and shut her door. It felt like she was going to prom with the devil. Tildy shook her head. The last time she had been on an actual date was with the son of one of her father's associates. How many of these awkward situations were just an extension of her father's influence on her life?

The drive was through the familiar narrow streets, turning left then right, a confusion of angles that Tildy would never become accustomed to. She held on to the handle of the door, her knees clamped shut and pointing away from Jude, who tried to make small talk. Her thoughts were distracted, though. If she had to walk back to the hotel from wherever he was taking her, she'd never know which way to go. She missed the grid of Manhattan. How could she think she could ever belong here?

They turned onto a familiar street, and her stomach lurched. The fliers on the light poles, the curve of the street, the sign of Aidan's restaurant. There was no blood in the street now. No police who didn't care taking statements. She turned to Jude, who looked at her with a small, questioning smile, inviting her to make a remark. Tildy set her jaw.

When they pulled up out front and he had helped her out of the sedan, Tildy felt ashamed of her dress and her effort. She was ugly and small, wearing a costume as if it gave her strength. She was already on the back foot, and they hadn't even begun this dinner yet. He put his hand on the small of her back and guided her toward the entrance. She'd have to do this now. She had to be strong.

Through the large glass window, she could see that there were a dozen small tables and one large one in the dimly lit space. Chandeliers with Edison bulbs hung from the ceiling, a monotone metallic wallpaper providing a backdrop for moss-green chairs draped with woven blankets. The tables were free of cloths, their light wooden tops lacquered to a bright finish. The floor was another shade of wood, gray and distressed, a muted stage for the furnishings. On the largest wall, to the right, paintings hung. One, an image of colors fading from one to the next, sharpened Tildy's focus.

At the large table, seated casually and with command, was her father. Alongside Mr. Sullivan were her sisters, Mr. Lee and his daughter Penelope, and two men she assumed were the investors. This was not a casual dinner date. And here? At Aidan's restaurant? The maliciousness of it all stunned her. She had underestimated Jude.

"Good evening. May I take your… Oh. Tildy?"

Katherine looked pale as she glanced at the pair of them. Jordie was answering questions at another table as Orla brought out a pitcher for refilling water.

"Hey," Tildy said, struggling for words. "How are you feeling?"

"Just doing the hosting for now." She looked at Jude with a cautious, closed smile. "Right this way, then, your party is already seated." Her tone was resigned.

"After you." Jude motioned.

Tildy was absorbed by her own stupidity. She needed to relax, she told herself. Her family liked places like this. Impressive places, unique places. In this city, this dinner could only have taken place here. And Aidan was the owner. He wouldn't notice them. Maybe?

When they reached their table, Katherine gave Tildy a strong look as she pulled out a chair for her. No, she realized, this was going to be a shitshow.

The table fell silent. Jude greeted everyone and unbuttoned his suit jacket before settling in. Her father nodded toward him.

"Jude, I have the wine list here. Surprisingly good selection. What do you say to a bottle of Domaine Leroy?"

Lee paled as Jude nodded. "I think that would be delightful. It's a celebratory meal, after all," he said, patting Tildy's hand.

"We'll start with that, but I'll keep the list for later," her father said with a smile.

Her father cleared his throat. "Well, Matilda. Meet Matthew Ormsby and his son Devon. Distant relations of mine, not your mother's. Her people probably worked in their estate though."

Tildy nodded at the men with a reserved smile. They looked at her with too much interest. She turned to Gisele, who was whispering something to Penelope and laughing behind her hand.

"That dress, where did you get it?" Gisele asked.

"Local shop," Tildy said curtly.

"It's charming," Gisele said with some venom.

"I think it's lovely. Black really suits your dark hair," Penelope said with a flashing smile.

Penelope seemed to be doing some maneuvering. Staying just viscous enough to be friendly with Gisele, but not so much as to alienate anyone else, Tildy thought distantly. She wasn't as good at this game as Jude.

He leaned close to Tildy. "Explain to me how you're friends with a waitress?"

"Most people in cities with heavy tourism work in the service industry." She wasn't really thinking about her words as she said it. Would she be able to avoid seeing Aidan? He was certainly too busy. It was his restaurant after all— how often would he be out at the tables? Those hopes were dashed immediately. She heard his voice nearby, from somewhere behind her.

"New York has more tourists than almost any other city,

and you have no friends who are waitresses there," he teased. He was probably trying to be charming. She didn't respond. Instead, she listened in on the activities behind her.

"Good evening, everyone. First time at Cluain?" His tone was easy, friendly, his voice like a warm embrace on a cold day. He loved this place. Tildy looked around at the restaurant, as much as she could see without facing Aidan, to appreciate what he had made. No detail had been overlooked. The fixtures, the upholstery, the ceiling, the paintings—everything was intentional. He wouldn't dedicate himself to something he didn't love. She thought of him gathering plants in her nana's field, clutching a fistful of soil to sniff, judging what was best for the people in his care.

She remained still, listening to the smile in his voice as he spoke to strangers. Soon, he would come around to her table and make his introductions.

Jordie's voice muttered to Aidan, "I'll get the big table."

A moment later, he appeared, flashing Jude a quick smile. "Good evening, folks. Have any of you dined with us before?"

One of the Ormsbys raised his hand, and Jordie nodded at him with appreciation. "We do a fixed course meal here. I see we have no allergies on file, is that correct?"

Most of the table murmured or shook their heads. Tildy noticed that her dad was leaning over to Penelope, telling her something. She carefully tucked her hair behind her ear as she listened, her lips parted with a soft smile for him. Yep, she was certainly maneuvering.

"Your wine will be coming up shortly." Jordie looked at

her and mouthed *what a fecking dress*, then left.

"The men here are quite handsome," Alexandra exclaimed.

Their father nodded. "No sun to ruin their skin here. But most of the women look like clowns. Makeup spackled on, heavy lips, heavy eyes, mascara like globby spiders. Your mother knew how far a light touch goes. And the spray tans!"

"Doesn't Aibell sell spray tan, Dad?" Tildy asked.

"Don't be stupid, Matilda. Of course we do."

"Tildy's right though," Jude said, casting a quick glance her way, "these are women who love makeup, and they are the core clientele for Aibell."

"It's true. That's a good point, Jude. Very good point. Clever thinking."

Jude gave her a smile that she forced herself to return. The wine arrived, and Jordie served her after her father had approved the sample. She thought of Benito, kind Benito, Evelyn's Benito, in miserable despair that could not be over-come as she took a swig of the glass. Hundreds of dollars of fermented grape juice sloshed down her throat, meeting bile on its way down.

"We're visiting the Carterets in Wicklow day after tomorrow, so we need to get right to business."

Lee looked at Tildy with apprehension. "Right, so. Matthew here has a proposal that he'd like to present, Matilda. We should all listen and absorb what is on offer, and how it may benefit the entire family."

Jude's hand touched hers where it rested on her leg. She resisted the urge to pull it away.

"Thank you, Peter." Matthew Ormsby nodded. In his tweed suit, he looked the part of an English lord visiting his Irish estate for the season. Tildy reigned in her emotions and steadied her gaze on him. He lifted out a paper from an elegant briefcase and showed her the diagram.

"Your father says you work in software, so perhaps you are already aware, but Ireland is home to many of the major internet services for Europe. The undersea cables traverse the ocean off our shores, and from various centers along our coasts. Recently, a cable was completed that connects Galway to Iceland."

He pointed a clean finger to the line that traced across the ocean. "It's about a 1,600-kilometer line, so quite extensive. A very difficult engineering process."

"I see," Tildy said.

"Now, this isn't common knowledge." Matthew Ormsby's voice dropped low as he conspiratorially smiled at her. "There's an opportunity to join a second cable connection. They are currently establishing a subarctic cable between Iceland and Japan. Asia is, as I'm sure you're aware, a major market for internet companies and so forth. Giving western Ireland a direct connection to Japan would be a boon for the local economy. And if you have any concerns, they will do it all environmentally friendly. Subterranean, no disturbing of bird nesting areas, so on and so forth."

She frowned and said nothing. A pause fell on the table, everyone watching her. Jordie walked around, sensing the mood and eyeing everyone as he refilled glasses.

"What does this have to do with me?" she asked, sipping her wine and looking sideways, where Aidan chatted with a pair of women, one of whom smiled up at him in a flirtatious way. Good, she thought, working to convince herself that it was good, that someone like that woman belonged with him.

"Isn't it obvious," Gisele laughed, looking at Penelope for confirmation. Penelope smiled blandly at her companion and at Tildy, darting a quick, nervous glance at Jude.

Tildy shrugged. "I'm sorry, you'll need to spell it out for me."

Devon and Matthew Ormsby exchanged glances, then Matthew smiled at her. "Yes, of course. You see, your grandmother's land is almost the entire breadth of the area cited in geological surveys as ideal for this second connection."

She swirled her wine. "And do you work for the data company or the team building this data connection?"

"Oh, no. But we have the local connections, you see, to make sure you get the best deal."

Tildy's dad looked at her with annoyance. "Matilda, don't be difficult. The builders have another spot they are looking at, one of the islands off the coast. We need to move fast."

She nodded. Jude's phone buzzed and he looked down, typing under the table in reply to someone. It reminded her of her call with Evelyn, and she steadied herself. She could just walk away right now. For her family, though, she needed to see this entire scheme with emotional distance. Aidan's voice came to her from somewhere, from where he spoke with someone. The setting wasn't helping. She felt like she was being pulled in four directions at once.

Jordie had returned, and the table fell silent again. Matthew Ormsby flipped the paper over. Jordie cleared his throat and began the introduction to the meal, while Jude continued to frown at his phone. Tildy stared at him while he typed, the wine bracing her. When he caught her eye, he nearly looked guilty, smiling at her apologetically as he put the phone away. "So sorry, just dealing with a minor emergency."

"All our food is sourced from the island," Jordie was saying, "with recipes derived from ancient Irish traditions. Tonight we have a variety of meats prepared and cured using techniques that have been passed down through generations of Irish history, mixed with some other good stuff. Shall we start with another bottle of wine?"

Her father ordered two bottles of a slightly less exorbitant type of Italian red, while Devon and Matthew Ormsby whispered to one another. Penelope and Gisele were sharing plans to go to the Riviera from Dublin, Alexandra was trying to talk to their father, and Jude was lying in wait to speak to her. She didn't want to speak to him. She looked around, surrounded by other people who were alone. She feared Aiden coming around the corner, she feared more looks from his friends and people who she'd dreamed were her friends, and she feared whatever Jude was preparing himself to say.

Their palate cleanser and first tastes arrived, distracting them all for few moments. The food was perfect. Even her father seemed impressed. It gave her a sense of pride, that the Irish boy he had viewed so disdainfully eight years ago was now creating immaculate meals, intricate works of beauty and taste. Tildy looked down, smiling at the sliver of purple seaweed atop the canapé.

"Delicious," Jude observed, cleaning his fingertips on a napkin before returning it to his lap. "It's going to be hard to convince you to come home to the city with food like this here."

Tildy sat up as straight as she could and braced herself.

"Why are you here?" she whispered. "Why is everyone here?"

He looked around, slightly bored. "They're each here for themselves. I guess I am too. But I'm here for you. They're here for what they can get out of you."

She imagined herself replying, laying out her accusations from Evelyn. The influence of his beautiful brown eyes and skin and exuded kindness began to fray her resolve. He was certainly guilty, that was beyond a doubt. And she couldn't be with him. But he was kind to her, and mostly honest.

He hadn't known her at the art gallery. Evelyn's words had twisted Tildy's memories, but on further reflection, she was sure he hadn't recognized her. His early infatuation had been sincere, and she needed to accept the compliment in that and then let him go.

Orla appeared with one of the bottles of wine, Jordie with the other. She smiled at Tildy, a kindness she didn't feel like she deserved. Jordie smiled at Jude and winked at her. Aidan was speaking to another guest, asking if they liked their meal. The couple were saying it was their first date night since having a baby. Aidan asked how old the baby was, and Tildy clutched her napkin. The yearning in his voice, unmistakable and intoxicating in its vulnerability.

The next course arrived, a soup with a design on the surface. Delicious and soothing. Would he make a soup like this for his wife after she had a long day at work? For his children when they were home from school with colds? His hands selecting the best ingredients, chopping them to size, measuring the herbs and spices, sprinkling them in, serving his effort, his love, to those who would accept his love. Love that he offered, that she had rejected, that was now withheld from her.

Jude leaned over, his shoulder touching hers, his face nearly against her cheek. "I know it's only been a few weeks, but I've missed you so much, Tildy."

He touched her hand as it rested on the table, tracing a vein along the pale surface. "You ran away from your life to come here. I see why," he said with meaning. "But you don't belong here. Don't you want to be part of someone's life? A cherished part?"

The way he whispered sent a shiver up her spine. Base, animal need. *Evelyn, Benito, this scam,* she repeated to a drum rhythm in her mind. His touch was so warm. And what would be the cost? He was going to scam her father anyway. What if she gave in here? Could she change him? Could she grow to love him? Wouldn't it be nice to be touched every day, each day, forever?

He would never leave her. Knowing his sins and his darkness, she could feel he would want her with him always. If she agreed to this, she would be his, forever.

She drew her gaze up to his eyes. There was eagerness and admiration, but no love. Beneath his beauty and need was a permanent void. She couldn't unsee it. And if she chose him, she would always know that she'd chosen the safety of being unloved.

Jordie arrived with the next course, and Tildy freed her hand, hiding it under her part of the table. He hit his mark to describe the meal, but before he could begin, someone approached over her shoulder. Jordie paled, offering her a brief glance of warning. He gave up his spot with a swift nod followed by a swifter departure. Tildy closed her eyes and breathed in, allowing herself the moment to prepare, then released the breath.

"Good evening. How is…"

She lifted her eyes as his voice faded. She had never seen someone look at her so thoroughly. He took in her dress, his focus lingering at the neckline, her hair, her face. His gaze was intent and searching. Then he frowned, looking from her to Jude, then to her father and sisters.

"Hi again. Funny to keep running into you," Jude observed with some bite. Tildy clenched her jaw but did not turn away from Aidan.

He was wearing the same style of white chef's jacket as Jordie, yet she hadn't even noticed it on him. Aidan seemed taller in it, more proud than in anything else she had seen him wear. The crisp fabric was perfectly tailored, tight in a way that allowed the buttons to sit correctly. With the sleeves rolled up, the cut and fit at the arms accentuated the indent where his bicep connected to his inner elbow. It was the sort of detail Tildy noticed in handsome men, the sort of men who had nothing to do with her.

Aidan wasn't looking at her with reserved disappointment anymore. No, he looked at her now like she was calling him to crash on rocky shoals.

At the other end of the table, her father and Gisele whispered. Tildy understood. One of them was reminding the other of who he was as they looked at him. And she could see in her father's eyes the disdain he wanted to have at war with his adoration for beauty. He couldn't deny Aidan now, successful Aidan, gorgeous Aidan. Just the same, she knew Aidan wanted none of their approval. Penelope flitted a quick look to Jude, then reverted back to smile at Aidan blandly.

"We're just here trying to convince Tildy to come home to New York," Jude explained. "This food is a temptation to stay, though. Bravo."

Aidan did not take the bait. He shifted his stance and smiled.

"For the first main course, we have three selections." He

kept close to Tildy, pointing to each bite-sized creation and describing the layers. His enthusiasm was markedly dampened as he described the intent behind each.

"Thank you," Tildy said.

"Enjoy." His voice was tight, and he looked at her with hurt.

Jude assessed her mood and decided to stay silent. They ate, listening to her father and Matthew Ormsby discuss yacht races and fox hunting, their casual disdain for the lives of those who lived or worked in those settings apparent. None of that was a surprise. Everyone else was silent, listening or thinking or both. Each person at the table had motives for this dinner and was mentally positioning themself for whatever came next.

The next course arrived, and Tildy braced herself. Orla approached, slightly confused, and delivered the description. She answered their questions competently—clearly Aidan was not the only person capable of delivering these speeches. Tildy thanked her and looked toward the kitchen. Aidan stood leaning in the doorway, as if anticipating her gaze. He slowly, victoriously, returned to the kitchen.

Jude took a sip of his wine and rotated the glass on the table slowly. "What if we pretend there is no family backstory to us."

Tildy laughed. "Hard to make that argument here, wouldn't you say?"

He nodded as he looked around. "I didn't want them to follow me. You know what they're like," he whispered.

"What if we pretend this is a communal table. It's just you and me, young New Yorkers who met at an art gallery, out for a date night at a local place. You liked me then, didn't you?"

"I did," she acknowledged.

"So. Why won't you let me care for you?"

Tildy resisted the urge to look toward the kitchen. In doing so, her face was clearly readable to Jude. He sensed her weakness and leaned in.

"Why won't you?" he asked huskily.

"You don't know me. And I know you."

"You know me?" He looked into her face, then sipped his wine. "Ah. Yes. Evelyn."

She didn't speak. It didn't matter what he said. She could see there was no remorse.

"What would you like to hear then, Tildy? I liked Benito. We were young and stupid. It was a gamble. He knew it was a gamble."

"But only you knew the stakes."

He didn't respond. She took a gulp of her wine, the spice of it strong and deep. She hadn't had enough water to drink today, and this was going to hit her too hard. She shrugged. Well, everyone else here was careless with her. Why not be careless with herself, too?

"Do you think my father is honest?"

"Your father?"

"Yeah."

Jude smirked. "Of course not."

"And Gisele? Alexandra? And Lee?"

"Unlikely.

"And Penelope?"

"I'm not following," Jude replied, his tone less even at the mention of Penelope.

"I'm surrounded by liars. I don't want to be a liar."

He shook his head. "Everyone lies, Tildy."

"Not everyone."

Aidan appeared and quietly refilled their glasses. The two of them fell silent until he left, and the impression that must have given him pained her.

"You're going to let all your mother worked for fall apart? Because of a business mistake when I was barely old enough to drink? When you could help me save it," Jude continued.

She breathed deeply but couldn't reply.

He whispered, his breaths casting a spell on her neck. "You know these people are going to fleece your father," he said, his lips nearly on her skin. "They think you'll cave, but when they see you won't, they'll bleed him dry."

"So better you than them?" Tildy whispered back.

Jude pulled away, shrugged slightly as he took a sip of wine. "I could go easier on him, if you wanted."

The next course arrived, and Aidan delivered it. Some of the other guests were looking at their table now, wondering why the head chef was giving their group such special attention. Tildy's gut wrenched. What if he was sacrificing lifelong customers to this nonsense? And she was the cause. Of course, her father would simply assume he was too important to be ignored. This only validated his ego.

"The next course is a palate cleanser before our seafood dish." As Aidan delivered the description, Tildy touched her collarbones absently, something she had always done to soothe herself. The movement drew his eye to her chest. She blushed and put her hand down. He averted his eyes, continued his description, then walked away.

The slight lift of air as he departed caressed her skin. His smell was intoxicating to her in all the ways Jude believed himself to be.

Devon Ormsby, visibly impatient, leaned back in his chair and looked at Tildy with thinly veiled disdain. "I guess I'm just curious what you plan to do with your grandmother's land, if you are so disinterested in our proposal."

"What I plan to do with it?" she repeated.

"Certainly. You must have some sort of clear notion as to how to extract value from it, how to bolster the community and increase tax revenue and international trade for the benefit of Ireland. After all, you're *Irish*," he said sarcastically. "Don't you feel indebted to this place of your ancestors?"

Matthew Ormsby put a steadying hand on his son's arm as he sent an apologetic look to Tildy. His son shrugged it off.

"Our family used to own that land. It was ours for generations, since my fifth great-grandfather was raised to the baronetcy by the king of England. And now you think you know what's best for it, because of a few vacations as a child? I heard your grandmother doesn't even like you, so why are you so protective over land she can't even use? That would help the people who in point of fact *deserve* the land."

"I must apologize—Devon had surgery recently, and I think the wine is having a reaction with his medication. We'll send Mannion back to drive you to the estate, Patrick. Lovely to meet you, Matilda."

The two men rose, one unsteadily, and left the restaurant, the younger muttering belligerently on their way out the door. Jude scoffed. "Surgery medications, uh huh."

His smug disdain for recreational drug use did not land as he had expected. When she didn't reply, he refocused.

"I'm sorry that man spoke to you like that. That was out of line."

"He isn't important."

"I know you love it here, Tildy," he whispered. "But look at that guy. You don't want to deal with people like him. Come back home. We could make something great, together."

Her wine glass was empty. She shook her head. "I'm not what you want, I'm an easy solution to a problem. That's all I've ever been to anyone."

Aidan approached as freshly arranged courses were delivered. She felt like a ping-pong ball, bounced between the attentions of these two men. After he had given a quick description to the other half of the table, he walked around to Tildy's, where he crouched between her and Jude, his hands relaxed between his legs. He looked up to her as if the restaurant was entirely empty. His eyes caught the light, and the background faded away. She was hypnotized by him now. She shivered under his examination.

"Next, here you have our final savory dish of the evening. Oyster paired with a selection of seaweed from north of here, near Kilkieran." The voice he used was soft, tantalizing, the same voice that he'd breathed into her ear after they kissed. "We all gather at the coast and collect it ourselves, to ensure the taste is perfect. The best in the world, right here, close to home. Alongside is a local cheese made of the sweetest cream. The pastry I rolled with my own hands this morning."

Tildy's palms began to sweat, her body protesting against her restraint. Her eyes were arrested by his, her face flushing, and she was sure her pupils dilated, the pair of traitors. Jude asked a question, and Aidan broke eye contact with her. As if nothing concerned him, he rose easily and answered the question, but remained right beside her. Tildy looked away from his hips, nearly at her eye level, and took a quiet breath. He tapped two fingers on the table, told them to enjoy, and departed.

How many courses is this meal? she wondered to herself.

Jude decided to pay attention to her father instead. He asked him for an opinion on a recent VC scandal. Sometimes Tildy supplied a word or two to the long-winded conversation, but her ears followed Aidan. First he spoke to a four-person table, then to the two women, where one laughed at his joke. Later, a small family with a child prepared to leave, and he used a stern voice to ask the little boy if he was safe to drive. She smiled and considered turning to see their reaction.

She felt more than heard him approach and froze. His hand brushed the back of her chair, fingertips casually sliding across her skin, exposed by the cut of her dress.

He continued on to his usual spot, where he stood and asked if the course was pleasant. The table nodded and smiled, and he left.

"The hospitality here is really remarkable," Penelope said pointedly. "You hardly see this kind of attention at most restaurants."

Patrick Sullivan simply nodded. "This is typical, darling. Michelin-starred restaurants collect a dossier on people of status. He must know of my investments, and of the Ormsbys, obviously."

"Speaking of the Ormsbys," Gisele said, "Matilda was so rude to them. I hope she's more polite tomorrow when we get her from her shabby little hotel."

"I'm not leaving my hotel, thank you."

Her father leaned forward. "Yes, you are."

"No, I'm not."

"Matilda, whether you like it or not, you are part of this family. And all this nonsense about Deirdre's land is finished. She doesn't even use it, for Christ's sake. You're selling that land, you're turning over your shares, and you're going to support this family."

Tildy breathed deeply. "Fine, Dad. You can have my shares."

Penelope and Jude gasped together. She spared them a glance, nothing more.

Her father looked pleased. "Good. And the land?"

"No, Dad. You will not have Nana's land."

He bristled. Katherine and Orla were refilling water glasses, eavesdropping with such disregard for subtlety it nearly made Tildy lose her train of thought.

"And you're going to, what, farm potatoes, then?"

"No, Gisele," Tildy said. She drained her glass and dabbed her lips. "No, I'm going to help Nana move home. She loves it there. She doesn't deserve to have her grandfather's trees torn up for a fucking data cable that sounds like a fucking scam, by the way. I love it here. I'm happy here. I'm not coming back. Enjoy Florida."

Overcome, exhausted, finished with them all, Tildy threw down her napkin and collected her things. She walked toward the kitchen, where Aidan had been watching her speak.

"Can you give me a tour of the kitchen," she said, her heels clicking on the hard floor in irritation.

"I, uh."

The eyes of the other patrons turned to her, their voices whispering in her wake. She passed Jordie in the short hallway, his face aglow with the drama. Tildy marched on, into the kitchen, with Aidan close behind.

The kitchen was the same as the day of the accident,

all white and stainless steel, but this time it was not empty. Seven experts focused on their work, hummed with conversation—until they entered. It sobered her briefly. These people were just trying to do their jobs, and here she was, drunk on several hundred quid of wine, decades of family resentment, and a few weeks of sexual tension. She looked around and noticed a small office beyond the bathroom to her left. The door hung ajar, and she could see the room was empty. Tildy steered that way. Once inside, she folded her arms and put her back against the far wall. Aidan shut the door behind them and leaned against it, watching her.

"What are you doing?" she demanded in a whisper.

"What am *I* doing?"

"You need to pay attention to the other tables. I'm leaving, so stop hovering at my family's table. You won't have me to scowl at."

He laughed softly, putting a hand to his face. "There was no scowling at you, Tildy."

"You're neglecting all your other guests!"

Aidan stepped away from the door, closing the gap to her. His voice low and soft, he said, "I don't neglect anyone."

She turned from the words as if struck. "I'm sure you don't."

"Why are you back here, Tildy?" His voice was silky and dangerous as he moved closer. "Shouldn't you be with your boyfriend?"

Emboldened by the wine, she tilted up her chin and met his eye. "He's not my boyfriend."

His eyes flashed, as if he had caught her in a lie. "Are you sure?"

"He's a con artist. He's here to destroy my dad. I mean nothing to him," she said.

He examined her carefully now, reading the sincerity she intended and the pain she did not. What anger he held for her faded before her eyes.

Tildy's hand clenched. His body was so close, the warmth of it passed through the air between them. There was nowhere to look that was not him. The torture of being so close, yet impossibly distant.

"I need you to stop," she whispered as she stared into his eyes.

He leaned down toward her, his face smoothly shaven and like silk as it brushed against hers. When he spoke, his lips flitted across her ear. "You want me to stop?"

Her breathing grew hoarse. "I know I lost you," she sighed. "Please. Just let me go."

He drew back, surprised. She took the opportunity to leave the room, and then the restaurant. Her family eyed her with disdain. Penelope watched her warily. Jude made to rise, but she shook her head and waved him off. She didn't want to play his games anymore. Whatever came next, he'd have no part in it.

It was raining outside. Tildy stood on the sidewalk, alone but relieved. She was done with her father. With her family. Never again would she hold them up. Freed like an object hurled from orbit, she felt the space around herself expand. Now, more than ever before, she was her own. It was a freedom her mother had never taken for herself, and she had it now. No one and nothing would prevent her from following her own path.

For now, the walk back to the hotel was going to be shitty. No dream machine would help her delete the curved streets and hills and rain. But she'd make it. There was nothing stopping her. She took off her shoes and began to walk toward the first turn, as familiar to her now as if this was home. Because it would be home. She'd figure it out, one way or another, on her own terms. All the mistakes, all the rewards—they would be hers to make and share with people who cared for her, in a place she loved.

She heard someone approaching from the restaurant. Expecting Jude, she steeled herself and continued walking, ready to ignore him and argue with him if necessary. A hand grabbed her by the wrist, slowing her progress, turning her near. Aidan, his face flushed, took her face in hands and kissed her.

His lips were soft, his touch pleading and tender. It sang with need and reverence, with apology and yearning. Tildy dropped her shoes and held his jacket tightly, afraid to see that it was all a dream.

Aidan broke away and held her to his chest. He whispered into her hair. "Haven't you seen it? I'm in agony, Tildy. How I've loved you. Only you. Téann tú go hanam ionam. Bhí mé lag agus tháinig olc orm leat. Inis dom nach bhfuil mé ró-dhéanach."

She sighed, too happy to speak, too happy to think.

"Tell me." He pulled her away and looked down into her eyes, his forehead to hers as he rasped out his plea. "Tell me now, Tildy."

"I love you," she said, her voice steady. "I'll never leave again, if you'll have me."

They embraced, oblivious to the rain and their surroundings, cold and sheltering in each other's arms.

"Let's get you someplace warm," Aidan said. He took her by the hand.

epilogue

A few weeks later, Tildy's little car bounced over the familiar potholes as Aidan steadied the box of pastries in his hands. She steered the car through the now-open metal gate into Nana's driveway. Packing materials bound together by twine rested against the freshly whitewashed house, along with moving blankets forgotten during unloading.

A moment later, Nana emerged, wiping her hands on her apron and smiling a wide grin. Mrs. Fegan waited behind, not wanting to miss any developments.

"It's about time, young man," Nana shouted. "Picking all my herbs, pining after my granddaughter without so much as a phone call or letter."

Tildy and Aidan shared a quick smile. He climbed out of the car, carrying the white box and a bottle of poitín.

"An buidéal ar fad! Ba choir duit é sin a thabhairt leat nuair a fhágann tú, a stócaigh."

"It's for you, now, Mrs. Halleran. I know the movers misplaced your last," Aidan replied with a laugh as he hugged her awkwardly.

"Who brewed this? I don't care for none of your big distilleries. The city smoke gets into the waters."

"It's a small-batch place, up near Achill."

"Achill, well now, that sounds grand. Come inside, now, with those delicious treats and that fine bottle, and let's have ourselves a celebratory cup of tea."

Tildy followed Aidan inside, where things were still in the process of being returned to their proper places. Nana had refused help unpacking. It would take weeks for her to settle back into her home. Of course it would—the woman liked her things just so.

"I see Jesus and JFK have returned," Tildy said.

"You don't expect me to be throwing away Jesus," Nana replied.

"But JFK?"

"Oh. He was my mother's. And he's a fine-looking man, isn't he."

Mrs. Fegan brought the tea tray with them into the sunroom, where four chairs had been arranged. The two nearest each other were theirs. Tildy began pouring the

teas while Aidan unwrapped the pastry box. Nana examined the lattice tops and glared at him. "What is this, now,
some kind of jackeen treat?"

Aidan looked over at Tildy and laughed quietly. In that
moment, she was overcome with a realization. He looked
at *her* when he laughed. He no longer looked down, as he
had done in the pub with his friends, or with her before
they had ended their eight years of separation. Now when
he felt joy, he looked to her, whenever she was present, and
that connection added to her own joy. The bond between
them was perfect. Their hearts were open, their feelings in
unison, as they prepared for a life together.

acknowledgements

Many of the experiences in this book are based on my visits to Galway, and my grandmother's love for Ireland. My grandma Mary Maude, not a native herself, spent happy months with her Irish family and friends in Galway City as well as in Ros Muc in Co. Galway. When I had a hard time sleeping at night, she would tell me stories in the dark; of myths she learned on her visits, of cousins who loved her but refused to speak to her in English, of being stranded on the road waiting for sheep to pass by, and of seeing the faces of her family on people in the street. As I grew older, she shared with me her love of Galway as a city of the arts, of language revival and poetry and music. She never really called herself Irish, at least to me, but I think she felt more at home there than anywhere else in the world. So, thank you to Galway for accepting my grandmother and thank you to her, wherever she may be, for sharing that love with me.

As always, I must thank my husband Jacob for his support, enthusiasm, and razor sharp criticism which I have grown to rely on. My dear children, for being mine and for sharing with friends, teachers, and strangers that "mom has to finish her book." Shame is a powerful motivator. My mother, of course, and my brothers who helped me workshop insults and my sister for being my "hype man." I must thank Andrea Brown for her care and attention translating. I will never forget how to spell "sutach" now! And Delphine Oudiette, neuroscientist, who took time out of her very busy schedule to patiently critique my dream machine. Thank you to Gallery Press for permitting me the use of *Geimhriú*. And Kara, my editor and fellow fan of *Persuasion*, thank you for helping me bring another novel home. And thank you to Jenn, for being my writing buddy and early reader, who kindly listens over coffees when I argue with myself.

And I want to thank you, reader, for choosing this book, of all the excellent books that hold worlds within their pages. I hope I entertained you for our short time together.

Norah Woodsey is the author of *The Control Problem*, *Lifeless*, *When the Wave Collapses*, and *The States*. After careers in the finance and tech industries, she has dedicated herself to creating fiction. Her subjects of intense interest but not quite expertise include history, physics, genetics, sociology, and gender studies. The product of four generations of Irish American Brooklynites, she now resides in California with her husband, kids, and their dog Saoirse.

For more information, visit: norahwoodsey.com